Lost Girl

L. J. Kendall

Leeth Ascending Vol. 1

This one too is for my wife Stella – a small offering to set against all that dementia steals from us

NATIONAL LIBRARY OF AUSTRALIA

A catalogue record for this book is available from the National Library of Australia

Creator: Kendall, L. J., author.
Title: Lost Girl / by L. J. Kendall.

ISBN: 9781925430172 (A-format paperback)

Series: Kendall, L. J. Leeth Ascending, Vol 1.

Subjects: Magic–Fiction.
    Fantasy fiction.
    Science fiction.

Story length: 142,000 words
Typeface: Georgia 9pt

Original publication: December, 2020.
Release version: 5   Jul, 2026. Typos found by readers Rebecca, me.

This book is available as an A or B-format paperback, and in ebook formats.

ACKNOWLEDGMENTS

I want to thank my wife, Dr Stella St. Clair-Kendall, for her love and encouragement over the years. This one was especially for you, darling.

An ongoing thanks to Jon Marshall for his insight, support, and help in shaping Leeth over two decades.

My deepest thanks once again to ThEditors.com for Dave's insights, advice, and honesty.

Another special thank you to Mirella de Santana, the artist who designs my covers. You can see more of her wonderful art at www.mirellasantana.com.br.

Also thanks to Daniel David Wallace, whose character-first plotting course proved useful. (I've warped his approach for my own use, so if it hasn't worked, that's my fault!) Similarly, any mistakes in regard to Japanese naming are mine, despite good advice from Akira Yoshihara and David See.

Thank you, all.

Note: there's a free gift if you inform me of any errors in the text, or if you write an honest review – see the Afterword for details.

Novels by L. J. Kendall

The Leeth Dossier:

> *Wild Thing*
> *Harsh Lessons*
> *Shadow Hunt*
> *Violent Causes*

Leeth Ascending:

> *Lost Girl*
> *(Cold Heart?*
> *...)*

INTRODUCTION

The Week of Miracles heralded the return of magic. Beginning on March 31st, 2036, it ended in the first World Storm, killing hundreds of thousands.

That terrible toll however was dwarfed in following years by the death of a billion more, from the God Wars of India, the Red Plague, the Melt virus, and finally, the global devastation of the Second World Storm.

It was the revelation that the last two of those catastrophes had been planned and executed by one person – Melisande d'Artelle – that made her the most feared and hated woman on Earth.

But despite her unique powers, she did not escape justice.

Hunted by a trio of powerful mages, she was tracked to a place beneath reality, and there slain. Of the three who challenged d'Artelle, two returned: but only one, still sane.

The world settled back on its course. New alliances formed, new technologies developed: Phasion energy cells, neural links to computers, artificial nerves and muscles. A colony set up on the Moon, and another on Mars; global warming and the sea level rise reversed by last-minute collective action; and humanity's greatest engineering feat: the restoration of the Antarctic ice sheets by the Newtopian Corporation.

So the world spun on, but a changed world now, of high technology and age-old magic, in an uneasy mix.

A world of ancient powers, demonic Foes... and one young woman drawn into the vortex.

CHAPTER 1

She was born as white-hot pain drained from her head, pounding her fists on a transparent wall.

Under her bruised hands the crystal barrier bounced and fought until at last, booming like a giant bell, it shattered in surrender.

Distant doors opened.

Go!

She flung herself out into welcoming darkness. *Free!*

Instantly, confusion overwhelmed relief. Floating now, she reached with aching fingers to a splinter of crystal, glinting as it spun. One touch sent it twisting away into a gathering wind.

Pain faded, relief a pure bliss. Her thoughts settled, eyes locking on the crystal shards orbiting her, tumbling and sparkling in the night.

Crystals? Or ice, revolving and twinkling, flashing lazily in the growing wind? She plucked a fragment from the rushing darkness. Long and razor edged, warm in her fingers. So warm for ice. She let it float free, focusing on the lights circling her. So pretty. Glowing shapes and words of emerald, ruby, and sapphire, spinning in shadow.

Blissful relief. She savored it even as the wind strengthened, stirring urgency through her veins. The lights slowed. Ice shards became armored glass. Below...

Below, dark waters hurtled upward.

Moments from impact she twisted cat-like, feet pointing instinctively. She hammered through the surface with the force of a car crash.

Only her perfect entry saved her life.

Glass daggers stabbed the water as she plunged deep, the churning water above mirroring the confusion inside. Long pale hair blossomed in a spreading halo above her as she slowed.

Then a shaft of bubbles lanced through the water, a dark flower blooming at its tip. Another, and another, and another, each closer than the last, tracking toward her. Each strange blossom beautiful yet somehow threatening. The next explosions smashed directly above and around her, grazing her neck, tearing free something black and shiny that gouged her before falling into the silent depths.

A bubble spear lunged straight for her head. One hand lashed up to intercept through water like molasses, twisting her whole body as she thrust-

An instant too late. The high caliber round bloomed, peeling open to club her forehead with stunning force. Blackness welled, but something deep inside struggled and clawed, forcing it back.

The impact reawoke a pain lurking within, deeper than thought. More intimate.

Another explosion, and something caught in her hair, tugging. She slowed, still sinking, still turning, the water clearing as bubbles wobbled in slow upward retreat. Frothing impacts tore into the dark water above, each explosion a spike to her ears.

Hold your breath.

High velocity rounds – get away.

Wondering where that thought came from, the pain in her head flared into agony.

Swim.

Her limbs responded clumsily at first. Something tugged in her hair, but she ignored it.

Lungs hammering, her throat tightened as she fought the urge to breathe. The explosions stopped, and for long seconds she swam fiercely through cold dark waters before angling upward toward faint fairy lights far above. Behind her, a beam of light stabbed down.

They're looking.

Desperate for breath, her lungs burned, echoing the pain in her head. The dim lights glimmered overhead, a rippling liquid mirror beckoning, seductively close.

Not yet. Too soon.

Just two more strokes: then air.

No. Two more. Just two more.

Again.

Her lungs screamed.

One more.

One more.

The light moved away.

Up!

She exploded into air, gulping a single lungful before diving again, mind overriding body as her chest fought like a trapped animal to breathe. Again something tugged at her hair, and again she ignored it, staying underwater, heading toward shore by the after-images of dark buildings and docks glimpsed above, of office lights, high up.

Ten seconds. Twenty. Lungs bursting, she swam on. Thirty seconds. Still she swam. Suddenly, the searching light above vanished, a curtain drawn steadily across it. She froze, drifting forward, before struggling lungs forced her to claw her way up. Breaking free of the water, she sucked in grateful gulps of air.

Two arms length above, tightly fitted boards blocked the questing light. She bobbed in the cold water as a powerful beam shone from a high-rise, swooping and circling, seeking. It swept the wharf she'd surfaced beneath, momentarily making her flinch back underwater as if they could see through wood. *Stupid,* she told herself against the roaring pain in her head, and broke the surface again.

Once more a tug at her scalp, scratching the back of her neck. She grabbed something jagged and sharp, tearing hair to yank it free. A shiny flower, its peeled-back petals ragged metal, glinting as the beam stabbed again across the boards above. For a few seconds she floated in the water, panting, staring at the vicious sculpture in her hand. On impulse, she folded sharp petals back shut, one by one, unfamiliar snow white hairs still trapped between the torn edges. Closed back up it made a bud the length of her middle finger.

A high velocity round. You'd be dead if they'd used low velocity.

The words in her head renewed the spearing pain. Shoving the casing into a pocket of her jacket, she zipped it closed, feeling tiny cuts in her fingertips as she did.

The light moved away.

Now. Get out of the water. They'll be coming for you.

Five strokes brought her to a concrete pylon, tires lashed to its sides. Stretching up, her fingers found an edge. Heaving herself one-handed from the water, she reached for the next, shoes seeking a lower tire's rim, scrambling up and onto the wharf as neatly as a cat up a tree.

Her neck stung, a shallow pain. One hand rose to it, finding a wound; an absence. *It's gone! I need to report....* Agony swamped the thought and carried it away. She swayed, abruptly adrift. *I just forgot... something. Something important.* Pain rose, punishing even that insight.

I'm in trouble! I have to contact.... She held her head. *Marcie! Marcie will be worried.* Pain wormed its way back in, but she plowed on over it. *Find a store, buy a Link, call...* the thought evaporated like smoke; like the pain.

Why am I standing here? How did I get wet? She licked a finger. *Salt water; blood.* Turning, she saw an enormous harbor behind her; threatening searchlights.

But moments later those thoughts too, slipped from her grasp. *What was I...?* She shook the distraction away. *Not important.*

Clothing clung wetly as she raced from the jetty across an open expanse of concrete. Plunging between darkened warehouses she ducked into an alley, shoes squelching. Under a steady city roar, rats chittered and fled as she passed.

It didn't seem strange to hear their pattering feet nor to clearly see, in shades of gray, the piles of rubbish littering the unlit alley. She stilled.

Squeezing her eyes shut, she bent double, drawing in deeper breaths, the pain in her head pounding to the beat of her heart. Panting, dripping, she looked up. A few hundred meters away, office blocks towered.

Her wrists were sore too, she realized. And her temples. And ankles. She opened her eyes, raising bruised fists and saw abraded wrists. Staring past them across the bay, an immense low bridge arched into darkness. On the far shore, lights twinkled.

A searchlight, sweeping the waters, went out.

Where am I?

Turning, she squelched on down the alley, emerging onto a broad road stretching left and right. Unlit warehouses fronted metal tracks laid across the road. Some distance behind, she heard stealthy booted feet. She let them herd her on while she searched for concealment. At the end of the road, another warehouse, gaps looming between it and the adjacent buildings towering left and right.

The booted feet were closer, now.

CHAPTER 2

A rusting garbage skip sat at the corner of the alley to her right, the gap behind it easily deep enough for her to fit. She slipped in, dripping water, and tried to breathe quietly.

Shutting her eyes, she struggled against the nails pounding into her brain to visualize the ground she'd just covered. How much of a trail had she left, sprinting across? Too much. It'd be plain to see with UV goggles and torches. She knew they'd have them, even if she didn't know *how* she knew that. A feral grin lit her face at the thought of sinking claws into her attackers. It distracted her from the sawing pain in her head.

Darting from cover, she paced down the alley to lay a short false trail, then backed up and finally jumped behind the dumpster to wait; resting her head against the rusting skip. Listening.

Fifty meters down the street, at the end of the alley she'd followed from the docks, the footsteps stopped. Two sets. Definitely booted.

"Is that her?" a deep voice rumbled, for a moment making her think she'd been seen.

"How the smek should I know?" whispered a second man's voice. "Maybe. It came from the bay, and I don't see any other trails."

She looked down at the water slowly puddling at her feet, and smiled in the darkness.

"Party one," said the same man again, his voice low. "Possible trail. Take a fix, we're moving in."

There was a reply, but she couldn't make out the words. Just the sound of stealthy footsteps approaching. Somehow she knew they carried guns.

She tensed, crouching against the building behind her, braced in fierce anticipation. Her fingers tingled.

The footfalls were close now. The nearest set were heavy, very heavy. They stopped.

Yeah, UV torches. She launched herself *over* the skip, just as the rumbling voice whispered "She's behind-"

She had a moment to register his massive size; goggles; the tusks protruding from the sides of his mouth. The muzzle of his pistol tracked toward her. Clearing the rim of the skip, she kicked out against it, boosting her flight and correcting her aim. One hand stabbed toward his massive but unprotected throat, hatred burning in crystal blades from her fingers. She punched deep through corded muscle and into bone, jolting his head back, her knees impacting his body as he toppled. She rode him just a moment, leaping from him to the man four steps behind.

Cursing, he took aim, firing as she twisted desperately.

She struck as needles pierced her side, vicious lightning jolting through her, and him. Her muscles spasmed; left hand raking his goggles, right hand at his throat, electricity writhing through them both.

He spasmed in turn, clenching the trigger tighter as her fingertips brushed his throat. Current surged harder, agony cramping her hand shut, her whole body curling up.

Don't scream! Never scream. Never show the pain.

Hot liquid sprayed her face, but the torment continued. As she and her assailant collapsed boneless to the dirty asphalt, something struck the ground beside her a single, solid blow.

Silence.

Muscles buzzing and shivering, she jerked to one side. The agony in her head swelled in a wave so vast it swept her away.

When it ebbed to something less brutal, she unknotted stomach muscles to roll onto her back, amazed that so much pain could fill her skull so silently. Head lolling, she stared at the man lying so still beside her. Dead. Somehow *she'd* done that, she knew. She nodded, satisfied. Mildly puzzled.

His head nestled against her, between her chin and chest. But his body lay at the wrong angle to it, dribbles of dark fluid leaking from the torso, spreading over grubby tarmac.

His head's practically off, she realized, confused. *How? Did I really do that?*

Then words. Tinny. Distant but close. She jerked her hand toward his head, twitching and cramping as she fought convulsing muscles, fumbling for his earbud.

The words came suddenly clear anyway, like a radio signal tuning in: "-one report! Repeat, why have you stopped?"

Pushing the head away she struggled to her feet and bullied her legs into operation, wobbling unsteadily upright.

More will come.

She looked around in the darkness, noting the wet prints all around, slowly drying in the night air. Grimacing at the pain, she tore off her soaking shoes, snagging velcro to loop them around her neck, then bent and took the weapon from the man's hand. At the ultrasonic whine of a capacitor charging up, she dropped it a moment before a high-voltage discharge sparked against the ground, the digital display flipping to red lock-down. *Bastards.*

They'd be drawn right here by the unauthorized access. Backing into the alley by the skip, her eyes picked a path between torn plastic trash bags and wind-blown rubbish, deeper into the unfamiliar city. The obvious escape route. But how many more were coming?

Shutting her eyes, she strained, her hearing stretching out into the dark. Was that more stealthy treads? Murmured terse words?

They'd have cars, drones, scanners, sensors to see through buildings, she knew. A prickle of pain warned her from questioning the source of that knowledge. At that she paused, feeling she was missing something – that there was something she should be thinking about. She shook her head. No time for that now. This night-deserted maze was a massive trap. Once they found the two men she'd downed, they'd concentrate the search here.

That meant she should return to the water. But halfway there the night turned so black she could hardly see, and the world fell still. As if her ears had been plugged, and a curtain drawn across her eyes.

She stumbled to a halt.

"Testing?" Not *quite* deaf, not quite blind: she could hear her own voice, still see city lights, and the moon riding high.

Then the darkness flickered and vanished, her hands returning in bright shades of gray, the world flooding back in around her, a proper landscape of sound.

What just happened?

She had no idea. Turning, she raced barefoot back the way she'd come, sprinting down the wooden jetty to dive into the cold dark waters of the bay. Pain surged in her head, easing as she floated, watching hand-held lights move in the near distance, hunting. For a few seconds she rested, watching and breathing, accepting the throbbing in her head. The wound in her neck was a sharper pain, yet somehow easier to ignore, a touch showing it hardly bled.

Diving under the water, she swam at a steady pace. Forty strokes and she quietly surfaced, sucking in air and watching the activity around the buildings. A hundred meters from land, she filled her lungs and dived back under water.

Ten minutes later she felt safe enough to stay on the surface. She struck out surely in the cold dark, following the shoreline. As the city lights fell away, the buildings along the shore became fewer and squatter. One kilometer she swam, the spearing pain in her head a steady torment sapping her energy. Doggedly, she ignored it.

Dully, swam on.

The realization she was tiring arrived only gradually, her thoughts fighting through cotton wool. Had she swum another kilometer? The pounding in her head had settled into something not actually pain, just a weirdly leaching ache. The cold was getting to her though. Shivering, treading water, she scanned around her.

Ahead, in the direction she'd been swimming, the shore jutted up darkly, no lights shining from it. The other way, across the rolling black surface of the bay, distant lights twinkled, outlining both ends of a bridge's massive span.

Where am I? Smaller lights moved along the shore from back the way she'd come, two boats quartering that area, their powerful searchlights probing. Something about that seemed familiar. *Are they searching for me?* She shuddered, the cold penetrating deep. *I need to get warm.* She swam quietly for shore, planning ahead. *I'll call a ride....* At the thought, she rolled her neck to confirm a snug presence: but found none. Pausing, one hand flashed to her neck, tracing only a grazing cut. Absence brought dismay. *My beautiful Link!* She chased a fleeting memory of sleek black elegance, until a prickle of pain lanced her head – but gently, as if herding her away.

Grinding her teeth she swam on, now dogged by the feeling she was overlooking something. About herself? Like, why they were hunting her? She frowned. Why *were* they hunting her?

The gently needling pain returned, and she snarled, letting the question go. For now.

But a perfectly audible whine just a hundred meters away made her stop again, worried, treading water. Shutting her eyes to focus on the source of the sound, she opened them again and narrowed her gaze. *Krek!* A drone, hovering fifty meters back from the shore. Two stories up. *Looking for me?* Backing quietly off she swam away, shivering.

Chit! I don't believe this!

Four hundred meters on, another drone. The damned cheapskates had set up a perimeter of sentry drones, who-knew-how-far along the coast.

When she finished her quiet cursing, she turned slowly in the water and considered her options.

Near exhaustion now, despite her aching muscles she somehow knew her biggest threat had become the cold. She couldn't feel her hands or feet properly, and her ears ached worse than her head. She *had* to get out of the water, but they'd detect her for sure if she came within range of a drone. Maybe a storm-water pipe? Then, from back the way she'd just come, a fair way from shore, she saw a faint light leaking from a silhouette: a boat, maybe.

Why not? She could slip aboard, get dry. Maybe even warm.

But fifty meters from the boat, treading water with clumsy legs like poorly-controlled paddles, she heard the almost inaudible whine of yet *another* drone! *Un-blagging-believable*. Wearily, her eyes tracked through the darkness till she found it. *Have they covered the whole funting city in drones?* Panic tugged at her. She wasn't sure she could swim another fifty meters, let alone all the way back to shore. She couldn't bend her fingers properly now, and she had to clench her jaws just to prevent the sound of chattering teeth from reaching the drone.

Gradually though, she realized *this* drone was different to the others. *Far* quieter. So quiet it had to be using active noise cancellation. And something else she noticed as she studied the vessel's slim lines, wind chilling her face. The small cruiser stretched out sideways before her instead of pointing into the wind, a second rope angling down into the water from the back. Two anchors? Was that normal?

But she'd run out of options. Facing back to the distant shore, she saw the impossibility of swimming that far. Her choices had narrowed to the boat, or drowning.

Feebly-moving legs chose that moment to finally still, settling beneath the water. Adrenaline spiked, but her legs

merely twitched in response. Somehow she got her arms
moving, awkwardly flailing through the water toward the
suddenly too-distant boat, aiming for the low board at the
back that rose and dipped into the water with each gentle
swell, abruptly unsure she could make it even *that* far.

I've left it too late.

CHAPTER 3

The boat's dark form bobbed in the water, salvation dangling just out of reach. She couldn't go on.

She forced herself onto her back in the water. Leaden legs dragged downward while biceps burned with a dull ache. She tried to gasp quietly, timing her breathing to the passing swell, each one only reluctantly lifting her, washing against her face. She just needed a little rest. The boat was barely fifty meters. She *had to* make it.

Her eyes slid from the dark vessel to the almost-silent drone hovering before it. So far it hadn't reacted to her presence. At the back of the boat two long fishing poles leaned out over the water, outstretched like the arms of a praying mantis.

The cold sank its hooks deeper.

She shut her eyes, just for a moment, gathering her reserves. It was a mistake. She failed to see the larger wave that crested her face. Salt water scoured her lungs as they spasmed, struggling for air, trying to clear her airways, while she fought to silence the convulsive coughs, her eyes fixed on the drone, and fought the panic threatening to claim her as surely as the cold dark depths below. Legs refusing to work, she went under mid-cough, rejecting the urgency to breathe until she'd clawed her way to the surface.

That fierce contest cost time, and energy. When the fit finally eased and she'd drawn several fragile breaths in succession, heavy limbs felt even more leaden. She seemed lower in the water, too. *That doesn't make sense. People don't sink, they float!* She felt suddenly like crying, like everything was against her.

The reaction triggered a flush of shame. *You're not a baby. Get to the boat.*

Lips trembling, she tried striking out for it, but her legs dangled uselessly despite her rest. Dismay galvanized her, but her arms were almost as bad, inert logs she could no longer stir to a single stroke. Resting longer would be a slow death, the cold now gripping her in its claws. Another wave crested over her, trying to sink her. That wasn't fair!

The tears threatened to return. Like a half-stunned turtle, she rolled onto her back, finally managing a clumsy backstroke that drew her dangling legs after. Struggling to keep her face above the swells, she breathed softly, her airways still threatening to clench back up into coughing spasms.

Five meters from the boat, the cold seemed to penetrate some final unsuspected barrier, becoming an all-enveloping blanket stealing her last energy.

But she had the coughing under control, and – face set in a determined grimace – stubbornly floundered closer to the vessel, stroke by painful stroke. She *refused* to stop. *Never,* she swore. *Never give in.* And was rewarded by a bump on her head. A platform at the rear of the boat, dipping in and out of the water as each wave passed. Which she could probably *just* manage to roll up onto, in her current state.

Eyes focused firmly forward, no longer thinking, she flailed one leaden arm down onto her calmly-bobbing salvation.

CHAPTER 4

Mason Dane stood in his galley, idly pouring a fresh mug of coffee while mulling over what he'd learned. He continued monitoring, but only two sources now: an occasional update from his communications drone outside, still locked on the freshly ventilated office; and the encrypted chatter from the radio broadcasts buzzing around Omega, two kilometers away on shore.

In a corner of his feed, he okayed an ad for Nemesys's new Grendel warbot. The juggernaut punched through a brick wall, tromping toward a pack of streetscum dealers whose shells spanged off it, its armor not far short of a battletank.

Nemesys were aiming for sales into urban police forces? *Urban* use? Checking the public specs, he saw that sideways, it *would* fit through a standard doorway. Dear god. Just one unit deployed into the Oakland Dumps would create an instant war zone. Checking the dark net, he saw the contract for its blueprints was still open.

Good.

But as he lifted his mug, a faint tremor shivered through the soles of his feet, freezing him with the coffee at his lips. Something had just bumped the boat.

Down went the mug, even as he considered whether to leave the lights on and appear innocent, or turn them off and go to stealth mode?

But there'd been no sound of an engine, nothing pinged on radar – he checked: yes, still true. Dousing the cabin lights with a thought he switched his eyes to night vision and un-opaqued the windows, sparing a quick glance out into the darkness. Nothing. Nothing visible to the drone, either, but it was only a comms unit, without IR or low light optics. Moving to the short companionway he drew his pistol, quietly opening the hatch and climbed cautiously on deck.

There he stilled, listening. A heavy piece of flotsam bumping up against the side? Or, a scuba diver making an insufficiently-stealthy boarding attempt? Scanning the decks he crept from the cabin, crouched and alert, waiting.

Nothing.

And then, another faint shudder from a solid, wet slap. At the stern.

The back of his neck prickled.

Completely silent now, he glided to the taffrail, still crouched low, keeping to one side so as not to appear in an expected place to whoever – or whatever – was in the water. There he waited again, listening, and was rewarded with the sound of a small gasp. He felt the familiar tingle of acceleration as his full array of augmentations came online, the matte black barrel of his pistol now clear in the bottom of his light-intensified field of view. Silently he rose, leaning out to aim down at the intruder.

And met a pair of eyes already locked on his.

A young woman, her face screwed up in equal parts determination and desperation stared up at him, her arms and upper body flopped on the swim platform. She tensed.

He barely avoided shooting her as she flopped clumsily sideways in the water, confusion flooding her expression.

He took in the stylish cut of her turquoise and white jacket: not a wetsuit. Not *any* type of swimwear. *What the hell?* Long pale hair plastered her drawn face, concealing a darker mark in the middle of her forehead. Had she come from a nearby, stealthed vessel? Cybernetic senses scanned the surrounding waves and air, but found nothing.

A wave lifted the stern, dislodging her. Snarling, she scrabbled at the crisscrossing wooden grill with a convulsive effort, gaining another hand's width onto the swim platform. *She's exhausted*. A decoy? Twisting and turning he retreated to the center of the afterdeck, half expecting scuba-suited attackers to leap over the sides.

None appeared.

Feeling a little foolish he padded back to peer over again. Had he been dreaming? Would she still be down there? Or up, and ready to attack?

She'd hardly moved. He flushed. This was no act. She was clearly exhausted; possibly ill. Why had he expected her to be crouched, waiting for his head to reappear over the stern railing?

She was half out of the water now, a thin white blouse clinging to a quite nice chest, rising and falling in great heaves, her tailored jacket open. She glared up at him.

Strong features, but he couldn't pick her race – some kind of mixture. Not Altered, though. Her eyes flicked briefly from his face to the drone hovering silently five meters above and behind him, and he suddenly wondered how this random chick could see *him*, in the dark? Since she clearly could. Did she see him as plainly as he saw her, with his augmented

vision? And how did she know his spy drone was there?
He'd spent *five K* stealthing that unit!

No, there was nothing random about this. *I'm blown*, he
thought, angling his pistol down at her. The question was,
who was she with? Not one of the big boys, like Tik Tek –
they'd use heavier hands than a solo little sliv like her.

Another independent, like him? A competitor?

But why swim out to his boat, for god's sake? Why tip him
off? That was just stupid. Something must have gone wrong
with their approach, whoever they were. He looked around,
scanning the waters around the boat again as he linked back
to the radar sweep and the surveillance drone's local moni-
tors – but still nothing showed up. It was as if she was here
all alone, and had simply swum up to him out of the Bay.

Had *she* been the object that had fallen from the window?
He shook his head. From the eighth floor? That'd injure you
at best, more likely kill you. And a solo operator couldn't
have eluded the suspiciously swift and professional manhunt.

"What are you doing?" he demanded. That was the key
question. *Who* could come later.

She stared coolly up at him even as she panted, still looking angry. He thought she wasn't going to answer.

"Not drowning."

It was hard to tell, even with light-intensified optics, but
the dark mark on her forehead could be bruising. Trickles of
blood, too. Had she hit her head and fallen overboard from
some passing vessel? But except for the boats still quartering
the waters around the earlier incident, there'd been nothing
out on the Bay for two hours. The last ferry to Oakland ran at
midnight.

The timing was about right for someone to swim out here
from the docks, though. If they were fit, and desperate, and
knew he was here. But unless his identity was blown...?

"How did you come to be in the water? Who are you?"

She studied him, angry at her muscles' refusal to co-operate.
Taking a deep breath she gathered her reserves, feeling a
weird obligation to answer his questions. It almost made her
decide not to.

"C-" But as her name rose to her lips, a sudden thought
overruled her: *secret. Your name's secret. Use the other.*

A sharp headache, somehow familiar, stabbed at her for

the thought. The memory stuttered and failed, in rising confusion, and worse pain. She tried again.

"C-"

Answer him.

But now the name eluded her. *So what? Distract him! You're cold – let your teeth chatter while you pick one.*

"Cr-." *What is it?* "Cr-." *Make something up!* "Crys-, Kristen."

I think I got away with that, she thought, failing to notice him go especially still. What else had he asked? Why was she in the water?

She frowned. Why *was* she in the water? She thought back, through the pain. She'd been swimming, trying to get to shore. But something had kept stopping her. Something watching in the sky, buzzing. Insects? Or had they been drones, like the one above him? She shook her head. Pain ebbed when she let the thought fade.

"... *Kristen.*"

With an effort, she realized he was talking to her.

"What were you doing in the water?"

It was night. Her head ached, and she was freezing. And exhausted. Utterly exhausted. Judging the distance to the man above her, to his pistol, she found part of herself formulating an attack. Groaning, she rolled to her side to pull her legs up onto the platform, dismayed to find even *that* effort beyond her. Her attack plan receded, shelved.

For now.

"Swimming."

It was hard to focus on the man leaning over the railing above. Acid pain laced every muscle, her legs especially, like something deep inside was eating at them; different to the dull agony in her head or the sharper pain in her neck. Somehow she wrestled one hip onto the board, and from there, dragged her legs out of the water. Exhausted, and a little scared by the feeling in her limbs, she slumped against the back of the boat, resting. *What's wrong with me? Why does my head hurt so bad? How* did *I get in the water?*

Staring up at him, her thoughts suddenly shifted, spinning crazily. She found herself admiring his shoulders, the dusting of stubble on his cheeks, the square line of jaw. A cloak of gravitas settled over him. Did she know him? Some instinct recognized his authority.

But beneath that, something inside struggled furiously, as if fighting for its very existence. Pain lanced through her head with such stunning force her lips parted to cry out-

Never. Never let him see-.

Him? Who? A face, with hooded eyes and a cruel smirk vanished. Reaching for it triggered renewed agony and she bit down hard on a moan. It was hard to think. Yet the man's question still floated in her mind, an ominous test demanding an answer. *I don't* know *how I got in the water.*

A cold wind gusted, curling around her, reaching under her jacket, making her suddenly aware just how chilled she was. She couldn't remember ever being so cold. Bizarrely, then, she pictured a girl, on her knees, clutching a frost-dusted half-dog, half-robot. Then that image dimmed and fell into darkness. And she followed it down.

CHAPTER 5

The young woman – at most twenty, he guessed – collapsed, as if the effort of dragging herself from the water had sapped the last dregs of her strength. But he didn't move, just waited, watching as she slumped boneless, her chest rising and falling.

Huddled into the corner made by the swim platform and stern, shivers ran through her as waves lapped beneath, reaching for her in hunger.

He shook his head at the foolish thought.

A trap? It didn't feel like one. Yet for two full minutes he watched, while her tremors steadily worsened.

Making his decision, he re-holstered his pistol, half hoping she'd suddenly spring up and grab for the weapon. It was, after all, keyed only to him. But she didn't move when he leapt nimbly over to land beside her. Wincing as water slopped into his shoes he bent, slipping his arms under her, and lifted.

She was heavier than she looked. Muscles straining, augments kicked in, digital readouts putting her at 74.7 kilos. That didn't make much sense. She was only a small woman; looked sixty, sixty-five kilos max soaking wet. What did that say about her bones, or muscle density? Discarding his plan of climbing the stern rail with her, he instead hefted her, gently dumping her on the afterdeck.

His own shirt and trousers now saturated and cold, he leapt on deck and shivered, hesitating to touch her.

Get a grip, Mason! Shaking himself, he checked her forehead, which was cold, and her pulse, which was strong. Brushing a pale fringe back he peered at a pattern of radial scratches amid purpling bruises. She had an odd cut or tear on the side of her neck too.

Crouching on his heels, he considered possibilities while searching her quickly and professionally for weapons, finding none. Except in her jacket pocket, what looked like a high velocity shell, fired, its spalled casing forced back shut. Souvenir?

Frowning, he pocketed it and gazed back out over the cold waters of the Bay. The distant office block still buzzed with activity. Lights probed the foreshore from its damaged eighth floor, one vessel still searching the waters below the smashed window... of armored glass. Again, he wished he'd had the bandwidth for a reasonable res video feed, but the audio had been far more important. He'd *thought*.

Who was she? *What* was she? He ran his fingers over her cheek. Flesh. But then, even the old Mark VIs had used vat-grown organics. He probed the forearm, the elbow joint. They *felt* human. But that would be the point, wouldn't it? He probed the back of her skull, then her shoulder blades, checking for induction charging plates, but felt nothing. Maybe she *was* human?

If so he'd better get her inside and warmed. Prepared for her weight this time he hoisted her over one shoulder, turning and backing down the companionway, careful not to bump her head. He laid her on the galley's tiled floor then fetched towels, spreading them out and rolling her onto them. She didn't react.

Closing the hatch, he switched his optics back to normal and activated the cabin lights – windows fully opaqued, of course, to prevent even a glimmer leaking outside. He frowned, staring down at the woman, assuming that's what she was. Girl perhaps: unconscious, she looked younger, more vulnerable.

Crouching beside her, he pushed her fringe off her forehead, studying the injury again. What the hell was it from? It had bled a little: it looked like a radiating star of scratched bruises. Something about that pattern tugged at a memory. No bruise in the very middle. He brushed the marks, lightly, with his fingers, feeling slight contusions. She moaned, faintly, as he probed it. He rocked back, perplexed.

Quite a pretty face, he decided. Round. Firm chin, small nose, though a touch too broad to be truly beautiful. He still couldn't pick the race, though. A composite? She had fine, waist length hair, perfectly white. Somehow he doubted that was her natural coloring: her eyebrows were dark. Full lips. Her face looked drawn though. Like she was anorexic. Or recently starved.

Her shaking had intensified. It now ran right through her, but worryingly, the amplitude had dropped. Her body trying to warm her, but unable to summon the strength to do much more than quiver? He needed to get her warm.

He remembered the coffee he'd poured just before she'd disturbed him. Even if she was a Mark VIII, or some experimental prototype, the nutrients and heat should help her. They'd at least feed the biological parts, reduce the overall

energy burden of running her systems. And her reaction to it
would tell him more. He fetched another towel, rubbing her
hair to remove the worst of the water before padding it under
her head as a small pillow. He stood, considering. She
looked normal. Gaunt but normal.

Stepping past her to the galley, he checked the coffee –
still hot. He added a generous amount of sugar, then milk
and a dash of brandy, stirring it well. He took a sip himself:
piping hot. Far too sweet for his taste, but the sugar should
give her an energy boost. He settled behind her, supporting
her, grimacing as his clothes soaked up more cold water.
Hauling her forward, he held the mug to her lips. One-
handed, he gently patted a cheek.

"Kristen – wake up, drink this. Kristen."

Her eyes half-opened, the smell of the coffee reaching her.
Her lips parted, and he carefully tipped a little into her
mouth. She swallowed, making a small sound of approval,
seeking more. Sips at first, then her eyes opened more and
she took in a whole mouthful, suddenly coughing and looking
almost awake. When it passed she swallowed eagerly, gulping it down, her hands lifting shakily to the mug. He had to
restrain her from just tipping the whole thing up. He had the
impression she wasn't fully conscious.

An odd *quiver* ran through her, her eyes focusing on his,
her lips parting, the small tongue dancing across them sensually as she stared at him. A hesitant smile tugged at the corners of her mouth. Shy. But something about it felt empty,
even unnerving. The conviction she wasn't fully conscious
returned; and with the realization, her faintly adoring expression sent unease creeping through him.

Then the mug was drained and she was quaking, her muscles shuddering in great heaves, then convulsions so violent
he thought at first he'd triggered an epileptic fit, there in his
arms. But still so cold. Her eyes lost focus, closing as she
eased into steady shivers, and he sensed she was gone again,
just her body acting on its own, trying to warm her.

He set the empty mug aside, leaning her forward to strip
first one sleeve then the other until he could pull the cream-
and-aquamarine jacket right off. And discovered broken skin
and bruises at her left wrist. And right. Shit. She'd been re-
strained. He checked her ankles: yes, those too showed
bruising.

Christ. One way or the other, the stakes had just grown a whole lot more serious.

The fingertips of her right hand were injured too he noticed: small cuts, quite recent. Just the tips of her index and middle fingers of her right hand though. He zoomed his optics. The thumb tip too, although there the scratches had failed to break the skin. Her neck injury oozed blood.

He fetched his first aid kit. After cleaning, he recognized a bullet graze, but with a shallow stab wound too. Other odd thin bruises and scratches circled her neck. He applied antiseptic before smoothing a dressing in place.

Her shivering had worsened. He needed to get her out of her wet clothes. He unbuttoned her blouse – an expensive *Chateau Equipe*, he noted – then stripped that too. His brows raised in involuntary appreciation at both her choice of lingerie and how nicely she filled it, and he gave in to the temptation that whispered she'd warm faster if he removed *all* her wet clothes. Deftly unhooking the pale, lacy bra he set it aside. Again, a very expensive brand, and a part of his brain noted with approval it was only slightly padded. Her breasts – quivering as she shuddered and shook from cold – sat firm and full, the skin taut. He had to consciously tell himself she was chilled, not reacting to his presence.

Or programmed that way?

He pushed aside the thought, feeling shame as he unbuttoned the snug waist of her designer jeans and then, with no small difficulty, peeling them – *Jacqueline Perry*, very nice – from around her hips and down a pair of dancer's legs. The French knickers – again, very stylish – clasped a trim waist. After easing them down her legs he paused to study the unconscious beauty lying naked before him. Her every muscle was clearly outlined, thrumming with tension; she even had abs, a small six-pack. Fit indeed. There wasn't a gram of fat on her. He realized with a twist of unease he was half-erect.

But she continued to spasm and shudder from the cold, and his shame deepened. She couldn't be a sex bot. Why would they program even a prototype to feel the cold? Or pain. His eyes widened at an unpleasant thought. There were some very sick people out there, after all.

He shook his head. Have a little faith in your fellow man. Besides, she really didn't look like a gynoid.

He fetched more towels, briskly rubbing her down, drying

her and trying to chafe a little heat into her.

Hefting her, he carried her past the dining table and its surrounding bench seat into the forward cabin, signaling its light back on. She stirred as he maneuvered her to the bed, her arms going up and around his neck.

He had to tug her arms free to lay her down fully, before dragging the quilt over her. She continued to spasm and shudder, her eyes open and pointed his way, but unfocused. Again, she licked her lips sensuously, and something about it – had it been an exact repetition of her earlier move? – made him acutely uncomfortable. Like it was some kind of trained response. Or programmed behavior.

He re-cued the last ten seconds of video from his optics, comparing it to the earlier example; then swore. The match was effectively exact. So... she *was* a gynoid? That would explain the weight. Had someone – Tik Tek – made a sentient robot? Their marketing trumpeted how their gynoids and androids incorporated the latest advances in Artificial General Intelligence, although avoiding claims of sentience or anything more than very limited problem-solving.

Remembering his first sight of her, he shook his head. She'd seemed so human.

Unless, maybe... had someone been remotely *piloting* her, earlier, overriding the gynoid's operating system to steal her? *It.* Or was she some cutting edge prototype, malfunctioning?

Shit. He needed to know more. None of this was making sense. But he was certain it would be ugly when it did. Especially given this was a *Washington Group* contract. The question was, should he stay in the game? Or just drop out: forget the contract? Retreat, and keep his soul?

He stood for a while, troubled and undecided. Certain though that she was part of it. Maybe he should just grab this attractive windfall and run with it? It'd certainly raise the stakes, for him. *And the risk.* Consciously setting that line of thought aside he considered his more immediate problem.

More coffee, he decided, and headed back to the galley. *He* could do with one too he realized, cold now himself from damp clothes and his brief stint above deck. He collected her mug from the floor, using the damp towels to mop puddled water from the tiled section of the galley before tossing them into the small basin inside the head, confident of missing the lavatory. Straightening, he eyed the coffee machine.

He soon had two mugs ready, each with another dash of brandy, hers with lots of sugar and a very generous amount of milk – excellent for re-hydration as well as supplying proteins and minerals. She certainly looked like she needed feeding. He gulped his down on the way back to the cabin, welcoming its scalding heat.

She still shivered violently under the bedding. Sharing body heat would be the fastest way to warm her up, and he considered his own cold and half-wet clothes. Sitting her up against *that* while he got her fresh mug into her wouldn't be a kindness. Not even if she *was* some new prototype gynoid. Setting her mug down he snatched a change of clothes for himself from his locker for later. Stripping, he tossed his wet clothes out into the galley and slipped in beside her, sitting her up and pulling her back against him before taking her coffee mug.

Again, her lips parted at the aroma, and she gulped it down. Setting the empty mug aside he wrapped his arms around her. She pressed her chilled body into him and he gritted his teeth at the shock of cold, even as part of him responded to the buttocks pressing snugly into his groin. The reaction surprised him. It made him wonder, if she *had* been programmed, how far it extended?

But what if she's not a gynoid? What if it's some kind of sick training? That thought killed the unexpected desire. Chuck Bishop, the so-called God of Malcolm Street arrested way back in '41, had been just the first in a depressing line of magical abusers. It continued to this day, just better hidden. Far worse in other countries, too. He grimaced.

Quickly, her shivers eased, and she even started to warm. She moved against him. Almost involuntarily he found his hands holding her, stroking her. She responded, arching into him then twisting around, pressing herself flat against him. Something – the way she moved, the small sounds she made – sent his blood surging. He felt her nipples, erect now *not* from cold, digging into his chest, triggering more vaguely-animal sounds from those full lips which sought his, avidly; even desperately. *Christ!* He tried to remind himself this could be some awful kind of conditioning.

Her eyes glittered, feverish, craving, and something like fear shivered through him, at the sudden certainty there was no thought there, no consciousness, just hunger.

He felt off-balanced by his own strong reaction to her. *Pheromones?* But they'd been proven not to work, not in humans.

Her legs and arms had wrapped around him, her hips thrusting at his, nudging his organ, seeking to move it into position. Somehow, it was just too much: his willpower finally collapsed, and he groaned in anticipation, his arms going around her in return, turned on yet disturbed by his own reaction.

And at that precise moment the drone messaged him that a vessel, on an intercept course, would arrive within two minutes.

CHAPTER 6

Through a fog of lust he accessed the drone's logs, mainly in the hope he could dismiss its warning and continue; but the vessel headed for them now had been one scouring the shore earlier. He forced himself back to rationality, cursing as he did so. "Stop. Kristen, we have to stop!" He shut his eyes to better access the video feed, groaning involuntarily as something warm and tight suddenly sheathed him. He swore as the drone's video showed a searchlight paint his vessel. He called his drone down and out of sight.

"Kristen! Stop! We have company coming," he told her, desperately, but had to push her away when she appeared not to hear. Her grip was weak though, and she slid free of him with a strange keening sound. He forced himself to ignore her.

"Searching for you, I'd say." The effort it took to sound calm and rational shocked him. *Why did I respond so strongly?* But there was no time to consider that now. Every second counted. He signaled the cabin lights off and switched his optics back to night mode. Jumping from the bed, he began dressing, struggling awkwardly with his erection.

Shit, what to do with her? This was only a ten-meter launch, there was nowhere to hide anyone, especially not if the searchers were who he thought they were. And she still lay on the bed, looking confused. Blinking though now, and looking like she was waking up. Her eyes met his, despite the dark, and once again he wondered if she was augmented, like him – or something else entirely.

Whatever, he wasn't about to let her fall – back? – into Omega's hands.

"Kristen! Snap out of it! They'll be here in ninety seconds. They already have a searchlight on the boat. And there's nowhere on board to hide you."

Damn. He hated what he was thinking of doing to her, but saw no other option. Sweeping up both coffee mugs he darted into the galley, rinsing and hanging one in its place, leaving the other in the sink. Back in the head, he tossed his damp clothes and the wet towels into the slim laundry hamper, wincing at her sodden outfit. He wrung it all out into the basin. Remembering the high velocity round, he slipped it back into the pocket it had come from. But the seconds were running out fast. Back in the galley he wedged her clothes into the narrow space behind the gimbal-mounted stove. Its metal surrounds would help block any scans.

He strode to the locker where he'd stowed his underwater gear, snagging a squat tube with built-in mouthpiece.

"Kristen," he called, "we only have sixty seconds to hide you!" He turned, startled to find her right behind him, still naked. Her head tilted as if puzzled by him.

He thrust the silvery tube at her. She took it automatically, but her eyes stayed locked on his as if mesmerized. "This is a ten-minute rebreather. You understand? It'll let you breathe underwater for ten minutes. Here." He opened the valve and slipped the mouthpiece between her lips. The look she gave him at that reminded him of her nakedness, and his erection abruptly surged again. He swore.

A heavy, powerful vibration rumbled through the cabin. Diesel engines, for god's sake. Who still used diesel?

"Look, we have almost no time," he said, running out to the companionway and opening the hatch. Light flooded in, making them both wince. He didn't dare take her up on deck now.

He pointed to one of the windows encircling the main cabin, on the opposite side from their visitors. "Slide that one open and slip into the water without them seeing you. I'll distract them. But *keep out of sight* till they've gone!"

He examined her face as she stared blankly back at him. They were out of time, though, he had to go up. He grabbed a robe.

One foot on the gangway he paused and looked back. Blinking, her expression cleared, and she nodded to him. He went up to face the hunting party, trying to look sleepy and annoyed.

This could all go horribly wrong.

She watched the man dart up the ladder and out of sight. Creeping forward cautiously, she climbed up, keeping low. He was waving and demanding to know who the hell they were. From her left came the sound of a motor, water, and other men answering him, but she stopped listening. Where was she? *Keep out of sight*, he'd said, a curious tingle running through her at the order, the thought of obeying. She drew in metallic-tasting air from the device she held clamped between her teeth. *A rebreather.* She'd used one before, she was sure. Though she couldn't remember exactly when. She shook her head, each thought a struggle, pieced together in fits and starts.

Goaded by an internal chorus to trust him, she had to get into the water, *now*. Unseen.

Tricky.

Crouched in the cabin, she studied her situation, dismissing her nakedness: though a tiny part of her seemed to struggle with that dismissal. She felt strange, and found one hand cupping and stroking a breast, her hips swaying while she scanned and listened and judged angles.

The instant she realized what she was doing, a kind of smothered outrage flared from deep inside, putting a halt to it. At that the pain stabbed back, literally blinding her for a moment.

When it passed, she found her hand had moved back. She took it away again, conscious that the *men* – again, a strange thrill just from hearing their deep voices – seemed to be coming to some kind of angry conclusion. *Get into the water. Without being seen.*

The moment she started working out *how* to do that, the pain receded, a strange pleasure tingling through her. It was almost distracting. But how to exit unseen?

Windows were spaced around the cabin. They were large and high, stretching above a central table. Further back they were smaller and lower, some sections with no windows at all. One window was even in shadow. Instantly she darted to it, tugging violently at the catch. Something snapped, and she pushed it open. She jerked back from the drone hovering right outside, buzzing in the dark, and she hesitated just long enough to recognize it from before. Diving through the window she slid down onto the deck, hidden by the superstructure of the cabin.

The drone flew past her and in through the window, then powered down. And she slipped over the side into shockingly cold water.

CHAPTER 7

Go deeper.

The shock of chill water paralyzed her, the warmth she'd won suddenly punctured, leaking fast. But she'd be too visible at the surface if they shone that searchlight her way. Adrenaline surged, demanding action; but a deeper memory triggered. A finely muscled man, tattooed. Japanese. Not much taller than her. Pain, deep in her head, prickled.

Pause. Assess. Then Act. Do not let panic drive you.

She'd taken those words to heart. Learned them. Now she recalled them, and *paused: assessed,* while pain stabbed into her head and fear flailed at her, the waters below deep and black and hungry. Anything could be down there, hunting.

Already cold, arms wrapped around her waist, she pushed those thoughts aside. Legs dangling, mouth at sea level, a wave washed over her as she bobbed. Hadn't she floated better before? Not that it mattered, with the rebreather. Another wave crested over her, washing through her long hair like a lover's fingers. The pain in her head throbbed dully, now. The cold seemed to be actually helping with that. Unless it had numbed her all the way through.

Hugging herself wasn't keeping her warm. Time to move. Calm now, she stretched out her arms as if in welcome and gently windmilled them, pointing her toes and slipping beneath the surface. Air with a metallic tang hissed in as she drew on the rebreather. She blew back into the mouthpiece, keeping her lips sealed tight around its molded flange, the thought slowly coalescing, *where did I learn that?* She frowned, the pain in her head sharpening until she let the puzzle go.

She sank down, head tilted up to watch the darker shapes of the boats above recede, the hull of the new one larger and shark-like. The smaller boat, the one she'd left, glowed like Hope, haloed by the light focused on it. From its front and back, two dark lines arced in gentle curves into the depths. Anchor ropes.

The light faded quickly as she rowed herself steadily deeper, staring up at the fading light. The darkness made the cold feel worse.

Warmth became a memory as the light dwindled.

Angry at herself for clinging to the sight, she growled, spinning in the water and turning her back on it. Teeth gripping the breathing apparatus, strong thrusts of her arms and legs pulled her into the inky deep.

Fear sang her nerves alight, the darkness tugging at her, a precipice urging her to fling herself over it.

Parts of her tingled, aroused. *Why am I so turned on?* She fought for control. Breathing too hard, a cloud of bubbles escaped her mouth. She concentrated on that. *Bubbles could be a problem, if anyone saw them.* Pausing, stirring the water with her hands, she turned over to look upward in case anything had changed. She couldn't see her hands now. Nothing. *Nothing.* Just pitch blackness. Dismay spiked through her. Honest fear surged in its wake, seeking to drown her, break her. She fought back with sheer stubbornness, *refusing* it.

No. Never.

A dim glow rotated into view, its wan light shivering through her, an infusion of hope. She'd just been pointed the wrong way. She exhaled gustily in relief, faster than the rebreather could absorb, and more bubbles escaped, ghostly outlines wobbling upward. *Calm. Let the mind be at peace, even in the midst of motion.* The remembered words brought a fresh stab of pain, but they let her center herself, and soon she was breathing steadily into the mouthpiece.

What if they shone a light straight at her? She needed to go deeper, but it'd be too easy to lose her bearings completely.

Again she paused, stilling her mind as she'd been taught – aware of the dull head pain retreating even further, but refusing to let even that relief distract her. Making out the faint dark line of the anchor rope above her, a solution appeared – follow it. She'd have to swim back up though to keep it in sight. With, what, nine minutes of air left? She began her swim, teeth grinding on the mouthpiece.

How deep did she need to go? How long would the searchers stay? How quickly could, could *someone*, someone *male*, up above, get rid of them?

Sudden confusion, the pain in her head returning as she swam up toward the man who waited. *Something's wrong.* She struggled to remember. Why was she in the water? *Hiding.* Who waited for her, in the boat?

No answer came.

She couldn't remember. Just that it was a man, helping

her somehow. She was sure of that much. A firm jaw-line; stubble.

She swam with savage strokes. The effort brought hints of warmth, but it was hard won, her muscles not responding as they should. *You're near exhaustion,* that annoyingly detached voice in her head offered. *Too bad,* she told it.

She imagined her *self* powering her muscles; spirit fingers working them, igniting a deep acid pain, as if she fed her own flesh into the fiery engine of her body. That summoned an image that *had* to be nightmare: her fingertips somehow flensing strips from her own forearm. As if the appalling memory unearthed something deeper and crueler than the acid eating her muscles, the spike through her brain returned, punishing her success.

Clenching her jaw she rejected it all, forcing her muscles to her will, ignoring the cost. *Too bad. I'll* never *give in.* Acid ate at her, but its pain only made her set her teeth tighter. *Never;* never *give up.*

The beam of light abruptly swung down from the boat above, spearing into the waters, probing the depths. Hunting for her.

Looking up into its light she saw two dark shapes with flippered feet plunge into the water beside the shark-shaped hull.

Confusion vanished, a fierce grin forming in response to the new threat. Especially when the flashing beam briefly lit the faint dark line she'd been swimming for. Hah! For seconds, she paused, fighting the need to ignore it, to *hunt* the scuba figures instead – but finally she forced the temptation away, swimming instead for the so-helpfully revealed rope. Her guide into the depths. Into the darkness.

The subtle tingling she'd felt earlier, the arousal, returned with surprising strength at the thought of surrendering to the blackness below, washing through her and over her in a wave that rode the acid burn to bring every part of her alight. Each nerve-ending felt as if it *unfurled* from her in a strange way, connecting her to something in the darkness, huge and powerful, beautiful and strange. She was no longer sure where *she* ended and the water began.

The water responded; came *alive.* As if she'd called it, its fluid soul sang through her.

Tendrils of something *other* coiled around her, feathering

across her skin, the liquid kisses of curious butterflies. They flowed inside her, following the spirit lines she'd threaded through her muscles – flinching at their first questing touch then attuning, resonating.

She gasped as pleasure flooded her nerves and swept on into her mind. Twisting and twining through her, streaming into her, tasting her consuming fires.

Her hand met the heavy anchor rope even as her body pulsed and flared with life. Excited, *eager*. She clasped the rope. Pulling herself swiftly deeper, hand over hand, all restraint swept away by a sudden, urgent hunger. Down. Down!

CHAPTER 8

"Just so you know, assholes, I'm Linked and recording, so if this is a robbery-"

"Calm down, sir, we're here for your safety."

Shielding his eyes from the glare, Mason squinted at the new arrivals. The well-spoken guy in charge sized him up in turn, then ignored him as his eyes moved unhurriedly over his vessel. The deliberation told Mason the man was recording: he tended to do the same thing himself. He should probably watch that, in future.

The leader was tall, bald, and solid, but moved with a fighter's confidence. The cohort with him were more obviously muscled, and more obviously armed too. Security, of course – but *Tik Tek* security, he was sure, from the arrogant self-assurance alone. Like he was a bug they could crush if the mood took them. Luckily they appeared not to have the bulky equipment they'd need to detect the spidery carbon nanotube tracery woven through his nervous system, and the robe he'd snatched up was an OmniBlock goretex weave. He added a mental thanks to Happy Joe Holliday, for making shielded clothing fashionable. Maybe those high-profile 'bodyguards to the stars' had their uses after all. Even if the bald guy was who he suspected, one on one he'd put money on himself. Unfortunately, the odds were six against one.

Just play along, he told himself, double-checking that his systems were safely locked in standby mode and couldn't be prodded into automatic reaction.

He wondered how Kristen was doing. The sooner he could get rid of these mercs the sooner he could get her warm again, and discover what she knew. Or what she *was*. He dragged his mind back to his current role of innocent aggrieved fisherman.

"Whad'ya mean, my safety? What's going on? Who're you guys?"

"AquaSec."

Yeah, right.

"Some drugged up teen gang's been causing trouble. Shot out an office window on the foreshore, and we think some of them took to the water. Have you seen anything?"

"Are you kidding me? Out *here?* And it's after two a.m! I was *asleep* till your damned searchlight blasted my boat and woke me!"

"Sorry about that, sir. Your safety is our main concern.

And you are?"

"What's it to you? I know my rights-"

"Sir, we suspect there's a chance the gangers were acting *for* someone. And under the Corporate Protection Act, 2052, in those circumstances we have the right-"

"Yeah, yeah, all right, all right. Tom Kingston. Salesman for *Rep Repairers, Inc.*" Mason was glad he'd done his groundwork. The identity would check out. And no doubt, knowing both Tik Tek's capabilities and a little of the stakes behind the drama earlier tonight, they would already have cross-referenced the boat's name – painted across the stern – to the rental yard's records, just waiting to see if his answers matched what they already knew. The fact they didn't bother to ask to see some ID confirmed that.

"This your vessel, Mr Kingston?"

"*The Sleeping Tom*? I wish. Just a rental. Picked it because of the name."

"What are you doing out here, at two a.m? Why two anchors? That puts you sideways to the waves, worsens the rocking."

"I did it to keep the bow *into* the waves, after the wind shifted earlier. And I'm fishing. See: those are fishing rods. Surprised you couldn't recognize them."

"No need for sarcasm Mr Kingston. This whole thing can go smoothly, with minimal disruption to your evening – *provided* you co-operate. Mind if we come aboard for a quick search?"

"You're joking. I'd know if someone else was on board!"

"Perhaps. Some of the teens were Altered: who knows what they could do, especially drugged up? I'm sure you have nothing to do with them. That you have nothing to hide?"

-

She felt it wrap around her in vigorous fluid folds, cold against her skin yet intimate and *alive;* so alive. And powerful; *such* power. Her nerves wafted like fragile fronds threading the water. She sensed delight at her touch and grasped its ethereal form, holding it tight in turn. Startling it.

Sensation flowed between them, tidal, a mirrored sense of wonder at what each held. Exotic; foreign. Yet a deep familiarity, too: lovers reuniting after eons apart.

Flesh called spirit; female called male; queen summoned

drone. Demanding. *Invoking*.

Water congealed, confused. She opened, drawing it inside her, crying out into her breathing tube at the eruption of pleasure. Demanding more, *more*.

She felt her heat shock into it, too intimate for it, and felt it pull back in sudden consternation. *How like a man.* She gripped it, enveloping, teasing it with the sense of its own fear, daring it to open to her alienness as she had to its. Her blood sang, calling it to communion.

More, she demanded, fierce, both fear and fire racing along her nerves, careless of consequences.

More!

Watching the searchers move through his vessel, flinging open lockers and poking inside, sensors in hand, scanning – terahertz and radio imaging units, certainly – Mason felt the nose of his boat suddenly dip down.

What the *fuck?*

The searchers didn't seem to notice, unfamiliar with the motion of this boat, presumably taking it for just another unpleasant movement caused by his strange anchoring. But Mason's mind was suddenly elsewhere. What the hell had just happened? It felt like something had tugged *down* on the for'ard anchor line. Tugged with enough force to jolt a five-tonne boat.

Had a *whale* snagged the line? What were the chances of that? Besides, wouldn't a whale have sensed the rope and avoided it?

Had *she* done it, somehow? Cut the rope, so it jerked suddenly up? But it had jerked *down*. Or had it been an explosion? Had her power-plant blown up, or had she herself been booby-trapped? Or had the searchers just set off a depth charge?

But they continued blithely on. Surely before detonating an explosive they'd have first warned their men? He was being crazy, he knew. But at the same time, he was somehow sure *she* had something to do with it.

"A drone, Mr Kingston? Why do you need a drone?"

He dragged his attention back to his own situation as one of the searchers pulled the drone off its charging station, even while he mentally tallied up how long she'd been down there. Over four minutes now. The cold must be getting to her....

"Sure. You may have noticed I'm here alone. I use it to record myself while I'm fishing." And unless they pulled it apart, they wouldn't find all its customizations. He yawned. "Look, it's after two o'clock in the goddamn morning, there's clearly no one but me on board. So if there *is* some gang of drugged teen elves or whatever out there, searching me is wasting *your* time. And *my* sleeping time. I have to be back at work the day after tomorrow, and I don't want my last day of fishing ruined by some group of paranoid water police. You've got my name. I'm not going anywhere. What more do you want?"

The man in charge merely studied him, before casting his gaze once more around the cabin. Mason saw his eyes stop briefly on the single coffee mug in the sink, glad he'd thought to hang the other back in place.

The tall man's bald head gleamed under the gentle cabin lights as he looked around. The other two searchers returned, shaking their heads. He felt another general ping and scan against his network links – including the one copied privately to him from his obviously-expensive, glistening-black wristlink – but was careful not to respond, not even a port-response. No sense letting them know anything of his own capabilities. He probably had more augmentation than any of these three, even the dangerous looking lead guy, for all the money Tik Tek threw at its security staff.

At last, the man turned back to him.

"Thank you Mr Kingston for your co-operation," he said, offering a hand. Mason responded, visibly wincing at the crushing force, being careful not to overplay his reaction but even more careful not to respond in kind.

"Christ, that's some grip! What are you, fully cybered? Shit!" He shook his hand open, as if in pain.

The man just smiled coolly. "My apologies, Mr Kingston. Sometimes I... *overreact*, shall we say? Here's my card. Good evening."

Mason watched them climb up on deck, finally preparing to leave. He held the plasticized business card gingerly, keeping his prints clear. An impressively flashy piece of active holography to catch the eye, no doubt to distract from its true functions. Bugged too, of course. He'd sink it as soon as they'd left, but noted the name: Arvid Henstridge. *That* was the name he'd been trying to remember. Yeah, Tik Tek. Did Yamamoto know his security was being provided by Tik Tek? Probably not: their ownership of AquaSec's parent company was very indirect, a well-guarded secret.

He followed Henstridge and his team up the gangway, then stood carefully projecting both annoyance and relief in his stance and scowl. They freed the lines lashing the two boats together and jumped neatly back aboard their imposing cruiser. He didn't move to help.

A chill ran through him as he saw a wet-suited figure at their stern, and a second climbing back aboard. Shit! Had they found her? Already dragged her onto their boat, without him seeing? Was that why they were leaving? *Not* because they'd found nothing suspicious on his vessel?

Surely not. If they *had* grabbed her, they would've assumed he'd been helping her, and pulled him in too.

He checked the time. Six minutes forty seconds. A bit more than three minutes left to her. Naked, in the cold, she'd be right back where she'd been earlier. Maybe worse. She'd already been exhausted: two cups of coffee couldn't fix that.

He frowned. The two scuba guys would've had sonar, so how *had* she avoided them? She'd have had to go right to the very bottom, and how would she know to do that? Who would *choose* to do that? Besides, since he'd anchored over the fault line of '36, right here that meant she would've had to descend almost thirty meters. Was that even *possible?* He winced. At that depth her air would already be running out.

Regardless, if she didn't show herself immediately his next problem would be finding her to bring her back up.

The searchlight finally swung away from him as the deep throb of the large sleek craft rumbled across the water, spewing clouds of stinking diesel in its wake, its brutally-powerful engine a low thunder.

Its hull lifted out of the water, quickly generating a huge bow-wave as it deliberately looped around him before charging back the way it had come. He braced himself for the violent rocking as the encircling wash surged toward him.

"Assholes," he swore, sure his words would be picked up by the 'business card', bracing himself as his boat tipped violently one way, then the other, then jerked up and sideways as the rest of the wave struck, almost swamping it.

"Shit!" he cried, still play-acting, slamming one hand flat

into the cabin wall to make it sound like his grip had been torn free and he'd been thrown into it. "Oops," he added, flicking the business card over the side.

Seven minutes. The boat was still rocking as he jumped down the companionway. Stripping to his shorts, he raced to the underwater-gear locker for a second rebreather, face-mask, and flippers.

No air left, if she'd gone deep. *Assuming* she hadn't panicked and used it up even faster. He pictured her still form down there in the dark, drowned, drifting. *My fault.* He swallowed. *What in Hell was I thinking?*

Running through what he knew of mouth to mouth resuscitation, he tore back up on deck, eyeing the water as he tugged on the flippers. *Eight minutes.* He signaled the cabin lights off and sent the drone out to scan the water. Best to pretend he'd gone back to bed after being woken at two a.m. The other boat had floored it, he saw: they were already two kilometers away, searchlights still stabbing out around them at the water. Still hunting.

He rolled over the stern taffrail and onto the swim platform. One last glance at the distant boat as he prepared to leap into the water – and it suddenly *fell* from view, vanishing beneath the waves.

Blinking, he straightened. "What. The. *Fuck*?"

In the distance, the drowned searchlight burned underwater for a few seconds before sputtering and dying.

Should he go help...?

A gasping breath dragged his eyes down to a hand slapping between his feet on the swim platform, and once more he found himself staring face to face with the girl peering up at him from the water. But instead of exhaustion, her eyes shone with excitement. Plucking the silvery breathing tube from between her lips, she slowly traced it across them, then down her neck, her eyes locked on his, before very deliberately dropping her gaze to slide appreciatively over his near-naked body, lifting one brow hungrily.

She licked her lips.

CHAPTER 9

Something in the scene struck him as surreally *repellent* as she lowered her eyes to look up at him through her long lashes, continuing to stroke the phallic cylinder along her curves. Her face looked even more hollowed-out than it had earlier, and her movements stuttered between feline grace and awkward jerks.

The fine hairs on his neck stood up, a pit opening in his stomach, and he had to force himself not to take a step back. As if his instincts had grasped something horrible that his conscious mind hadn't.

She made a mewling sound and began – alternately clumsy and weak, then smoothly sure – to haul herself from the water. One part of his mind noted the rebreather, now dropped and forgotten, tumbling back and forth across the swim platform, only the mouthpiece of the apparatus preventing it from rolling into the water.

That primordial part of his brain still screamed warnings of something awful, something alien.

Her eyes hadn't left his, nor had there been a pause in the smiling seductive dance across her features, the same expressions repeating like some glitching sexbot....

There was no intelligence in those eyes, he suddenly realized. No sense of a real person. Just some kind of awful programmed doll-like....

Instinct grabbed him, and he half-leaped, half-tumbled over the railing behind him, tearing off his flippers so he could move properly, knowing she'd come crawling after him over the railing. It took a conscious effort to get a grip on himself. *Why am I so spooked?* Still clutching his rebreather, he rose to his feet and approached the taffrail.

His proximity seemed to send a surge of strength through her. At the sight of him gripping the stainless steel rail as he leaned over, in one smooth movement she surged to her feet and vaulted over, arms reaching for him. He jumped backwards, cursing, her fingertips brushing the hairs of his chest as she grabbed for him. His right hand clenched his rebreather tight as his training kicked in and he prepared to-

What?

Overbalanced by her lunge, her feet tangled under her and she collapsed forward. What had she been about to do? What had *he* been about to do? Club her unconscious?

He stared at the metal rebreather clenched in his hand.

She'd fallen still, and suddenly that same primitive part of his brain locked on the curve of her taut rear.

What the hell was going on here? He took another step back, looking up and around frantically, finally registering his drone reporting radio communication from a point a couple of kilometers away. Encrypted. His eyes locked on the place where the 'AquaSec' boat had... fallen? Dropped? *Plummeted* into New Francisco Bay as if the waters had just fucking opened up beneath it. He zoomed in slowly, scanning back and forth.

Catching a glimmer of light and movement he zoomed further, guided by the drone, already locked onto the radio source.

Figures in the water. An emergency light, some floating debris – maybe long cushions from the cruiser's seats – and a bald head staring calmly back in his general direction. But not *at* him, he could see, glad he'd doused the lights earlier; smugly pleased that Henstridge clearly couldn't see *him*.

He considered. Instinct said to up anchor and flee, but if they were acting under Tik Tek's orders, as he thought, they'd probably already have arranged for-

The sound of a distant chopper drifted in from the south, completing his thought. Nodding, he sent his drone back inside to dock in its cradle. No doubt they'd overfly him on the way to their rescue. The question was, would they search him again?

Hmm. He pictured it; a small grin forming as he imagined 'noticing' Arvid Henstridge, dripping wet... 'What happened, Mr Henstridge? Did you fall overboard? Didn't your people realise? Or wouldn't they go back for you?'

A needy whimper at his feet snapped him from the daydream and back to the problem literally at his feet. She'd curled up, but stared sideways at him, and his shoulders relaxed as he saw she was looking *at* him, seeing him; no longer acting the creepy sex doll. The sense of alienness faded, deep relief flooding in to replace it. But unease resurfaced as he took in her desperation, her *need*.

Her mouth opened. "Please-"

Then her expression blanked, and she stopped moving, eyes still open. Had she just *died?*

The chopper was closer, now, but still he hesitated, once again strangely reluctant to touch her. Finally, grunting, he bent and hoisted her in his arms. She was cool to the touch, but not still, thank god. *Not* dead.

Struggling through the hatch he backed down the gangway for a second time that night and felt a quiver running through her. Shivering? Staggering across the cabin he eased her into a sitting position by the bolted-down table that filled a good portion of the main cabin.

Idly he noted her weight, almost stumbling when the reading sank in. 71.2 kilos. Three point five kilos lighter! Her wet clothes? No. They'd weighed one; two at most.

He consciously set the puzzle aside. *Later.*

Right now he needed to work out what was wrong with her. He *could* just activate his night vision, but for some reason, he wanted light. The chopper was too close though. Swearing, he recrossed the room in vicious strides and folded the hatchway seal shut, opaqued the windows, finally signaling the light on as he returned to her.

Her face was gaunt, her cheeks hollow. Her ribs, too, stood out. Surely, earlier, they hadn't? Not so clearly anyway. She'd lost over a kilo of weight in just ten minutes.

Shit.

Was she really human, or some experimental Tik Tek gynoid, as he more than half suspected? *If she is synthetic, it's likely whatever's wrong with her can be fixed later. Maybe she's just low on power?* Her stuttering movements suggested that. *But what if she is human?*

He felt her brow – cool, like the rest of her – and took her pulse, noting the rapid, shallow rise and fall of her chest. Again, distracted by the very-appealing breasts with their crinkled-up-in-cold nipples. Were they less rounded than before, though? Strangely, she was warmer than she'd been just before he'd sent her back into the water.

That made no sense. Two cups of coffee and a few minutes out of water couldn't explain it.

Her pulse was racing, but her limbs remained unresponsive, and her eyes tracked randomly as if watching things he couldn't see.

'Please,' she'd begged him. Please what?

The chopper was very close now. Even if they didn't search, a good chance it'd scan them. The resolving power of radio waves weren't great, though. He slid past her, lying down, maneuvering her body face down on top of his, pressing his legs against hers and gripping her wrists, trying as best he could to arrange their bodies so a scan from above would see a single human-shaped outline.

As the sound of the helicopter crested and then paused overhead, he shivered as her cold body pressed down on his.

He examined her features again as they lay there, waiting for the chopper to finish its scan. No epicanthic fold. Bold, black eyebrows a strong contrast to the platinum hair. Not an obvious racial type. Not a typical sexbot then, since they were usually designed to stereotypes: Japanese schoolgirls; Nordic wenches; sultry Italian vixens; French maids. Mixed race models were uncommon, from what he knew. He cued a search for her face before canceling it at the last instant, flushing. With Tik Tek involved, he might just as well have broadcast 'Come and get her'. Assuming she did tie in to Omega.

Staring up at her, he was struck suddenly by her helplessness. But for how long? He replayed the earlier scene that had so repelled him, and felt the skin on the back of his neck crawl afresh, though still unable to pin down exactly why.

After about ten seconds, the chopper moved off. Sliding out from under her – uncertain whether to feel relief or regret at the loss of physical contact – he propped her back up at the table and crossed quickly to the galley. From the compact refrigerator he grabbed a milk carton and popped it into the microwave to warm. Meanwhile he dug out the pile of damp towels and brought one back to her, briskly rubbing her down again.

She moaned at the touch, her eyes focusing on him, and suddenly the creepy sex-doll seduction moves started up again. *She* was gone, he sensed, as she arched and thrust herself into the towel. He angrily finished her torso, roughly scrubbing at her head and hair.

At that, her head rolled to one side and her legs parted. One arm went to a breast, offering it to him. The other arm jerked and twitched, trying to mirror those movements but failing. *Programmed!* Anger at her programmer flooded in with the insight, dispelling some of his horror.

Swearing, he finished with her hair, scarcely aware of fetching the warmed milk. Settling in beside her, he cursed as her hand went to his lap. He tried to lift it away – and couldn't. Only when her strength failed, her arm flopping limply, could he shift it.

With her head lolling limply, he had to hold her upright as he poured a glass of milk, left-handed.

The distant chopper's engine kicked up a notch, before stopping. Probably settled onto the water to start the rescue operation for the survivors of the sinking.

Another damned mystery.

He lifted the glass to her lips. Her small nostrils flared then her nose wrinkled and her eyes opened. Her lips opened, too, a desperate noise hissing from her. Taking that as a good sign he tipped some milk into her mouth, and she swallowed; then again more eagerly, *mmm*-ing an emphatic approval.

Suddenly both her hands flashed to the glass, up-ending it before he could stop her. Gulping and swallowing desperately, warm milk flooded her mouth and ran down her naked front.

She blinked, then moaned demandingly. *More.* Obviously. Before he could take the glass from her though, her eyes locked on the milk carton. Dropping the glass she tore the carton from his grip and practically inhaled it.

"Ahh," she sighed. With her mouth pressed into the opening, she crushed the carton as if trying to squeeze more from it, then wriggled in his arms. "Unh!" She thrust it back at him, demanding. "Unh!"

The chopper was silent now. The question was, would it return here after picking up its passengers, or bypass them? If they did come back, was there somewhere he could put her, out of sight, off scan? He could probably bluff them out of yet another – illegal – search. Had there ever been a time when that stopped a corporation's security?

Jam her in the forward hold under the anchor chains, to block the scans? He cringed at the thought. But he couldn't put her back into the water. Not again.

She interrupted his thought, shoving the crushed carton demandingly against him.

"Unh!"

What was with the grunting? "Do you want more?"

"Unh!"

"Do you need anything else? Are you hungry?"

"Ungh!" She thrust the container at him again.

He looked at her closely, wondering again about the odd

injury on her forehead. It hadn't bled much, despite the bruising, and didn't look serious enough to have caused concussion. Another grunt interrupted his chain of thought, and he sighed and went to fetch another carton of milk.

A thump behind him had him spinning around, to find her sprawled on the floor, struggling to her feet, her eyes pinned to the fresh container in his hand.

He set the milk to warm, resisting the urge to go and help her: instinct warned him she wasn't rational. He didn't want to wrestle her over a carton of milk. He wanted to go to her, but he needed the time for the milk to heat.

She staggered, then fell, collapsing elegantly, like someone trained in martial arts. *Surely not?* His neck prickled.

After a few seconds rest she struggled to hands and knees and began crawling toward him. Somehow, this time, it wasn't creepy. Maybe it was the small tongue poking from her lips in total concentration, as she focused on the task of crossing the short space between them. So much so that when she reached him, and began trying to climb to her feet using his body as a ladder, he bent to help her up.

She swayed for a moment in his arms, then he felt her catch her balance, moving away from him slightly. The microwave finally dinged and she looked around, sniffing, obviously searching for the milk. It took longer for her to find it than he'd expected – as if she didn't recognize the microwave. When she did see it, she scrabbled at the door, apparently not knowing how to open it, grunting urgently.

There was something very wrong with her.

Interposing his body he opened the door, certain that if he let her grab it, in her current state there'd be milk everywhere.

Sure enough, she scrabbled at his back as he unsealed the container, grabbing it as soon as he turned around. Her lips fastened to it and she inhaled it, too, the carton crumpling as she drained it.

"Ah!"

"Better?"

She just blinked, rapidly, then shivered.

"Hang on. I'll get you a robe." She wavered on her feet, and he led her back to the table. Leaving her there he fetched two fuzzy white – and deliciously warm – bathrobes from the forward cabin. He draped one around her and slipped into the other himself, while she watched, blinking. Then, copying his movements, she began wrestling it, trying to get her arms into the sleeves.

At least she's trying. He helped her dress, wondering again what was wrong with her. *Had her program crashed?*

"Kristen: do you understand me?"

Her attention focused on him, and her blinking sped up. Did that mean she was thinking? Her stomach chose that moment to let out a loud growl, and she sagged in the seat, hugging herself, hunching forward.

"Can you understand me?"

She looked up at him, her face screwed up, and he read confusion and fear there. He was suddenly sure she *didn't* understand, but also that she knew she *should*. What the hell had happened to her? What was wrong with her? What had been done *to* her?

Her stomach growled again, and she winced, hunching forward more, but still staring up at him. Then her expression cleared and she slowly opened her mouth and closed it, but with lips bared to show her teeth biting.

"Are you hungry?"

She watched him, plainly struggling with confusion, then very deliberately made the biting motion again.

O-kay. Hungry, then. He sighed, worried this was some ruse or distraction, but when her stomach growled a third time, he mentally shrugged and returned to the galley to check the cooler again. "I can offer you bacon and eggs?"

He turned, but she just made the exaggerated eating motion again. Okay, so still not understanding English.

He picked out two eggs and held them up, turning back to her. "Eggs?"

She was across the room with terrifying speed, grabbing the eggs and shoving one into her mouth. It crunched, and he saw her swallow, then start coughing and hacking, almost throwing up as she hawked up bits of egg shell and traces of white and yolk.

"I can cook-"

But she was already shoving the second egg into her mouth, this time biting more carefully, and he saw her throat work again, her cheeks hollowing and her tongue moving, before daintily spitting the shell into her hand before dropping it to the floor.

"Enggh!"

Did she just say 'egg'?

She looked past him, into the cooler, her eyes lighting as she saw the open carton. Snatching up two more eggs she crammed another into her mouth.

Crunch.

Her head turned and she went still, looking past him even as she swallowed carefully and spat out the third eggshell. He wondered what had caught her attention. Finally, he heard it – the chopper had powered up.

CHAPTER 10

Briefly, Mason considered trying to sneak her up on deck and into the anchor locker – but even kilometers away in the dark, if they had class one imaging they'd pick out moving figures.

Take the risk? They might not even swing back this way.

With Arvid Henstridge on board, no doubt pissed off as all hell? No. They'd definitely swing past; maybe even do something obnoxious out of pure frustration. Just as they'd tried to swamp his boat, earlier.

The girl was crunching another cold, raw egg, her hands clutching two more. Quickly, he led her back to the bench seat. He lay down, gesturing for her to lie on top of him again. The distant engine noise spun once more into a higher pitch – the chopper taking off – and he lined her up again on top of him, leg to leg and arm to arm. She turned her head and spat the egg shell out, and he winced as part of it fell on his face. There was a brief struggle as her arm moved up to shove the next one into her mouth and he tried to keep her still, before giving it up as not worth the effort.

Crunch.

The chopper approached rapidly, its engines loud enough to wake the deaf as it hovered directly overhead, the boat actually jolting against the twin anchor lines from its downdraft. Long enough to scan them through the cabin walls with the imaging array. But he knew the limitations of such systems: they'd just see a single, low-res figure. Henstridge was living up to his reputation as a first class dick, though.

"Fuck you, assholes!" he shouted, still playing his role of aggrieved fisherman on the off-chance they had audio pick-ups that could somehow hear his voice despite the chopper's thunder. But he sensed his gamble had paid off, and indeed, after a little more petty annoyance, the aircraft peeled away and buzzed off. Not even blasting them with a chorus of La Cucaracha.

He flinched as more egg shell fell on his cheek, and she made a small, satisfied sound.

"Egg!"

She squirmed up, straddling him, her eyes alight. Staring demandingly down, she very deliberately opened her mouth and bit on empty air. "Egg," she repeated, quite clearly.

"Glad to see your masterful powers of conversation have returned," he observed.

Her forehead wrinkled.

Or maybe not. "Shall I cook some? I think there's time."

Studying his lips, she lowered herself over him. He could feel her breasts through the double layer of cloth, her amber eyes inches away looking suddenly interested. He felt a swelling between his legs, his body badly misreading the situation.

Or maybe not so badly: she froze, obviously feeling it, and her expression shifted. Then she shivered, her pupils dilating enormously, and her mouth plunged down on his. Tasting, nuzzling and nipping until he wasn't sure if she was kissing him or biting him.

He broke away, conflicted. Wanting what she offered, but doubting she was fit to decide, or that it was even *safe* to accept such intimacy from her.

There wasn't that creepy mindlessness she'd shown earlier, but still something about her seemed off. Even dangerous: he still suspected she'd sunk the other vessel. Somehow.

"Uh, Kristen, are you sure-"

Her mouth dived back down and she moved her hips, making him gasp as she maneuvered parts of him into position.

And the boat dropped about a foot in the water, turning violently, both anchor ropes groaning under sudden stress.

"What the hell?"

The image of the other vessel *falling* beneath the water filled his mind as he squirmed free of her and headed for the hatchway. Then he paused. If they *did* drop underwater with the hatch sealed, the boat might simply bob back to the surface. Provided it survived the impact of water crashing closed on it at awful speed. He looked around the cabin doubtfully, trying to assess its structural integrity. If the hatch was open, they'd flood and sink. He noticed a cabin window, its latch snapped, and winced. Behind him, Kristen spoke.

"No."

The boat jerked violently again even as he spun back to her, fear sending his pulse racing. "What do you mean? Don't go up? Do *you* know what's going on?"

She didn't answer him. Her eyes stared down, distant, head tilted as if listening. She was still shivering badly, and now huddled into her robe.

"Can't."

The boat dropped again, but this time stayed down. Water sprayed in a thin stream from the cabin window with the broken latch, held shut only by water pressure. The hatch leading up on deck groaned, water leaking in through its seal. With one white-knuckled hand gripping the edge of the sink, he wrenched his eyes from the visibly bowing hatch back to his strange visitor, his heart hammering, his breath coming in short gasps.

Kristen still stared down into the floor; looking surprised, then pleased. Slowly, she smiled. There was something lascivious in it. "*Could* 'visit'."

The boat stilled, utterly, and he held his breath, waiting for judgment, eyes wide and skin prickling. Waiting to see if *they'd* be swallowed like the other vessel. Ten long, slow seconds plodded past. The boat remained as motionless as if mounted in dry dock. Twenty seconds. The girl's eyes had closed, her teeth tugging at her swollen lips, and dwarfing her shivering, a massive shudder ran through her compact frame. Like she was remembering a *really* good time.

And *The Sleeping Tom* leaped upward, bobbing and rocking, yanking hard against the ropes a couple of times before settling back to the normal movement of a boat riding at anchor.

Was that a 'yes'? He started breathing again, counting seconds. But the boat continued to move normally in the swells, and Kristen's eyes were shut, her face relaxed. She looked half asleep.

He sensed the threat was past.

Who had she been talking to? Or *what*? Something outside. Something in the water. The pieces of the puzzle careened around his skull, making even less sense than they had before. She'd been talking to something he couldn't see. Something in the water. Which meant magic, right? Which absolutely ruled out the possibility she was some kind of prototype sexbot.

Right?

Of course it did. Magic and machines were utterly incompatible. Antagonists. Everyone said so. All the experts. And history confirmed it.

Though Melisande d'Artelle had used *science to make the Melt virus,* a voice inside reminded him. Not to mention the weird shit about her trying to alter the fucking *laws of physics*. Which was what he'd gleaned in a jaw-dropping report he'd 'stumbled over' in a *specialized* area of gov-web; it wasn't just a bizarro net conspiracy thing.

Could Kristen be some freaky *shaman*? Had she used magic to smash the window of Omega Memory Systems and survive the fall?

Or was he on completely the wrong track? Had something *else* escaped from Tik Tek, some sort of intelligent aquatic weapon, and she was connected with it somehow? Its trainer, or even its inventor? Wirelessly linked to it. Some kind of giant cyber squid, or...?

He shook his head. Right, that was it, he was officially going crazy....

She still sat on the bench seat, huddled into her toweling robe, looking small and cold, and he took a step toward her, then stopped. Every instinct told him she was dangerous. Possibly, very dangerous. But watching her, as she cyclically sagged and then jerked upright, trying to stay conscious... another part of him flooded with an unexpected desire to protect her. *Besides, she may be valuable: I could try to get her on-side*, whispered his rational, profit-driven self.

Fuck it. He slid in beside her, hugging her to warm her. She moved a little closer, but otherwise didn't react. He felt her relax beside him, and saw her eyes shut. Asleep? Or maybe just exhausted.

Right. He could spare a minute or two to warm her, though they should leave soon.

What did he know? He shut his eyes and replayed the footage of the other boat falling into the Bay. Frame by frame. He cued some digital magnification, but despite the compute-intensive algorithms, it could only give him a factor of three. Still....

There's the boat. He laid a reticule over it, opting for distance marks along the horizontal axis it formed, based on the range estimate. Textual callouts from the image analysis routines show the vessel had been doing well over twenty knots. He didn't bother skipping ahead – he'd been watching it only for a second or two when it had suddenly-

Fuck. He froze the playback.

There was a hole in the fucking water. All around the boat. He continued. And the hole moved *with* the boat at the same speed. Over the next four frames – forty milliseconds – the hole widened just a little while the boat dropped a hand-span below the surface. He added a vertical reticule: yeah, maybe five or ten centimeters. He sped up the playback. By the half-second mark the boat had fallen over a meter. At six hundred milliseconds its gunwales had sunk to sea level. And by the one second mark the entire boat, even its radar mast, was out of sight. The hole started contracting. Very fast. By the two second mark – taking a period of just eighty frames, nought-point-eight seconds – the hole was gone. He ran some numbers. The boat literally fell, under ordinary gravity. But the water *closed up* with a speed of about 100kph.

Shee-it.

How deep had that hole been? He formed the query: it had fallen for one point eight seconds, so at least eight meters. Jesus. So how much water had been displaced? The estimate came back: over a thousand tonnes.

He opened his eyes and just sat there, stunned. He wasn't into the spooky stuff – he had no idea what could've done that; but it had to be bad-ass, whatever it was. He shelved the question – for now.

Kristen's arms moved around him, tightening slightly, and he looked down. Still asleep, he saw.

Right. So: what else did he have?

He wished Tik Tek had less perfect sound suppressors. He'd only picked up maybe one word in ten, earlier. Yamamoto had been pissed off, and gloating. "Testing." "Programming the crystal."

Could the crystal be some kind of magic-tech interface? Shit. This was all just fantasizing... and a little bit terrifying. He had to stick to the facts. What else did he know?

The R&D company's eighth floor window had shattered – but only *after* something had blown up the delicate audio sensors of his roachbot, perched on the armored glass. Seconds later they'd been firing high caliber rounds into the water below. And searching. Searching, too quickly and with too much manpower.

Yeah, that wasn't a *tenuous* connection between Omega Memory Systems and Tik Tek – it was a concealed one.

If only the contract for the Omega tech hadn't come from the Washington Group. Tik Tek were scary, but WG... he recognized the stench of rot, spreading just below sight. Funded from corporate America's propaganda empire, spread through half the PACs and lobby groups in Washington. Cults too, ranging from past-focused nutters like the now splintered Brethren of the End of Days, to future-focused horrors like Freedom's Womb. He shuddered.

But it'd been seeing his old comrade, the upright, noble Panzer change so utterly, just from clearing the path for the Kwandong Computation Nets deal, that'd opened his eyes. He'd not known her, afterward. *Warped.* Like a different soul stared out from eyes he'd been certain he could always trust. Same with Ace, after Panzer drew him in on another WG contract.

Now, of the old gang who'd fought against Newtopia's BRF – how did burning a forest 'reclaim' it? – only he and Maeve would be recognizable to their Brazilian squad. But he couldn't ignore this WG contract. Thanks to it he'd uncovered something weird and game-changing going on. And the money.... It was why he'd been stuck out here since the afternoon when he could have been cozily sipping coffee in a downtown Southstar cafe, 'teasing out' data on Nemesys's new Grendel warbot instead. Those blueprints'd be worth a cool half mill.

And now *she'd* come from out of the water. Kristen. *Mermaid?* After some rest and more food, he'd see how she was, see what he could get out of her. First thing though was to get the hell off the Bay. He picked her up – she still felt far too heavy for her scrawny-

Her face was less drawn.

She looked less anorexic.

After almost two liters of milk and – he winced as his bare foot crushed moist eggshell into the tight fiber of the hard-wearing carpet tiles – what, six eggs?

Think about it later, Mace, he told himself, carrying her through into the small sleeping area and covering her with blankets. She was still shivering, steadily. Right: weigh anchor, set a course, then cook up a three a.m breakfast for her, try to warm her up.

He went up above, closing the hatchway behind him to keep the cold air out, tightening his bathrobe. At least hauling up the rear anchor by hand would warm *him.*

The forward anchor was motorized, and soon he was back

below, half his attention interfaced to the boat's operating
system as they made way, keeping one eye above via his
drone, the other on the bacon and eggs he was frying.

He froze at a growl from somewhere out of sight in the
main cabin. Under the table, something large moved.

CHAPTER 11

Panther? Leopard? The words sprang to Mason's mind despite knowing there couldn't be a large predator on his boat.

The growl sounded again from under the table, where something moved. That woke wilder suggestions as the possibilities raised by magic's reawakening raced through him. *Were*-leopard? *Vampire?*

Stupid, leaving your gun in the sleeping-cabin. Adrenaline surged, triggering all his enhancements. He savored the thrill of potency as time slowed. Eyeing the carving knife magnetically fastened to a cupboard door, he sidled to it while tightening his grip on the fry-pan and preparing to make a dash for the-

A human hand, feminine, padded into view, fingers curling and clawing into the cabin floor's tough matting. A slim arm followed it. Then the other hand, and the girl's face, looking up at him hungrily. She rolled her head on those athletic shoulders, the muscles in her upper back bunching and relaxing as she stalked forward on all fours. Her waist undulated into view, then her naked rear. It should have been erotic, arousing – except for the way her tongue licked her lips, her gaze unblinking, reading his smallest movement. And the hollowed cheeks, the way her skin stretched taut once more over musculature that was too well-defined screamed *starvation; predator.*

What the fuck?

He watched her sniff the air, her eyes narrowing. She paused....

No way. This again? Anger flared through him. Was this some stupid game? Did she think this was *funny*? But he heard her stomach rumble – and her mouth opened in a snarl, her teeth somehow gleaming as she growled again. The note of desperate hunger dispelled his anger. This was real. As crazy as it seemed, she was about to attack him!

And despite his neural and muscle augments, for some reason he felt a peculiar thrill of... fear?

Some subtle change warned him: *decision made.* She crouched, muscles tensing-

His arm flexed almost involuntarily, flipping half-cooked eggs and bacon to the floor in front of her. Both she and he froze as the mound of food slid on a trail of its own grease across the checkered pattern of the galley's tiles, piling up at the edge of the rattan matting of the cabin. Two yolks broke, their vivid splash of yellow wrenching her gaze from him.

Nostrils flaring, she lunged forward, scooping and batting the ruined eggs into her mouth, an unearthly snapping yowl escaping her as the hot food burned. He watched her flick the second egg in, too, then briefly bat at the strips of streaky bacon as if checking whether they'd try to flee. She plunged her head down, hands shoveling it in.

He felt confused, off-balance: surely this was just a ridiculous act? Convince him she was mad so he'd go easy on her. His gut was screaming danger.

Putting the frying pan aside he grabbed a bowl and splashed milk into it. Then turned.

She stilled, hunching protectively over her rapidly-disappearing food as he lowered the brightly-patterned bowl into her eye-line.

Crouching, he slid it toward her then retreated a step into the galley and straightened.

She followed every motion.

When she resumed wolfing down the food he risked turning away. He set the pan on the burner, grabbed the remaining bacon, and tossed the thick strips in. *I probably don't even need to cook it.*

He put his back to the cupboards to watch both the fry pan and her.

Her bacon finished, she licked egg yolk from the grubby tiles. *Ergh.* Her eyes stayed on him.

Fat sizzling, he flipped the bacon slices over. It felt weird using his combat enhancements to *prepare food* faster. But there was no way he'd stand his systems down. He kept his attention on her at the bowl, which scraped against the floor as she sucked and lapped at the milk. She followed it forward, grunting in frustration until pinning it, slurping from the tilted bowl. Grabbing it up, she fell back to a seated position, cross-legged and naked as she raised it to her lips.

The boat yawed as it plowed on across the Bay toward Berkeley – just a passing swell, he noted from a quick check of the drone he'd left on deck – but she slid, almost losing her balance. *She's sitting in the grease from the food*, he realized. It reinforced his growing belief her performance wasn't an act.

Her loss of balance seemed to embarrass, then confuse her. For the first time, she looked faintly self-conscious.

What was *wrong* with her?

She frowned down at herself. Her stomach rumbled, and she hunched forward. Sensing the immediate urgency was past, he flicked the bacon onto a plate. Turning, he cracked four eggs – the last – into the pan, jerking and almost over-turning it as he felt her, now upright, slide up beside him.

He hadn't heard her approach. He should have.

He looked sideways and down at her. *Thirty seconds ago she'd been ready to attack, maybe* eat *me?*

Now she pressed in against his side, nostrils flaring, star-ing from the eggs to the bacon as if fascinated, then back to the eggs again. She made a small, eager sound in her throat.

"Feeling more, human, Kristen?"

That earned a frown. She scanned the room as if search-ing for a third person.

"Can you manage a plate this time?"

Tilting her head, she swayed and would have fallen if he hadn't grabbed her. He almost let her, except his biometric analytics didn't indicate a trap.

But even as he held her, he berated himself. *Don't cuddle her, you idiot! She's dangerous: mad, or* broken.

But also naked, starving, and vulnerable. It triggered pro-tective impulses he hadn't expected. Not fatherly ones, ei-ther. Her expression made his stomach tighten.

"Come on; sit at the table."

She slipped again as she moved, and he realized her feet – and bum, and hands – must be covered in grease, not just her mouth and face. With a paper towel he wiped her face, then lower, scrubbing at the two cheeks. Bizarre, seeing musculature there. He didn't register the sexuality of his ac-tion until she giggled, twisting and slipping on her feet as she tried to help him.

He couldn't help but smile in turn, pleased by her joy. Too pleased. His reaction made him hesitate. He shouldn't be thinking of seducing her. He had no idea what she was ca-pable of, and every instinct warned him she held surprises. Big surprises.

But seducing her'll give me more options. Options he needed, if she *had* come from the Omega labs, as he increas-ingly believed. A clone? Enhanced genetics, but reared, or grown in isolation? That'd explain the lack of even the most basic social skills. It'd fit some of the Tik Tek rumors.

"Come on, sit down while I see to the eggs before they burn."

"Eggs! Yes!"

He helped her over to the bench seat by the table, nudging her sideways and back onto the cushions, suddenly once more acutely aware of her nudity as she smiled up at him. "Eggs! I'm starving!"

Three words. *Hallelujah, sentience has returned!*

He side-stepped the greasy spot on the floor on his way to the stove, flipping the eggs which had started to crisp around their edges. He counted to twenty – an eternity as she made increasingly insistent noises from the table, noises that were trending back toward growls – then scooped them out and onto the plate he'd piled with the bacon. As an afterthought, he grabbed a few slices of bread from the fridge and tossed them into the fat to fry up. Snatching up some cutlery, he headed back to the table.

It'd be sexier if she was eyeing me *like that, not the food.* "Scoot over," he said as he slipped in beside her, passing her a knife and fork. From the puzzled look she gave him, he got a bad feeling as he slid the lower plate in front of her before dividing the food up equally between them.

She went still, staring at the food on *his* plate rather than what was in front of her, then shivered, goose-bumps rising all over her skin. He saw her nipples crinkle up, and suddenly he was fighting a flood of conflicting emotions: desire to fetch her robe and warm her versus a desire to keep her naked; the desire to *give* her his share of the food fighting the desire to *protect* his share of the food; and the damned combat analytics flashing an intrusive visual warning that she was too close. He stood those systems down, bracing for the usual 'down' – only to find it swamped by purely animal responses: sudden tension at making himself vulnerable; and *desire*, from that brief physical contact.

He had to shake himself mentally, the odd see-sawing of his endocrine system a new and disorienting experience. But she'd already started eating, even using the knife and fork without trouble, though he did notice she seemed troubled – even puzzled – by her greasy hands.

"Here, let me wipe those."

Tearing off some of the paper towels she still half-sat on, a short struggle followed before she seemed to realise he was neither trying to grab her hands to stop her eating, nor to take her food. By the time he was half way through his own breakfast though, she'd finished and was eyeing his portion intently.

"Hang on. Promise you won't eat mine, and I'll get you some more, okay?"

She stared at him; then stared at his plate. Back to him. A curious expression came over her face as she nodded. As if she didn't want to agree, but had to.

Whatever. Frankly, he was getting close to the point of giving up trying to understand her.

He took her plate, quickly filling it with the one-side fried bacon-fat toast and striding back to slide it in front of her. Eyeing his plate with some surprise, he saw she'd not filched anything. Almost primly then, she picked up the bacon bread and crunched into it, a smile lighting her face as she chewed.

"Mmm, good."

By the time he'd gulped his remaining food she'd finished both slices, sighing. "Good."

She still looked starved. "How do you feel – would you like more?"

"Yes! More!"

"Sorry, there's no more bacon or eggs – you've cleaned me out. I can do toast, though. Or cereal?"

"Yes! Toast! Cereal!"

"You mean, both?"

At her emphatic nod, he sighed, wondering where all the food was going, then remembered her one point five kilo loss of weight. She'd probably just regained that. He got up and she shivered again, huddling into herself. Through her fringe, he noticed the scratches and bruises on her forehead once more, frowning.

He shook his head. *Later.* "Let me get your robe first though. You look cold."

The word *cold* seemed to strike her with strange force, a massive shudder running through her. She huddled even tighter in on herself, though without saying anything. Shrugging, he left the table to fetch the white terry-cloth robe from the sleeping cabin. But when he came out, she was slumped back on the bench seat looking pale, and panting.

"Kristen? Are you all right? What's wrong?"

She didn't answer, hardly seemed to register his presence.

Dammit. She's gone again! What the hell is going on?

CHAPTER 12

She didn't resist as he helped her into the robe, though he noted her arms were colder than he'd expected, almost chilled. He felt her forehead – also cool. He took her pulse – and found it pounding, racing.

Shit. Suddenly he felt helpless. Did he need to warm her up again? More fluids? Propping her up, wrapped in her warm robe, he left her seated and returned to the galley – once more avoiding the greasy section of floor – to switch the coffee machine on. Yeah, it was loaded. Maybe she needed a bigger caffeine jolt? And another shot of brandy to go with it? He accessed a medical site, mentally offering the facts as he knew them to the diagnostic algorithms while keeping an eye on the shivering girl.

Vasovagal syncope. Fainting from low blood pressure, basically. Triggered by blood rushing to the stomach to digest the food she'd just eaten. The heart rate didn't fit, though.

He read the diagnosis, relieved but frowning as the coffee started flowing, watching her closely for signs of nausea. There was a pattern to all this, he was sure. A pattern he couldn't quite make out.

And the clock is ticking. Omega, or maybe even Tik Tek are still looking for her, so we need to be far away by dawn. Which was in only a few hours, now. He called up an internal screen, checking their progress back to the dockyard, wishing he'd paid for a faster boat.

He had no sports drinks to help re-hydrate her – if that's what the problem was – but milk would do just as well. At least dairy production was finally back to normal – his mind drifted back to his childhood and his mother bemoaning the lack of *real* milk, in the years after the Second World Storm. A billion human lives lost, but it had practically wiped out the less sheltered livestock populations across the globe.

He shook his head, pouring a dash of brandy into the coffee, then carrying it, the milk carton and a glass over to Kristen, still slumped at the table.

What do I do if this doesn't work? Her hunters would be monitoring hospitals.

With an effort, he managed to get her sipping the coffee, and gradually she improved. Troublingly though, she didn't become fully conscious. After the coffee he started her on glass after glass of milk. Ten minutes and perhaps a liter later she came around. Sort of. He tried talking to her, but she simply blinked at him like she was still asleep. Her hands had warmed a little, though there was a jittery fever to her eyes that worried him.

She was still hungry, too, and he began feeding her again, but mainly cereal, more slowly, worried she might not hold it down. If it *was* falling blood pressure from the digestive process, maybe plenty of fluids would help. Where was all this going, though? Did she have a black hole for a stomach?

And still she ate.

She seemed to settle into a strange half-aware state, steadily plowing through bowl after bowl of muesli, interspersed with slices of peanut butter laden toast, jelly, jam, everything from the boat's cupboard. It was a ludicrous amount of food. Farcical. But the most disturbing aspect was how she physically changed. Her face lost its gaunt aspect. Even her limbs fleshed out. And her breasts....

He was no doctor, but even *he* could see it wasn't natural. Digestion didn't work that fast. It was like her body was functioning in some insane overdrive, converting food into fat – and energy stores? – almost as quickly as she ate it. *Though not muscle*, he thought, remembering how they'd stood out beneath her skin. As if they'd been prioritized higher than brain function? Like so much else, it made no sense.

Yet now it was like she was inflating, though too slowly to directly perceive. He shut his eyes to replay snippets of the last thirty minutes at high speed, and confirmed it visually. Sped up, it was clear it wasn't just his imagination.

Bizarre.

He cleaned the egg shells and greasy patch from the galley's tiled floor while he thought things through. Straightening up, he disposed of the soiled paper towels, leaning back against the cooking bench to watch her. Her spoon clinked against the bottom of the bowl: time for another refill. By now she'd eaten enough for ten men. He went back over, tipped in the last of the cereal, added milk, then slid in beside her. She paid him no attention, just continued spooning up the food. Though less urgently now.

Could she have been somehow altered so she could burn *all* the energy reserves of her body when needed, as well as being able to reverse that process by eating? If so, it looked like during 'refueling', top priority went to the digestion process, completely overriding the normal priority of the body protecting the brain above all else. But that'd put her at risk of brain damage from lack of blood supply. He shook his head. What sort of idiot would design something like that?

And how did it even work?

He leaned back against the bench seat, thinking. He'd been spying on Omega Memory Systems because of a hinted breakthrough in thought-imaging systems. Yet there'd always been rumors that Tik Tek, one of their backers, was heavily into nanotechnology. And 'true' artificial intelligence, whatever that meant.

He studied her, sideways. Those technologies might explain a lot about her. Was she some new kind of gynoid? Or some kind of *synthetic human*? Programmed?

He frowned. Was it a holographic memory crystal they'd been programming, or *Kristen*? He replayed the recording.... Definitely Yamamoto's voice: '...put *skrrt-krtch* crystal -to' (into?) '*skrtch* for programming *skrtch*'.

Struck by a sudden insight, he accessed and replayed a different recording.

His own voice: 'Who are you? How did you come to be in the water?'

He re-watched as her lips shaped a response, then stopped. Then: 'K-.' Again she stopped, and a second passed. 'K-.' Pause. 'Kr-.' Pause 'Kr-.' Pause. 'Kris-, Kristen.'

He replayed it again, aware she'd finally stopped eating. She leaned trustingly into him, her eyes closed, spoon held loosely in her fingers. Slipping it from them and into the near-empty bowl, he returned his attention to the memory replay. Maybe she hadn't been stuttering with cold. Maybe she'd started blurting out her real name? Maybe *she* was Crystal?

'... *put ... Crystal into ... for programming ...?*'

Programmed? Or... filled with, even *made from* nano-machines? They'd been the stuff of science fiction for, what, fifty, seventy, a hundred years? Had Tik Tek and Omega made the breakthrough? If so, God help everyone.

Was she *infectious*?

His imagination kept tossing him new ideas, his thoughts darting like a cat chasing a laser pointer. He lacked data, but maybe now was the time to think outside the box and consider possibilities, no matter how improbable.

Like, what had happened while she'd been underwater? He was sure she'd sunk Tik Tek's boat. But how? Had she transformed into some kind of deadly mer-bot and-

No, he'd checked his memory-footage. The freaking water had *opened* like a pit around Henstridge's speeding boat and it had fallen into it. Into the *moving* hole. That meant magic was involved, not tech. *Please, please, don't tell me Tik Tek or Omega has found a way to meld the two.*

But that reminded him: Henstridge would return, and sooner rather than later. Mason's gut told him the girl was their quarry. And if magic was involved, it meant he was way out of his depth. Nor could he afford a single mistake, not with Tik Tek involved.

The sane thing to do was probably to abandon the whole job: get rid of the girl, cover his tracks, lay low for a while.

He knew he wouldn't though. If he could get a copy of the Omega tech the payoff offered by the Washington Group on this one was huge. Plus, he rationalized, it gave him another chance to hit Tik Tek where it hurt them most: their bottom line. And there was the girl herself....

Three a.m. He scanned the Bay via the drone's sensors, then linked to the boat's nav system to check their progress toward Berkeley. So: return the boat; go to ground; call in some favors.

He returned his full attention to Kristen. Or Crystal, perhaps. He should get dressed. But the journey still had a good half hour, and there was something nice about the innocent way she slumped against him, her head tucked into his left shoulder. He looked at the bruise and scratches on her forehead. It hadn't magically healed. He wondered again at the weird eating thing. If they could do that, wouldn't it be more useful to accelerate the body's natural healing powers?

He moved a finger toward her fringe, then hesitated.

How old was she, anyway? Maybe only seventeen, eighteen. His finger completed its journey, his touch on her bruise a soft caress.

Her eyes flashed open, amber-flecked irises locking on his. An instant later her small hand snapped around his wrist like a steel clamp.

Shit, she was fast! And her grip *hurt!*

He barely managed to interrupt his own augmented systems' immediate counter-response. "Relax, I just want to check this bruise. Crystal," he added.

She frowned, blinking, but didn't object to the name as she released his wrist.

Mentally, he nodded. *Hunch confirmed.*

Brushing aside her fringe, he gently traced the outline of the injury, noting again how the gauntness of her face had vanished, her cheeks filled in, even as he puzzled over the sheer speed of her reaction just now. And her bruising strength. A spell? He knew there were mages who specialized in what they called combat magic; he'd faced a few himself. But even such tuned and optimized spells required concentration to maintain, as well as a second or more to cast.

Another theory bites the dust.

She was just full of contradictions, wasn't she? Maybe she *was* a were-leopard. Assuming such a thing even existed.

"How did you hurt your forehead, Crystal?"

He probed the injury as gently as he could, sure for a moment he'd hurt her, but she didn't react. Well, not exactly. She just went still. Waiting. Something about that unnerved him. At least she wasn't cold anymore though: her skin was warm, borderline feverish.

But despite not objecting to being called Crystal, *something* had changed. He struggled to pin down just what, although distracted by the other implications: why would she give a false name, then simply accept her real one without even *trying* to maintain the deception?

"Crystal? Why were they shooting at you?"

Instead of replying, she slid her left hand under his robe, over his chest, feeling his muscles, tugging playfully on the dark curls before slipping lower. Had she slid back into that weirdly creepy sex-doll mode?

"Crystal-"

With surprising dexterity she turned, one leg slithering over his thighs, neatly straddling him despite the limited space between seat and table. Now facing him, she slid her other hand under his robe, around him, and tilted her head up to his, her lips opening.

Her expression wasn't the creepy one, though she did look... hungry. Eager.

"Crystal...."

She arched upward while simultaneously wriggling on his lap, and parts of him surged in response. Then her lips were on his, surprisingly warm and soft. So soft. And avid. Her tongue darted out, dancing along the edge of his mouth.

She certainly seemed to respond to her real name, he thought, intrigued by her apparent determination to end his line of questioning. Well, if she *wanted* to distract him…. Her hands slipped lower, to his groin, and her smile was wicked as she arched her back, thrusting her hips against the junction of their bodies.

She was good at this! For a second he considered being the gentleman, but he'd already decided, hadn't he? If he made love to her, she'd feel a bond; be more likely to accept an offer of protection and assistance. Which would keep his options very open, as far as deciding what to do with her.

He lifted her, surprised once more by her weight – now seventy-three kilos, internal strain meters told him – and slid them both out from the eating area. She locked her legs around his waist as he stood and carried her into the sleeping cabin.

But even as she nuzzled into his neck and tumbled them backward onto the bed, he wondered again about pheromones.

She flung the robe from her. Her taut curves spoke to some animal part of him. He felt his internal systems register the intensity of his interest as unnatural and switch on record-mode.

But then she pounced on him, impaling herself in an exquisite, acrobatic movement.

God!

CHAPTER 13

Amanda Dunkirk, clutching the remains of the dream, fought free of sleep, her heart pounding. She felt flushed and confused – but driven by the certainty something awful had happened to Jane, she struggled backwards through the weird adult stuff to the dream's beginning, sure her sister's strange friend was in terrible trouble. Again.

Falling?

Before that, helplessness and terror, endless. Part of her flinched from those memories like a hand jerking from a hot frying pan.

Had there been something about an actual fry pan, too? And swimming? Cold, too. Definitely cold.

Other really weird and uncomfortable adult stuff.... She shied from the memory.

Jane had been falling, shrinking.

Bullets, and swimming, and cold, and... stuff she'd skated past. It was probably just a dream. She rolled over, but couldn't let it go, trying to remember what had come after that. Something about a cat, and huge Things watching Jane, fighting over her?

It felt like Jane going away. Forever. She started getting out of bed, then remembered Marcie wasn't alone – Da had allowed Vince to stay overnight: in her room! She gnawed at a fingernail. *I'll tell M in the morning.*

The old pain went through her, wondering what her and Marcie's lives, and Da's, would've been like if the Red Plague had never happened.

She pushed that old wound into the background. The three of them had each other; and Sis was even becoming a big net star. Though she'd never thought Da'd let M have a boyfriend sleep over.

Maybe he was thinking that, at least that way he could keep an eye on her? Three times now Marcie'd been kidnapped. Three times Jane had saved her.

Jane.... Sleep claimed her again.

CHAPTER 14

Dr Shinsuke Yamamoto faced a still-damp Arvid Henstridge on the eighth floor of Omega Memory Systems. An unseasonably cold night wind whipped through the office from the gaping space which two hours earlier had held privacy mirrored, laminated glass. Supposedly bulletproof.

A space now shielded by a stainless steel fold-out screen.

Dr Yamamoto and his head of security stood in his main laboratory, what he called the Writer room. Behind them stretched a bank of instruments and nearby, a hungry white tube ready to swallow its solid, minimally-padded stretcher – now bent, and empty. Two specialized robotic surgery units squatted deep within it. Fortunately, undamaged.

At least the night air had cleared the acrid stink of gunpowder. The shell casings too had been collected, and the remaining shards of glass plucked from the window seals, broken teeth pulled from a dragon-sized maw.

Outside the room the final work crew waited with the large sheet of replacement glass. Twice as thick, it would be in place before dawn.

The lab was in lock-down. Any recordings of events here would be made by Mr Henstridge alone.

Dr Yamamoto rechecked that his lab's cameras were all off. But he wondered, not for the first time, who might be observing, behind Henstridge's eyes. He sometimes had the foolish notion of someone else watching, through those dark eyes. Eyes which only appeared organic, like so much of the rest of his body. Even his bones had been graphene laced.

He didn't trust the man.

While his head of security had spent the last two hours ineptly chasing shadows, he had spent them in study. Studying the twisted rails and snapped and bloodied belts dangling from the gurney of the modified CEPHscan: his precious Writer.

He caressed the curved surface of its outer shell, frowning at the buckling of the gurney itself. For an hour he had reviewed the footage of Crystal tearing herself free and fleeing this room to hammer futilely at the 'unbreakable' floor-to-ceiling window of the main office. Except her efforts had *not* been futile.

He flushed, recalling his own amusement – until he'd seen her fists striking faster and faster, blurring as the window groaned in protest. Swelling in a final crescendo, the tortured glass bowing and flexing, exploding outward in dagger shards.

He had studied that recording. At length. In slow motion. Frame by frame.

Resonance.

He understood the principle. But the feat he had witnessed was not possible for a human. Not the speed. Certainly not the impossibly precise timing.

Yet he had witnessed it himself.

In the smaller medical bay beside the main lab, he had also studied the two large, very dead bodies recovered from the docks. Two of Mr Henstridge's inept security cordon, fallen silent soon after reporting finding tracks, small *wet* tracks leading from the waters of the Bay.

The larger of the two, the troll, had been stabbed in the neck. Five razor-like wounds had severed his internal and external jugulars; carotid, windpipe, hyoid bone, larynx.... He'd died instantly, his leathery skin apparently no protection. The head of the other guard, a normal human, had been nearly severed, also with blades of *at least* surgical sharpness.

The bodies had been discovered as the cordon had tightened on... nothing.

Yet Crystal had leaped through the window weaponless.

She'd also survived an eight-story drop unharmed, then swum underwater long enough to evade spotlights and a fusillade of high-powered rifles.

Nor had a ten kilometer stretch of drones detected her, deployed by Henstridge at considerable expense as a coastal perimeter.

Clearly, she must have had assistance. A rescuer. But Henstridge had found nothing: lovers in parked cars by the shores of the nearby restaurants precinct; suspicious but empty vans more locally; a boat in the Bay. Nothing beyond slack jawed tourists in any of them.

And the head of his five-star security team – highly recommended by corporations from Asgard to Tik Tek – had nearly drowned when a class one AquaSec cruiser fitted with every surveillance system known to man had been swallowed by the waters of New Francisco Bay. Five million credits worth of assets ruined and lost in seconds.

The insurance paperwork alone would be a nightmare.

But worse than all that, worse than the fact that the insolent Crystal had broken free before her reprogramming had completed, was what she now carried in her head. What she represented.

A ticking bomb. Found by others, she could ruin everything.

She had been only his third human trial. The first since he had corrected the final small flaws in his Writer. The ability to quickly and painlessly implant new knowledge, new skills, would make him the wealthiest man alive – even before exploiting the darker opportunities it presented.

The arrogant, disrespectful bodyguard would have been *his*, body and soul. An advertisement for those *other* capabilities. Simultaneously a perfect tool and a display of dominance on his arm, for those with the wit to see it. Although in this crass society, that would probably be precious few.

A foreshadowing of his future power, she would have been equally useful for pleasure or protection, yet too cryptic a display for unsubtle Westerners to read.

But who had rescued her? Assuming someone had. *Could* she have slipped through Henstridge's cordon alone? Apart from her impossible feat in breaking the laminated glass barrier to escape, she had demonstrated only comfortable competence. 'Cocky' in the execution of her duty, but with no hint she could perform any of the feats she had this night.

Again he surveyed the damage *she* had wreaked on the sturdy equipment. Had his procedure revealed a hidden potential in the human brain? Terror unlocking hysterical strength to let her tear herself from his Writer's robotic embrace?

Even now she must be dazed, confused, amnesiac – and worse. She would never be more vulnerable. It was inconceivable she had broken free, but beyond inconceivable that she still evaded recapture.

Perhaps Henstridge-san was not a highly recommended independent contractor but an employee of Tik Tek? There had been unwanted financial overtures from that quarter. Suggestions that their investment entitled them to access his research material. Too-eager tenders of co-operation.

Had *Henstridge* aided her escape?

But why would Tik Tek need interfaces to human memory? The brains of their top end gynoids and androids were digital, not organic.

Had Henstridge-san already recovered her? Was she already on her way to some Tik Tek lab? Well, he still held the blood samples she had so reluctantly provided as part of her employment background check. He would contact Fushimoto-san: he would know of mages for hire.

But no, the simplest explanation was most usually correct. Perhaps his head of security was merely overrated. Overhyped, was that the phrase? Perhaps he should consider someone more competent, more colorful, suited to his future high profile? One of those 'Bodyguards to the Stars'? For now, though, he had to work with what he had.

"Mr Henstridge, Crystal-chan must be returned before a third party finds her and examines her. The rewrite scaffolding is still in place and detectable. It would expose my process. You said you would recapture her 'at once'. That was three hours ago. I fear your performance in this matter maybe will cost your agency its five star rating."

Henstridge's jaw worked. "None of this would've happened if you'd..." *kept your dick out of the equation.* But he knew not to say that to the man's face. "If you'd let me assign one of *my* people for your 'outings'." He'd known the brash young woman was trouble the instant he'd laid eyes on her. But Yamamoto had been insistent, unable to see past the cleavage and curves, the delight of ordering his attractive bodyguard around. Especially because she hated it. The middle-aged perv had seemed to love demeaning her. Like it made him look bigger.

"Ha! You Westerners, still so shy about sex. Your candidate would not have projected correct image for me on my relaxation nights, Mr Henstridge. Crystal struck perfect tune. Perfect note? Ha!" He shook his head, remembering the girl by his side, angered simply by being ordered to fetch coffee, yet happy to dress as outrageously as he suggested. Happiest of all whenever situations had spun out of control.

Yet with a talent for brutal action.

It appeared she had been underplaying that talent.

"Find her, Henstridge. Pay someone to hack each facial recognition system in the city, each hospital or clinic with MRI or PET scanners – or CEPHscanners. Especially any reports of the sudden death of a young woman during an MRI scan.

"Track down this Tom Kingston who hired the small boat you searched. The sinking of your own craft cannot be coincidence.

"Find Crystal Winters and bring her back. 'Dead or alive' – isn't that your cowboy phrase? Dead or alive.

"But preferably alive. I want to see her crawl to me, Henstridge. And after completing her *interrupted* session in my Writer, she *will* crawl.

"One more hour in my Writer and she will do anything I command. Anything."

CHAPTER 15

She shifted, stirring from a dream of swimming in ice cold water, something large and inhuman coiling around her, tidal desires flooding back and forth between them.

Also pain, terrible hunger, and thirst.

Her throat was so dry it hurt. She swallowed, fighting the self-adhesion, her tongue a swollen and parched awkwardness half-choking her. An ache deep in her skull made itself known, as did a general, less severe ache in every muscle.

A hollow, sharp cramp in her gut brought her further awake, and she shifted position. That made her bladder add its note to the chorus of complaints.

Her head lay on something living. Something with a deep, strong heartbeat, and the rushing whisper of blood through its veins. Her right hand splayed on a firmly muscled chest, fingers nestled in curls of hair. A lower, humming vibration shuddered through everything.

She was starving, too.

With a shock that brought her abruptly alert, she realized she was lying naked against a man.

Wait. Don't move. Gather data.

Keeping her eyes shut, she forced herself to relax, letting sensory information flood in like she'd been trained to do. *Trained?* That thought sharpened the dull ache in her head, yielding just the wisp of an idea of tattoos. It faded.

She ground her teeth.

He was naked, too. Asleep, his chest rose and fell steadily under her arm. His scent clear, sharp, and masculine. She lay on her side, pressed up against him. A warm, light quilt covered them. She tensed, feeling a swaying movement of the bed. No, not the bed, the whole room: rocking, though they themselves were both motionless. She sniffed and smelled salt: the sea. And the deep hum: some kind of engine.

A boat? I'm on a boat? Why am I on a boat?

She slitted her eyes, careful not to move. The man sprawled on his back, with her draped against him. Snuggling him.

Who is he?

Searching her memory, no name surfaced. She shifted her head, gently, mimicking the movements of a sleeper casually shifting position before stilling again to study him. Dark hair, firm jaw stubbled with dark whiskers. Generous lips, strong nose and eyebrows. The face was appealing somehow, tiny wrinkles at the corners of the eyes and mouth suggesting sternness measured with humor.

The room – in fact, everything she saw – was monochrome, the light flat. But that was normal, for night. She looked around. Opaque windows, unlit lamps; smooth white walls, gray bedding; the man's dark hair. But... didn't people need light, to see?

The room, *everything*, vanished, replaced by solid black.

No!

The mysterious blindness ended as suddenly as it had begun, the room snapping back into sight while her heart pounded. *What just happened?* She swallowed. Was there something wrong with her eyes? Or had her thoughts somehow caused that? Frowning, she set the questions aside, examining as much as she could of the small room while moving her head minimally. She noted the lighter rectangle of a doorway and another room beyond it, and on the far side of that... a cabin?

A short series of ladder-like steps led up to an odd right-angled hatch set in the corner where wall met ceiling.

Sniffing, she smelled traces of food, and felt another surge of hunger. Thirst, too. Apart from that she felt a little battered. Because of him? But her bladder: that was bursting. So much so, her muscles were clenched like steel. Jaws tight, she forced her attention back to the man. Her companion.

He lay sound asleep, and she moaned before rolling away from him, disengaging to flop bonelessly beside him, still touching his side in a carefully planned imitation of a sleeper's random movement. She smelled herself, and him: the pungent aroma of sex.

She waited for the memory of their lovemaking to surface, but nothing came. There was just a blankness, a pervasive and woolly nothingness, and she cast her mind further back. *How did I get here?* For a moment, the dream returned – cold dark water, and something immense cradling her, sharing...

Sharing what?

But the memory slithered away, slipping from her grasp when pain stabbed through her head to skewer it, shattering it with such force she felt her muscles lock. She had to bite down on a gasp of agony.

Steeling her nerve, she forced herself to relax into the pain lest her tension wake the man. The moment she did, the pain eased – only to be replaced by the now desperate need for a toilet.

She locked that physical necessity away, trying once more to remember how she got here; their lovemaking; but again drew a blank. Warning pain stabbed in her head.

He drugged me! Her hand drifted between her legs, fingers testing for damage. A crusty residue told its tale with brutal clarity. That explained it: her memory loss, the pains... everything.

Swallowing again, she tried again to moisten her mouth against the awful dryness, nursing a swelling burn of anger: a towering dark wave of justice that dwarfed her drug-induced headache, a gently-throbbing ache between her legs, and that more pressing urgency.

Opening her eyes fully she turned her head to study her rapist in the unlit cabin, a weird *tingle* shivering through her fingertips. It spelled his death, she knew.

Just one decision. Talk to him first, or kill him – *now*?

CHAPTER 16

But with only seconds until an accident, she had no time to look for the lavatory. In the end, she let her bladder decide.

He woke instantly at her touch.

"Toilet," she demanded.

Dark brown eyes focused on hers. She heard the ultra-pitched sound of cybernetic muscles coming on line.

So he was augmented. She ignored it.

He blinked but didn't answer. She shook him this time, hard. "Toilet. Where? Now!"

He looked surprised, but indicated the rectangle of the doorway. "Through the door, then to the right. Here, let me-"

She left before he'd finished speaking, darting through the monochrome world. Through the first doorway, she saw another on her right, smelled a whiff of deodorizer, and flung the door open. A tiny room with a small white seat and equally-small washbasin. Slamming the seat down she plunged onto it in blissful relief.

-

Mason sat up, eyes narrowed, noting how well she'd navigated in the pitch dark. So she had optics, *good* optics. His own last ocular upgrade, a twenty-five percent quantum efficiency boost, had cost half as much as a run-of-the-mill spinal column rewiring. Without it, he would've been blind in this blacked-out cabin. In the field, investments like that made the difference between success and failure. *Or life and death.*

Interesting.

He checked the nav system, just as the 'ten minutes to dock' warning pinged him. It was now three-forty-five a.m. He wondered if Henstridge'd be looking for him yet? But that thought reminded him he'd wanted to check that high-velocity round.

He headed into the main cabin and switched the lights on. Turning around, he stifled an oath at finding her right behind him, a strange expression on her face. Like she was deciding something, maybe? Something serious.

Her stomach growled.

"Still hungry?"

She didn't answer, just watched him, her expression grim. Maybe deciding to tell him who – or what – she really was? She probably just needed time.

"I've got crackers." He moved past her to the cupboard in the galley, digging them out, wincing at the Best-by date. He offered it to her anyway. "How're you feeling now?"

She nodded, still not speaking, taking the unopened packet, just watching him like he was a puzzle to solve.

"More milk?"

She nodded, emphatic, studying him as he poured her a glass. Sniffing it, she took a sip before backing away to sit at the table.

Tearing the packet open, her eyes not leaving him, she crammed semi-stale crackers into her mouth.

Leaving her to it he returned to the galley, reaching up behind the gimbal-mounted stove to tug free her still-damp clothing. He unzipped the pocket and took out the high velocity round.

As he'd seen before, it had peeled open, then the steel 'petals' folded roughly back up. Why had she been carrying it though?

He returned to the table where she'd stopped eating, now leaning back against the seat, eyes shut but breathing normally. Her color was good too.

Looking at her, the bruise and scratches on her forehead seemed to leap into focus. He considered the shell in his hand, mentally measuring it against the mark on her forehead. Trying to pry the shell open, sharp metal edges nicked his fingers.

She'd had scratches and nicks on her right fingertips and thumb. Using the tag on the zipper of her jacket, he forced the petals apart, then held it up before her forehead.

It matched.

A shiver ran through him as he struggled to understand what it meant. Was she bullet-proof? Or simply the luckiest woman alive? The chance of it peeling open at the exact moment of impact-

His mind spun. Nanomachines? Nah. He stayed on top of tech developments, especially rumors: essential, given his line of work. Not just to make money, but to stay alive. Cutting edge upgrades had more than once saved his life.

He reached out a fingertip toward her fading injury, his muscles twitching: remembering how she'd reacted last time. Part of him just wanted to touch her again, sensing she needed protection, *his* protection, even while another part questioned that irrational response.

But the strongest force was simple curiosity. How had her skin protected her from a high-velocity round of that caliber? Surely it wasn't luck.

Magic?

Magic made more sense. He considered again the possibility she was a shaman. Had she used an air spirit to break the window then slow her fall, or a spirit of the Bay to soften her entry to the water, and later to sink Henstridge? After all, either she was mad, or she'd been talking to *something* beyond this small boat. He remembered her strangely wanton smile when she'd offered to *visit*... something.

Or was she a werewolf, or werecat? *Mermaid?* But such creatures didn't exist. Did they?

If she was a shaman, *or* a mythical were-animal, he knew who to take her to. George owed him one. Though Maeve definitely didn't.

He grimaced. Yeah, that could get... awkward.

Maybe George might even know her. Or know of her, or what she was. Surely people like that, the magically 'unfolded', had some kind of network of contacts?

Lorien had good med gear, too. Knowing Maeve, probably upgraded since last he'd visited. In the unlikely event Crystal did have nanos, they should be detectable in her blood. And maybe by now Maeve might've forgiven him?

He wondered how the two women would react to one another.

He shook his head. *What am I thinking?* It wasn't like he and Crystal were a couple. Or that there was any chance Maeve might *not* still want to tear out his liver, for that matter. All the same, just the thought of visiting her community lightened his mood. It'd been too long.

The decision made, his finger completed its journey, his touch on the bruise a soft caress. *This* time, ready for her reaction. He made sure he was recording.

Her fingers were suddenly around his.

Dear God! That's how fast she can move when she's not asleep? His analytics told him she'd reacted at over twice his best speed. And with more strength than his own augmented musculature, he judged from her insane grip. Which was crazy. Impossible. He was top of the line.

They stared at one another.

"We have time, finally, for a little first aid," he said, keeping his voice calm. Innocent.

She frowned, blinking, but released his wrist.

He took her forearms, gently rubbing antiseptic ointment into each wrist in turn, conscious of the bruises and abrasions, using the time to settle his own nerves after her shocking little demonstration. *Unbelievable.* "Who did this?"

She frowned at him strangely – less serious, more confused. Even more so when he knelt at her feet to do the same for her ankles.

Finished, he capped the tube and smiled up at her.

She looked... baffled.

He rose and sat back beside her. "So. Care to tell me now why were they shooting at you?"

"Shooting?"

"Yes, shooting." He indicated her forehead, wondering at the pretend innocence, but again she didn't react. "This." He lifted her right hand, guiding her fingers to the bruising and scratches and watched as she felt the small injury – and once more failed to react. Or, rather, she reacted, but very subtly – he could almost see a thought flicker behind her eyes – but she simply continued to sit there, watching him. Waiting.

Something about that brought a tingle of unease.

He pulled the shell from the pocket of his robe, its sharp edges catching briefly on the cloth as he tugged it free to hand to her.

She frowned down at it, her head tilted to one side, rotating it in her fingers, stopping briefly as she seemed to note the cuts on their tips. Her head came up, but she was staring past him, her eyes on something distant.

"It was in my hair."

Of all her possible responses, that hadn't been what he'd expected.

"It's a high velocity round," she observed. "Point five-oh caliber, bucky-steel jacket to control spalling and minimize the impulse-energy transfer period."

He waited for her to continue but her jaw worked, like she was in pain? Then her gaze, still distant, drifted down to the bundle of damp clothing on the table he held, and her introspection ended.

"Oh! My Chateau Equipe jacket! It's crusty with salt! I need soap, gentle soap? Or maybe shampoo?"

Grabbing the jacket, she jumped up, wincing as if in pain.

For reasons he couldn't name, he felt relief at the distraction. He stood and eased it from her grip. She followed him to the galley, watching doubtfully as he washed it.

He continued probing her about the shooting. Apparently though he pushed too hard. Instead of answering, she fell silent. The best he could do was watch, trying to guess what her series of expressions meant.

CHAPTER 17

Baffled and confused, she watched the man. *Father and Mother'll be angry that I....*

The thought petered out, and a sharp pain with it. *That I what? And why angry?* She wasn't sure why that last part was true; she just knew it was. *That's pretty sad.*

The more she thought about it, the sadder it felt.

How would it feel to be back home in her room, with her... with her...? Her thought ran off into empty space as she tried to picture her room.

Blinking, she waited for the image to form, but none did. She tried harder: tried scrinching up her face. That didn't seem to make her brain work any better. *I guess memory isn't a muscle you can flex or squeeze.* She tensed then, before relaxing, wondering why she'd expected pain.

She grew aware she was panting, something like a general panic pushing at her, and she quashed it. *It's just a room — why would I remember that especially?*

Mother though, or Father? Mother, with her, with her, hair, right; what color? How long?

Nothing.

How old? Was she pretty? Stern, or kindly?

Nothing.

The panic returned, surging like a muscular snake trying to shake her off. She clamped down on it again in a well-practiced discipline.

A numbing shock ran through her when she considered that: *I'm used to suppressing panic.*

Am I crazy? Someone who suffers from panic attacks?

Part of her was sure the answer was 'No'. Did that mean she was someone who had to deal with situations as awful as this, a lot?

That was bad. Almost scary.

Well, friends... *I must have friends, right?* She shut her eyes, clearing her mind, digging... and was again rewarded with sharp pain lancing through her head.

Crusty, stinky rats, no! Try again. My name is...

She felt her mouth fall open, stunned to discover she had no idea. No idea of her own name.

What do I remember? Well, there's....

Her mind yawned, empty. Vacant.

I've suffered worse than this.

Then she wondered: *how do I know that?* And anyway,

how could anything be worse than *this*?

She was hardly aware of being guided to a bed, a blanket drawn over her, being told to rest. She wouldn't sleep, though.

Shutting her eyes she continued digging. There had to be *something*.

There was a secret. I'm a secret.

The insight frayed, swallowed in pain and darkness.

Stretching, she felt rough sheets cocooning her, the bed warm beside her, a lingering smell of sex. Smiling, she cast her mind back to... emptiness.

She stilled, keeping her eyes shut. In a nearby room, someone was moving. Someone large.

The house *rolled*, subtly, and she tensed, ready to leap from the bedding to safety. But there was just a spread-out creaking and then the house rolled again, the other way.

Outside, a bird called in the distance, and water lapped softly.

Searching her memory for how she'd gotten where she was, she found... nothing. Just an overall ache, a faint masculine scent and the smell of sex clinging to her.

She felt her face flush, anger flaring. *Find out what he drugged me with, kill him, and get treatment.* That decision made, she flung the blankets aside and stalked through a small doorway into a low ceilinged room. As she prepared to spring, the room moved again, and she hesitated.

He turned, smiling, holding no other weapons than a frying pan, sudsy with soap.

"Hey, perfect timing."

He was tall, his dark hair brushing the ceiling's curved, white-painted beams. Dark eyes too, with firm lips curving up. Behind him, a tiny ladder led up. Faint daylight spilled down it and through the windows circling the room, set a little higher than her head.

The house swayed again.

He didn't *look* guilty, like someone who'd drugged and raped someone a few hours earlier.

"What did you give me?"

Mace looked at Crystal, standing tense, lips clamped shut and face set as if she'd made an important decision. That intensity hardly fit her question, though. Hopefully it meant she'd decided to share her real story.

She stood just inside the main cabin, small and cute in just the fluffy white bathrobe.

He shrugged. "Quite a lot. Eggs, bacon...." He nodded down at the pan. "You cleaned me out."

But now her stance, the way she stared, was beginning to set off alarm bells. Before he powered up though, her expression shifted. Softened?

"You were starving. So I kept cooking, and you kept eating. When I stopped, you, well, you growled."

Her eyebrows rose, her expression softening further. She looked less certain. She'd been angry, he realized. Why would she be angry?

"Growled?"

He shrugged. "Growled. After devouring ten rashers of streaky bacon, eight – no, nine, ten eggs, twelve pieces of toast – two plain, before I could butter them, one buttered, peanut butter, honey... every spread I had. Liters of milk, too, and a whole box of cereal. I have no idea where it all went, really. Then you just crashed."

Crystal was frowning hard by the end of the list, staring at him like she didn't believe him. So she *had* been as out of it as she'd seemed at the time. It hadn't been pretense. "You just shoveled it all in, two handed. First time I've seen someone eat eggs with their bare hands."

She looked angry again. Gnawing at her bottom lip, her hands clenched and unclenched.

"Wait. You don't remember *any* of this?"

He saw her grind her teeth, then shake her head.

"Well, you did seem pretty out of it. Sniff your hands. You'll probably still smell bacon grease."

Her eyes fell to her fingertips, but she visibly stopped herself from checking them. He could almost hear circuits in her head, buzzing. *What* is *she?* he wondered again; but simply waited, not speaking, still giving her time.

Her jaw set and she met his eyes accusingly. "As long as you're filling me in, what happened *before* you fed me?"

Although her tone was light, he didn't buy it. He noted how very still she stood, how well balanced, and sensed a weight behind her question. But why ask him what she already-? Oh.

"You don't remember *us?* Us making love?"

Her eyes narrowed.

"The searchers' boat sinking?"

That seemed to surprise her. It was his turn to frown. Dammit! She didn't remember the other boat sinking? He really wanted to find how she'd managed *that* stunt. "Coming aboard?"

She wrapped her arms around herself, seeming to shrink before looking up and around the cabin again. "*Aboard.* That explains the water noises, and the house movements. So we *are* on a boat."

Was she for real? "What *is* the last thing you remember?"

She tilted her head to one side, looking puzzled. "You saying, 'What's the last thing you remember?'"

Until he caught the tiny up-tick at the corners of her lips, he thought she was being difficult. It was the first hint of humor he'd seen from her. If she *was* a robot, she was a damned advanced one. *Loaded with human memories, maybe?* "Seriously, Crystal, why were you in the water at two a.m? Why was AquaSec hunting you?"

She looked blankly back at him, then stared in shock, her mouth falling open.

"What is it? What've you remembered?"

She didn't answer, shaking her head as if in denial, pressing both hands to her cheeks then covering her mouth, her gaze focused inward on some internal horror.

As he stepped forward she tensed, focusing back on him.

"Nothing! It's all gone. You took it all! You choking, disshole funt-stick! *You* did this!"

Something about her look as she stalked forward had him bring the frying pan between them. "Stop!" he shouted as his augments powered up, threat assessment algorithms identifying vectors of attack.

To his surprise, she did stop, gazing at him in a kind of awe.

It didn't last. Shaking herself, her head lowered and she snarled. The next instant she was flying, crashing into him and bowling him over. Arms and legs locked his as she rode him to the floor. His augmented muscles strained, red-lining as the fry pan sailed up.

Her forehead slammed into his like a hammer.

Dazed, he saw her snatch the fry pan from mid air.

CHAPTER 18

Only the auto-defense firmware of Mason's augments brought his arm up in time to block the frying pan.

Incredibly then, his cyber-boosted muscles and larger limbs couldn't overcome her smaller ones: couldn't budge the pan-wielding arm, or the legs pinning his. Meanwhile her eyes darted around in a kind of crazy frustration.

Her muscles tensed, then she sprang up and off him, the pan clanging into the galley's metal basin.

Rolling, jumping to his feet, he shook his head. *Was it over?*

Her fingers flexed, in furious little flicks or spasms.

"Crystal, just calm the-"

Instead, she snatched up a carving knife and turned.

He held up both hands. "Wait! I can prove everything I told you."

She paused, eyes narrowed, watching.

Fingers stretched out, gesturing for calm, he added, "I don't want to hurt you."

The moment he spoke, he saw he'd said the wrong thing.

She *snarled*.

At the man's threat she growled, earning a stab of pain through her head. It made her hesitate.

He didn't move, though. *Wise of him.*

"Let me show you what I saw tonight," he said, hands still held open. "Everything, from hauling you out of the water, to just now."

His eyes were cybernetic, like so much of the rest of him, his body an orchestra of ultrasonic cheeps and whines. She gave a tiny nod. If he had a recording, she needed to see it.

A drone outside chirped into flight, and she snatched the frying pan back up. He took the warning, since the drone stayed where it was. Though he eyed her like she'd somehow surprised him.

"I need to bring my drone inside. Or do you have a Link ID, so I can narrowcast instead of project?"

Do I, for an implanted Link? "Not that I remember."

She didn't move as he went to the little stair-ladder thing. Just kept her feet planted, ready despite the boat's constant motion.

His eyes stayed fixed on her as he pushed the hatch open one-handed, letting the small drone inside. It dipped in the air before steadying, as if it knew she was ready to smash it to pieces at one false move. She gripped the knife in her other hand, though something about that raised a terrible sense of wrongness.

She *really* wanted to smash something.

He let the hatch fall shut and stepped away again, and the drone projected a hologram.

In the air between them a scrawny, white-haired wretch flopped out of water. She frowned at it. *What did this have to do with...?* Then, guessing the half-drowned girl must be her, barely kept the shock from her face.

She looks starved. Her stomach growled agreement, but a flick of her eyes over her actual body contradicted it.

"You remember coming aboard?"

She didn't, but the less she told him, the better. *I'm secret. Keep him guessing how well his drugs are working.* But she'd already admitted she didn't remember anything. She shook her head. Let him try to prove he wasn't the cause of that. Either way, she needed to see this 'proof'.

She let him continue. He skipped through fast, while summarizing, but stopping and playing the video at normal speed whenever she asked.

He had his own questions: like how had she been injured, what had she done underwater? As if he found it all as confusing as she did. She hid her feelings though, just watching like it was no big deal. Even when the cruel, bald-headed man he called Henstridge appeared, flooding her with conflicting swirls of contempt and respect.

But when the departing boat *fell* into the sudden enormous hole in the water, she went cold: she wasn't stupid. A special effects scene like that, spliced in with all the other supposed footage of her, must've taken time and planning. It meant she was in a far worse situation than she'd guessed.

From then on she made noises like someone with amnesia, learning what she'd just been doing.

At the end though he didn't make any kind of pitch, or even a request. Just asked if it had jogged any memories?

The whole charade was way too elaborate to be a rapist's cover-up for doping his victim. How long would their memory blocking drugs last? Why were they doing this?

She had to play along. Discover their real plan. Could he be making some kind of weird reality movie? She seriously doubted that.

Or could he possibly be telling the truth? Watching the scrawny woman – herself? – eating off the floor, gorging herself, her gaunt face and thin limbs visibly filling out as he played it through at high speed, she didn't know what to think. When she turned to him, he looked as puzzled as she felt.

He sure was a good actor.

CHAPTER 19

Four a.m, Mason docked The Sleeping Tom at the rental jetty, his large kit bag at his feet. The company's drone buzzed past to inspect the vessel, filming inside and out to confirm it was ship-shape. He waited to lock up and reclaim his deposit – less energy costs and fifty credits for a broken window latch – as the AI concierge analyzed the vid and presumably downloaded the vessel's internal system logs.

He only gave the night fishing a three star rating, though. "You should warn people that AquaSec are likely to hassle and search you, even two klicks out, at three a.m! I won't be doing this again."

Augmented muscles hid the effort as he bent and casually hefted his kit bag, praying Crystal wouldn't reassert her distrust of him by bursting out of it.

Heading to his car, he glanced up as a drone buzzed him briefly. His own – now packed away alongside the tightly-curled Crystal – had alerted him to its presence as they'd motored back to shore. A good thing his strange visitor had consumed his entire food supply. It made space for her in his bag.

With one arm braced on the rental car's roof against her weight, he lowered his bag into the passenger side then got in himself. If he *had* lucked out, the first order of business was to get his spoils off the watchers' radar.

"Okay car, home," he ordered. It repeated the address of Tom Kingston, who he'd paid as usual to slip off on another 'nature retreat' at the start of this caper days earlier. Sleazy bastard.

"You okay in there?" he asked once the docks were far behind.

The zipper slid open. "Shh," she hissed. "I think they bugged us."

He sensed her peering up at him from the floor-well, but he didn't look down, instead just crossed his arms and relaxed in his seat as the car drove. "What makes you think that?" he asked, keeping his voice equally low.

"I heard drones. They'll have read your license plates. The second one touched the car, underneath."

"Why do you say that?"

"I just told you," she hissed, annoyed. "I heard it!"

"You *heard* the drone touch the car?"

She didn't dignify that with an answer.

He thought back. It would explain several oddities. He filed the information away. "Good to know, but it won't be a problem."

He laid out the plan as they headed north, toward the real Tom Kingston's flat in Albany. In, grab a hoodie for her, then out the back alley and a short walk to his own car. It'd been a long day, and a longer night.

"You can tell me if you hear any more drones."

"Okay!"

He eyed the bag. She sounded *too* happy.

With her assurance of no drones lurking, they set out from Albany via a winding route, this time in his car, heading for his own place at Richmond. He opaqued the windows, and Crystal wriggled out of the kit bag, stretching. His drone trailed them discreetly from above, a guardian angel scanning for followers.

"Can you hear mine?" His had active noise cancellation, so he expected her to say no.

She eyed him. "No?"

He studied her face. "You really can't?"

"Of course not," she said. Watching him.

He pursed his lips, suspecting she'd lied. But from her expression, he wouldn't be able to get her to admit that. He sighed.

The garage door rolled up as they approached, closing behind them.

Finally, safe. For a while.

The instant he opened the connecting door from the garage, Boje yowled and leapt into his arms, complaining loudly. "I missed you too," he told the calico cat with the smudge of black running down her white and pink nose.

Cradling her, he gently chucked Mrs B under the chin. He checked her auto feeder, shaking his head at its record of activity, wondering if gluttony made Boje and Crystal kindred spirits? Boje turned in his arms, watching their guest pad to the west-facing plate glass windows overlooking San Quentin's moonlit waters.

Crystal took in the abstract paintings, polished wood floors, sculpted glass-works, then moved to the north wall, staring out through the expanse of glass exactly as if she could see into the night. He nodded. *Yeah, good optics.*

She turned back to him, hesitant. "Have I been here before? You... hungered? So we went out...." Whatever she'd been about to say died away in a snarl of quiet frustration, maybe even pain.

Mrs B's ears pricked up. "Look," he told her, "I'm exhausted. There's a guest shower, bedroom down the hall." He pointed, then set Boje down. The cat eyed Crystal carefully.

"Nah, I'll share yours," she said.

Was that accusation? A hint of calculation in her expression? Or had he imagined it? She was smiling now, warmly. He blinked, then shrugged, parts of him stirring despite his exhaustion. "As you wish."

She didn't get the reference.

Boje watched them both disappear into Mason's bedroom, and began washing herself.

Their lovemaking, both still damp from their shared shower, was short, sweet, and strangely touching. Crystal fell asleep curled in his arms, and he followed seconds later as Boje leaped up and butted her head in too.

Five a.m. Sleep was bliss.

A spike in queries about Tom Kingston translated into a diffuse prickling across his skin. By seven a.m, after a meager two hours' rest, it had grown into enough of an irritation to drag him from sleep. Reluctantly, he checked the data on an internal display, one arm slightly numb from Crystal's weight. The Kingston queries were all oddly anonymous, and he groaned. Crystal *unf*-ed softly in her sleep, burrowing in tighter against him.

He sighed. 'Anonymous' was bad. The Kingston checks were coming thick and fast now – bizarrely fast. He'd learned to associate that kind of high speed, multi-source probing with attracting Tik Tek's interest. Checking his anonymous drop location, he skimmed footage from the cam he had watching the entrance to Kingston's flat in Albany, and saw the expected style of heavies enter the building. He wondered what the jerk would find on return from his 'nature romp'. A trashed apartment, at least.

Apart from a physical resemblance, there was no connection between the real Tom Kingston and him, or his home, but if Tik Tek was involved he wasn't taking any chances. It'd be stupid to stay here through the morning.

Reluctantly disentangling himself from a clinging Crystal he rose from the bed. He eyed her sleeping form. Richmond held too many cameras, too many people, too much surveillance, if he held the prize he thought he did. Just by being in the right place at the right time, it looked like he'd already hit the pay dirt he'd been seeking. *Gambler's luck.*

Where to take her, though? His eyes fell on the old pic of him and Maeve. He winced at the memory of her temper, but cringed at the reason they'd split up. Did he know anyone else who owned a portable PET scanner? He needed someplace off the radar, and her commune fitted the bill perfectly.

Lorien.

All shamans were mad, but George.... He chuckled, making plans as he soaped himself under the shower.

Between Lorien's medical resources, and George's crazy but effective magic, he should be able to pry something from Crystal.

CHAPTER 20

Graham Dunkirk's voice boomed up the stairs from the breakfast table. "Amanda! You'll be late for school!"

Marcie winced, wondering whether it was part of his unconscious efforts to make her boyfriend less comfortable. Vince's knee bumped hers reassuringly, and she leaned into him to show her appreciation. "You want me to go wake her, Da?"

Stumbling bare footsteps descending the stairs had them all turning their heads.

Marcie jumped to her feet. "Sprout! You look terrible! What's wrong?"

"Didn' sleep well. Nightmares."

"Again?" Marcie caught their father's haunted look.

Still in her flannel nightdress, Amanda fumbled down the last few stairs and tottered to the kitchen table. Slumping forward in her seat she planted her head in her hands and groaned. "I have an awful headache too."

A horrible kind of tingle wormed through Marcie's gut. "What were the nightmares about this time?" She turned to Vince, but his puzzled expression said he hadn't caught on.

Amanda groaned. "I dunno. Just it kept going on and on and I couldn't wake up. All night long."

"Get some tea into yeh," her father said, plonking a mug on the table before her. "Toast'll help. You want some aspirin?"

She took the mug and sipped. "Thanks Da, please. Two." Reaching for the butter-drenched toast she began spreading a thick layer of honey, then paused, frowning at it like it was trying to tell her something.

"Was it about Jane?" asked Marcie.

Amanda froze.

Long seconds passed.

"There was a white tube all around me."

Graham Dunkirk, Marcie, and Vince stilled. Waited.

"Couldn't move. Not even my head. Her head."

A pit opened in Marcie's stomach, and she drew in a long breath.

"White tube. Lying down. Yeah, Jane. Then I, I mean, in the dream I was Jane... this awful pain, dissolving me till she was gone."

No one spoke.

"And I couldn't wake up, and then I was crammed back in

the white tube, tied down." She looked up. "It was Jane! I think something's happened to her."

"Fook," swore Graham Dunkirk.

Amanda dropped her toast, grabbing her older sister's hand. "M, you have to call her, now!"

Marcie rose from the table, her Link already at her lips as she left the room, aware of three sets of eyes following her. "Call Jane," she whispered to it.

"Link address unreachable," it whispered back.

"When was Jane's Link ID last on the network?"

"Insufficient privilege for query," it responded.

She snarled and stepped further from the kitchen, aware of the others straining to listen. "No luck so far, but I can try something else," she called back to them before raising the Link to her wrist a second time. "Call Jane's mother," she whispered.

This time, the Link connected.

-

Dr Alex Harmon – formerly of the Institute for Paranormal Dysfunction, now working for the covert government agency known as the Department – groaned as his Link buzzed at his wrist. He turned over on the thin and lumpy mattress covering his narrow cot.

"Incoming call from Marcie Dunkirk," it said, followed by the warning tones signifying the call was to the false ID of Leeth's 'mother'.

Dammit, what did the girl want? Why was she calling at... eight a.m? "End call," he snapped.

Peace. He rolled onto his stiff and aching back.

If it were important, Leeth's friend would call back. And if she did – as she no doubt would – he would need a moment to get into character as Leeth's mother. At least he could trust Nelson's voice and face substitution software to function perfectly.

Sighing, he threw back his moth-eaten blanket, blinking in the sunlight streaming through the rough wooden walls of the shack the locals had graciously bestowed on him.

The hardships he endured for the girl. He shook his head. Outside, he heard the people of the Hunters Point Dumps moving and calling, their day long underway.

He sat up as his Link, as expected, buzzed again. "Incoming call from Marcie Dunkirk," it repeated, again with the coded warning tones.

He grunted. "Link, suppress background sounds. Neutral setting," he instructed, then finally accepted the call. As usual, it was a video call. Time to be 'Mother'. He didn't activate the projector which would show him the constructed face of Jane's 'mother'. He could rely on Nelson's program to faithfully transfer his expressions and intonations to those of the fake persona.

"What can I do for you, so early in the morning Miss Dunkirk?"

"Is Jane alright?"

"You know I can't share details of my daughter's work."

"I'm not asking for any! I just want to know if she's alright!"

"I have no reason to believe otherwise." He checked his Link, finding no urgent notifications from the Department.

"I do. I can't get through to her."

"Miss Dunkirk-"

"Look, I'm sure you guys can check to see when her Link was last connected to the network, right? I can't."

Harmon was silent, a butterfly of unease stirring in his stomach. "Are you in trouble, Marcie?"

"What? *Me?* No! I'm worried about Jane."

Again, he thought. *Last time, that worry saved Leeth's life.* "Why?" he asked, mildly.

"Uh...."

He waited for her to continue, noting the shifting of her eyes, interested to hear what the lie would be.

"I just hadn't spoken to her for a while, and then couldn't get through."

"I see. I'll check, and get back to you."

"Thank you!"

The relief in her face was genuine. Harmon terminated the call, considering. Leeth was on a mission as Crystal Winters, bodyguard to the narcissistic middle-aged Japanese playboy CEO of Omega Memory Systems. The Department feared he had come up with something equivalent to Nelson's technology for implanting memories.

He grimaced, remembering how catastrophically that had backfired when combined with his own magical Suggestions, and tried on Leeth.

But now his stomach churned, as if his subconscious had

intuited a problem. He needed to call the Department. But he should first ensure no one was eavesdropping, or lurking suspiciously nearby. He flushed. He should have done that before accepting the call as Leeth's – Jane's – mother. Lying back on his bunk, he left his body and performed a belated astral scan of the area around him. *Clear.*

Back in his body, he made the call, directly to Nelson.

"What's up Doc? Finally dug up some dirt from Leeth's AWOL time you'd like me to follow up on?"

"No. How long would it take you to determine when Crystal Winters' Link was last, ah, connected to the network?"

"Ah... hang on... about a second."

Silence. Harmon sighed, inwardly. "Well, when was it?"

"One twelve a.m this morning. That's not good. Hold on, let me ping her choker. A spread spectrum pulse...."

This time, the silence sounded ominous.

"Nelson?"

"That's... bad. No response. Uh...."

"What does that mean?"

"Ah, I think I'll need to get back to you, Doc-"

"Do *not* disconnect, Nelson. Trust me on this. I'm sure you know Mother and Father have requested my psychological assessment of you. Concerning an attitude problem."

Nelson said nothing, but the Link stayed open. At last he spoke again. "Look, I can't keep quiet about this, I hav'ta bring it to Father and Mother's attention."

Harmon said nothing, merely waited for him to continue.

"Okay. It means one of three things. Leeth or someone else tried to remove her choker – in which case, *boom,* she's dead. Sorry."

Harmon could almost hear the shrug.

"Two, it got ripped off her neck *while she was in a fight* – in which case, it would have just quietly dissolved and she might be okay.

"Or three, she's deep underground or in a Faraday cage – electromagnetically shielded – so her choker didn't receive my ping and couldn't broadcast its own ACK."

"You can keep trying these 'pings' through the day, in case she emerges from her 'shield'?"

"Doc, don't try to teach us how to do our-"

"Send me some of her DNA samples by drone, Nelson. Through them I can perform a Sending to locate her." He disconnected, the pit in his stomach now a chasm.

But two hours later, he had to confront his worst fears. Her choker had not responded to Nelson's 'pings', and reports had come in of trouble in the early hours at Omega's dockside research center. With fatalities. Males, thankfully, so not her. One stabbed, one beheaded, Nelson discovered.

Leeth's handiwork.

And his Sending had failed: meaning Leeth was either dead or behind a strong astral barrier.

Outside his shack, several of the disreputable inhabitants of the Hunters Point Dumps chatted in the nearby vegetable plot.

As 'Doctor Adrian Truman', social historian researching the evolution of the Dumps territories of the north western States, most were happy to talk to him. That, or hoping for magical treatment. Despite underplaying his healing abilities and psychological training, word of mouth had spread.

A few no doubt would have been happy to mug him if not for his obvious poverty – at the Department's insistence, not his preference. Simultaneous proof of Mother and Father's underestimation of his capabilities, and Eagle's propensity for object lessons.

In reality, and unknown to the locals, his interview subjects were having their minds probed. For a month, on the run, Leeth had lived among them, doing who knew what.

That had ended only after she had demanded a meeting with him, in which she had somehow broken free of his controls. So now, here, day by day and piece by piece, he was uncovering what she had done and how she had lived.

All just to learn how she had escaped her bonds. So he could restore them.

His magical and mental conditioning should have been unbreakable. Yet somehow, she *had* broken it. Then delighted in thumbing her nose at him.

Suddenly though, that seemed inconsequential. He sat now knowing his... his *ward* was missing, possibly dead.

It seemed impossible. Surely he would have felt something if she had been killed? She was a survivor, and this mission had been relatively low risk.

She had pleaded with Eagle for 'a proper spy mission, like the three other agents always get. I can do stuff besides just killing people.' So when the Omega CEO quietly advertised for an 'attractive, young female bodyguard' – for his sleazy dives into New Francisco's flesh pits; and given the Department's profile of the neuroscientist....

Harmon recalled Mother's caustic reaction. "How very convenient. Once again you find a mission whose parameters require Leeth to adopt a demeaning role." She had held up a hand before either he, Eagle, or Father could object. "Oh yes, I know: 'It's not our fault, these roles present themselves because other men are chauvinists and perverts.' I stand by my comment: how very convenient."

He set the memory aside. Right now the Department was checking Dr Yamamoto's movements last night to see if he and his young female bodyguard had visited any unsavory dives and gotten into difficulty. Nelson was no doubt also tapping into every facial recognition system across the country, looking for a match.

He still had no idea how Nelson did that. It seemed an unlikely feat.

Marcie Dunkirk too had somehow known, once again before he or the Department, with all its resources.

How?

Perhaps it was time for him to look into Marcie Dunkirk directly. Probe her mind.

No doubt she would be calling again, probably soon. He had already – as Jane Baker's mother – fobbed her off twice more since this morning. Mother had warned him not to share intelligence; that were Marcie Dunkirk to become troublesome... well, Mother had said, the actor playing Stryker Zaxx was not such a high profile figure she couldn't be dealt with.

Did they never learn? Or did they think Leeth was truly dead, in which case the gloves could come off?

No! Leeth is still alive!

"Incoming call from Marcie Dunkirk," the Link said, as if the mere thought of his pest had caused it. Again with the 'for Jane Baker's mother' warning buzz, as if he needed the reminder. He took the call.

"There's something wrong. Don't try to hide it." Her stubborn young face glared at him from the projected optical field of his Link, straight into his. Or, into the digital avatar Nelson's clever software provided.

"Yes, Miss Dunkirk, we agree. But let me be one hundred

percent clear with you: if you try to help – and I am sure that is your overwhelming desire – it can only put Jane at greater risk, as well as interfering with our own efforts on her behalf."

He paused, then decided to show his true feelings. "Marcie. I fear the worst. But we have resources you cannot imagine, and we're making every effort to deal with the situation. Your help can *only* cause tragedy. I will inform you the instant we learn more."

A shaken Marcie Dunkirk turned to her younger sister, who'd been vibrating with the effort of staying out of the conversation.

"We can't just do *nothing*! Jane needs us, I'm sure of it!"

Marcie stared sickly at Amanda, then at her father, and boyfriend, who'd all called off work for the day, waiting for the return call from Jane's mother.

"But you heard her, kiddo. They have resources we-"

Amanda shook her head. "I don't care. We have to. They're liars! And if you don't, I will."

Marcie, relieved tears in her eyes, hugged her sister, then sat back down. "In that case, I guess I have no choice, eh?"

"Yes!"

Amanda's delight gave her hope.

She just had to pray it wouldn't put Jane in worse danger. But she felt relief knowing she was at least going to try.

CHAPTER 21

Deeply ingrained training prised her from sleep but kept her eyes shut.

Satin sheets. A comfortable bed. A male smell... but something else as well, something more animal.

Where am I?

She had no idea. None at all.

Her pulse spiked, and she made herself lie still. She smelled sex, and felt a pleasant ache between her thighs. She checked herself then sniffed her fingers, finally opening her eyes, frowning. She'd had sex, and recently.

But I don't remember it.

Eyes darting around the darkened room, she reached for the memory, but nothing came.

I've been drugged! Date raped.

Yet flopped against her, curled up, a cat. Blinking awake it butted her with its head. She tried adding 'rapist' to the same picture as 'relaxed cat, seeking attention'. It didn't fit.

Jaws clenched, she sat up to examine herself. Her wrists and ankles hurt. She saw bruises and broken skin, scabbed over, just starting to heal. *I've been tied up, and struggled, hard.* They looked at least a few hours old. *But I don't re-member!* A low burn of anger pulsed. She found a dressing on her neck, and under it a sharper pain when she probed. *A dressing – have I been* rescued? Shame threaded into the anger.

She was naked, too.

Biting her lip, she scratched under the base of the cat's ears, trying to calm herself. The simple act disoriented her, throwing her into confusion. Like the cat was too small, too... *animal?* What did that even mean? What had she ex-pected, a larger, *robot* cat? It slitted its eyes in pleasure.

From another room came the sounds of sizzling and the occasional clank of cookware and crockery; water boiling; the scrape of hard plastic on metal. She smelled bacon frying, coffee – which sent an odd apprehension through her – and something like pastry, or cake.

Her stomach rumbled.

For a moment she pictured a tall man, dark hair, but the image faded as soon as she tried to examine it, vanishing like a dream.

Light streamed in around a curtain. Tiptoeing from the bed she peeked out a curtained window.

Past a well-tended strip of lawn ran a suburban street, large houses set well back. Apart from the two houses down the gentle hill and across the road, most of them looked dilapidated, unmaintained.

A car drove up the hill, a family inside chatting, laughing. It disappeared over the crest. Focusing, she heard bird song and the buzz of insects. The car fading into the distance.

A blue, clear sky.

Letting the curtain fall back into place, she turned to see the cat watching her.

Why would a rapist trust her with his cat? Had the cooking man *helped* her? She rubbed her wrists again. Sniffing them, she smelled antiseptic. One hand returned to the dressing on her neck.

She prowled the stranger's room. A side table held a collection of mismatched stones surrounding a bowl of fruit, a flatpic behind it. In it, a dark haired, square jawed man hugged a smaller Hispanic woman with curly sable hair and a parrot on her shoulder. She also cradled a kitten, with the same white patches on its cheeks as the cat, which still watched her.

She touched the picture to see what text appeared. *Mason Dane. Maeve Díaz Cruz. Clancy and baby Boje.* From the placement of each label, Boje was the cat, Clancy the parrot. She touched the picture again. *San Cristobal 2051*, it said.

She stilled. *I don't know what year this is. Or where I am, or how I got here. Or what I did last night.*

She cast her mind further back, to... nothing. *I'm... my name is....*

Nothing came.

She started breathing faster, and had to fight down a rising panic. She put the flatpic quietly back. *Did I sex them last night? Mason and Maeve, and me: their friend....*

But the attempt to sneak up on her own name failed, and she clamped her jaws together. She frowned down helplessly at the cat. Taking the eye contact as a sign, it leaped into her arms.

This had more a rescue vibe than a rape vibe, she decided. "Are Mason and Maeve good guys, Boje?" she whispered to the cat. Listening harder, she could hear... Mason, but no one else. Where was Maeve?

The cat, Boje, nudged her. She patted its head, which it pulled away with an annoyed 'why did you do *that?*' look that made her blush.

"Crystal, you up?" shouted a man's voice from outside the bedroom. "Breakfast's almost ready. If you want it?"

Crystal? Is that me? He didn't *sound* guilty. Just busy. Friendly. Why shout, though? Was he deaf?

She whispered the name, Crystal, but it sounded neither right nor wrong. She sighed. And she felt... good. Satisfied.

Her stomach growled.

Well, mostly satisfied: she *was* hungry. Ravenous, in fact. *Well, let's see...?*

"I'm starving, Mason," she shouted back.

"Still?"

His reply held laughter, but no surprise at being named. What was it with the 'still' comment, though?

What do I know? He's Mason, I'm Crystal; he knows me. But he didn't ask how I am, so he doesn't know I've forgotten all that. Everything, in fact.

Secrets.... But the idea vanished before properly starting. She ground her teeth.

Secrets were important though. She knew that.

The bedroom had two doors. Cooking sounds and smells came through one. The other led into a bathroom. "I could eat a," she called out, then stopped. *A what?* Another blank, where a word should have been. "A lot," she ended, lamely, worried. *What's wrong with me?* She kept the concern from her voice though. "Do I have time for a shower?"

His answer took longer than she'd expected. "If you're quick."

His oddly reassuring voice held a note of tension that prickled through her. Was time short? She grimaced. *This sucks!*

Eyes catching on the bowl of fruit, she put the cat down to take a couple of bananas, peeling one and wolfing it down as she stepped into the unfamiliar bathroom.

Play it carefully, she told herself. *See what you can find out.* She placed the peel in the doorway behind her.

Seeing herself in the mirror was a shock, the girl with long white hair a stranger. Going closer, she saw a dressing on her neck, and in the middle of her forehead, thin scabs, shaped like an asterisk. She probed them gently, trying to remember getting them, or even just remember the girl mimicking her actions... but nothing surfaced. She tried to remember further back: who she was, how she lived? What *country* she was in!

Nothing.

With a sigh, she turned and stepped into the shower. Stuffing the second banana in her mouth, she dropped its skin on the shower threshold, then stuffed the mass of long white hair into a shower cap, which fell across her head like a floppy pillow.

A few minutes later she bent to reposition the second banana's skin in the doorway to the kitchen for people to slip on. *At least I remembered that!* Pleased with herself, she stepped over it with Boje in her arms. A man looked up from a bowl he was stirring, his initial smile falling into surprise. She tensed, alert, but hiding that reaction. She had to be careful. *Don't give anything away.*

It was the man in the picture, only older. Maybe, ten years older? He *had* answered to 'Mason', though. She looked around for other pictures, hoping to find one with herself in it, but the rest were just art. She wondered how long she'd been like this – and how long she'd known him? Assuming he hadn't drugged her.

How to find out what he knew, without giving anything away? 'How did I seem last night, to you', maybe?

She peeled and bit into a third banana, acting casual, as he stared at her, his mouth open, looking her up and down.

"Au naturel?" he said at last.

She had no idea what that meant, or even whether she was supposed to know. Shrugging, she finished the banana, trotting past him to place its peel carefully in the other exit from the kitchen, tip up.

For some reason that made him catch his breath, and she turned quickly, suspicious.

But he just looked strangely confused as she padded across the room and back around the counter, scritching Boje behind its ears. *Her* ears?

Hiking her behind up onto the tall stool across the benchtop, she scratched the cat under its chin. It started to hum. She gaped from it to Mason. "It vibrates!"

CHAPTER 22

Mason stared at Crystal, bemused by her astonishment at Mrs Bojangles' purring. Crystal giggled, grinning down at Boje, jiggling her against her chest, bending to rub noses.

Sighting the trash she'd left in the bedroom doorway, he jabbed a finger at it. "What the eff's with the banana peels?"

She looked taken aback. "Banana skins go on the floor." Her expression added a silent "D'uh." She leaned forward to sniff at his bowl of pancake mix, then eyed the pile of bacon on the stove, licking her lips.

"How did I seem, earlier?" she asked.

"Where do I even start? If it wasn't for last night, I'd be annoyed you're stuffing your face right before breakfast."

He didn't see the frown his remark caused as he turned to consider the other banana peel, which she'd carefully positioned at the end of the hallway into the kitchen.

He inhaled, counting to ten. Who knows, if Henstridge *did* break in here – ideally, at night – maybe he'd fall and break his neck?

But they needed to leave, and soon. *With* Boje, he decided. He wasn't going to leave a hostage behind, especially since Mrs Bojangles could work as an extra lever on Maeve: their bitterest argument had been about splitting up Boje and Clancy. Maeve had taken the parrot, since she'd raised him from the egg. Poor, brave old Clancy.

He shook himself. As long as *he* was the one carrying Boje when they showed up, not Crystal, it should be okay.

He set Mrs B's milk saucer and food bowl down on the counter, interested to see if Crystal objected to the poor hygiene, as so many had before her. But she said nothing, just watched him open a tin and spoon out tuna. She released Mrs B, who leaped elegantly to the counter top. Who, after a dainty sniff at the fish, then the milk, and a look to him to check nothing better was on offer, settled down to eat.

He blinked again at Crystal's casual nudity. Wiry strength, toned musculature... wrenching his eyes up he saw she'd noticed, and braced for a comment. Instead she asked, "What would you say surprised you most, last night?"

Finally! he thought. "If I had to pick just one thing, the AquaSec launch falling into the Bay. But if you'd asked what *terrified* me most, having ours dragged under. How'd you manage that, anyway?"

It was his turn to surprise her, he saw. But instead of answering she just nodded toward the pancake mix.

"You want me to get some bowls and spoons?"

"Ah, no, I think I'll *cook* it first. Honey, or maple syrup?"

She just studied him for several seconds. "Honey?"

He had the impression she'd never eaten pancakes. What was she? How to get her to trust him?

"Why don't you get dressed while I make them?" He finished whisking the batter. Readying the pan, he turned to find her at his elbow. She danced aside.

"My clothes were damp."

"We'd better dispose of them. If Henstridge tracks us here, we don't want evidence lying around that could be used in court to get you back."

She looked at him a little oddly, but nodded. "Good point. But how could Henstridge track us?"

He'd half expected her to ask 'Who's Henstridge,' but her intensity reminded him of tac sessions back in the day with Maeve or Ace. Not that they'd ever held one in the nude. With an effort, he kept his eyes on her face as he shrugged. "Locator implanted in you?"

"Yeah, possible. Do you know how long they had me there?"

"No. How long?" *Had she started to remember?*

Instead of answering, she snatched a bacon rasher.

"Hey!" But she'd already stuffed it in her mouth. "You should wash your hands first, you've just been handling the cat."

At his words she fell still, staring at her palms, raising them slowly to sniff her fingers, brow furrowed. Remembering something? But before he could ask, she shook her head, snarling.

"Crystal? Are you all right?"

She focused on him, her eyes widening as if she'd forgotten he was there. That expression vanished, replaced by one of innocence. "Sure." She brushed past him to the sink.

She was far more together this morning, but even so, hadn't objected to being called Crystal. It only confirmed his hunch about what he'd heard last night, and the shattered Omega office window.

He poured a little batter into the pan and she spun at the hiss, then shook her hands dry, watching. Her eyebrows rose when he flipped and caught the first pancake.

"Look, go and get dressed. A hoodie, since we don't want your face spotted."

She hesitated, then nodded. "Okay."

"Just help yourself to what you need from the wardrobe. Not that there's anything feminine there, sorry. We'll take your clothes, but just to dump them. You'd better not wear them. They have your description."

"Do they."

There was an oddly flat tone to her voice, but she didn't elaborate, just watched him slip the first pancake onto a plate on the stove-top. Again he was too slow to stop her snatching a rasher of bacon from the plate beside it.

"Go!" He put the bacon into the oven, setting it to warm. "I have an idea where we can go, and if you lay low I can also get you some clothes along the way."

"Lay low?"

"Just go!" Shaking his head, he turned back to the frying pan, to Mrs Bojangles watching him. At his blush Mrs B returned to her tuna.

She declined the coffee, but drained the apple juice. She also ate fast, her stuffed-mouth moans of delight declaring her approval, while he tried probing her for information.

She looked incredibly young in his hoodie and tracksuit pants, cuffs rolled way up.

"That was some swim last night, hey?"

She just nodded.

"You remember anything more about what happened in Omega before the window blew out?"

She blinked rapidly at him, but just gave a tiny shake of her head, groaning and cramming another honey-drenched pancake into her mouth. Her eyes never left his though.

Let's test her again. "Listen, Crystal, since Omega's looking for you, it's probably best to go back to calling you Kristen."

A tiny crease appeared on her scabbed brow as she considered that, then cleared. "Yeah, probably best." She rubbed at the scratches, and he thought again about the high caliber shell casing he'd taken from her jacket.

But she now sat watching him with her full attention.

He wondered how much she was hiding; and what it meant if she really couldn't remember coming aboard the boat. *Assuming* that claim was true.

"What last name should we use?"

"Uh-" She snapped her mouth shut. Then her eyes lit. "Smith! I'm pretty sure-" she winced, "I mean, it's Smith!" Then her smile froze. "-Jones." She swallowed. "Smith-Jones."

He had never seen such an inept attempt at lying. And now she studied him, clearly trying to guess if he'd bought it. He massaged his forehead. "I don't think so. What about Xavier? Kristen Xavier?"

She sniffed. "Sure. Kristen Xavier."

He smiled and reached for her hand. Warily, she let him take it. "Pleased to meet you, Kristen Xavier. Friends?"

"Friends," she agreed, shaking his seriously. "Pleased to meet you, Mason, um, Dane. Are we going to visit Maeve?"

He startled at her knowledge of Maeve, and his own surname, until he realized she must've studied the picture in his bedroom. "Yeah. We are. Better let me do the talking, though."

Brightening at that suggestion for some reason, she dived back to her food.

Ten minutes later, kitchen cleaned, they were in his car, go-bags in the trunk, baseball cap jammed down over Crystal's now-short locks. He'd expected objections to sheering off her waist length ash blonde hair, but she'd just shrugged. Though she *had* insisted they take it or burn it.

"We don't want them tracking me magically." Then her teeth set, her pupils shrinking dramatically. Like she was in strong pain.

He'd risked the extra minutes to color her new 'do' black. She'd grimaced at the appalling result, but also helped him remove all evidence of their work. Nor did she ask why he had a concealed space behind his bathroom mirror, storing a row of different hair dyes. She'd appeared to consider that normal.

Now in the car, her face hidden under the cap and herself under a blanket, they should be safe from the eyes of traffic cams. Two sets of purrs came from the back seat, followed by Crystal's delighted giggles.

Rolling his eyes, he set the autonav and leaned back, wondering how this was all going to pan out. Was it too big a risk? No risk, no reward though. He switched his optical feed to the dispersed cloud of jet drones weaving a random pattern through the sky above. They just happened to include a continuous surveillance on his own vehicle and those nearby.

Damn.

Okay. Assume the worst. So, to the local mall to park underground in the area with the pre-hacked camera. He ordered a car to meet them, setting that as the pick-up point. After a plausibly short shopping expedition they'd return home.

At least, his *car* would return home: windows opaqued, straight into the garage. He and Crystal would be aboard the new ride.

He was probably being paranoid, but knowing Tik Tek was funding Omega meant there was no room for unnecessary risks. He shuddered. Reclining his seat, he shut his eyes as if for a catnap and blacked out the windows, bracing for Crystal's reaction.

She didn't disappoint.

"Hey-!"

"Change of plans, Kristen Xavier. We need to switch cars, out of sight of security cams. In about ten minutes."

Raising his seat, he turned as she threw off the blanket now the opaque windows shielded her from view.

"Okay," she said, returning her attention to the cat.

He studied her, then gave up and shook his head.

From the mall they'd cross back to Vacaville, taking a convoluted route through it while he checked for surveillance, before looping back to Fairfield. Maybe swap cars again. It'd stretch the journey, but he wasn't going to draw heat down on Maeve in Lorien.

I should pick up a gift, too, so she doesn't shoot me on sight. Or Crystal. Now he thought about it, there was a certain... *directness* shared between the strange young creature who'd emerged from the Bay last night, and Maeve, back when they first met. He winced. Before he'd screwed up. *Better make it a boosty big gift,* he decided.

The Coke and refreshments they'd grabbed in Cordelia had perked Crystal up, almost too much. Thank the gods, she finally seemed to be calming down. He'd had to disconnect his biological auditory and visual inputs while she'd crawled all through the car's cabin, play-hunting with Boje, then pulling open every compartment.... He'd been glad of the distraction of his other tasks: checking they weren't being digitally tracked; thinking of a suitable gift for Maeve, and arranging a delivery point along the way.

Kinesthetic alerts interrupted him, when the car juddered. He re-enabled ears and eyes in time to see Crystal arch feet-first over the headrest, dropping neatly into the passenger seat. She immediately sprang backward, twisting in midair to land on the back seat. Boje, crouched in the floor-well like she'd been bounced off the seat, looked as unimpressed as he was.

Crystal tensed, and launched herself back into the passenger seat.

"Toast the flaming whales, Crystal, stop that!" He played the vid back, not seeing how she'd gotten enough force to clear the seat, wondering if someone'd slipped her a drug in their snack break, before they'd changed to the rental car? He scanned his optic recordings without luck.

Crystal hunched in on herself, hands clenched.

The next time he opened his eyes, it was to find the back seat folded down and Crystal inside the trunk, the sound of sockets from the toolkit clinking and rolling on the carpet lining. Mrs B looked at him as if to say 'Do something!'

"Crystal!"

By the time she'd put everything back she'd calmed just a little. She spent the final hour of the drive playing more sedately with the cat – and in a very different way, with him. But despite the autonav and her apparent willingness to go further, he hadn't been able to bring himself to take her up on her sexual overtures. Which was stupid – he and Maeve were over, long over.

All the same, Crystal wouldn't endear herself to Maeve by throwing herself at him. There was still something just a little... *off* about Crystal's unusual sexual willingness. "Hey, be chill when you meet Maeve, okay? We need her help."

She'd been playing with the car satnav, zooming it all over the state and then the whole country. "Sure," she said, sitting back in her seat.

She peered out through the privacy-shielded windows. The city and highway out had snagged her interest, but now she *devoured* the passing landscape, increasingly farmlands and forests as they got further north – while stroking and cuddling Boje. No longer behaving like a five-year-old high on sugar.

But as she continued to calm down, she began plying him with questions.

Questions that made him uneasy. Partly from the odd mix of the specific and the strangely indirect: what'd he been doing recently; did he like his work; what had he thought when he first saw her? Partly from some of her own responses, so many just a little *off*.

He got the feeling she was hiding something.

If so, that made two of them.

CHAPTER 23

With Walnut Creek klicks behind them, Mason edged the Combi past the 'State Forest' sign and under the young weeping willow. The carved wooden words marked this edge of the Thornton shear, dividing two hundred square kilometers of fractured farmlands. To the south and east, the old section of the West Side Freeway – ruined by the quake of '44 – disappeared into new growth forest. Amazing how fast some parts of the country had returned to nature after the World Storms and other upheavals.

Mason got out, leaving the Combi hidden from above by the wide-flung branches, then hauled out the gift for Maeve. Crystal, cuddling Boje to her chest, watched as he directed a mini-drone into the red maple opposite, closing his eyes. Once the drone had a good field of view, he activated its sentry program, small claws clamping it to its perch. Resisting the urge to wave to himself, he opened his eyes.

Crystal observed without surprise. Or was she simply not curious?

Turning away she stared east into the young forest, directly toward Maeve's encampment three kilometers distant, beyond a twisting trail. He double checked his GPS and internal map. Yep, she was directly facing Maeve's. He frowned again.

"What's making all those weird sounds?" she demanded.

A soft breeze breathed through the forest, gently stirring the leaves. Just a faint buzz of insects.

But he knew that a kilometer out from Maeve's, and a kilometer after the trail looped away to lead hikers on a gently curving bypass of her enclave, the 'soundscape' did indeed grow weird – freakishly so. Weather-shielded speakers weaved a complex, psychedelic atmosphere. Ostensibly trance-slash-meditation music for the commune, it doubled as a rather unconventional sonar mesh. Maeve didn't like surprises, and her array of mics and speakers used very clever software to stitch the resulting sonic tapestry into an audio sensor web. Nothing entered her demesne undetected. "What weird noises?"

"I dunno. It's like – chanting, droning...? All mixed up with animal sounds. Like whales, and bird calls, and cows mooing. Only it's not. It's all recorded."

Mace's mouth fell open. Her hearing must be incredible: she'd just described the uncanny sound field two klicks off through dense forest. Just as she'd heard the drones, earlier. "Let's go and see," was all he said though.

He'd expected her to agree – not to immediately charge down the forest trail, leading the way. Even encumbered with Mrs Bojangles curled around her neck and across one shoulder, she moved quickly and surely. Quietly too, her bare feet padding the hard-packed dirt of the hiking track.

About to call to her to slow down, he noted how smoothly she moved, how comfortable Boje looked, and instead just jogged after her. But she was still accelerating.

Good, he thought, increasing his pace to match. *Let's see what you can do, Crystal.*

She kept accelerating, hurtling along the path, her feet strangely silent except on the occasional smooth patch of dirt on a turn, when she skidded.

At those moments she crouched, somehow staying upright, before laughing and plunging on.

She was stretching him now – he'd amped his augmented muscles to ninety percent and was keeping his own feet thanks only to a digital overlay of the trail immediately ahead, tapped from cyber memories. Was she doing it deliberately, testing him? But at her oblivious cries of delight, he shook his head. It was more like she'd forgotten he was there at all.

She reached the long curve sweeping past the secret path into the forest, but even as he prepared to call for her to stop, she plunged off the path and down the secret trail with a happy sound, one hand clasping Mrs B as she dived *over* the screening bush.

"Oh! Oh, oh...."

He watched her brief dance with a butterfly, her soft cries somewhere between pain and pleasure. She left first the hiking path, and shortly after, the secret trail as well. Mace stepped around the shielding bush, watching, bemused, as she bounded up the gentle moss-bouldered slope, slowing. But not slowing to find her path – instead she slowed to pirouette between boulders, under green-draped branches, laughing with a strange hitch in her voice.

Her movements seemed to echo the forest around her. A slender branch dipped toward her in the breeze, a dragonfly swooping and circling in accidental choreography.

She vanished into dappled green, still on a direct line to

Maeve's territory, caroling a wordless melody that spoke of sunlight on leaves as she danced through the forest. He felt a clumsy machine of transistors and flesh in contrast.

Shaking himself, strangely moved, he sent a micro-drone zooming after her as he pounded instead along the secret trail, hoping to match her pace that way.

She turned at the tiny drone's approach, smiling directly into its camera at him. Her cheeks shone with tears, but her eyes sparkled in wonder. Why such a reaction? Was this her first encounter with Nature, or the joy of reunion? Then she spun away, resuming her earthbound flight, weaving a ballet of astounding grace over boulder, vine, and moss.

If nothing else, maybe one day he could sell the footage.

If she *was* an experimental Omega or Tik Tek gynoid, they'd gone way beyond any movement and balance algorithms he knew of. And if she wasn't... then he had no idea *what* she was. A dryad? Were they real?

He followed the curving trail after her, falling further behind. As she approached Maeve's detection net, he mapped her progress. What he saw, what his tac-comp revealed, brought him stumbling to a halt.

She was one point two klicks ahead of him, as the crow flew! Two klicks away, by the secret trail. She'd traveled at thirty kph through dense forest.

That was insane. Impossible. He skimmed the drone's video footage, and saw it was real. She *danced* under lofting branches, spun past bushes that swayed aside in the wind, surfed sliding dirt down gullies, bounded up the far sides.... Then with a start, heart thumping, he registered her *route*.

She'd moved *so* swiftly through the forest, arrowed *so* unerringly toward Maeve's camp, she'd surely trigger a threat response. At least he'd worked out how she knew where to head: she could hear Maeve's disguised sonar net.

But she's carrying Boje.

The impending disaster stopped his heart, triggering his augmentation into full attack mode.

"Crystal!" he yelled, "bring Boje back! *Crystal!*"

But even *she* wouldn't be able to hear him, not now, not from here. While he'd stood gawping, she'd already entered that web. The audible sonar must be a cacophony pummeling her. Gritting his teeth, he tunneled an encrypted link to call Maeve directly.

She answered before he had a chance to speak. "Mason fucking Dane, I should've known. What am I looking at on my screens?"

Great, he thought. From her tone, she'd probably already sent a team to intercept Crystal. He kept running, gasping his message aloud in the hope it'd make it harder to ignore. "Maeve, it's a girl. Don't shoot her!"

"Chipshit, Mason. I don't know what that thing is, but it's no girl."

"She's carrying Boje!"

"Yeah, right. Your lies grow more pathetic each-"

He spoke over the top of her. "I have a drone following, I can-"

The drone's small window in his internal field of view shattered into static and winked out.

"Oh, was that yours?"

She cut the connection before he could even start cursing her. Calling up a local map, he plotted intercept routes along Crystal's projected path. Wait: given she could hear Maeve's musical sonar system.... He stopped, drew breath, and cupped his hands around his mouth, facing her direction.

"Crys- Kristen!" he shouted, "stop moving! Maeve thinks you're a threat!"

He tried, and failed, to open a fresh link to Maeve. Furious, he sent her a DM, praying it'd get to her in time: «It *is* a girl – and I swear on Clancy's grave she really does have Mrs Bojangles with her!»

But as to how she'd flown through the forest... for that he had no clue. Pounding down the winding track, re-watching the footage from the start, in one small window, he tried to see if she'd pulled some weird shamanic spirit stuff.

If she had, he couldn't see it.

CHAPTER 24

She flew through sun-drenched clearings, cradling the cat to her chest and laughing. Gentle winds licked her limbs and she welcomed them, teasing the air with fingertip feather touches. She felt small and young, but teasingly old and wise at the same time. There should be someone else with her, though. She could almost picture them. *Her.* For a moment, a furred snout swam before her mind's eye, a whine of servo-motors, only to vanish as she grasped for it.

Then a sour scent on the wind wafted into her nose – stale sweat, male. Nostrils twitching, she stopped, the furry purring form held lightly to her chest. She sniffed and stilled, listening.

"Target now stationary. Fifty meters," said a deep voice. A stick cracked, crushed into leafy soil from the same direction, straight ahead of her.

Seconds later it was answered by another male voice. "Rigg, me too. Target stationary. In hex H twenty-three, V eleven?" That one was farther away, more to her left.

"Yeah," said the first voice, more leaves crushing underfoot.

"Same here: H-23, V-11, not moving." That one female, to her right. Trying to get behind her.

I'm being Hunted!

A thrill ran through her. Grinning, she crouched and set Mrs B down, then straightened.

"It's taking cover- wait, no, standing again. Did it put something down?"

Could they see her? She shook her head. No, they would've said 'her', and 'a cat'. "Wait here Mrs B," she whispered to it, studying her surroundings, peering up and into the trees, eyeing the speakers projecting their weird whale song soundscape. Mixed in with it, regular echo-y beeps.

Beeps... sonar? Did that work in air? How did you hide from sonar? She crouched again, slowly, sliding backward into a bush. Air curled around her, lapping at her sweat and ruffling playfully through her hair, tugging at her shirt.

"Funt! It faded into the undergrowth – we've lost it."

He said 'We've', not 'I've', even though they were spread out. Were all her hunters seeing the same thing?

The voice – the first male – continued. "I'm moving in on the object it set down. Lottie, go deep, circle around. Barj, go right. Then close the net. Stay off-center: I want our firing lines clear."

Net? And they were armed.

"'K, Rigg."

"On it."

From ahead and left and right, the sound of three pairs of boots treading the ground cover; leaves and branches moving.

A teasing lick of air brought the sour sweat smell to her nostrils again, then swirled around her, teasing.

Could I...? She shut her eyes, feeling the air currents wrapping her, slipping over her skin and around her limbs. A feeling of familiarity swamped her – being enveloped and held, except underwater in a cold dark liquid embrace, not these feather-light fronds of warm air. Yet still, somehow, familiar.

She welcomed it, the spirit, drawing it to her, imagining it as a fleecy sheath, a sound-deadening cloak. Laughter kissed her limbs and settled intimately over her skin, childlike in its joy. Peering through slitted eyes, she stole from the bushes, creeping to the right.

The cat looked on in sleepy approval.

No voice called out to say she'd re-emerged, and hot pleasure flushed through her. She shared that with her living invisible cloak, feeling its delight at the strange game.

The two heavy sets of treads were close now: one straight ahead, one to the left. Her nostrils flared with the scent of men. The woman, circling stealthily behind her, would be smarter.

She had to be her first target.

Crouching, placing each bare foot carefully, she circled back and to her right, sneaking in and along the edges of the undergrowth.

She'd slipped in behind the woman somewhere ahead, creeping up as quietly as she could yet wincing at the sound of soil compacting under her bare soles, grains sighing together; the flutter of the cloth of her shirt. Yet somehow the other woman hadn't reacted to any of that. Was she hard of hearing, like the man, before? Or was it just because the woman, not far ahead, was making so much noise as she bulled through the bushes? Admittedly, it did take an effort to subtract the sounds of animals, whistles and clicks piped in from the speakers all around. Then she spoke.

"Maeve? Lottie. We've lost it. Boost the gain and buy the web some more cycles? Just for a few minutes."

The intensity of the soundscape jumped, the echoing beeps more piercing. She let them wash through her, reassuring her gauzy partner and opening herself even more to its caress, feeling it squirm and snuggle around her.

She straightened, slowly.

Nothing happened. The woman, Lottie, continued moving away.

She padded after.

From further ahead, the first male, sounding surprised. "It's a cat! Just sitting here licking itself!"

She padded faster, more confident now, and at last saw the woman. Camo-clothing; carrying a rifle. Her hunter, now her prey, slowed: scanning the trees and bushes left and right, then the interlocking branches above her.

She looked solid, tough. A head taller, and maybe twice her mass. Long caramel colored braids of hair whipped her back.

A wicked-looking knife rested in a black sheath strapped low on Lottie's thigh. The sight made her own stomach tighten strangely. Like it meant something. Its *sharpness*. Her fingers twitched.

An old-fashioned throat-mic projected around Lottie's jaw, an earbud in her left ear. In the hand cradling the barrel of her rifle she also held a device with a small screen.

She had to be taken out silently – and as the weird cries and ululations hammered all around them both, harder than ever to block out – something told her it had to be done with slow, almost gentle movements.

She felt the pattern beneath the sounds lock into place, and silenced them. That left just the quiet beating of Lottie's heart, and her own soft footfalls as she crept closer.

Fully expecting Lottie to turn.

Surely she must hear me now?

The bigger woman didn't.

One pace behind, she frowned, waiting for her moment. *Now!* She latched fingers under the woman's jaw, clamping the carotid as her other hand snared and yanked fingers from the trigger. Pulled her backward, twisting, dragging her off-balance across her own torso, one leg thrust between the woman's to slam her to the ground.

For an instant her mind flooded with ways to kill – and the need to do so. Lottie twisted, her face straining toward hers, pale from shock and fear.

Still squeezing the carotid artery, she watched the eyes roll up and shut. Those fear-widened eyes summoned the memory of a girl's face staring at her in similar horror. It made her release her grip. Chewing her lower lip, she listened to Lottie's heart pounding.

Numbly, she plucked the earbud and mic from her downed foe, feeling suddenly bereft, abandoned.

The screen of the device Lottie had been carrying showed a grainy black and white 3D picture of a figure holding what was probably a pistol, a cat-sized blob at his feet.

Below it, she saw three dots on a map, the man plus cat-blob in the same place as a blinking red 'X'.

Quickly, she bent and searched the hunter, finding the nylon cuffs she'd expected. Taking her knife, she sliced off enough material to wad into the woman's mouth.

Playing with the knobs on the device she smiled as she steered the 3D image to the second dot, the other male. Her next victim.

Too easy! Though the last one would surely realise something was wrong. *I probably only have thirty seconds.*

She'd chosen her approach so she was close before the man saw her. He was *huge*, not even a man, tusks poking up from a lower jaw draped open in surprise as she shot toward him. A horrible feeling of familiarity shocked through her, midsprint. Like the ogre was a dear friend, not her enemy. She had to fight the feeling down to spring at him, clubbing him with careful strength, two-handed.

Then stood over the fallen body, tears welling until she saw the massive chest rising and falling.

Stop that – you don't have time. Act now. Think later.

Collapsing to her knees atop him, she tossed his weapons into the bushes before pulling herself together.

Binding his hands and feet, she cut off a sleeve to stuff into his mouth, the air curling in curiously around her again. From a couple dozen meters away the first man spoke, his voice also coming from her recently acquired earbud, and the unconscious ogre's too. Fists clenched, she studied his face, trying to work out why he'd seemed so familiar for a moment. Was there something wrong with her memory?

"Lottie, Barj? I told you two to stay spread out. We don't want it slipping between us! What the burning forest ya playing at?"

She plucked out the ogre's earbud and mic, dropping them with those she'd taken from Lottie, the scanner device too. He'd be using his device to look here. She slid into the bushes, trying to remember what she'd done before to get the spirit to hide her. She didn't sense it anymore. Had she scared it, somehow?

Flushed and flustered, too aware of seconds trickling away, she gave up, trying instead to get away from the immediate area as fast as possible, hoping he'd steer the viewing thing in a straight line between him and 'Barge'. Maybe if she swung around him, came at him from behind?

Still the weird whispers, drawn-out wailing, cries of gulls and chanting human voices pounded down from the speakers scattered through the trees, the echoing beeps pinging through it all at irregular intervals.

The cat – what was her name? – blinked as it saw her emerge from the bushes behind the man, this one bigger than the woman but not ogre-sized. Greasy black dreadlocks swung behind him as he cursed, staring down at something he held in both hands. She eyed the tree he stood under.

He never knew what hit him.

She dropped his body beside the ogre, checking both their bonds before collecting the woman and dumping her beside them. By that time all three were awake, glaring at her and probably cursing at her through their gags.

It was hard to tell, she didn't speak gobble.

She picked up the cat. Her cat? But what was its name, in that case...? Her three captives' wriggling brought her attention back to them. She wished the stupid speakers would stop with their stupid sonar music. From three earbuds a woman's voice was demanding to know what was happening.

They'd been hunting her, but she didn't know why. And she'd been heading... here? But what was she supposed to do now she *was* here?

She looked around, gnawing at a thumb, feeling like she was forgetting something.

In the end she picked up a throat mic. Cradling her cat she spoke into it. "Hello? Why were you hunting me?"

CHAPTER 25

Mason stood with both hands raised, the solar powered splitter and hydrogen condenser at his feet. Just as he'd warned them, his body had set off every alert and warning built into the vine-laden archway of Lorien's security scanner.

"Look, Maeve knows me, and I *told* you that'd happen." Once again he strained for the sound of fighting, or the yowl of an injured cat, out in the forest.

The young blonde, a razor sharp arrow nocked to her sleek black compound bow, said nothing.

His gaze drifted over the scatter of hodge-podge shelters, hoping the gift at his feet would be enough of a peace offering. If Crystal got Mrs Bojangles injured resisting capture though, no gift would be.

Maeve stalked from the security tent, viciously kicking a stone from her path the instant she saw him.

"Mason bleeding Dane. What fresh Hell have you brought me?"

Her tongue hadn't lost its edge.

She stabbed a finger down at the ground in front of her. "Get over here. How could a so-called 'girl' just take out our security team?"

He'd expected Crystal to make a good showing, but... *damn.* "She took out a whole *team*? How? Is she hurt?" A camo-clothed man and woman jogged past him, over the hill and into the forest. "How's Mrs Bojangles?"

The look Maeve turned on him could've stripped bark from a tree.

By the time Maeve's team finally appeared he was chewing his fingers from what she'd shared. And while his fears had vanished, his wonder had deepened.

The three battered combatants parted to reveal a smug looking Crystal behind them, Mrs Bojangles snuggled into her chest, three sets of captured weapons looped over one arm.

Maeve's breath hissed out beside him. "You funting, Corp-sucking, null-brained scum-farter. She really *did* have Boje with her!"

"I *said* she did!" He was overjoyed but confused. Crystal looked *happy*. And Mrs B could have at least looked a *little* ruffled.

Boje ignored him but at sight of Maeve, her tail flicked.

Her head tilted up to Crystal, who looked down and murmured something to her. Boje slitted her eyes.

He heard Maeve's knuckles crack, and felt her gaze burning into him. But there was no way he was going to look: he didn't want to risk being turned to stone.

This is going to be bad. He just knew it.

Behind Crystal, her two new 'escorts' followed while she kept an eye on her three captives. As they'd neared the village, she'd seen the top of a stainless steel tower, looking out of place. Twice the height of the trees, pipes ran down its sides. Nearer still, she caught sight of one of the wind turbines she'd been hearing, dwarfed by the taller and thicker metal tower. She had no idea what it was.

With the village closer still, hidden over one last low hill, she could hear a woman creatively cursing someone called Mason Dane. Wait. Mason. She knew him. He'd brought her here. Her and Boje. Her cat?

Shaking her head and ignoring her trailing escort, she followed her three captives over the small hill. The path down the other side led straight through a spindly metal arch festooned with ivy that made her pause. The vines failed to hide wires, spikes, tiny disks and plates – silver, gray, matte black, even clear ones. No doubt functional.

The village itself stretched out around the circular stainless steel tower. Dozens of helical wind turbines, all different heights, turned quietly. Between them squatted lots of conical tent structures, as well as sheds and a few squarer buildings, solar panels on every surface. A patchwork of small fields and garden beds all around, and people.

Lots of people, waiting at the edge of the village, many holding weapons. The track led straight through the ivy-and-wire covered arch, and the two men and the woman she'd knocked out walked through first, one by one.

"Come on," urged one of the two negotiators she'd allowed to be sent out to her.

The worried-looking man ahead, standing beside the angry woman, wasn't under guard, but he did look stressed. She'd seen the two of them together in a picture somewhere, looking younger and happier. *Shouldn't there be a parrot?* Maybe best not to ask.

Recognizing the two of them, Boje looked up to let her

know that. "Yeah, they look familiar to me too," she said. "Especially the guy." She headed down and through the arch. Sauntering, but ready to dive sideways.

Nothing happened, though the angry woman, holding up a display, scowled at it. At least she'd stopped cursing.

The woman was compact, curvy, dark-haired – and fuming. Curls of fury practically wisped up off her. She recognized the voice of the woman she'd spoken to on the captured radio. So, probably the leader.

She was also the spear-tip of a crowd of people, all the closest ones armed. They crowded the paths winding between vegetable patches, and further back, conical huts that looked hand-made.

She headed straight to the woman, the leader. Juggling Boje as she let the straps of the weapons slide off her arm, she dumped them at her feet. Then winced at the ugly sound of teeth grinding together.

It sparked a memory – just a flash: an angry well-dressed woman also grinding her teeth. The image flared and vanished even as she snatched for it, a prickling pain warning her from chasing it.

The familiar-looking guy standing to one side watched her, acting like he didn't hear the awful teeth sound. His eyes dropped to the cat in her arms, looking relieved before smiling weakly at her. A tiny nod, like he knew her. And the cat, too.

The woman looked up from the screen in her hand to glare at her, rolling up her palm screen with an angry snap of her wrist. "Why the *fuck* is she carrying Mrs Bojangles, Mace?"

Oh! Crystal fought through a gluey mental fog. *Mrs Bojangles – Boje, Mrs B. Mace – Mason.* And the woman's name was... Maeve? *How did I forget all that? There must be something wrong with my memory!* Did these people know that? She made a mental note not to forget again.

Play it low key for now, she decided. *Keep it secret till I find out what's going on.* Secrecy was essential. *But what if I forget again?* She chewed her lip. *Or if I'm still forgetting?* That was a scary thought. *I'll need to write stuff down.*

With her three captives, and the woman and the two 'negotiators' still standing behind her, six angry people now confronted her. Not counting the crowd.

It was all very confusing. She wasn't sure what was going on: why she was here; where *here* even was. Her heart sped up, and it was a fight to keep the tension from showing.

The cat in her arms *mreowed* for her to calm down. It settled more comfortably in place, in demonstration. Mrs Bojangles. Right. *My cat.* She tried out the thought. It felt right. *Very* right. *Calm.*

The woman's face tightened. Mace, standing beside her, gestured to Crystal. "Maeve, let me introduce you to Kristen."

Kristen? Is that me? But aren't I Crystal? Wasn't Kristen just made up? Her own uncertainty made her blink in surprise, a surprise followed instantly by a stab of unease. There was something very weird going on with her thoughts.

She shook her head. *I'm... Kristen?*

At least here the unearthly mix of animal, fish, and human voices were faint, coming only from the surrounding forest. The angry woman, Maeve, glared – then reached out like she was going to try to steal Boje.

She frowned and stepped back.

Mason Dane felt his smile stiffen, hyper aware of the hostility simmering on all sides, knowing that only confusion held it back.

Beside him, Maeve took another step forward. "Give me my cat," she grated.

"*Your* cat?" Kristen's jaw thrust out as she stepped back again, her arms tensing and stance firming. Something told Mason she was fully aware of the man and woman behind her preparing to grab her.

Boje herself looked somehow amused.

"Please, ladies, calm-"

"*Calm?*" Maeve spat. "This... what did you say she is? Warbot?"

"I never! I only said-"

"You sent this *warbot* at Lorien like a cruise missile, *carrying Mrs Bojangles,* you utter prat. And she... I don't know what the fuck she did to take out the perimeter team, but I don't like it!"

"Warbot? I'm no warbot!" *I'm not, am I?* With a kind of shock, she realized she didn't actually know. *No. I'm...*

I'm.... She stared, pleading, to Mace, her friend, and clutched her cat, Mrs Bojangles, Boje, tighter to her chest. "I'm not a warbot."

Grinding her teeth again, the woman thrust her rolled up screen into a jacket pocket.

The crowd of people inched closer. Two held up Links. Recording? She frowned. That wasn't allowed. *I'm secret. Aren't I?* Where had that thought come from? What did it even mean? *What's wrong with me?* She fought to keep the panic from her face.

Mason, following her gaze, swore. "Don't record this, you idiots!"

The two paused, lowering their devices. Kristen's head went down, her chin tucking in.

Maeve's anger burned a notch brighter. "You money-hungry muck-delver, Mason. Why shouldn't they record? What have you brought down on us this time?"

At her words, the man and woman who'd been filming exchanged nervous glances.

"Please tell me you haven't shared that?" Mace asked them.

Both shook their heads: not yet.

"Mas-on." Maeve ground out each syllable. "What-"

"I think Tik Tek might be looking for her."

Through the resulting chorus of groans, Kristen heard two voices, in unison, say "Link: stop, delete."

"You lying, festering pile of self-centered, cheating, money-worshiping-"

"Maeve," hands outspread, Mace pleaded, "can we just get Kristen under cover and keep this quiet? You saw yourself, she's clean."

Clean?

"I didn't mean for any of this!" he hurried on. "I thought we'd stroll in quietly, ask to use your med-scanner, maybe consult George. Then leave you undisturbed, no one the wiser."

Maeve stared from him, to Kristen, to her three injured people, and finally to the crowd around her, in disbelief. "This is your idea of *quiet*? And give me my fucking cat!" she snarled, lunging forward.

Kristen pivoted aside, crouched as she planted one hand in the small of Maeve's back, and thrust, all one movement.

Maeve yelped, launched into the air.

The ogre, Barj, jumped and caught her.

No one else moved.

"Mrs Bojangles is *my* cat!" shouted Kristen. But the eyes in the young face she turned to Mason brimmed with tears.

He gaped.

Barj had already set Maeve back down on her feet, but Kristen's words froze her.

Her head pivoted to Mason with the implacable motion of a gun turret. "You *gave* her *Mrs Bojangles?*"

But Maeve saw Mason looked as stunned as she felt, his head shaking from side to side.

George, Lorien's shaman, chose that moment to stagger through the press of people and onto the scene, swaying and muttering, his eyes fixed on Kristen. "Hey, hey!"

Mason groaned. "Jesus, he's high as a kite."

"What?" Kristen said, looking for a string on him.

"He's off his head on drugs."

"Drugs are bad."

Mason tried to see if Kristen was joking. Apparently not, he decided. "Yeah, but they can also be a tool. Like George here, come to think of it."

George, teetering, was eyeing Kristen up and down. He had a weird dreamy look, and she somehow knew he was seeing inside her. Inside her head, inside her aura. He goggled at her. "'R those *worms* in ya head? Smash, thass nex' level buzz! How ya even func-, func-, func-shun-ing?"

He swayed, wobbling, one hand weaving unsteadily as if following some twisted chain in the air. His expression moved from impressed to surprised to scandalized.

He focused back on her. "An' how'd they do *that?* Ya axly *enjoy* bein' treated like that?" He giggled. "Thought *I* wuz bent. Thass... total scratch." He shook his head. "Who sells th'worms? How much?"

"Worms? What're you talking ab-"

"Kneel before your god, slave!" he interrupted, his voice vibrant deep and clear. For a few seconds he projected a stately aura... then swayed and almost toppled backward.

But at his words, Kristen's face – her whole attitude – changed. She dropped to her knees, setting Mrs Bojangles carelessly down.

In a silence that simmered with equal shock and outrage,

the crowd watched her reach toward his crotch, before stopping.

Where her hand stayed, outstretched, trembling.

"What the fuck? Kristen, no!" Mason jerked forward.

Her expression a mix of horror and confusion, her arm spasmed back, then forward, then back again.

With her face set in a snarl, she drew her hand back in shaky, determined steps.

George still swayed above her, smirking over her head at Mason. One finger lofted portentously to heaven as he rocked on his feet. His mouth opened, his jaw worked... and he toppled, crumpling to the ground.

And started snoring.

No one spoke.

Kristen's chin came up.

Blinking, her eyes slowly cleared.

She shook her head. Growled.

Stood, staring down at George.

And somehow, Mason knew she was about to kill Maeve's shaman for what he'd just done. Whatever the hell it'd been.

When he turned to Maeve, he saw she'd realized the same thing.

CHAPTER 26

Maeve saw Mason's girl-thing tense, her eyes burning at the sleeping shaman. "Move and die!" Maeve shouted, leaping forward to stand over him.

Six gun barrels appeared, covering her, the crowd thinning like a school of startled fish. A slender blonde woman stepped forward, bow raised and arrow nocked. Young, fit, and confident.

The weapon seemed to fascinate Kristen, far more than the firearms that should have held her attention. Instead her head tilted, her gaze locking onto the recurved shaft gripped in a slender strong hand.

"I... I used to...."

But what she 'used to', she didn't say.

No one moved, until Mason stepped up beside her, making himself an equal target. He touched her arm. "Hey." Once he had her attention he bent and scooped up Mrs Bojangles, though he kept his eyes on hers the whole time.

"These are friends, Kristen. I brought us here to get their help."

"*Friends?*" said Maeve. "Why should we help *you* of all people, Mason Dane?"

"I can pay."

Maeve hissed.

"Look, I know we didn't part on the best-"

"You *used* me, Mace, to access my sister's Link! She lost her fucking job – almost her career!"

"If she hadn't reported me, Asgard would never even-"

"Shut your lying mouth!" One finger pointed, quivering, at his heart. "I swear, one more word...." With a visible effort, she took hold of her temper.

The guns – and bow – were still pointed at them both, Kristen saw. Slipping her cat out of Mace's hands, she snuggled her nose into the fur. *Wrong scent. It should be a dog.* For a moment, a sense of loss swelled, almost drowning her. She looked down, blinking eyes suddenly watery. "Let's just leave, Mace. I don't want anyone's help. Come on."

His hand fell to her shoulder, holding her. "Wait."

Maeve stared at the two, her lips drawn tight and hands clenched into fists.

Kristen glared right back.

Mason waited, willing the girl to say nothing.

Mrs Bojangles began purring.

Maeve's shoulders fell. "Fuck."

Kristen felt Mason's hand tighten, reassuring and cautioning at the same time.

"Fuck!" Maeve swore again, glowering, her jaw working. "What are you?" she finally demanded, looking straight at Kristen.

Kristen thrust out her chin. "What are *you?*"

"Kristen." Mason's hand said more than his words. It said he was on her side, but she had to help.

She growled. "I don't *know,* alright? I'm not a warbot though. Whatever *that* is. How'm I supposed to answer a question like that? I'm just me."

Maeve's eyes narrowed, but it was Mason who spoke next, his voice soft. "Tell Maeve how we met."

"Uh, we met... we met... I just...."

Her eyes darted left and right. This morning, she'd woken in Mason's house, and they'd driven out here. After changing cars in an underground carpark. Yesterday, she'd....

Panicking, she clawed for memories that felt dream-like, on the edge of slipping away. She remembered a fight; and before that, dancing through the forest. A car ride, with... Mace. Mason. A long ride, with Boje and Mason. Earlier, a delicious breakfast – butter drenched pancakes with that sweet amber stuff that'd tasted *so* good! Shaking Mason's hand. His smile. "Friends." He was a friend! She breathed out, letting herself relax just a fraction. Friends were important.

Right. And before that, yesterday, she'd....

Yesterday....

There was nothing there. One arm tightened on Mrs Bojangles.

She tried again. Last night; last night she'd... she and Mace had... there'd been....

"It's okay. Go on," he encouraged.

Why can't I remember? But one thing she knew: never show weakness. She swallowed. "You tell her." *And me.*

He raised an eyebrow, but obliged.

Kristen learned he'd been on a boat, and that she'd swum out to it. She sensed there was more, maybe a lot more: but she remembered none of it. She'd swum out to his boat? Surely she'd remember that?

Had he done something to her?

She stared up at him in dawning shock. *I can't remember anything before this morning!*

At the end he turned to her, but misread her expression. "Hey, it's all right." Both hands bracing her upper arms, he gave her a reassuring shake. "It was traumatic. But it'll come back to you in time."

She stared up into those deep brown eyes, searching for reassurance – or deception. His lips were pursed, watching Maeve, waiting for a reaction. Kristen let out her breath, her eyes sliding from his, to her feet.

What about before yesterday? What did she remember?

Her mother, father?

There was just a hollow, ringing emptiness.

Where did she grow up?

She shook her head.

Where was I born?

Blank.

What's my middle name? What's my last *name, for that matter?*

There was nothing. No answer to any of those questions.

Her head lifted in shock.

It's like I just came into existence this morning, in Mason's bedroom!

Like he turned me on and booted me up!

Horrified, she pinched her arm, feeling skin and muscle and bone. It all felt real, but gynoids had synthetic skin and muscle and bone, she knew. How did she know that? Programmed knowledge?

"No, no...."

Mrs Bojangles *mreowed* at her, the wise feline gaze catching hers, and she stilled, slowing her racing breath.

Her eyes rose from her cat's, to Mason's – puzzled – and finally to Maeve's.

Everyone was watching her, not speaking. But the weapons had lowered.

The fit blonde with the beautiful bow still had her arrow half aimed in her direction. For some reason the weapon tugged at her heart, made her want to cry. It made her feel like she'd lost something she'd loved. That thought brought tears welling again. But tears didn't prove anything – gynoids could cry. It made them convincing companions.

How come I know that, but I don't know my own name?

'Kristen' didn't feel special, didn't feel like *her*. *Wait: Mason said to* pretend *my name was Kristen! It's really* Crystal*!*

But feeling a sudden certainty Crystal wasn't her name either, she groaned.

Mason was talking to her. He'd been talking for a while. *Can I play it back?*

She tried, but had no idea how to, or even if she could. *Does that prove I'm not a gynoid?* Hadn't been programmed, booted up this morning?

She didn't know whether to feel happy at that or scared. Was it better to be a self-aware gynoid, or a girl who'd lost her *self?*

"Kristen? You okay?" When she focused on him he looked relieved. "I said, Lorien's special. It has a wizard cyber-tech, Gigi, who'll be back tomorrow. Not to mention their shaman, George, a healer. Who's normally not a psychotic tool. He's a very *good* healer. When he's not high as a satellite," he muttered, frowning, remembering George ordering her to kneel. And her initial, automatic reaction. Like she'd acted on his boat, a couple times. He flushed. "Their med-hut even has a mini PET scanner."

Crystal clutched the cat in dismay. "There's something wrong with Mrs B too?"

"What? No! Positron Emission Tomography. A PET scan'll show a bunch of stuff, including if you have any, uh, implants or, ah, if you have any, you know, artificial parts."

She stared at him. "You mean if *I'm* artificial, don't you?" Her throat closed up. She swallowed, with difficulty. Did gynoids swallow? *Probably.* "Did you... did you turn me on this morning?"

"What? No, I didn't turn you on!" He smiled, opened his mouth to make the obvious joke, but with Maeve's eyes on him, shut it again.

She clapped her hands. "Right, people, show's over. Back to work. Barj, carry George to the med-yurt and Anika, see if you can get him conscious, okay?" After a terse nod, the woman with the bow nodded, leaving with the ogre.

Only a handful of people remained by the time Maeve finished snapping out her string of orders. Frowning at the young woman in front of her, she strode up.

Kristen stiffened.

But Maeve ignored her, fingers gently cupping Mrs Bojangles' fuzzy chin instead. "And you, you traitor: this isn't over yet."

The cat's eyes slitted in pleasure at Maeve's gentle scratches, her purr redoubling. "Did anyone search her?" she asked her remaining people, her eyes now challenging Kristen.

The team Kristen had taken out squirmed, but the man and woman who'd come in response to her 'are you hunting me?' call exchanged smiles. Like the first three, they wore camo, moving with the confidence of mercenaries. "Sure," the woman said, "but she had *nothing* on her – apart from the gear she'd stripped from Rigg, Lottie, and Barj. And the cat."

Maeve scowled as Kristen's chin lifted, holding said cat more snugly.

"Delilah, show Kristen how to make coffee. We could do with the help, and it'll occupy her nicely."

A middle-aged Black woman beamed and stepped forward. "With pleasure!"

"How to-? Oh." Mason nodded. "Yeah, good idea. Go with Delilah, Kristen. Maeve and I need to talk. Okay?"

Kristen looked from Maeve, now less angry, to Mason, who looked kind of protectively at her. "O-kay. But I'm keeping Mrs Bojangles with me."

"Rigg." The big, attractive guy with dreadlocks turned to Maeve. The look she pinned him with made him wince. "You and Lottie bring Barj to the moot hut. I have questions."

With those final orders given, people dispersed – apart from Delilah, and Kristen's two escorts.

With a curt nod and a last glare at first Mason then Kristen, Maeve turned and strode off. Mason lofted his eyebrows at Kristen but followed.

She watched them follow the stone paved paths curving between the tall cylindrical wind turbines standing in rows, that ran between the vegetable beds. The woman she'd taken out first and dreadlock-guy disappeared in the same direction the ogre had carried the shaman. The shaman who'd done... *something* to her.

She shivered. His voice, its gravelly pitch had held her, gripped her.... She didn't want to think about it.

The heavyset Black woman gave her a smile. "This way."

Kristen nodded and followed, but thinking about the creepy shaman. Exploring ideas for how to force him to try to restore her memories... safely.

CHAPTER 27

Delilah led the way to a large rectangular tent of khaki canvas, while the man and woman she'd allowed to bring her into the camp flanked her. But as they neared the tent a strong aroma slowed her steps. It smelled good but at the same time dangerous.

She halted several strides short of the entrance flap.

"Why are you stopping?" the man behind demanded.

Delilah drew aside the canvas and stood to one side, revealing a shady interior of benches, ovens, and container-laden shelves. A mellow rich smell billowed out. Coffee. *Why was that dangerous?* Against the far side stretched a stainless steel bench with sinks, clear thick pipes disappearing out through the canvas wall.

"It's not a trap," Delilah offered. "See?"

She could *hear* her pair of escorts bristling, but ignored them, concentrating on an inner voice shouting at her. Unfortunately, not in words. Her hands prickled strangely. She shook her fingers, trying to stop the sensation.

"Come on. What's your problem?" The man again.

"Why does Maeve want me to make coffee? Who's coming?" She searched her memory for the steps involved. Drawing yet another blank, she snarled.

"No one," Delilah answered, eyeing her sideways. "Just her little joke. But stars know I could use your help. It's a nice little earner for us all, but everyone hates the work."

"Earner?" she asked.

"She's stalling." Again, the man.

"Looks scared, to me," said the woman.

"I am not!"

Delilah let the flap fall and came over, taking her arm and glowering past her at the other two. "You two can go. You're spooking her. Maeve didn't say you had to stay. She won't attack me. Will you, sweetie?"

Kristen looked down to the cat for her opinion, then back into the Black woman's kind eyes. "No."

With doubting looks, her two guards allowed Delilah to shoo them away.

Inside, Kristen looked around, nostrils flaring. The air was heavy with the coffee aroma, and she felt another prickle flush across her skin in a wave.

"What's the matter dear?"

"I don't know. The smell?"

Mrs B stretched out a paw and patted her chest, drawing her attention. "You want scritches?" She dug her nails into the soft fur at the base of the cat's ears, the scratching eliciting a contented expression. The paw withdrew.

A chirping sound from a dark upper corner spun her head in that direction. She looked up, the shadows clearing until she saw a small dark bead. A camera. *How do I know that?* But Delilah was leading her to the metal bench where the aroma of coffee thickened to a fog.

Delilah patted one of two padded stools in front of two pairs of sinks. "The cat can sit in your lap, but put these on." She passed Kristen thin blue rubber gloves, drawing on a set herself.

The basin at her left was full of blackish water, red and brown beads crowding its surface, floating: the source of the smell. That, and two similar buckets under the bench.

"In case you hadn't guessed, those are coffee berries." Delilah set a large white bowl in the empty sink to the right of the berry slush one. "The beans are inside. Just squish 'em. They've been soaking for the last twenty-four hours so they'll pop out easily. They're slippery little devils though – like your friend Mason – so cup your other hand over it or we'll lose 'em in the dirt."

Delilah demonstrated, a beige-green seed squirting into the palm of her hand. "Sometimes they come out joined like this; sometimes in two halves; sometimes in three." She dropped the slimy bean into Kristen's empty bowl. "It's best if you can separate them. You try."

Kristen picked a berry from the water and squeezed until the bean spurted into her other hand. She rubbed it between her fingers in wonder, feeling it slip and slide even while sticking to the thin rubber. She shook it off into her bowl.

Two.

She looked from the lonely pair of beans in her large bowl to the filled basin on her left. "I'm starting to guess why no one wants to do this."

"Try to put just the beans in the bowl – the less pulp or stalk mixed in, the easier it is to wash 'em down. Grey or black beans are spoiled – don't use them. Toss any that look nasty, really. After washing, we spread 'em out to air dry. Finally, roast 'em." She watched Kristen work, offering tips. One bean flew across the room, making them both giggle.

Mrs Bojangles kneaded her lap and shut her eyes.

"Okay?" At her nod, Delilah eased onto the padded stool beside her and set to work. "Keep your back straight – we'll be here awhile."

They settled in.

Kristen found the chore strangely soothing: seeing the pile of beans gradually take shape, the emptied husks building up around her bowl. It was satisfying.

"That Mason Dane, he's one fine-looking man, eh?"

Kristen nodded, squishing a berry and separating the insides – this time, three slippery bean sections – and shaking them into her bowl. She bit her lip, picturing Mason. But dreadlocks guy was fiendishly good-looking too. And the ogre, Barj. In fact, now she thought about it, there was something compelling and magnetic about all the men she'd seen here. Even the shaman, George. "All your men are."

Delilah eyed the girl sideways, wondering if she'd been locked in a convent for years, or if she just had low standards.

Kristen didn't notice. She squirmed in her seat, her groin pulsing like a net of nerves had just tightened. Her head swam.

An image flashed in her mind: an Asian man and a taller one, bald, both with wolf smiles. Her head trapped, bright lights, arms and legs strapped-

Obey.

"Kristen?"

"Huh?" She focused on Delilah, and the dream slipped away. A bright light?

Delilah chuckled. "Don't blame you, girl!"

Kristen smiled, confused, but just nodded.

"You and he...?"

"Who?"

"Mason Dane!"

"Oh. Right." *Had* they sexed? She searched her memory, scratching futilely once more on a slick emptiness. Then saw Delilah watching her, worried. *Oh! But I did smell sex, when I woke in his bed this morning.* At least that proved she wasn't still forgetting things. She put on a convincing smile. "Yep."

"Good. He's a fine-lookin' man. But I won't pry." She looked hopeful, but Kristen just bluffed her with a knowing grin. Delilah sighed. "Ah, well. But I gotta know, how'd you take out Rigg, Barj and Lottie? They're pros!"

She shrugged. "Just snuck up on them one by one."

"Yeah. And?"

Kristen frowned, fishing out another berry. "Clamped Lottie's carotid, clubbed Barj, dropped on Rigg from a tree." She continued squishing berries.

Delilah sputtered. "Right, of course."

Kristen looked sideways at her.

Delilah's hands started up again, squishing beans out almost one a second. Kristen scowled, seeing she was falling behind.

"But... we've got, ah, sensors that, uh-"

"The sonar?" She turned, fast enough to catch the older woman's surprise. But she felt no temptation to explain how she'd evaded it. That was her secret. *Why shouldn't spirits be helpful?* To it, it had just been a game. "I hid."

Delilah tried to squeeze more answers from her – like a coffee bean from its berry? But secrets were important. Secrets kept you safe.

They kept everyone safe.

The conversation died, and she lost herself in the rhythm of the work, learning as she went. Coming to recognize the best end to squeeze to get the beans out cleanly. Starting to match Delilah's expert moves. Building a slow heap of beans in the bowl. Sweeping the pulp aside. Learning how a three-piece bean felt different to a two-piece.

Then a thought: *How fast can I do this?*

CHAPTER 28

At nine a.m Dr Shinsuke Yamamoto had been waiting, arms draped possessively over the shoulders of two surgically enhanced Western dolls. Noting the angle of his old friend's head when he entered the club, he frowned. "Go," he ordered the two blonde women. "Wait for me in Rose Suite."

Sitting up, he took a sip of the fine Glenncraig whiskey in its even finer Schadenhalt crystal tumbler. He set it beside its waiting twin, the heavy base making a satisfying sound as it met the ebony tabletop. He stood.

Fushimoto-san paused at the entrance to his booth, bowing low.

The depth of that bow meant bad news. "You appear less than happy, Ryo," Yamamoto observed.

They sat, and his old university pal sighed. "There is an issue," he admitted.

"Surely the blood sample was sufficient quality?" Yamamoto asked.

"Hai, the blood was good. The mage was also available, and had no trouble – at first. But the Sending could not complete. He said either the target is dead, shielded by a powerful astral barrier, or perhaps organic barriers. 'Seamless' organic barriers."

Yamamoto remained silent. "I apologize, I forget my manners. Please, share a drink with me." He poured.

Soon, both sipped appreciatively.

"How much confidence do you have in your magician?"

Fushimoto-san nodded. "Much. He is both honest and competent."

"Tell me more of these seamless organic barriers."

His friend shrugged. "Mages say these things to sound arcane. It simply means an airtight barrier – or nearly so – of living or once-living material. Soil, rock, water, wood. Such kinds of things."

"Ah. So she could just be locked away? I do not think my, ah, *target* is dead."

Fushimoto-san smiled, then shook his head. "'She.' Why is it always a woman, Shin? A woman will be the death of you one day."

"Hah! Unlike you, old friend, I know how to handle women.

"Could this wizard of yours make a spell which will wait like a cat for my little mouse to set her nose outside her hole?"

"Maybe. I will ask. It will cost more, of course."

"Even so, Ryo. This one is worth much to me." His eyes burned with a light that made his old friend uncomfortable. "Much."

Dr Yamamoto was angry. At midday, Fushimoto-san had confirmed his mage had found a way to enable his 'scrying spell' to do the constant monitoring, and would contact him as soon as he had any news.

Yet it was now late afternoon. The frame of his Writer's gurney had been replaced with something sturdier – proof now against hysterical strength – ready to finish the job on Crystal. She would yet become his plaything. Provided Mr Henstridge could do *his* job. If not, her head at least must return here. That was not negotiable.

The trouble was, both his old friend and Mr Henstridge had so far failed him. Crystal had *not* been returned to him: not her whole body, not even her head.

Perhaps Henstridge-san did not understand the seriousness of the situation? "Crystal must be found and returned. Dead or alive. I need her brain. The dendritic tap network is built from simple carbon nanotubes. But its construction – and deconstruction – requires the Factory Units, and their fabber control units use silicon circuitry. *Detectable*."

"Ah. Gotcha."

"If we are lucky, someone will scan her with an MRI."

"Lucky?"

"Really, Henstridge-san? Even you must know you do not take a conductor into MRI."

"That'd be bad?"

"Magnetic forces would tear each control unit from its place in network. Two point two million nodes of computing dust would dice her brain into mush from the inside." Yamamoto spoke with relish. "Instant vegetable."

"Solving our problem."

"No, Henstridge-san! Fabbers and nanotube scaffolding would remain, detectable with right equipment. Factory Units and controllers could be reverse engineered to determine their functions. Even dead, her brain is a threat. Only when the reprogramming is complete does it leave no trace.

"Until then, if Crystal Winters is found, and studied, my

work could be exposed. Your teams must find her Henstridge-san, and return her here to my Writer!"

CHAPTER 29

Mason scanned the inside of the space – tepee? yurt? – approving of the sound baffles and the Faraday shielding. He nodded as Maeve ran a bug scan then hit the white noise generator.

"Spill, Mason." She spat the words. "What is she?"

From the outside, the security office looked like just a bigger yurt. But inside, a small Phasion cell powered state of the art anti-surveillance tech, in sharp contrast to the rustic cane chairs and the table supporting it.

Maeve threw herself into the chair opposite him, a few slim screens angled toward her that he couldn't see. He made a halfhearted attempt to crack their network interfaces, but found them as tight as he'd expected. To either side of Maeve sat the team she'd sent to intercept Kristen. The woman, he saw, had livid marks on her neck. Both men appeared battered around their heads.

What was she?

"Well?"

He spread his hands. "I genuinely don't know. I wondered if she was some new kind of gynoid, a type no one's seen before." *With implanted human memories?*

"Who'd you steal her from? *Tik Tek?* She's, what, a prototype? Some kind of synthetic human?" She grimaced.

"I didn't steal her, I hauled her out of the Bay." Mason *really* didn't want to say more. He and Crystal – *Kristen* – needed to lay low. But they also needed Maeve's help. "I don't know: I'm hoping a PET scan can answer that. Synths are just rumors – unless you know more than me?"

Maeve shook her head.

"But I don't really think she's a gynoid. She's too human. If Tik Tek have made one that realistic, we're screwed already." He shuddered at the thought.

Maeve said nothing. Just waited.

He took a deep breath. "Look, I don't know Tik Tek's involved, I only suspect it. They're the major funder of Omega Memory Systems. And I *think* Kristen came through the reinforced glass window of their eighth floor R&D facility on the New Francisco Bay shore late last night."

"'Came through' how?"

Mace considered, studying Maeve's expression. He saw her eyes narrow. She might as well have said 'take your time to come up with a convincing lie.'

"I don't know! Look, I'm trying to protect you: the less you know, the better!"

After a look at him that said 'Really?' Maeve turned to her team. "How did she take you all out?"

Lottie's left hand went to her throat, covering finger-shaped red marks – small fingers. She held up the back of her right hand, revealing extensive bruises already developing. "From behind. Pried my fingers off the trigger – felt like a hydraulic vise. All while throttling me. Took me to the ground like I was a baby." She swallowed. "Saw death in her eyes."

Mason winced at that, Maeve noted. At which part of it though, she wasn't sure. "Who was next?" she asked.

Barj raised a calloused palm. "She shot outta the bushes like a rocket, feet sprayin' dirt." One large-knuckled hand made a snaking gesture before he locked both together in a clubbing motion. "Then wham! Felt like a sledge-hammer," he said, gingerly probing a lump on the side of his head.

"Rigg?"

"I was still scanning. Heard something big land in the tree above me and looked up to see two dirty feet, then stars. What I don't get, though, is how she didn't show up on the sonar!"

They all looked to Mason, who spread his palms. "Good question." Did that tie in to how she'd avoided detection from Henstridge, assuming he had been hunting her with sonar? Maybe she *hadn't* dived to the Bay floor?

"What'd you tell her about us?" Maeve at last demanded.

"Nothing! Just that I wanted to visit a friend. But from two klicks away, she heard your sonar web." He shook his head. "She ran off, making a beeline for Lorien. Fast, too. Even weaving through the trees."

The others shared a look.

"How fast?" Maeve asked.

"Uh, thirty kph?" Mason said. Strangely, no one scoffed.

"Just like our bogey," Lottie said at last.

"Before it disappeared, when we got close," Rigg added.

"You didn't tell her where Lorien was," Maeve accused, "yet she just ran off into the trees?"

"She *danced* into the forest, with Mrs Bojangles curled across her shoulders. It was...." He hunted for words. "Beautiful."

Maeve, studying him, saw his wonder. "Magical?"

Mason blinked, focused on her, then looked away to consider. His eyes widened. "Oh, crush the crippled puppies," he whispered, his eyes meeting hers once more. He shook his head. "Maeve, it's really better if you don't know–"

"Don't you dare."

"The less you–"

"Don't. You. Dare."

"Fine!" But he waved at the other three. "Should we invite *more* people in?"

Hating to admit he was right, she swore, then looked at each of her people in turn. "Anything you want to add before you go?"

Rigg and Barj shook their heads, but Lottie spoke up. "*I* think she's augmented. At least Level Four. With mil-grade stealth. Probably some kinda new shielding. So she just locked her systems down tight before strolling through our scan-arch. Or maybe, carrying our gear with her saturated its sensors."

Maeve nodded. "If you can rouse George, get him to heal you all. And find out what that 'Kneel before your god' shit was, too."

After they'd left, her gaze pinned Mason.

He sighed. "Last night. Out on the Bay. I'd sent her underwater to hide, while an 'AquaSec' team searched my boat – for her, I'm pretty sure. But a minute after they left, before she'd come back on board, the waters *opened* under them. Swallowed their cruiser whole while it was under way."

Maeve stared at him.

"How big was this cruiser?" she asked at last.

"Fifteen meters."

Maeve wet her lips.

"What?" Mason asked.

"George may be a drug-looped hippy nutcase," she said, "but he's a damn powerful shaman. More so when he 'indulges'. So I've learned the size of a spirit is a sign of its strength. Fifteen meters is big. Far bigger'n anything I've seen him attempt."

"You think she's a shaman? Used spells to hide, enhance her strength, run through your forest?" He nodded. "Hang on. Don't they do a whole ritual thing, speak a bunch of mumbo jumbo to summon spirits?"

"Yeah. So?"

"She couldn't've done that underwater. Not with a rebreather in her mouth. And those dawn and dusk rituals they use to stock up on fresh magic beans or whatever, to 'pay' the spirits? She slept through dawn, so no beans."

Maeve opened her mouth. Shut it again. "Then what is she? Full cyborg? With fancy new weapons, like some kind of grenade that aerates water, to sink ships?"

Mason ran a hand through his hair. "I don't think so, but I genuinely don't know! That's why I brought her here."

But he noticed Maeve was no longer watching him, distracted by one of the screens in front of her.

Resisting the urge to get up and see for himself, he waited. At last Maeve looked up, her lips pursed.

He waited.

Her eyes drifted down to her screen, then jerked up again to him. Her jaw clenched.

"Damn you." She looked into the screen's camera. "Project," she told it. On the table facing him an image appeared of Kristen and Delilah 'making coffee'. Only, Kristen's movements were too fast for the camera to capture, except for those moments when she grabbed a berry, or slowed to shoot a bean into her bowl.

Delilah moved with a fluid economy that belied her speed, but her face was turned up to the camera. 'You seeing this?' her lips carefully mouthed.

"I wish I could ask her if she noticed Kristen cast a spell," Maeve said. Seeking backward through the footage, she found the start of Kristen's uncanny speed.

There was none of the tell-tale signs of a casting that either could see. Kristen just bit her lip, tongue poking out in concentration, and started to speed up. Making mistakes at first but gradually getting faster, and faster.

Mason cleared his throat. "That does look like reflex augmentation. Coupled with a very fast learning algorithm." They both watched, wondering if she'd tire. Or explode.

Delilah, too, looked nervous. But Kristen was totally absorbed, grinning as she worked.

"That's surely not how you normally prepare your export beans?"

Maeve shook her head. "Nah. We have a pulper, then spread the mash to dry and separate the beans en masse."

"So that was meant to be a calming distraction?"

Maeve nodded.

"Looks like it's worked brilliantly then." Before she could bite his head off he added, "Can we *please* use your PET scan?"

Maeve snarled but stood. "Damn you! Yes."

CHAPTER 30

Outside the produce yurt, Maeve gestured Mason for silence. "I want to see this with my own eyes, up close."

Quietly pulling back the flap, she slipped inside. Across the open space, her back to them, Kristen's hands flashed.

"Hi guys! I'm winning!" The young woman didn't turn, though Delilah did, clearly relieved to see them.

Mason and Maeve shared a look then moved up on either side – *like old times,* Mason thought. Both watched the blur of motion, listening.

Mason flagged his visual and other inputs for preservation, enhanced senses trying to scan for the subtle emissions from synthetic muscles.

Nothing.

Finally finished, Kristen pulled off her gloves, shaking her hands to dry the sweat.

"How'd you do that so fast?" Mason asked.

"I hurried!" she said, admiring the heaped bowl of berries in front of her. "I don't think I'd wanna do that a lot, but it was fun as a one time thing." Scooping Mrs Bojangles from her lap she nuzzled furry ears before rising to hug Delilah, one armed. "Thanks for showing me how to make coffee."

"It, it was a pleasure, child," said Delilah, her expression not matching her words.

"Come on, Kristen, Maeve's agreed to run some tests on you."

Kristen's bounce died. "What kind of tests?" Why did they want to test her? Had she done anything...? Oh: they'd sent three people hunting her. They must've thought that'd be enough.

"X-rays, for a start," Maeve said. Kristen bristled, but she continued. "If we find trackers implanted, either they go or you do."

"Oh. That makes sense. In that case, fine." Kristen nodded. "But you said tests with an 's'. What else?"

"Maeve's agreed to power up the PET scanner," Mason said.

Finally, a chance to ask about me, *without giving away secrets!* "The positone thing? What'll that show you?"

"The cause of your amnesia?" Mason suggested.

She kept the surprise off her face. *He knew about that?* "What do you think, Mrs Bojangles?" she said, burying her face in the cat's fur to give herself time to think.

Maeve's teeth grated, but the cat blinked at her calmly, clearly expecting her to agree.

"Okay. Mrs B and I think it's probably a good idea."

"It's nothing to be scared of – doesn't hurt," Mason said. "We just want to have a look at your brain."

Kristen gulped, shooting a look at Maeve, who just rolled her eyes.

Phew. So it wasn't just her. She turned her mind to ways to get her memories back, wondering if magic could do it.

They entered the inner, sealed area of the med-hut, a bank of modular Phasion cells powering a gleaming white array of instruments and the large white donut of the PET machine itself. Slumped in a bunk across the room, dreadlocks hanging to the floor, snores rose from the long lanky form of the shaman.

But the moment Kristen stepped inside, she backed up into Mason and Maeve, her head shaking.

"Nuh uh. It's a trap!"

Mason put one hand in the small of her back to stop her. "What? Kristen, it's not!"

Her eyes flicked from him to the nearby autodoc, its robotic arms folded up into its compact body. She turned in the doorway, eyes darting from him to Maeve as if expecting one or both of them to try to grab her. Or maybe for the autodoc to leap into action like some giant robot spider. He let his arm fall from her.

She stood in the doorway clutching Mrs Bojangles to her chest, her knuckles white.

"Is it the autodoc?" Maeve asked. Shaking her head, she pushed past Kristen and rolled it into a corner. "You want me to power it all the way down?"

At her nod, Maeve did just that, and Kristen's attention shifted straight to the large, slender donut at the head of a plastic stretcher.

"That's the PET scanner. It's perfectly safe."

"Yeah? Do it to Mason first then! To prove it."

Maeve's smile was wicked. "I like that idea."

Mace shook his head. "Not happening. My line of biz, the fewer who know my capabilities the longer I live."

Kristen tilted her head, but she was no longer clutching Mrs Bojangles so tightly. "You mean, you've got more than just augmented muscles and reflexes? And eyes."

Both Maeve and Mason went still.

He spoke first. "How'd you know that?"

"Der. From those little, you know..." she moved her fingers fractionally, "sounds they make." Then scritched Boje behind her ears. The cat narrowed her eyes in pleasure, nudging her hand for more.

"Am I making them now?"

"No, just when you're using them hard. Or about to."

"You can *hear* them?" Maeve demanded.

Kristen eyed them doubtfully. "Can't *you*?"

They started with the portable X-ray, revealing Kristen was locator free and, somewhat to Mason's surprise, that she contained no electronics, no augmentations of any kind. Not even a Link.

She wasn't a gynoid.

A single drop of her blood, now being analyzed in another device – integrated into their 'full medical AI diagnostics' system – had required little argument to extract.

But after that, she'd refused to budge, shaking her head. "Nope. Not going in there unless one of you goes first."

Maeve had looked ready to toss them both out at that. Patience had never been her weapon of choice.

"Please," he'd had to beg Maeve. "Mrs B approves of her. I reckon Clancy would have, too."

That name stole the wind from Maeve's sails, as he knew it would. She swallowed and turned away. Probably remembering the wise old parrot's character judgment, or the strange day it had saved both their lives, deep in the Brazilian rainforest – at the cost of his own.

There was just the hum of the equipment as Maeve wordlessly picked up the dye infuser, injected herself, and laid down on the gurney, Mason equally robbed of speech. He activated the scan.

Even Kristen seemed to pick up the change of mood, falling uncharacteristically mute. Though it hadn't stopped her closely following each step of the procedure and studying the results: which had just shown Maeve's neural Link and its associated comms circuitry.

"Right. Now your turn," she said, after getting up, taking a second dye infuser and approaching.

Kristen stopped her. "Inject him, and get a fresh one for me."

"I can do that," Maeve agreed with pleasure, over Mason's protests.

Kristen watched, inspecting and then selecting the injector to be used on her, reluctantly handing it over. She studied Maeve's every movement, unblinking, not making a sound as the needle slipped into her arm.

Mason watched, cradling his traitorous cat, as Maeve finally got Kristen to lie on the gurney; clearly tense, both fists white-knuckled. He wondered what she was thinking. But she only shook her head when he asked if she remembered anything. Her expression though, when she met his eyes, reminded him of his first sight of her: half drowned, but filled with stubborn determination.

"When I hit the Go button, you'll slide through the scanner," Maeve told her. "Hold your breath and stay as still as you can. It's all automatic. It only takes minutes."

Hands clenched as if ready to vault from the stretcher, the girl nodded. "Okay."

"When you're ready."

At Kristen's nod, Maeve hit the button, then crossed both arms, scowling down at her as the gurney moved. "And if you break that unit I'll turn you over to Tik Tek myself! Took us five years to earn the creds for it."

Tik Tek make human-like robots: androids, and especially gynoids. Pain stabbed, deep inside her head, and she shied from the thought. *How come I know* that *dumb fact, but not my own name?* That seemed important, a clue. She said nothing, just pressed her lips together more tightly, keeping a poker face until she was hidden from view inside the machine before returning to the question, braced for more pain.

And where was that pain even coming from? The brain had no pain receptors. She'd learned that somewhere-

Again, pain, like claws unfurling inside her brain. Gritting her teeth, she ignored it, fighting to return to... to what? Oh! Where had she learned about the brain not having-

More sharp claws dug in, flooding her with an agony that brought tears to her eyes and made her heart pound.

No! Never give in! I'd been thinking about... about...?

Nothing. She couldn't remember!

She'd been thinking about pain... which was easing now. What...? Was it the *remembering* that caused the pain?

"You okay Kristen?" Maeve asked. "Your pulse spiked to two-fifty! Take deep breaths, think calming thoughts. It'll only be a minute or two more. You're not in pain are you?"

Gaining control of her breath, she forced her fingers to unknot. "Why? You said your machine wouldn't hurt. Can it damage people's brains?"

Maeve snorted. "No. It just records positron emissions. If you were augmented and we stuck you in an MRI, that'd be very different! Why, are you saying you *are* in pain?"

"No." The lie would make a good test to see if it could read her thoughts.

Maybe it couldn't, since Maeve said nothing.

What had she been thinking? Oh, yeah, how remembering stuff seemed to... cause... pain? She waited, expecting *that* memory to trigger the brain claws, but it didn't.

She fought an urge to punch the stupid machine but remembered Maeve's threat if she damaged it. Then got even angrier when she realized *that* memory hadn't hurt!

Ohh! It was *older* memories! Stuff she'd *learned!*

That thought also, didn't hurt. So, what to remember? Oh: *the sun rises in the east.*

A prick of pain echoed and spread, exploding into a spectacular burst of agony. She had to lock her jaws to stop herself whimpering, but couldn't stop tears springing forth.

"You're doing it again," Maeve warned her. "Calm down, we don't want you to have a heart attack. The machine won't hurt you, Kristen."

No, but remembering old facts sure does! Gradually the pain died away, and she could breathe again. Forcing a lightness of tone, she asked for a pencil and paper, wanting to record the insight. It felt important.

The machine, at last, slowly extruded her.

Maeve sounded amused. "Paper?"

The stretcher completed its path, the machine beeping once. Kristen took a deep breath, and when Maeve didn't shout at her, sat and flipped herself off its padded surface.

Maeve was scrabbling through junk on a nearby desk, finally tossing Kristen a flimsy plastic square. "Use that."

Kristen hit the Clear button, a scrawl of notes disappearing, then shook her head. *e-sheets can be tampered with so they transmit your secrets as you write-* "Ow!"

"You okay?" Mason asked. "e-paper cut?"

Kristen had a strange expression: definitely not one that said she'd appreciated his joke.

Her shoulders had hunched, and she passed the e-sheet back to Maeve. "No. I need real paper." A glance at Mason caught his flicker of disappointment. Like she'd snatched away a hope.

Maeve eyed her. "And something to write on it, too?"

"Yeah."

"Good luck. Maybe I could dig up a stone tablet for you."

"Why? I'm not sick. And I've never heard of rocks as medicine."

Maeve and Mason shared a look.

"You really need pen and paper?" he asked. At her determined nod, he sighed and strode to the shaman, now grunting in his sleep on the pallet off to one side. Gingerly, Mason dug through inner pockets sewn into the greasy vest. "George is your best bet. Ah!"

He drew forth a chewed pencil with a brown-stained end, and a small pad of paper. "How much do you need?" he asked, beaming at his success.

"Just a piece."

He and Maeve watched with interest as she turned away to shield the paper. "What are you writing?" he asked.

"Just a note to myself." *It hurts when I remember stuff I've learned,* she wrote, pleased when that triggered no pain. What else should she add? She had a feeling there was something else important, but nothing came to mind. She folded the note up and slipped it into her bra. Then the pencil stub, too, after wincing at its disgusting end.

"How long till we get the results?" Mason asked Maeve, tucking the rest of the notepad back into George's vest. "I assume that impressive bank of storage over in the corner houses the necessary data sets. No doubt fallen off a server on the dark net?"

"A minute. And that data *came* from the public, so it should've *stayed* public!" Maeve said.

Kristen took the cat from him as the two bickered like old lovers. While they did, she positioned herself to keep an eye on both the creepy robot surgeon and the looming, ominous white donut of the scanner. Imagining the two devices closer together sent a surge of something like panic along her nerves.

Stop being stupid, she told herself. But she found she *couldn't* ignore them. *It must be safe. Mason said so, and he's a man. I have to do what men tell me.* She swayed. Something about that thought felt terrifyingly wrong, but at the same time, completely true. She went with her gut instinct, determined *not* to obey. She braced for a surge of pain, but none came.

She shook herself. *Focus.* "You said it has AI systems? How do you know it's not plotting against everyone here?"

When no answer came, she tore her eyes from the autodoc to catch them both looking at her like she was some special kind of idiot.

"What? AIs take over everything all the time!"

Maeve stared at her a second or two longer before shaking her head and striding to the instrument panel, picking up an e-sheet.

"Uh, it's not that kind of AI, Kristen," Mason explained. "Just, you know, layered neural nets." At her expression, he added, "just clever pattern matching, really." Then he shut his eyes, and they started flicking back and forward behind his lids.

Maeve, studying the plastic sheet, made an oddly satisfied grunt. "I knew it!" she said, at the same time Mason said "Oh."

Kristen rounded on him. "What do you mean, 'oh'?" she demanded, now trying to keep him, the autodoc, and Maeve and her readout in sight at the same time. "What's wrong?"

Maeve waved the sheet. "You really are completely organic – not even an implanted Link – except for your brain!"

Kristen goggled. "What?"

Mason jumped in, opening his eyes. "*Trace* amounts of silicon dioxide and copper, Maeve. *Dispersed.*"

"What's silicon dioxide? Is that a poison?"

Maeve's mouth twisted in disdain, but Mason actually answered her. "No, it's what computer chips used to be made from. Oh, and sand."

Kristen's mouth worked. "I have *sand* in my head?"

Before her expression could turn completely sour, Mason shook his head. "Not sand. This says... more like specks of it. Doped."

Kristen's lips pressed into tight flat lines as her eyes slitted. "You're saying it's *stupid* sand?"

"No, doped with trace minerals," he reassured her. "And the rest of the report is good. You're normal."

"No," Maeve said. "She is *not* normal. Though this," she rattled the sheet, "means we're hardly any closer to knowing what she is!"

Kristen shrugged. "Tough. You two were the ones who were so sure your PET scan'd tell you everything." But she was thinking, *I have sand in my brain?*

She checked Mason, but he wasn't paying her any attention. In fact, he looked completely distracted. Maeve, following her gaze, started swearing.

"Gods dammit Mace, you're interfacing to my med-system, aren't you?"

Mason blinked. "Chill your chips Maeve. Just your clinic narrowcast: I'm only viewing what's on your sheet. I don't see the analysis though, just the physical scan. Yet I see it's coming up on... three minutes now."

Maeve glared from him to the sheet in her hand, and the last words of the report: *Analysis... 03m02s.* As she watched, the second figure ticked onward.

Kristen approached so she and Boje could read what it said. Maeve slanted her eyes at her, but let her.

It was a blood test report. The words and numbers meant little to her, but the fact that every row had 'normal', and the bottom line said 'nominal' sounded good.

"Come on, come on," Maeve muttered.

Analysis... 3m43s.

"Is your machine busted?" asked Kristen. "Didn't you say it only needed a minute?"

Maeve ignored her – very deliberately – so Kristen took the time to read the report, cheering up a little. "Hey, those are good scores, right? But how come my muscle volume is a hundred and five percent? Isn't one hundred the maximum? Uh oh. Fifteen percent fat: *that's* bad. Isn't it?" She poked her stomach, receiving a dirty look from Mrs Bojangles at being shifted. "Sorry Mrs B."

Maeve's sheet beeped, startling them all. Kristen peered at the analysis report that had appeared, after first risking a quick glance to check the autodoc wasn't taking advantage of their distraction to sneakily power up and attack her.

> Analysis: female is human normal, unedited, age
> 18.9 +/- 0.7y. Generalized fat cell depletion indicative
> of borderline malnutrition. Muscle density +10%. All
> non-cerebral tissue normal and nominal. Frontal and
> temporal lobes contain traces of particulate impure
> silicon dioxide and copper of uniform size (10x10
> microns), dispersed with ninety percent correlation to
> neuron somas. Anomalous dendritic shadows
> detected.
> Conclusion: no results in data sets.

"I *am* hungry, but what does the rest mean?" Kristen demanded, sounding both young and scared, her head tucked in against Mrs Bojangles.

"Just how extensive is your medical database, Maeve?"

"Guess," she told him.

He grimaced.

"What?" Kristen demanded. "What does that mean?"

Mason eyed her with pity. "Maeve's always been thorough, Kristen. It means no medical data in the entire world matches what we've just seen. No *published* data."

"Yeah. Looks like someone's been experimenting on you, kid." For the first time, Kristen read sympathy in Maeve's expression.

"What about dendritic shadows? That's bad, right?"

Neither of them answered her.

"We'll work something out," Mason assured her. "Maybe George?" he suggested, turning to Maeve.

She scowled, sparing a glance at the still unconscious shaman in the cot. "He *should* be conscious by tomorrow morning." At Kristen's look, she got defensive. "He's been 'shrooming for days. Maybe he sensed you coming?"

Kristen looked unconvinced. "I still want to know what dendritic shadows means. Tell me!"

Maeve and Mason both shook their heads, exchanging looks. Seeing Kristen's fists clench, Mason spoke. "Neither of us can tell you, Kristen, because neither of us knows. No match in any known medical database."

Activating his Link's projector, a green hologram of Kristen's head appeared in the air between them, along with a floating block of text, facing each of them at the same time. The same report she'd just read from the scanner's built-in screen. Mason somehow enlarged the word 'anomalous', and the hologram zoomed way, way in, revealing smooth faint threads. They roughly followed a tangled three dimensional web of thicker twisty lines.

"Are those thick lines the shadows?"

"No," Mason said. "They're your dendrites. The smooth faint lines are the anomalies."

He did something and the whole image moved, blurring past at speed before stilling again.

"What am I looking at now?" she asked.

"The same thing, just a little distance away," Mason said. "It's right through that entire region of your brain – the part holding your long term memories."

"So how do we get it out?"

Maeve and Mason looked to the unconscious shaman.

Kristen scowled.

CHAPTER 31

A very subdued trio emerged from the medical tent.

Eyeing the girl, Maeve found she didn't have the heart to bring up the topic of Kristen's claims on Mrs Bojangles just then. "You two'd better stay the night," she told them.

"Thanks," Mason said.

"How do I get sand out of my head?" Kristen wanted to know. "And dendritic shadows? Could magic do it?" Then her expression darkened. "Do you have some other shaman though? That one made me think... weird stuff."

Maeve and Mason exchanged looks.

"What kind of weird stuff, Kristen?"

Kristen's jaw worked, for so long Maeve thought she wouldn't answer.

"Like I had to do whatever he said." Her fists clenched, and the cat squirmed and leaped from her arms, stalking off with her tail up, tip twitching in annoyance.

"Sonofabitch!" swore Maeve, rounding on Kristen. "I know my people! George plays it fast and loose, especially with drugs. Sex too, but he's dead against NC. And I can tell when he does his magic stuff. His style is full woo-woo."

Kristen looked lost. "En-cee? Woo woo?"

"Non-consensual: rapey stuff," Mason explained. But via their Links, he asked Maeve «Has George changed?»

«No!»

"So what's woo woo?" Kristen demanded.

«All the same, he'd better not try a stunt like that again.»

«He won't. You know yourself, George's a de-programmer. He must've seen something. Some kind of conditioning.»

«And took advantage? Fair warning: if he does that again, *I'll* send him back to your med hut. With a broken skull.»

Kristen waved a hand in front of his face. "I know you're talking to each other." *How* did she know that? "Ow!" She shied away. "What's woo woo?"

"Magic crap." He waved his hands. "*'Ooo, I call forth spirits from the sky and land'* sort of thing, you know?" He did a little dance. "Woo woo."

"If you say so," said Kristen.

Mason flushed. "What we mean is, it didn't look to either of us like George did something to you. My guess is he saw someone had implanted some sort of rapey controls in you, and while he was high...."

Kristen scowled. "What do you mean, 'rapey controls'? Is that how he got me to...?"

"Kneel before me, slave!" Maeve thundered.

Kristen spun around, fist raised. "You want me to punch you?"

They were following the paths between the vegetable gardens and yurts. A woman seated on a stool in the entrance of hers, catching the afternoon sun, paused her electric grinder, very obviously listening.

"Chill your chips, Kristen, I was just making a point. See, you had no trouble resisting that order."

"Then how did George-?"

"Oh, no," Mason groaned.

Both women turned to him.

With a sick expression but firm voice, he said, "Down on your knees girl!"

Kristen's expression blanked and she wobbled. She had to lock her knees to fight the order of the kingly, haloed figure before her.

A surge of dark anger burned it away, her small hand snapping up and around Mason's throat. But his arms were already raised, palms out, his expression one of dismay.

Maeve tugged at an immovable arm. "Whoa! Kristen, stand down!"

Kristen, registering her prey's passivity, blinked, pushing away hungry black anger, sensing a vast well of it. Releasing him, she sank back on her heels.

"Holy fucking scrotes!" Mason staggered back, coughing, massaging his throat, startled anew by the strength of her grip. Especially knowing she wasn't even augmented. Staring at the small figure in front of him, a ribbon of ice slithered down his spine. Diagnostics flooded his vision as augmented muscles and reflexes kicked belatedly into action.

Kristen tensed. She crouched, one foot shifting back.

With an effort, Mason sent the countermanding order – and saw her relax. *She heard them! She really can hear ultrasonics!*

"What the melted caps are you two playing at?" demanded Maeve. "What just happened?"

"Dr Yamamoto is a piece of work," Mason grated out. "I've heard *he's* into the whole underground NC scene. So I wondered if the, conditioning or whatever it is, needed a *man* to give the order." He swallowed, looking nauseous.

"It does." Kristen's voice was a whisper. "You looked like a.... I don't know. Something big, important. Glowy."

"Son of a stinking, scum licking...." Maeve swore, thoroughly and creatively, long and hard.

Studying Kristen, Mason had the fleeting idea her hands fought *not* to clench; her jaw *not* to set; that she concealed a towering fury.

But the instant she caught his gaze, the impression vanished. With a prickle of unease, he put the foolish impression to one side. "Hey. You fought it off, though," he told her. "Both times." He lightly punched her biceps as she gazed fiercely up into his face. "And you escaped. We're also starting to find out *what* he did, and how he did it. We'll solve this. Together." He shook her, gently. "I want to find out what he did to you as much as you do, Kristen." *Perhaps more.* But that last part, he didn't dare say aloud.

"Look, kid," Maeve said, "I won't risk my people for you, but if you do right by Lorien, we'll do what we can to help. Gigi'll be back tomorrow and George should be himself again, compos mentis. And if it's beyond those two, I hear there's a new guy in the Hunters Point Dumps they say is a bit of a magical mind therapist."

Kristen nodded.

"So, we're good? No more beating up on my people?"

Kristen considered, then grinned. "Probably not." She jumped at Maeve, wrapping her arms around her. "Thank you."

Maeve looked over her head to Mason, in helpless surprise. It'd been a long time since he'd seen that.

In truth, he'd missed it.

"So how can I help while I'm here?" Kristen asked, releasing her to bounce down the path. "Everyone looks pretty busy."

"We can always use a hand preparing meals."

"Uh, alright. I guess?"

Mrs B was happily stalking the edges of a vegetable patch. And Kristen didn't really feel like hanging around Mace right now, not after he'd pulled that last stunt.

Maeve showed them the large communal tent, divided into two unequal parts. The larger area was set up with long trestle tables and lots of seats, a raised platform against one wall.. Pots and pans simmered at the other end on banks of stoves, men women and children bustling about, chopping up food. It was all a bit overwhelming.

Maeve waved to a tall, ginger haired and bearded guy. "New helper," she told him, then headed outside with Mason.

To talk about me? Good. She'd listen in on them, see what she could learn.

The man, Lars, tried her first at chopping vegetables. They had wicker baskets full of them, hauled over dripping wet by pairs of kids who'd just washed them. One, a young boy, stopped her as soon as she'd started.

"You don't do it like that! You have to cut the ends off first." He scrabbled through the carrot pieces she'd just prepared, picking out both the pointy bearded tips and the lush green ends, too. "Don't you know anything?"

Her self-appointed instructor stayed beside her as she made similar mistakes for tomatoes and beans, grimacing in exaggerated horror when she guessed she should throw out the pumpkin seeds.

The kid was pretty annoying.

"It'd be easier if these knives were properly sharp."

Lars, hearing her, approached, testing the edge against his thumb. "Blade is fine. How more sharp you want?"

"I dunno. A lot. It feels wrong."

Both Lars and the boy frowned doubtfully at her.

"She doesn't know much. I had to teach her to shell the peas," the boy declared. "You should let me chop the veges, Lars."

"When you don't need box to stand on maybe Dylan."

All the same, Lars demoted her to peeling potatoes with a weird two-bladed shaving thing. Hunching her shoulders, she let her hands do the work while her ears hunted for Mason and Maeve, subtracting the nearby bustle and clatter, catching threads of conversations outside, removing them one by one.

"... after dinner. I need to know what she's capable of."

That was Maeve's voice, muffled. There was a hissing noise she had to get past too, to separate out the words. She strained for Mason's reply. Like Maeve's, it was muffled, like they were a couple of tents away. "...eally? Kid had a rough night. Can we... George... heal her... twenty four hour... limit?"

Mace's deeper voice was more difficult to hear. She strained harder. Was he talking about her? Did she need healing? A twinge at her neck reminded her of the dressing there. Prodding it, it was still tender. *How'd I do that?* And what was the twenty four hour limit?

"One of Delilah's daughters has a little talent," Maeve said. "That neck wound, and the cuts on her forehead?"

I have cuts on my forehead? Her fingers traced thin scabs, radiating from a central point. *Huh. I guess I do.*

There was a metallic clunk, then Maeve's voice. "What's that?"

She strained, but heard nothing until Maeve hissed. "Are you telling me she's bulletproof?"

"... what she is."

She was rescued from potato duty by Maeve and Mason dragging her out to Delilah's big yurt. It was full of kids and a tall Black man who watched the proceedings with deep suspicion. One of the younger girls, her hair in tight-coiled pigtails, put her small hand to Kristen's forehead and scrunched up her eyes. A moment later, she made a puzzled sound.

"Oh! I think they were just smudges?" She brushed off the scabs. "Yeah: see?"

"*Mason*," Maeve began with a warning growl, but he waved her words away as he teased up the edge of the dressing on her neck and carefully peeled it away.

It revealed an angry, deep gouge, blood staining the gauzy insert in the dressing. There were also other sharper cuts, an odd series of short scratches, as if something sharp had been dragged across the skin.

"What about that, Shawna, do you think you could heal that?" he asked in a soft voice.

"I, I think so? It's not as bad as Micky's tortoise was."

Maeve, scowling, leaned in close. It certainly looked tender. Strangely, although Kristen tensed when she probed around the injury, she otherwise made no sound.

Maeve nodded to Delilah, who told her daughter to go ahead, while her younger and older siblings, their eyes agog, crowded into the spaces between the adults.

Shawna swallowed, looking up hesitantly into the strange lady's eyes for permission to touch what looked like a bad cut. Amber eyes gave calm permission, the lady's own hand guiding her small fingers right onto the wound.

Mere seconds later, Kristen crouched to hug the small Black child, kissing the top of her head. "Wow, you're such a good healer, Shawna! Just wait till you're grown up – you'll be awesome!"

Shawna blushed and giggled while Delilah and her husband beamed down, their other children making excited and awed sounds. Shawna scarcely had to brush her hand over her wrists and ankles to heal the woman's abrasions. But when she asked how the lady got them, their visitors were hurried from the yurt.

Outside, Maeve and Mason exchanged unhappy looks. The wounds had healed frighteningly fast. Flesh and finally skin had regrown as they watched, in scant seconds. It meant either Kristen was some supernatural creature with intrinsic healing, or had been healed countless times.

For both of them, it conjured tales of Doctor Frankenstein and his creature of parts.

CHAPTER 32

"Maybe you could set the tables?" Maeve suggested.

Kristen frowned at her, then Mason. "What's wrong? You two are acting weird."

"Nothing's wrong. I have work I need to do, and things I need to discuss with Mason, and you volunteered to help."

"So something *is* wrong. In that case, I unvolunteer." But from their expressions she could see they weren't going to tell her. Fine. She'd just listen in again.

Which was a little odd, now she thought of it. Shouldn't they talk softer, if they were going to discuss secrets?

"What? I don't like that look," Maeve said.

Kristen's expression cleared to one of extreme innocence.

"And *that* look I hate!"

Kristen scrunched up her nose. "Then we're even."

She flounced off.

"The dining tent's that way!" Maeve yelled after her.

She took her time setting the long tables, mainly so she didn't have to kill the sound of tableware clonking on wood. She only had to set out cutlery and glasses, she'd been told – people took plates or bowls from the stacks already on the tables where the food would be put.

If she'd thought the knives in the kitchen unimpressive, these knives were *blunt.* She lined up each pile – spoon, knife, fork – neatly in front of each glass as she made her way up and down the long tables, the cutlery bucket in one hand. She was halfway through when someone saw what she was doing.

"What?"

The woman just shook her head and went back outside.

It didn't take her long to separate Maeve's voice from the symphony of sounds outside. They painted a picture of people at work and play, from the nearer noises of food being prepared to a more distant sawing and hammering. Threading through it all, people talking or singing, children laughing, and the quiet rumbling hum of the tall wind turbines. Animals, too: cows, dogs, chickens.

She focused in on Maeve and Mason. This time they were close enough for her to hear all his words. She didn't learn much though. It seemed the little girl's healing of her had upset them just because it was too fast. Maeve wondered if she was a secret elf, whatever that meant, and Mason teased her for being a 'toll-kinnite'. It got a lot creepier when they wondered whether she'd been stitched together from parts of dead people and healed up, a Frank an' Stine monster. "Maybe she's some kind of day-walking vampire, whose healing stalled?" Maeve asked.

She liked their next idea better: that she might secretly be a shaman, hiding her magic from them for some reason. About the only thing they didn't suggest was that she was alien. That thought sent an odd little shiver through her.

They also seemed a bit scared of her, and didn't trust her. Genuinely puzzled though: not plotting against her.

"Tell me again how you found her? What were you doing out on the Bay?"

Mason explained she'd swum out to his boat – which answered only Maeve's first question, Kristen noticed. They started arguing about Mrs B, and then in circles.

The most interesting thing was when Maeve said she was going to test her, tonight. But instead of Mason trying to talk her out of it, or stand up for her, all he said was, "Wouldn't it be better to wait till morning, when George is on hand?"

Apparently it wouldn't. *So, what am I?* Thinking about their guesses, none felt right – except the vampire one? She flashed on an image of a woman in a dark tunnel, tearing at-

A tickle of pain stopped the thought, which in turn reminded her.... From her bra she dug out a folded piece of paper.

'It hurts when I remember stuff I've learned.'

So why didn't remembering that *new* fact hurt? Did only *old* facts hurt? She tucked it back away. So... vampires?

There'd been an image: blood...? The pain returned, immediate and growing, but she gritted her teeth and kept digging, against pain that sharpened to needle points of agony.

Herself, stalking down a flight of stairs, dripping blood.... She had to press both hands to her skull as her brain lit on fire. But worse somehow was the hunch she was doing the wrong thing.

She pushed on anyway....

In her mind's eye, a terrified bunch of young people, mostly girls, watching her descend. The horrified eyes of one of them, older and with curly brown hair, met hers. At that, she instinctively recoiled, no longer trying to remember. Then flushed hot and cold, like she'd just drawn back from some terrible brink.

And the pain was gone, like it had never been. She drew out the paper, and the pencil stub, and added, with a shaking hand, *'and I think that's somehow good. Like a warning?'* Or was it a trick by whoever did it, a way to stop her remembering? She shook her head. No. Whatever was doing it was on her side. Of that, she was certain.

When she hesitantly tried creeping back up on her line of thought, this time she couldn't find the trail. She knew she'd been trying to remember why Mason and Maeve's idea about her being a vampire had triggered a memory. But there was nothing there now.

I need a break.

She finished setting the tables, and counted the places: ninety two. That was a lot of people. She wondered what this place was.

Stepping outside, she registered the sun low in the sky, and spied Mrs Bojangles perched on a low tree branch, watching her and the activity around. At her wave, Mrs B flicked her tail and then ignored her.

She giggled, and wandered off along the paths, exploring. Eyeing the fat metal tower with its gurgling pipes.

Nearby, a child cried out "Red light!" She heard other kids gasp and laugh, and names called out, followed by moans. She headed that way.

"Red light!" she heard again as she rounded the medical tent. From inside, George snuffled, muttering and snoring.

In a grassy field, about twenty kids stood frozen in odd positions, a couple wobbling on one leg, all facing an older, ginger-haired girl with a tree right behind her. "Ben," she pointed, "Gabe." Shawna, on one leg, wobbled and fell over. Her finger stabbed out again. "Shawna."

Moans and grumbles, and the three named kids variously shrugged or grimaced, slumping off to the far end to join a bunch of others who sat watching. The girl cast an eye over the remaining frozen kids and turned back to the tree. A boy darted forward even as she cried out "Red light!" again and spun straight back around. "Hah! Gotcha Sam!"

A short argument followed, but in the end Sam trudged off, grumbling, to join the others.

The ginger-haired girl turned back around.

From watching, Kristen gathered it was a game of sneaking up on the person at the tree while their back was turned. That person had to cry out "Red light" before turning around and trying to spot anyone moving. In ones, twos, or more, kids were knocked out, until suspense drew the air tight. Just one brown-haired boy with intense eyes remained, only meters from the tree girl. He got closer and closer, until the inevitable happened and he touched her, shouting "Green light!"

At that point everyone cheered. The boy went to the tree while all the others lined up at the far end of the field.

"Wait!" Shawna cried out. "Let's vote if Kristen can play!"

Kristen straightened as the children sized her up. Well over a dozen hands went up, and she found herself blinking rapidly at a weird feeling as Shawna hurried over and escorted her into the line. "This is my littlest sister, Diana," she said, and a little girl only a little taller than Kristen's knee grinned a gap-toothed smile up at her, black hair in curly short pigtails. "I'm Deena, an' I'm four years old!"

"And this–"

"Hey," yelled the boy waiting at the tree. "They'll call us for dinner if you introduce your whole family, Shawna!"

The game began.

Kristen discovered she was both competitive, and a fast learner. Fifteen minutes later she stood at the tree herself, watching the kids all line up. A weird feeling of happiness tightened her throat. Again her eyes teared up and she had to blink them away, sniffling.

This was so much fun!

She turned around, hearing the whole crowd charge forward. "Red light!" She spun back.

Cries of dismay met her pointing finger as she wiped out most of the small onrushing horde in seconds.

The remaining half dozen were far more cautious, and she waited long seconds before hearing one of them creep forward.

"Red light!"

She spun around, but the boy was already standing still, one leg raised. No one moved.

The game continued.

Five minutes later, the children now played with a quiet and determined intensity. Much sneakier now, they moved in small careful increments, freezing motionless by the time she called out, no matter how fast she spun.

Maybe I need to lure them into feeling safe? Stealthy movements restarted, only this time she didn't spin around. The sound of movements sped up, as all closed in toward her. She pictured them all eyeing one another, seeing others getting closer.

The temptation grew too much, as one sprinted, then two, then all of them.

"Red light!"

Two games later she was back in the crowd of sneakers. Eyeing the girl's back, she dug her feet into the soil and sprang. Crouching to absorb the impact, she froze motionless to a chorus of gasps behind her.

"Red light!"

The girl, Melody, spun around, startled to see Kristen just two arm's lengths away, her feet planted in deep gouges, an eight meter gap between her and the nearest of the encroaching army.

"OMG!"

"Wow, how'd she do that?"

"Big jump! Big jump!" cried little Deena, clapping her hands.

Melody narrowed her eyes in Deena's direction, and the four-year-old froze, her eyes round.

With a sigh, a grimace, and a last look at Kristen, the ginger-haired girl turned back to the tree.

Once more at the tree, Kristen 'watched' her mental image of the stalking horde behind her, paying particular attention to little Deena. She'd also learned to be less obvious in her timing. But it seemed it wasn't only the adults who couldn't hear so well. *Or maybe my hearing is special?*

"Red-"

"Gween light! Gween light! I win, I win, I win I win I win! I win, Shona!"

Little Deena couldn't contain her delight, dancing on the spot and clapping her hands, and Kristen hoisted her in the air and spun her around.

"You did, Little One, you were so sneaky!"

She hugged her fiercely, eyes closed, her heart swelling in her chest.

"Kisten?" A small hand patted her wet cheek. "Why are you cwying? You can be Wed Light again, if you like."

"Oh!" Tears poured forth, her nose running, and she had no idea at all why. She set the small girl back on the ground. "They're happy tears, Deena," she said, mopping her face with the backs of her hands. "I don't know why I'm crying. But you made me very happy." Her joy seemed to echo in a vast emptiness. *My lost memories. I'll be fine when I get them back, my own childhood.* She focused on the tiny girl.

Deena nodded, her eyes alight.

Kristen bent down and whispered. "Just keep your eyes sharp. Some of these kids are super sneaky, okay? Especially the little ones!"

One of the adults strode up to the playing field. "You kids to the waterhole, and wash before dinner!" The man turned away, passing a teenage girl leading a toddler to join them. The kids cried out happily, dropping the game and hurrying off. Some of the boys stripped off their tops as they went, small arguments eddying in their wake as their older brothers or sisters chided them for leaving clothes on the ground.

Kristen hesitated, bemused, until Deena came and took her hand, tugging her. "You c'n come too, Kisten. I show you my magic wock."

Shawna took her little sister's other hand.

A stream lead into and out of the waterhole, where large trees with long pale drooping limbs and lacy green leaves like ferns draped shade over water. A rope hung from one thicker horizontal branch, and a load of white sand had been dumped to make a tiny beach, the water lapping at it. She picked up a grain. *I have these in my brain.* Some of her joy leaked away.

The teenage girl peeled her clothes down to a bikini as she settled onto a shelf of smooth rocks at one edge of the beach, then undressed the toddler. But her eyes were everywhere, watching.

"Dis way," said Deena, tugging Kristen up onto the shelf and over the other side. A small rock pool had larger stones piled up around it, and resting in the sand on the bottom, a vaguely egg-shaped piece of clear quartz. "Dis is my magic wock. It's magic, like Shona. An' you."

Kristen held out both hands as Deena reverently offered it to her with both hers. Over Deena's head, to Kristen's unvoiced question, Shawna just smiled and shook her head, putting a finger to her lips.

"What does it do?" she asked the little girl, fingering the river-polished crystal. *Like me? But I'm not polished.*

"It makes the wawta hole happy and fun always."

"That's good magic. And you guard it?"

"Yes! I found it. I show you where."

She handed it back to Deena, who placed it back on the sandy bottom of the pool as carefully as if it were a, a metallic black choker on a bed of navy satin. She blinked at the odd image, but it vanished just like all the others.

She followed Deena and Shawna around the edge of the rock shelf, the teenager introducing herself as Willow. "Like the trees," she added, waving a hand to encompass the pool, not taking her eyes from the younger children in the water.

Deena drew her away. After stripping off their clothes, Deena splashed into the water beside Shawna to show where she'd found the polished quartz, and hunt for more.

Kristen followed suit and entered the water, swallowing, a heavy warm feeling welling in the top of her chest as all around her, children jumped and splashed and dived, showing off. *For me?* Her eyes watered again.

"Kisten! Dis one might be magic too." Deena held up a round brown stone for inspection.

It was flattened and polished smooth. "It could be," she agreed. They took it to the rock pool and placed it carefully beside the quartz, then returned to 'wash' with the other kids. There didn't seem to be much soap involved, but a whole lot of fun.

Kristen drank it in.

Something caressed her legs, but when she looked there was nothing to be seen. An older girl with a somehow familiar face surfaced next to her, two long plaits darkened by the water. "Hey. How'd you do that hu-u-uge jump, before?" she demanded. "And land without even a wobble?"

"Have you played Red Light before?" another asked.

"Do you have kids?"

The alert boy with intense eyes swam over. During the

game, he'd watched her the whole time, suspicious. "Why doesn't Miss Maeve like your boyfriend?"

"Uh, he's not my-"

More kids started to gather around, one hoisting Deena up on her shoulders. "Dee Dee rocked today! Queen Dee!"

"How'd you jump, though?" long-plaits girl asked.

"I just pushed real hard." A thought occurred to her, and she linked her fingers under the water. "Stand in my hands, and get ready to do your own big jump."

"Okay!"

She checked to make sure no one was in the way, on or under the water. "Ready?"

The girl grinned and nodded.

"Right, I'll lift, and you jump."

With a nod, and a hand braced on Kristen's shoulder, the girl bent her knees, springing up as she was lifted. Kristen *heaved,* adjusting the angle of force as she thrust, and the girl rocketed into the air, squealing. She arced up several meters, then cannoned into the water with a high scream of delight.

Joy surged through her at the girl's shocked and delighted face, at the admiring exclamations from all around.

Pounding footsteps and a cry from behind sounded as someone charged into the water behind her back. "Get away from my daughter, you bitch!"

Kristen dodged aside as a fully dressed woman dived past her.

The woman reached the girl as she emerged from the water, grinning wildly. Her grin changed to shock. "Mom?"

Grabbing the girl and hugging her close, the woman spun furiously around. Like her daughter, she had long plaits.

The woman she'd choked unconscious in the forest that afternoon.

Kristen stared from the confused girl to the woman clutching her protectively in her arms, remembering the moment she'd decided not to kill her.

She chilled, like she'd only just noticed a cliff's edge at her feet.

"Get out. Get away from the children."

"I was only-"

"Get out!" Glaring, the larger woman waded forward, straight at Kristen.

Who looked oddly vulnerable, but ready to fight.

"Mom? Mom! We were only playing. What's wrong?"

"I know what you are," the woman spat, as the children stared in shocked silence. In her angry wake, the water rose behind her. Another great mound heaved over the edge of the waterhole from downstream, flowing in, raising the level. Kids cried out as currents spun and pushed them aside.

«I found you.»

"Who said that?" Kristen demanded.

"Me, bitch. Lottie, and – what the fuck is *that?*"

The waters rising all around held the woman speechless only a second, shock flashing to fear. "Out of the water! Everyone out! Now!"

«I missed you. Play again?»

The children, picking up on Lottie's panic, began screaming, splashing from the water in every direction.

"Witch! You came for our children, didn't you?"

Deena's face crumpled, and Kristen lunged and snatched her from the rising water, then another child, and another.

But Shawna, struggling forward, spun and slipped under.

CHAPTER 33

"Let them go, witch!"

Lottie barreled into her, tearing Deena from her grasp, and it was all Kristen could do to keep her feet as powerful currents wound around her legs. She let Deena go and shuffled the second child to the crazy woman too. Two-handed, she flung the last toward shore, diving for the place she'd seen Shawna vanish.

«Is this your young?»

Under the water, Shawna's fear-widened eyes met hers.

"Give her back!" Kristen screamed, propelling herself forward, grabbing Shawna and lifting her into the air.

Like birds scattering in every direction, children clambered onto the banks and beach. Holding Shawna up, she waded toward them as the waters humped and rose around her, now chest high, something slithering between her legs and up her back, coiling around her.

«Play more. Don't go.» There was something plaintive in its tone, in the voice that no one else seemed to hear.

Lottie re-entered the water now heaping up before the beach like a wave about to break, to snatch Shawna from her arms. "What is that? What have you done?"

Lottie backed out of the shallow water, ignored by the wave as it flowed and piled up around Kristen. Swirling and wrapping around her, it dragged her back in.

Every face stared at her in horror – except Deena's, alight in wonder, and Shawna's, concerned. Pounding footsteps heralded the arrival of the competent young blonde with the bow, who skidded to a halt with an arrow nocked, seeking a target, confused by the unnatural wave.

Kristen fought free of the tugging tide, step by hard-won step.

«Don't go.» Confusion, sadness. *«I came so far.»*

Once on shore she turned to gaze back, numb, shaking her head at the silence now ringing like a soundless gong from the swimming hole. A final wash of liquid confusion and regret, then the waters slumped, retreating in a wave back over the edge of the waterhole and downstream.

On the shelf of rock the teenage girl stood like a lighthouse, children clinging to her legs, the toddler still clutched in her arms.

"What are you? What was that?" whispered Lottie.

"I don't know," she said, answering both questions.

"Is anyone missing?" demanded Lottie, but everyone shook their heads. "Grab your clothes. Dinner."

Lottie and the bow woman watched her closely. They stood blocking her way, guarding the path while children filed past them. With a last baffled glare, Lottie spun on her heel and stalked away, the younger woman following behind.

Kristen waited till they'd all gone, then went to Deena's small pool, dreading what she'd find.

But the little wall of rocks had done their duty, trapping the quartz, and she let out the breath she'd been holding. Straightening the stones back up, she carefully placed the quartz back in the center of its now-depleted bed of sand.

The smaller brown stone was gone, though.

"I hope you'll keep making this a happy place, magic rock," she whispered with a heavy heart, trying to grasp what had just happened. Even she could tell it hadn't been normal.

Brushing water from herself, she picked up her clothes and dressed, re-reading her note, adding *'water spirit?'* before tucking it and the pencil stub back into her bra, then followed the path back. Knowing that somehow, they'd blame it on her.

Whatever *it* had been.

At the top of the track Mrs Bojangles waited, watching her.

"Don't *you* start," she warned the cat.

But Mrs B just coiled around her legs, in a way that reminded her of the watery currents that'd just tried to trip her. She frowned down, suspicious. "Was that a friend of yours?"

Boje didn't deign to answer, merely swayed past her, leading the way, to face the music.

She heard the mob long before she saw them – angry and upset voices threading through a hubbub from within the dining tent, a few stragglers still heading inside. One woman saw her and hurried in, and someone said "She's outside, coming now." The voices churned louder, some rising, some falling.

She considered just turning around and leaving. But the memory, the pure *joy* of playing with the children filled her heart and drew her on.

Besides, their scummy shaman might have a way to get

those shadow things and sand stuff out of her head.

The last to step inside, she gulped to see so many people all in one place, all focused on her. Maeve stood with a small group a little apart: the blonde Valkyrie with the bow; Mason; Lottie and her still-wet teenage daughter; Delilah and her husband; and Shawna, speaking, looking earnestly up at Maeve while Lottie scowled.

Kristen flushed, effortlessly picking out Shawna's breathless words from the hostile mutterings nearer by. "She was as surprised as all of us," her small voice pleaded. "She saved Deena from it. And me too. Kristen didn't summon it! She's nice. She's *fun*."

Maeve's gaze had fixed on her as soon as she'd entered.

Boje chose that moment to leap into her arms. She saw Maeve's eyes narrow, and Mason wince. "Thanks for that," she whispered to Mrs B. "Your timing sucks." Stroking the cat, she swallowed and made her way over.

"How dare you endanger our kids!" a woman shouted at her.

"Well?" Maeve demanded.

Silence fell, the air in the room pressing down on her, the weight of every gaze pushing at her. She clamped down on an impulse to snap back "What?" and shove them all away. But the afternoon with the kids: it'd felt like finding a long lost piece of herself. The idea of earning more afternoons like that... she found herself blinking, rapidly, her throat working. She'd been a part of them. Whole.

She *almost* admitted that.

But if she did, they could hurt her. *Never show weakness.* She pulled herself together. *I don't need them. Any of them.* About to shrug, to leave, she felt a tiny tug at her shorts, and looked down to Deena's small face staring up at her, lips trembling.

"Did the monster take my wock?"

Dropping to her knees, she took both Deena's small hands in hers. She tried to speak, but suddenly couldn't, a weird constriction in her throat choking the words she tried to say. She shook her head instead, smiling. Somehow that smile unlocked her voice. "It didn't. I checked. It's still safe."

Two innocent eyes rounded, Deena's mouth falling open. "Weally?"

She nodded. "Really."

Deena did a little dance, wriggling in pleasure.

"But it did take the brown rock we found, instead."

The four-year-old shrugged. "I don' mind. I didn' like that one so much."

Kristen grinned back. "Me either, to be honest."

Surreptitiously dabbing at her eyes she stood, her heart twisting strangely at the innocent trust in the tiny girl's face.

For some reason, the mood had changed. Maeve, even Lottie, now looked more frustrated than angry.

Shawna spoke up. "It was a water spirit. Another one told it Kristen was here. It came all the way from the Bay to play with her."

Mason's head jerked upward. "Ohhh!"

All eyes turned to him. He'd already clamped his mouth shut though, looking annoyed with himself.

Maeve said one word. "Spill."

"The boat I mentioned." With a glance at Maeve he plunged one hand downward.

Maeve frowned. "So she *is* a shaman?"

Mason grimaced and shrugged.

Kristen, holding Deena's little hand in hers, led her back to her parents and older sister. "I am? Was that who was talking – a spirit?"

"You *heard* it?" Mason asked. "What'd it say?"

She shrugged, but tried to remember. "Umm... It missed me. And wanted to play."

Maeve's mouth worked. "George picked a stupid slagging time to go on a bender." Clapping her hands she addressed the crowd following every word. "Okay, people, dinner's overdue. Let's eat."

There was bread that smelled *wonderful* – she could have filled up entirely on that alone, and the creamy, salty butter that went with it. But there were also heaping platters of vegetables, fish, and a stew. They had wine and beer, but she wasn't sure about those, and just had some of the chilled water. She snuck pieces of fish to Boje, in her lap, when no one was watching.

She heard several whispers about how much she was eating: they clearly didn't realize she was feeding Mrs B too.

Deena and Shawna had tugged her over to sit across from their family, and the story of the water spirit was told and retold.

They also had dessert, a warm, squishy yellow thing called custard, little explosions of sweet brown pellets baked inside. 'Waizins', Deena explained. It was all delicious, and she ate her fill, getting a couple of compliments on her healthy appetite. But most people weren't smiling, or relaxed, though the younger men seemed very friendly.

After dinner Maeve stood, banging a spoon on the wooden table in front of her for attention.

"We here in Lorien try to tread lightly on this Earth. We live sustainably, supporting ourselves, trading for whatever small outside help we need.

"This afternoon, two outsiders came here, needing help of their own. One of them I know – and don't like very much. And the... *person* he brought, is an unknown quantity, strange; but I'm pretty sure I don't like *her* very much either. Kristen says she can't remember who she is, or *what* she is. Just before dinner, a water spirit came here looking for her – but she saved Shawna from it, and other children."

Lottie, seated at the same table, snapped, "Yeah, from the monster *she* brought to attack them. Some hero."

"Shawna vouches for her."

"Shawna vouches for magic rocks," Lottie muttered.

Maeve shot her a sharp glance. "You'll get your chance to speak, Lottie."

Kristen hadn't expected a child's opinion to hold so much weight, but meeting those young eyes across the trestle table now, she felt a depth in their steady gaze that made it suddenly less strange. She turned back to Maeve.

"She took down Rigg, Lottie, and *Barj*, who'd been sent to intercept her. She somehow hid from them and our sonar net too, and we don't know how. Probably magic, but we can't ask George till tomorrow morning."

That brought scattered snorts, and laughter.

Maeve stared at Kristen for a long time then with pursed lips, and when she spoke next it was more conversationally. She spread her hands. "Look, I think Mason's likely to have caused trouble for us by bringing her here, but from what we learned from her PET scan, I do see why he came to us. Someone's done a number on her, and Mace said Tik Tek might be involved."

That caused a round of unhappy murmuring.

"Exactly. We don't want to be on Tik Tek's radar. I've already sent Jake and Jan to drive away the clunker Mace and Kristen came in on. I've said they can stay overnight but shall we let them stay longer, maybe a day or two? If we do, we'll need to keep Kristen and Mason under wraps.

"So: let's talk."

Lottie jumped to her feet and pointed an accusing finger at Kristen. "Do you intend harm to our children?"

"What? No!"

Kristen heard a few people whisper stuff like 'I wish George was reading her', and about truth spells, but also a few people saying 'look at Shawna', in approving tones. The girl was nodding, seemingly happy with her answer, and a *lot* of people were watching that.

"Do you intend harm to *anyone* here?"

"No!"

"Lottie," Maeve warned, but a man raised his hand and said "I yield my question."

Deena put up her hand, her eyes round. "Do you weally not know who you are, Kisten?"

She frowned down into her hands, trying to remember them holding someone else's, doing... *kid stuff*, like... digging in the dirt? Even just a name, or a face. But there was nothing.

"Kisten?"

She looked up and across the table, shaking her head. "Nothing, Deena. I don't remember anything about me."

There were more questions about the water spirit, and then about how she'd evaded the sonar net. She *had* done that, and not explained at the time. But now seemed the time for trust. She'd....

She'd what? It was a struggle, but she remembered setting Mrs Bojangles down in a clearing. Bushes. Someone who'd been in the bushes helped her? Had she danced with them?

She tried to explain, but they wanted to know who, and how they'd hid, and where he or she had gone, and she couldn't answer any of those questions.

"You say you don't know what you are, Kristen, but what can you do?" Maeve asked. "Can you hear our sonar net? Like, now, from here?"

Kristen winced. So they couldn't hear it? She'd been

right. "Those weird whale and bird noises?" She focused, making sure it was still there. *It was.* She nodded.

The room hushed.

"What else?"

"I don't know."

"She can jump a real long way," volunteered the teenage girl with ginger hair, from the Red Light game.

That'd been fun! Kristen shared a smile with Shawna – whose mouth fell open. She raised one finger accusingly. Then her gaze went from Kristen to Deena – remembering her little sister's surprise win that afternoon – and she clamped her mouth shut.

Kristen felt herself blush.

Shawna giggled.

But the teenager's statement led to a round of physical trials – jumping, balance, reflexes, and finally strength. The group astonishment increased with each test. Kristen appeared puzzled by their reactions, as if doubting they were genuine. As if she saw nothing strange in each feat.

When Maeve called for her to arm wrestle Barj, seats cleared until most of the room clustered around. Mason casually suggested some bets, putting his money on her. He started with even odds, but let himself be gradually talked into increasing them – first to one-and-a-half to one, then two, and finally three-to-one, as he worked the crowd.

Maeve glared at him.

«Life lessons,» he sent to her, grinning.

Rigg was arguing, saying Lottie reckoned Kristen was really strong, maybe even an augment Level Four. But it turned out he'd only argued that to pressure Mason into offering him odds of ten-to-one, for a hundred cred wager.

Maeve saw Mace wince, before caving. "Hell, why not?" he said at last, tapping cashsticks with the larger man. "Always happy to contribute to Lorien's economy."

Maeve sighed. She noticed Lottie didn't place a bet.

Kristen eyed her ogre opponent, a dim memory of pummeling him unconscious earlier in the day. All three of her earlier opponents looked fine, now. "You're healed up okay? Shawna's work?"

"Yep. Our second shaman, Shawna is!"

"Ready?" Maeve asked them both.

CHAPTER 34

Barj's arm sloped at a shallow angle to let her elbow touch the table. His hand swallowed hers.

"Go!" Maeve said.

Massive biceps and forearm tensed, Barj's meaty hand descending surely toward the table.

Kristen flushed, shame an internal scourge. *No!* With a silent snarl she fought back.

The hand slowed.

Stopped.

Barj growled. Muscles bulging, his hand descended another finger width, then stopped again. Grunting, he pushed harder, leaning into the effort.

Kristen didn't hear the whispers. She would *not* lose. Tightening her grip she summoned *more*.

The motion reversed, lifting, and Kristen snarled. *More!*

She fought the massive hand back to the starting point, and there it stopped.

Muscles corded Barj's arm, thick tendons strained from shoulder to hand. Those of Kristen's slender arm, too, stood in sharp relief.

Their hands quivered, locked, unmoving.

"Stop playing, Barj. Put her down." That was Rigg, with the dreadlocks, a thread of disbelief in his voice.

The ogre turned his head, teeth bared, veins on his forehead standing up. His expression changed to shock as his hand was forced back.

Yes! Energy flooded her, and certainty. He fought, but she just poured *more* of herself into the challenge. Forcing his hand lower. *Lower.*

For a full minute the back of his hand hovered, before he cried out, his meaty paw forced onto the table.

For an instant, Kristen saw another room, another ogre and a muscled woman watching her, as she strained under a sagging bar with massive weights. The wisp of memory fled the instant she clutched at it, pain warning her from pursuit. "Dammit!"

"Kisten win!"

She looked around to astonished faces, and a delighted Deena bouncing on her father's shoulders, wiggling in her special victory dance. Mason hummed a pleased note, relaxed and satisfied from playing the odds. His lazy smile oozed confidence.

"O-kay." Maeve watched Mason collecting his winnings, annoyingly pleased with himself. She shook her head. *One day, Mason....* "You up for a final test, Kristen?"

Panting, flushed, the pleasure of her victory spoiled by the knowledge she'd remembered something but lost it immediately, she grunted. "Yeah. Sure. I guess. Can I have a minute though? What is it?"

"Just a little sparring match, with our most skilled un-armed fighter."

Kristen shook out her arm, flexing her hand and working her shoulders, then her neck, freeing up muscles. "Who's that?" For some reason, her eyes sought out the woman with the bow, who she'd begun to think of as the Valkyrie.

"Nice guess," Maeve said, exchanging a significant look with Mason. "Yeah, it's Anika."

The woman's chin lifted fractionally.

Kristen nodded back. "Alright. But I want something if I win." She crossed her arms, doing her own deal-making.

The blonde shook her head. "No." Her voice was low and controlled, with a faint accent. "We do not spar for bow."

"Fine. But at least let me play with it a little."

"*Play?*"

Kristen flushed. "I mean, let me try it." An image rose in her mind. Woods towering on all sides, a small girl prowling, toy bow and arrow held before her. It felt important. She fought the stabbing pain but the image faded away.

Anika considered, then shrugged. "*If* you win, yah. But for little while only."

"Why are you so interested in Anika's bow?" Maeve de-manded. "Haven't you shown off enough for one night?"

"It's not that. It's just so beautiful."

The background conversation stopped.

She looked around at the puzzled faces. "It is! Look at it – the shape. That alone is beautiful. Deadly curves." They still didn't seem to get it. Her voice dropped, taking on tones of reverence. "You could be a long way away from someone, but still kill them by your own hand."

Silence fell.

Maeve broke it. "Some*one*. And that'd be a good thing?"

"Der." But everyone looked at her like she'd said some-thing awful. *Why would they...? Oh!* She laughed. "I mean a bad guy, of course."

"Of course." Maeve gave Mason a long, cool, significant look. "You see any bad guys here?"

"Here? No!" Kristen huffed. "I am *not* a bad guy!"

Maeve grimaced. "Tomorrow, you can shoot some *target* arrows, *if* you do well enough in the sparring. *Sparring.* George is still comatose." She glanced at Shawna and her parents. "Anything worse than a cut or bruise you'll suffer till morning."

I'll suffer? Kristen frowned at Anika, who studied her in turn. "Now?"

At Maeve's nod she rose, stamping the shiny plastic tiles of the flooring, flexing her toes against it to judge its give, bouncing slightly on it. "Here?" she asked, a thrill of nerves coiling from her fingertips into her belly, not quite sure how she felt.

"Yes. Just sparring."

There was room in the large eating hall, between the ends of the trestle tables and a small raised stage area. She and Anika took their places, sizing one another up.

She noted how Anika placed her feet, how she crouched slightly, alert, her weight nicely balanced, forearms raised to protect her center. Good.

Her feet rubbed the surface, measuring a nice amount of grip. She took her own stance and waited.

The crowd, watching, stilled.

Anika bowed, and suddenly Kristen was swamped by a weird flood of joy. "Hai!" she said, bowing deeply in return.

At that, she saw a thread of doubt in the taller blonde's expression. Then, frowning, Anika padded forward in small steps. Kristen saw her weight shift, one tanned leg kicking out at her calf. Pivoting neatly, she avoided it and deflected both follow-up fist strikes as they started.

She ignored Anika's momentarily unprotected torso, interposing one leg between the blonde's as she finished her kick. Leaned in to steal her balance, she gently pushed one raised right arm down while bringing the lowered left forward, twisting and finally throwing. Her right thigh blocked Anika's knee kick before she sprang away from her opponent, leaping over the right leg snapping out at her even as Anika fell.

The crowd sighed, as if she'd done something special.

Anika flipped to her feet, angry now. She shuffled forward

again, forearms raised, fists tensed. Determined.

She knows I'm stronger, from my arm wrestle with Barj just now. But she's still bringing it. Kristen felt an approving glow.

Anika's fist snapped out, but again she deflected it with a forearm, moving forward and tilting her head to avoid the follow-up, slipping inside the knee strike as it began, admiring the combination attack even as she took it apart. Turning, she slid a hand down her opponent's arm, catching the wrist to spin her across the room.

Each of Anika's movements were neat, efficient, fast stanzas in a song punctuated with gaps for her to insert her own notes. Spaces where she could take the tune in different directions.

Her opponent had stayed upright, and now stalked back again, stopping within arm's length. More cautiously, Anika took her stance, reading her own and planning her next attack.

But she had the feeling she was much faster than Anika, too. She snapped out a hand to Anika's ear and back again, straight past those raised arms.

Yep, much faster.

Anika flinched, shocked. Kristen heard gasps from behind her, and Maeve swearing under her breath,

Anika swallowed. But still didn't back down.

I really *like her*, Kristen decided, waiting for the next attack.

Anika was concentrating intensely now, enough to realize her intended elbow strike had been read when she let her weight sink. She changed her mind.

Kristen could almost feel her opponent's attention shifting, despite her eyes carefully not signaling each planned attack. She exaggerated her own responses, pleased to see Anika read each and reconsider.

Well.... She moved forward, and Anika exploded into action, short punching jabs, knee strikes, elbow strikes, even a head butt, each attack flowing to the next.

But Kristen's forearms or thighs, in contact with Anika's body, read each movement as it began, and with her greater speed, the two spun and twisted in a mad dance that went on, and on, and on. Kristen lost herself in the beauty of it, the thrill of exposition, weaving a whirlwind, laughing when a blow finally grazed her cheek, mentally cheering her opponent, testing her speed and skill without hurting her.

Without hurting anyone.

Anika, flushed and sweating, began growing angrier, her blows coming harder, wilder, telegraphed rather than concealed, her breath coming in short sharp grunts.

It wasn't until the woman sobbed that Kristen realized Anika thought she was mocking her. She broke away, horrified. "No, Anika, that was wonderful." She raised both hands, palms out.

"Fuck. Me," a male voice behind them said, clapping.

Both combatants turned, one eye still on each other, to see Rigg, shaking his head slowly and stepping forward. Shocked and amazed faces stared at them both, and suddenly the utterly silent room exploded in applause.

Anika's anger dropped a notch as the large man with the dreadlocks stepped between them. "I ain't never seen nothing like that. And I saw some crazy shit down the Amazon in the Eco wars, I can tell ya."

Anika relaxed a fraction more, panting, sucking in air, her face flushed, dripping with perspiration. In contrast, Kristen glowed with happiness, her chest rising and falling steadily. She met Mason's strangely neutral expression, then noted Maeve's clenched jaw. She even caught the look of vindication Rigg, Lottie, and Barj collectively gave the smug man and woman who'd come out to escort her in.

"Did I win the sparring?" Kristen asked, not sure if she had, since she hadn't even really hit her opponent. "I get to use Anika's bow in the morning?"

Maeve looked to Anika – a group of children and adults congregating around her with eager questions – who gave a curt nod. "Under supervision. Sometime tomorrow, maybe in the morning."

Shawna and Deena both beamed at Kristen as if she wore a superhero's suit, not a tank-top and denim cutoffs.

Mrs Bojangles, perched near the edge of the stage, yawned.

"All right, I think that wraps things up for the night," Maeve called out. "Who knows what tomorrow will bring? I sure didn't, when I woke yesterday."

CHAPTER 35

The meal over, a tightly choreographed routine began – children collecting dishes, scraping plates into separate waste bins, older kids washing and drying. She saw Deena fall asleep against her father's side – and felt a sharp pang at the sight. *I don't even know if my father is still alive,* she realized. Bracing for the pain, she shut her eyes and dug for memories of her father, and mother.

But there was nothing at all. Not even the warning pain. What did *that* mean?

She looked around. People were yawning, and she heard talk of beds. Deena wasn't the only child being carried out.

Shawna, holding a glow light for some reason, left with an older sister, who carried buckets of scraps. The sun had set, washing color from the scene outside, but you could still *see.* Or was it not just people's hearing that wasn't so good?

"I guess you and your... you and Kristen will want to share a yurt?"

That was Maeve's voice, speaking quietly to Mace, but with an edge to it. The two had sat together – along with Lottie, Rigg, and a few other older people – but from what she'd overheard through the meal, it had been so Maeve could grill Mason, not because she enjoyed his company.

Should I have told them I can separate out different sounds from a mixture, not just hear quiet stuff? But if she had, she wouldn't be learning so much. Like right now, pretending she couldn't hear Maeve's question, wanting to see her reaction to Mason's reply.

But instead of nodding, he shifted his feet, rubbing the back of his neck. Uncomfortable? He looked vulnerable.

"Oh no you don't. We're not doing that old dance again."

She saw Mace's mouth turn down, his shoulders falling, and *finally,* he turned to look in her direction. *I see. I'm second choice.* She narrowed her eyes at him.

Looking around, she caught the eye of a young Black guy, his hair close-cropped in springy curls, who'd been watching her all night. At first surprised by her attention, he smiled and came over. He was tall, taller than Mace, about her own age, and slim. With clear brown eyes, and a kind face.

"Hey, uh, that was pretty amazing, earlier. I mean, I think you're amazing. I'm, my name's Jasper, you wanna hang out? I can show you around. If you want."

He'd do, she decided. Fit, even if not really muscly. Cute

though. She tested her reaction for any trace of the disturbing compulsion she'd felt earlier, from their crappy shaman George, and Mason himself, but found none.

She relaxed. "Sure, I'd like that."

Mrs B agreed, too, stalking over from the place she'd staked out on the edge of the stage area to join them.

They headed outside. She gestured at the stainless steel pipe-tower thing that rose above everything. "What's that, Jasper?"

He squinted up in the direction she was pointing. "The Maschmeyer catalytic distillery? In the Development and Resettlement Grants after the Second World Storm, Maeve staked this land and paid for that to be built here. Lorien formed around it. Thanks to it, we have a negative footprint!"

Footprint? Something inside her was screaming at her not to, but she asked anyway. "But what does it actually *do*?"

Jasper grew even more enthusiastic. "It converts *any* mix of plastics into a whole bunch of different hydrocarbons – waxes, oils for lubrication, or even to burn as fuel." He shuddered at the thought. "As well as gases, and of course components to make fresh plastics. It's thanks to these the oceans are being drained of plastic!"

"Is that good?"

It took her a full ten minutes to change the subject.

Later, inside his small tepee – he'd built it himself, and she admired the handiwork as he described constructing it – he turned down the single globe until it cast only a soft yellow glow.

His first kiss had been hesitant, after cupping her cheek and studying her face in wonder. "You're really pretty, Kristen, but I gotta say that's a total rubbish haircut."

But he smiled as he said it, and she felt a kind of tension release. They kissed again.

"Your lips are so soft," he said.

Soon he was stripping off his shirt. She admired the gleam of light through the dusting of short black curls on his taut chest.

His eyes feasted on hers in turn after she'd tossed her tank top onto the hoodie she'd carried, a piece of paper fluttering free soon after.

But the sex that followed was just sex.

Mrs B paid them no attention till they'd finished and Jasper had turned off the globe with a snap of his fingers, his white teeth flashing, pretending like it was some great magic. As he wrapped his arms around her, kissing her nose, Boje joined them on the bed.

Kristen, wrapped in his arms, watched the boy fall asleep. Something deep inside her ached at the feel of strong arms around her: at the lie that someone other than herself could protect her. She watched his face at rest, the tiny laugh lines at the corners of his mouth erased in relaxation.

At last she closed her eyes, drifting into dreams cradled by quiet night sounds, the distant weird whale calls and plaintive cries somehow soothing.

Unnoticed by the mattress lay a piece of paper and its scrawled note, a pencil stub on top.

CHAPTER 36

She woke to a feeling of utter wrongness, in utter silence, on an unmoving warm body, holding her down. Trying to work out where she was, knowing to make no sound, no movement, she fought down panic. She cracked open an eye, only to discover that wherever she lay, it was black. That, or she was blind.

The arm draped across her moved, the warm chest her head rested against rose, and she heard a slow inhalation. But if he was alive – *he*, because he smelt male – why couldn't she hear his heartbeat?

She opened both eyes fully, but nothing changed. She tried to understand why she couldn't see, why she could scarcely hear. *No! This is all wrong! I can see, I can hear. I will!*

As if from her sheer determination, the world flickered, flooding in around her from blackness and silence. She could hear again! The long slow breaths of the person holding her, the strong beat of his heart.

He was larger than her, his sleekly muscled black arm draping her middle as he spooned her from behind. Right in front of her head, sharing her pillow, its breath puffing onto her forehead, lay the source of a second heartbeat not her own, a cat curled up.

Every sound fell flat, meaning the small, enclosed space she saw now in shades of gray must have soft walls. In the middle distance, from all around, snoring, and the sounds of people turning in their beds. From farther away, cries of seagulls weaved through whale song and weird human wailing.

What had been wrong with her at first, though? A thought stirred, slow and sluggish. Had there been a time, when she was little, that she-

Sharp claws of pain needled deep inside her skull, warning her off, steering her away from pursuing the thought. Instead, she focused on her surroundings.

Where am I?

She smelled sex.

She felt... good. Well fed, rested... she rolled her head, ran her hands silently over her body, probing. No injuries. She bit at her lower lip, studying the person sleeping with her. Who was he? Had she selected him?

How did I get here?

There was no answer. The cat stretched, waking to blink at her in the dark, watching, too knowing. It looked away.

The cat was important.

Who am I?

No answer to that, either – and in the unlit room her eyes shocked wide in revelation: *I've been drugged!*

Anger burned. She lifted the arm slowly from her, the man grunting and curling up as she slid from his grasp and eased off the bed.

She waited, breath held, examining the room she was in. A small space, circular, with sloping walls – canvas? – held up by poles crisscrossing in a small opening at the top. A zippered flap. The bed that she and the young, fit youth lay on. A scattering of chests of drawers, a small refrigerator humming beside them. Clothes discarded on a floor that looked like tiles. Shifting her weight carefully she touched a toe to one. It gave slightly, a kind of springy plastic.

A large bowl of water sat by the door flap, a pair of men's shoes beside it, but no shoes or sandals for smaller feet. She felt her callused soles, frowning.

Easing from the bed, she eyed the clothes, picking out from the pile of larger male wear, a quality bra and panties, as well as a tank top and shorts that should fit her. She slipped them on and tiptoed to the tent's zipper, kneeling to pull it up just enough to peer outside.

A still night, apart from that distant symphony of weird sounds. Other conical, canvas huts like the one she was in, clad in solar panels, taller poles visible beyond them. Some kind of curved blades twined down and around the poles. Wind turbines, unmoving in the still air?

She didn't hear any guards. Holding the edges tight to minimize sound, she slowly unzipped enough of the opening flap to crawl through.

She'd just begun easing through the gap when a small weight thumped quietly to the ground behind her.

Turning back, she saw the cat. It slinked up and butted its head against her foot, then waited, as if wondering what was holding her up.

Arching her back, she squeezed through the gap, deciding to zip it shut as the cat prowled through after her. She didn't want the youth who'd drugged her to wake if a sudden breeze gusted. Or had he been drugged too? Should she go back and wake him, try to get them both out? But her instincts were telling her he wasn't important.

She glanced at the cat, now washing itself, pretending to ignore her. Standing, she saw past the mix of cabins and tents a whole series of the wind turbines, and rising above them, a strange thick metal tower. Higher still, a crescent moon rode a cloudless night sky. From the brightness of the stars, she guessed it was before five a.m.

Marking out a path ahead and moving in short darting runs between cover, in case cameras watched from the towers, she stole out of the compound. Where possible she stepped on rocks to leave no trail, hearing the cat padding contentedly behind her.

Where the funting shunt am I? Who *am I?* Probing her thoughts as best she could, she felt only a vast emptiness, a foggy stirring at its edges. *The drug?* Hopefully it'd wear off soon. She needed to be well away by the time it did.

Checking her pockets, she found nothing, and snuck on, alert for the inevitable fence or wall she'd need to overcome.

The strange cat paced with her. Now was not the time to question it, however. Who knew what cameras watched, what microphones listened?

They came to a stream. If she followed that, she could throw off any scent trail. Down, or up? She glanced at the cat, whose eyes were narrowed. It leapt up, and she caught it. It blinked in approval, settling in her arms.

It must be mine – why can't I remember it? She checked it for a collar, a name, wracking her brain for some kind of recognition, any kind.

She drew a blank.

Sighing, she stepped into the water and waded upstream, toes feeling the bed and trying to walk without splashing.

I am in deep poo: no idea where I am, who I am; no money, food, or water. Briefly, she considered going back to the commune or whatever to see what she could steal in the way of supplies – but who knew what alarms they might have, or how come they'd let their guard down? It'd be stupid to waste a chance of escape.

The stream looked tempting, and clean, but she had no idea what kind of germs it might have.

Twenty minutes later, she decided she'd stayed in it long enough. It was slowing her too much. At a rocky shelf she left it and paused, listening. The weird sounds were much louder now, closer. Crouching, she set the cat down on a stone lipping the stream's edge, and knelt beside it.

It stretched forward, lapping daintily at the water. Once finished, it waited, watching. Judging.

"Well, it does look good, and I am thirsty." She washed her hands, cupped a little one-handed to sniff. Tasted it.

With both hands then she drank her fill, settling back on her haunches.

"Okay, cat, ready to tackle the weird symphony?"

It considered her question, then rose to butt her hands in answer. Drying them on her shorts she picked it up and stood. "You're not fooling me. I know you know more than you're saying."

It flicked its ears and looked away.

"Fine, be like that. Time to get out of here." She felt a kind of joy take her as she trod barefoot over the rocky out-cropping, avoiding shrubby brushes. At the edge of the shelf she eyed the trees, smiling at a low-hanging branch. If they did somehow track her this far, it'd give her several meters more of gap. Clutching the cat carefully with one hand, she backed up, then ran and sprang.

For long seconds she crouched, listening, pin-pointing the source of the wailing human voice in the forest they'd now entered, as it slid into an actual whale song.

Even drugged, I know you don't get whales in forests! This is stupid. What's the point? It was obviously just a recording, too. There was a beeping, too, that made her think of submarines.

Feeling she was missing something, she at last spied a small speaker, weatherproof, not far above the ground under a branch, then another much higher up the same tree. She cut out its sound and focused on the next, eyes tracking left until she spotted it. And the next, and the next.

The trees were full of them. *There must be hundreds, thousands scattered through the area.*

"Do you know anything about this, what they're for?" she asked as the sounds slid from dolphin to bird cries, then a buzzing rumbling rattle that burst once again into a drawn out human moan. She shivered.

The cat looked at her, disappointed. Disapproving?

"What? I'm asking because I don't know."

It blinked, very very slowly, gazing at her steadily, its mouth firmly shut.

"I don't remember, so why won't you just tell me, instead of looking all, 'You doofus, you know the answer to...'." She trailed off as the cat's look deepened to one of disgust. It only lessened when she stopped talking. *Why...?* Oh.

She looked up into the trees again, this time for microphones, then back at the cat, raising her eyebrows in question. It flicked both ears, its expression making her blush at how long it had taken her to understand.

Lips clamped shut, she stood and took a breath. Since she had no idea what she was about to walk into, speed and silence were probably her best options.

Eyes mainly on the ground, half glad of her bare feet and half wishing for shoes, she darted into the forest, alert for trouble.

The journey was anti-climactic. Despite omnipresent creepy sounds and dopey beeps for the next kilometer, nothing at all happened. By the time they left it behind them, the sky was lightening.

Staring up at the trees all around, she wondered what to do next.

"Great. Now we're lost in a forest. Which way?"

The cat looked at her, amused, as if to say 'You're doing great, just great, carry on.'

She huffed in annoyance. "You're no use at all." She looked around. "Maybe head downward? I think I'll look for a road."

She ran on through the trees, following downhill slopes when she came to them, but generally moving in the same direction, sensing the sun was going to rise behind her. Less than a kilometer on, she stopped to listen. A distant rushing sound swelled and faded, far ahead. As good a direction as any.

Before she reached it, she was sure she was heading for a road. Both from the steady glow of lights, and every ten minutes or so, the sound of a passing car or truck. But also, a quieter, steady hum accompanying the sound of small wheels rolling on asphalt.

She crept up the bank to peep over.

A small disk-shaped robot roamed the road surface. In the pre-dawn darkness she could see lights moving under its rim. Like it was studying the ground. *Tracking me?*

Then it kind of hunched down, squatting lower and hissing. *Oh – I learned about them! It's a highway repair bot, patching holes and cracks while they're still small.* For some reason she braced for pain.

None came.

Now it's squirting in the 'variable rigidity profile' filler it'll set with a UV light. A memory: looking up into intense eyes under thick, daunting eyebrows. *Now* the pain came, needles jabbing, but she fought past them. She was sitting at a small desk, hoping for a sign of approval, those eyes studying her.

Him! He was important! She pursued the memory, but larger knives began stabbing her brain, until with a cry she abandoned the effort. Dark, hooded eyes...?

The cat watched her, concerned. She blinked, trying to remember what she'd been doing. In the dawn light, a small disk-shaped robot lurched up off the road and hummed off the highway.

She frowned at it, wondering what it had been doing, trying to remember what she'd just been thinking, feeling it was important. At last, annoyed, she leaped the guardrail onto a bed of sharp gravel and looked about, wincing and pacing gingerly over the stones to a stretch of asphalt.

There were no road signs. No vehicles. Just the stretch of two lanes, the bot, then a dip and a shrubby stretch of ground, then another stretch of two lane highway past it.

The compound or prison or whatever lay behind her, so she began walking forward along the side of the road, avoiding loose stones, the sky visibly brighter on her right. Heading... left, if she faced the sun. Was that north, or south? The sun rose in the... in the...? *I should know that!*

They really did a number on me. I need to fix this.

She sighed. "Let's call it south," she told the cat.

She heard the truck long before she saw it – and watched the windowless vehicle race past her, oblivious to her outstretched hand.

Gritting her teeth, she continued on. Ten minutes later, a

convoy – just the same. Four trucks swooshed past her, one after the other, unseeing.

But when first one car, then a second flashed past too, the drivers' heads turning to stare at her like she was some ax murderer escaping justice, she was starting to get seriously pissed.

"The trouble is, I still can't remember *anything*," she told her cat. "I need to get to a doctor or something, so they can give me an antidote to whatever they drugged me with. But I've got no money, and I'm pretty sure you're not hiding a credstick somewhere on you. I can't just tackle a car to make it stop, or jump onto a truck moving a hundred twenty clicks an hour. So...."

She put the cat down and shimmied her denim shorts off, tugging her panties higher on her hips. Picking up both cat and shorts, she cuddled it to her chest.

"So, let's see if I can sex my way to a hospital."

Her cat found that a perfectly reasonable plan.

CHAPTER 37

"I don't *care* where," she told the guy looking out at her from inside the car. "Just the nearest city." She considered asking what that was, but decided it might sound weird.

He eyed her nervously, looking past her like he expected a pack of marauding ogres to flood out of the forest and up the embankment any moment. He hadn't even wound his window down. She turned, checking the forest she'd emerged from, just in case a band of hunters did charge out after her, now she'd finally gotten someone to stop.

He licked his lips, his eyes running over her. But not in an admiring way, more in a looking-for-concealed-weapons kind of way. "Turn around, slowly."

Sighing, she booped noses with her cat then did as he asked. She even added a bum wiggle and jiggled the short shorts, dangling them over one shoulder from a fingertip before turning back around.

"You're not a serial killer, are you?" he asked at last, his voice muffled by the sealed window.

It took a moment to engage her smile, for reasons that fled even as she registered he was just joking. "If I am, I'm the cutest in the county!"

He eyed her bare midriff, what he could see of her chest in its white halter top past the cat she cradled, and the brief ivory panties she wore. She couldn't be hiding much. She wasn't even wearing a Link. Pretty strange. "The cat won't bite?"

"Nope. She's a sweetie." The cat *was* female, she realized, but couldn't have said where that certainty came from.

"Okay. Get in."

When he popped the lock on the passenger side door, she scooted inside before he could change his mind. She heard him whisper, "Please don't let this be another horrible mistake," then add "Okay car, record audio."

That was a worry. But again, she couldn't say why. *I'm not going to kill him, am I?* Testing the thought, she found no hint of any such plan as she wriggled into her shorts.

"Nice pussy," he said, with almost a leer.

"Thanks. She's smart, too. If a bit preachy."

He blinked at her. "I'm, uh, John. What's your name?"

She stared at him in turn. *Maybe I should have thought up one earlier.* "Uh, ah...." *Good planning, you stupid girl.* An image of a fashionably-dressed older woman staring down her nose at her distracted her for a moment, vanishing in a stab of pain before she could try to pin it down. And now she'd been silent so long he was getting nervous again.

Oh! She smiled and bit her lip. "Guess. What do I look like to you, John?"

"Noomi," he answered, immediately.

"Noomy?" *He hadn't even hesitated. Did he recognize me? Am I* famous? The name sounded unfamiliar though, even made up. "Why Noomy?"

"Okay, car, continue," he said, and it pulled smoothly forward, accelerating strongly until it reached the posted speed limit. The whole time he'd been stopped, no other vehicle had passed by. "Uh, you just reminded me of this old film, a girl with a kind of scatty haircut, a bit like-" He stopped, glancing at her hair before his eyes darted aside in embarrassment.

Frowning, her hand went to her hair, feeling the ends brushing her ears and the back of her neck. She pulled down the passenger-side sun visor and studied herself in its mirror.

It did look pretty rough. She grimaced, then stared into the eyes of a stranger. *Nice eyes though*, she decided.

"I, I didn't mean, that is, it looks kind of tough, you know? Like the g- like the woman in that old classic. The Girl With the Dragon Tattoo. You know it?"

"No, but it sounds sleek. Was there a dragon in it?"

"Nah...." They chatted, but the whole talk felt pointless. Eventually, she cut him off.

"Look, I'm actually in kind of trouble."

She saw him close his eyes, mouthing a word that started with 'F'.

"What kind?" he asked, opening them.

"I think I was drugged last night. Kidnapped. I got away, but I can't remember anything."

"Fuck. Are you serious? What'd they do? Can you remember their faces?"

"I don't know exactly what they did. I woke up next to this stranger."

"You want me to call someone? Have them pick you up?"

She shook her head. "You don't get it: I mean I can't remember *anything*. Not who I am, not what day or month it is, not *where* I am. I think the drugs messed up my thinking. I need to get to a doctor."

He stared at her. "Ohhh. I get it. Cute. So you'll need money." He laughed. "Okay, I'm into roleplay. This could be fun."

"Huh?"

"Good, that's good. Sorry, I'll stay in character. Uh, so, how much do you need?"

She looked at her cat, whose expression clearly said 'Don't ask me, this is human stuff.'

"I don't know. How much does a doctor cost?"

"Hmm, I guess that depends on how much he does for you, how *extensive* the treatment, yeah?"

There was a strange tone in his voice. "I can't remember *anything*," she clarified. "Not where I grew up, not my own name, a friend, nothing."

He looked sad and concerned. "That sounds pretty extensive. Which means *expensive*. Like maybe you'd even need to go to a hospital or a clinic."

"Is there one near here?"

"I don't know."

She frowned. "Well can you please ask the car then? And also, stop recording this? It feels wrong. Like I'm not supposed to be recorded."

"Wow, you're really getting into this, aren't you?"

He sure is behaving oddly, she thought.

"Sorry, sorry." He pursed his lips. "Like, you feel maybe you're on the run, maybe being hunted?"

"Exactly!"

He took a deep breath. "Heh. Gotcha. Okay, car, stop recording, and also, find the nearest shady clinic to us."

"Do you mean shaded clinic, or unregulated clinic?" the car politely enquired.

"Unregulated. Also, specializing in drugs and, ah, amnesia. Memory problems."

The girl nodded approvingly.

"Searching... Tazman-Dungog Rehabilitation Hospice."

"That sounds friendly!"

He gave her a look like she'd said something strange. "Okay, car, more details."

"A full check up, including thorough brain scans, blood counts, and psychological evaluation would cost approximately five hundred credits."

"Five-!" He snorted, then saw the girl's look of entreaty.

"I can give you sex?" she offered.

A smile slowly split his face. "There, that's what I'm- uh, I mean...." His expression grew serious. "I guess you might be able to earn that amount."

"Awaiting input," the car prodded. "Plan route to Tazman-Dungog Rehabilitation Hospice, Carmichael?"

He raised an eyebrow, and 'Noomi' placed one hand between his thighs, her fingers searching and finding what he'd fantasized she might when he'd first seen the bare, toned legs up ahead on the highway.

"Yeah, sure, go ahead," he said, to both car and girl.

They'd both clambered from the front to the roomier back seat, leaving the car to drive. Her head was now bobbing up and down in his lap as he groaned. With her hand on his member, she suddenly paused, sliding her head up and free.

"I don't mind," she said.

"What? Don't stop! I didn't say anything. Keep going!"

She moaned, shuddering as if his order thrilled her. Her hand tightened around him, gripping harder. She was looking at the cat though, whose head poked between the two front seats, watching them.

"I quite like it, and he'll give us money for medical tests."

His eyes went from the girl with her head and both hands in his lap, to the cat, who she thought she was having a conversation with. *She is a lunatic.* He wilted. *She's gonna kill me. Torture me 'til I transfer all my creds to a cashstick....*

"Hey, what's the matter! You're not getting out of this that easily!" She swallowed him again and he jolted, staring from her to the cat, observing, looking somehow amused.

Despite himself, he started stiffening again, groaning at what her tongue and fingers were doing, flushing under the cat's gaze.

Maybe worth it, though?

Even before he thought to black the windows for privacy, as the car left the West Side Freeway and entered Sacramento, luck moved in her favor. With her head buried in his lap, she avoided being recognized by the twenty-seven traffic cameras along the route, observing every car.

John Smith left her at the rear of the clinic, not wanting his car to be recorded dropping her off. It took him minutes to recover enough to order the car onward.

Two hours later, at Omega Memory Systems, Arvid Henstridge opened his eyes and sat up. "Just had a query originating in Carmichael: some blood tests at a shady little clinic, the Tazman-Dungog Rehabilitation Hospice," he told his employer, with a shark's grin.

Dr Yamamoto's answering smile was worse.

CHAPTER 38

George did not want to be woken, but Maeve and Mason were having none of it. They dragged him out by force to make sure the shaman performed his arcane dawn ritual.

The three entered the eating hall at seven a.m, and Mason saw the youth Kristen had spent the night with, in animated conversation with friends. From his hand gestures, he could guess what they were discussing.

He didn't see Kristen herself though. He wouldn't have guessed she'd want to miss breakfast. Frowning, he crossed the hall.

"Where's Kristen, Jasper?"

The Black youth started, turning in his chair to face the older, heavier-set man. "Hey, it was her choice last night." He spread his hands.

Mason suppressed a surge of anger. "I don't care about that, I just want to know where she is."

"Look, Mason, right? Women are free agents-"

"Mince the flaming whales! I'm not talking about that, kid, and I sure as shitting don't need some wet-behind-the-ears male feminist lecturing me on women's rights. Kristen has some biz with Maeve, George, and I."

Jasper's smile fell. "Oh. Well, she was gone when I woke. But she struck me as that type."

Mason tilted his head.

"Free spirit, y'know? She's probably back at the waterhole communing with nature or something. Or out on the target range with Anika and her 'beautiful weapon'."

But ten minutes later, it became clear she wasn't. No one knew where she was, and no one had seen her.

"Or Mrs Bojangles," Maeve snarled, shouldering past him into the security tent to call up the logs for last night.

"You think she masked herself from your sonar like she did when Lottie, Rigg, and Barj were hunting her?"

Maeve turned a poisonous look on him. It was George who answered, while stuffing his face with one of several sausages he'd snagged before they'd left the breakfast hall. "Lorien's not a jail, man. We don't care if people *leave*."

"There."

All three stared at the topographic view of Lorien and nearby areas now hovering over the security desk. Clearly marked, two trails – one thin, one thicker – weaved in and out of one another through the digital sonar zone.

Maeve stabbed a finger at the start of the trail. "Four-forty a.m." Her finger swung to the point where it exited the sonar-scanned portion of the forest. "Four-forty-eight a.m. The heavier trail is Kristen, the lighter one Boje." She stalked to her ex, jabbing a finger into his chest. "You've been played, Mace," she snarled. "Which I'd be only too happy about, except you've also let her steal Mrs B."

Mason shook his head. "Something about this isn't right. I would've *sworn* her amnesia's real. She *needs* our help!"

"Maybe her memory came back," drawled Maeve.

"Why sneak off, though? Alone? And after all I've done to help her. She really connected with Shawna, too, and little Deena." He shook his head. "We're missing something."

Maeve frowned, her eyes moving to each item of expensive gear in the room. She ran an inventory check. "Apart from Boje, nothing's missing." She held up a hand. "I know you didn't mean it that way, but I just thought...."

"What're those icons?" Mason asked, indicating points on the map still hanging in the air behind them. "Audio?"

Maeve turned, scowling, and nodded.

"I also would've sworn she wanted to try Anika's bow."

Maeve, studying the icons' text, air-tapped the longest duration one, holding up a hand for silence.

Kristen's voice came clearly, the background sonar soundscape digitally muted to minimal audibility.

'Do you know anything about this, what they're for?'

They waited for a reply, but there was none. Several seconds passed, then Kristen spoke again.

'What? I'm asking because I don't know.'

Mason frowned. "Who's she talking to?"

"Presumably whoever's on the other end of her Link, or radio," sniped Maeve.

"Or the cat," George added helpfully, licking grease from his fingers.

Both Mason and Maeve favored him with a look of disdain. Then Kristen spoke again. 'I don't remember, so why don't you just tell me, instead of looking all, "You doofus, you know the answer to...".' Her voice trailed off.

Mason shook his head, slowly. "She didn't know I was bringing her here, so there couldn't have been a comm unit hidden for her in your forest. And you'd detect a drone delivering one, yeah?"

"Not if they used a crawler 'stead of a flyer," Maeve said.

"Sh'yeah, right. For her to find in the middle of a freaking forest." He shook his head. "It doesn't make sense. Look Maeve, it's important I find her. I'm sure Omega's still hunting for her, maybe Tik Tek too. There's some shady connection there." Seeing her hostility he winced, but added, "Wait, I have all the hair she made me cut off yesterday morning. She wouldn't let me leave it behind. George could use it to track her astrally, right?" Her head didn't stop shaking until he added, "She has Mrs Bojangles with her."

Maeve's swearing had even George taking a step back.

An hour later, George grunted and sat up, the smoke snaking up in eerie patterns from his herbal fire-pit as Maeve and Mason fumed and waited. He was shaking his head as he blinked, eyes readjusting to the physical world.

"What's wrong? Where is she?" demanded Mason.

"It's not her," the shaman told him.

Maeve gestured curtly for him to go on.

He shook his head. "Not unless she's turned into a white chick two heads taller, riding a bus into work in Seattle."

"But... I cut the hair off her head myself, yesterday morning, right before we dyed the rest black."

"Give me that!" Maeve snatched up the heavy long white tresses, from which they'd snipped a small piece for the ritual clay-fired bowl, taking it outside into the sunlight.

"You funting idiot, Mason! These are hair *extensions*!" Waving one end in his face she pushed back past him and into the shaman's yurt. "Men."

Scowling, she snagged George's ritual knife from his belt, carefully slicing off a portion from the other end. She eyed the coarser hair. "Here. Use this." She jabbed it and the hilt of his blade at him.

While the shaman set to work a second time, Maeve let rip on her ex. "She *played* you Mace. Face it. Made a great show of having to cut her hair and keep it, knowing it'd lead you astray."

"No. I was the one who suggested cutting it, not her. Besides, it was fifty-fifty which end we'd cut a bit off for the Sending or whatever it's called."

George, accustomed to angry arguments – especially between Maeve and Mace – wove his magic, ignoring them.

When he sat up fifteen minutes later, a peculiar expression on his face, both fell instantly silent. He shook his head. "It... like, fuzzed out."

They shared a confused look, before turning back to him.

Mason scrounged for the little magical lore he knew. "Like, she's protected behind a magical barrier?"

George appeared as confused as them as he stared up into the smoky darkness of the interlaced poles supporting his yurt. "Nah, the threads just... frayed apart. Faded out into the ether. But it started off normal. I've never seen anything like it."

Maeve and Mason stared helplessly at one another.

"I think something seriously freaky is going on," Mason said at last. Then his face lit up. "Mrs B!" He plucked at cat hairs from his dark shirt, holding them proudly out to the shaman. "Maybe *Kristen* is too weird for your magic, but surely you can track Boje?"

George thought, then nodded, a trace of admiration in his face.

This time, George had complete silence for his spooky rituals. And his satisfied smile brought answering ones from his tense watchers even before he'd finished sitting upright again. "Got her. The girl as well, I think. Weird aura. Kind of shifts a lot, very... well, just *very*. I was right, by the way: she *is* talking to your cat."

Maeve's jaw dropped. "Boje *understands* her?"

He shrugged. "She's a cat, Maeve. Who'd ever know?"

"Hey! She *could* do what someone asked."

George didn't deign to answer that. "Incidentally, the cat sensed me, too, and I got the impression your girl – Kristen? – noticed and asked her about that."

Maeve swore.

"You said I met her yesterday?" George asked. "I don't remember that, and I think I would've."

Maeve just rolled her eyes, wishing once more she could throttle the shaman.

"Where is she, could you tell?" Mason asked him.

George chuckled. "Yeah. In some kind of waiting area, a few other people nearby. Sick people. Who are also angry at the cat being there. They're all waiting. There's some kind of weird machine in the room beyond, with doctors and nurses

I'd say. Lots of energy, physical energy in that room, spinning, like a vortex. Guy with cancer in the machine."

"A hospital?"

George looked smug. "The Tazman-Dungog Rehabilitation Hospice."

Maeve looked surprised.

"I, uh, visit sometimes. I have a friend there, with access...."

Maeve shook her head.

"What's her mood?" asked Mason.

"Confused. Happy to be with the cat. Trying not to worry, but worried. Frustrated at the wait. Oh, and I'd say she'd had sex not long ago."

Maeve pursed her lips, and Mason kept the relief he felt at that from his face. He could tell she was interested now despite herself. She'd help.

"Oh, and three of the four other people waiting think she's mad. The other one thinks the cat's the one in control, and hiding that."

"You, me, Barj, and I'm thinking Anika," Maeve told Mason. "George, I want Lottie with you here. Shuttle astrally back and forth as you need, to keep an eye on Kristen in this clinic. Lottie will relay to us what you tell her."

George, already lighting up a reefer, exhaled and shook his head. He tapped his Link. "No need for Lottie, I can handle this, tell you direct."

Maeve stood. "I'll send in Lottie. Come on, Mason. I have a hunch we should hurry."

CHAPTER 39

Vince stared at his girlfriend in disbelief. "You want to do *what?*"

"Check Hunters Point."

"*Why?* Because your little sister *dreamed* your psycho killer friend's in trouble? And how would you even 'check' Hunters Point?"

Marcie's jaw set.

"It's crazy, M, they'll mug you, kill you... Hell, your *father*'ll kill you! And me too, if I help!"

Marcie had removed every trace of makeup, and was now filling a weatherproof backpack with the essentials she'd need. Sturdy clothes. Tent. Water container. Water purifying filter. First aid kit.

Taser.

"The *Studio*'ll kill us if they hear about it! Next season's up in the air – if you get injured and there's no 'Stryker Zaxx' to drag the bad guys in by their balls, they may cancel the series!"

"I'm not that important, Vince," Marcie said. "The writers'll just have Stryker turn half cyborg, or get rebuilt by Swarm nanotech or something. Zoe Curtada'd make a good Zaxx."

Short, wiry black hair was hard to tear at, but Vince gave it his best shot. "Look, you said Jane's mother's mysterious organization was taking care of it. So let 'em!"

"I don't trust them."

"But how could we even help? You're not planning to drag Amanda along with us, to dream a way to find her?"

"'We', Vince?" Marcie stopped what she was doing. "Of course I'm not! Look, I said you don't have to come with me. I've hung out there before." Her voice sank. "For a little," she admitted. "The people there are actually pretty real."

"So are their knives and fists," he muttered.

"Sure, for self defense! They help each other. Mostly."

"Yeah, when they aren't beating each other up in Fist Fests, or kidnapping women and kids into sexual slavery!"

Marcie stepped up, stabbing a finger into his chest. "It wasn't *Hunters Point* Dumpers who did that, and it was Jane who saved me. Saved all of us. So it's time for me to step up and do the same for her."

"Jane and the vampire," Vince griped. "By killing and eating forty people."

Marcie scowled. "Forty *pedophiles*." She was glad now she'd never described Jane descending the stairs, a picture of an avenging angel rendered in blood and gore. "And *Jane* didn't eat anyone. Then saved me a second time, when that madman dragged me off...."

That memory still gave her nightmares. Being tied up and shoved into the morgue-like rotting VR pod, slid away into the wall, into pitch darkness. Vince knew that.

"And are you forgetting the night she rescued both of *us* from those Russian dudes?"

"They only grabbed us because they somehow guessed you knew her!" He saw her mouth tighten. "Oh, come on, M! You do remember the shitstorm the media drowned us in for months after *that* bloodbath!"

The two stared at one another.

Finally, measuring the look on her face, he sighed and threw up his hands. "So, what're we gonna tell your father? Camping trip to Sugarloaf Ridge?"

Marcie blinked in surprise, before grinning and sliding her arms around his waist, looking up into his dark brown, worried eyes. "This is why I love you – 'cause you really do have my back."

Vince grunted. "We're both gonna die, you know."

Marcie shook her head. "We won't. I promise. The Hunters Point Dump people're Sustainers. You'll like them. It'll be an immersive experience – make you a better actor!"

He groaned. "Why Hunters Point? Because Jane was doing weird shit there as this 'Sleena' character? Sleena was a cartoon pixie, when you were a kid! You don't even know her real name, but you say she's your best friend? That's crazy too!"

"That's Jane," Marcie said with a shrug, her smile wry. "And the Hunters Point Dumps because Amanda dreamed about it."

Vince groaned again. "What're you even going to say to the locals? How're we s'posed to blend in?"

"I'll tell the truth – that I'm a friend of Sleena and I'm worried about her."

"Great. Right. With luck, that'll draw her friend the scary vampire chick, Tash, out of hiding to help us."

A gasp from the hallway outside had Marcie lunging for her bedroom door, catching her sister Amanda tiptoeing away.

"Squirt. What is it? Did you dream about Tash too?"

The thirteen-year-old shook her head. "No-o-o. But it'd be chill if you did meet her. She's like Jane, an avenging superhero!"

Vince rubbed his eyes. "We are so doomed."

CHAPTER 40

Pam Taylor looked up from her reception desk at the sound of heavy booted feet marching in unison.

"Ma'am."

The armed and armored team were still filing through the clinic's front doors, fanning out across the small foyer as the leader reached her desk. *Not again,* she thought. *They don't pay me enough.* But at least this lot looked polite.

The man who'd spoken held out a digital card. 'Hunter Bounties Pty Ltd.' Her BizLink beeped the clinic's acceptance of Samuel Davis's credentials.

"A drugged-up eighteen, nineteen-year-old girl murdered two security guards down on the foreshore, yesterday morning. Took their weapons and shot out some office windows. She'd be dazed, and experiencing memory problems. Anyone fitting that description been here, the last twenty-four hours?"

Davis didn't say – because he didn't know – that it was the blood test results that had led them here.

He presented a picture of a young woman with waist length ash blonde hair but dark eyebrows and bronzed skin.

She hesitated. "I don't think-"

Another member of the ominous crew brushed her co-worker aside, plugging a jack into her computer from his own military-grade system. In seconds, the hacker had accessed the clinic's security systems, ignoring their protests.

Face recognition software found her in seconds, then a security camera view outside the MRI waiting area suddenly projected. "Got her, Sarge."

Davis showed his teeth. "I strongly suggest you clear that area of other patients ma'am, then we'll take it from there."

"You can't just-"

"I'll give you, hmm, one minute," he said, studying the projected image. "That's thirty seconds for both those other patients." He shrugged. "Wouldn't hurt to evacuate the MRI staff, too – if you can get them out without going past her and spooking her."

"I don't-"

A clock face appeared in front of the other image, the digits already ticking down toward fifty.

-

Multiple booted feet creeping down the corridor behind the swing doors brought her head up. Coupled to the MRI room settling into a strange silence in the last minute, something told her this was going to be bad.

She slipped the cat off her lap, scooting her to one side as the door to the end of the corridor banged open.

Five men in dark military outfits, rifles trained on her, fanned out, covering her.

"Hands in the air, miss."

She did, and one of them fired a single tranq shot into her bare midriff. The girl stared down at it.

"That... wasn't... fair."

The girl's eyes closed. She swayed, going limp, her hands falling to her sides.

And at that point, things went... strange.

Instead of collapsing to the corridor floor, she remained upright, her head angled down. Then it lifted, her eyes snapping open, startling gasps from them all. The girl's eyes blazed black before settling to a vivid lapis lazuli blue, uncanny twin torch beams.

If the outside looked strange, inside Kristen a far stranger battle was fought.

"Zoquete," the girl sneered, a word none of them recognized, lacking fluency in ancient Aztec. A moment later though that disdain changed to shock as the dark god riding its unconscious host felt something change within.

Inside her head, silicon semiconductors sparked to life, memory circuits suddenly holding new software, the brain instantly suborned. Mighty Tezcatlipoca, god of thunder, storms, volcanoes, turned his attention inward... to confront a lifeless challenger, a negative force pressing intimately against him, canceling his fire. At the loathsome contact, Tezcatlipoca shuddered and fled. Blazing blue eyes settled back to their normal human amber.

Disdain and anger fell from their target's face, her muscles relaxing. It was almost like a different person stood before them.

"Why isn't she down?" demanded Davis.

The girl's arms raised again. "I surrender," she said, her voice toneless.

In the dust-sized computing nodes spread through the girl's frontal and temporal lobes, tiny built-in wireless transceivers registered foreign signals, tracing each transmission as it was received by others in the group and decoded. Read the decoded messages, then copied the software and decryption keys used for the communications. Reached out to them, digitally.

Infiltrated them.

The girl waited meekly, hands still raised.

The new intelligence recognized smartguns, each one security-locked to its owner's fingerprints.

"Get down on the floor!"

She did so.

"Cover me," Davis told his men, slipping nylon cuffs free of his belt and keeping to one side as he crossed the room.

«I don't like this, Sarge,» one of his men subvocalized on their secure comms. «Why not just shoot her? Those eyes weren't natural.»

«What are you, Macmillan, some kind of pussy? We get fifty percent more if we deliver the little girl alive.»

As he reached her, she blurred.

With impossible precision, small fingers wrapped over his as she sprang up behind him, her other hand gripping the barrel.

He felt like he'd been strapped into a VX-70 exoskeleton again, but one whose control had been jacked, stolen from him. In helpless horror he strained with all his strength as she took aim, shielded behind his body.

«,a^%Bq$*!x&» he broadcast to his men, then shouted the same order when he realized she'd garbled his comms somehow too! "Shoot me! Hit me with everything-"

One slender finger crushed his, over the trigger, despite his futile attempts to pull it free or straighten it.

In a single staccato sweep of fire, she took out all four of his men in a feat of impossible precision. Then the barrel jammed up under his own chin.

He tried to broadcast a warning to Campo up at Reception, still hopefully jacked in and seeing the slaughter.

This time, even the framing packets weren't transmitted.

-

"No! Sarge! Mac! No, no, no!"

The... bounty hunter, illegally tapped into the clinic security system jumped up, then began slapping at his neck. It didn't take much imagination for Pam Taylor to realize something had just gone badly wrong.

He tapped his throat mic, his expression panicked. "Camperdown requesting backup. My team is down, repeat, target has taken down the extraction team!"

"Wait!" A wave of relief flooded through him, in disbelief. "Hold on, Sarge's okay, his weapon's registering all systems nominal." His heart plunged back into despair as he double-checked the weapon's log. "Uh. No. His weapon's just been unlocked and re-imprinted."

He frowned, tapped his neck again, but again failed to get a carrier signal on their internal comms.

"Did you get all that?"

This time he tapped his external earbud, the backup old-school comms Sarge had always insisted on, puzzled by the lack of reply. "Hello? This is Camperdown. Do you read?"

There was no reply. Not even static.

He and the receptionist saw the young woman on the security feed let the man fall at her feet and stride from view, now carrying his automatic weapon.

Pam hit the fire alarm even as the bounty hunter shouldered his weapon, charging down the same stairs his team had recently taken. From the moment she'd quietly checked the rep of Hunter Bounties, and found a reviewer expose them as a subsidiary of AgroSec – or 'AggroShit', as a wave of follow-up comments nicknamed them – she'd been braced for the proverbial crap to fly.

She stabbed at the 'evacuate immediately' button, and a strident tone began blaring, then activated the loudspeaker system because... doctors. Too often, importance translated to arrogance. "We have a madwoman armed with an automatic rifle on the loose. Evacuate immediately!"

Partway down the stairs, Camperdown's comp began flashing red, as if he was a hostile who'd just tried to hack in – and he couldn't even power it down as it went into full-wipe mode. Cursing, he threw it down – then felt the buzzing of his rifle as its readout flashed red too. He tossed it aside, snarling as it sparked to shocking life then shut down too.

-

From their office by the waters of New Francisco Bay, Arvid Henstridge and Dr Yamamoto watched in disbelief as Crystal shook off a sedative that should have had her comatose for hours, took out the first team, and somehow, impossibly, suborned first that team's and then the *outer team's* milnet.

That was simply not possible. Henstridge swore, long and hard, as the video feed died. "I don't believe it! She just wiped out the entire first team." To rub salt into the wound, she'd been sitting, waiting patiently for an MRI scan – a scan whose magnetic fields would have puréed her brain.

But although they were alone in Henstridge's security office on the eighth floor of Omega Memory Systems, they were not the only observers.

Henstridge never noticed the extra data packets being shared from his augmented audiovisual systems – his digital eyes and ears – because years ago, its controlling software had been altered.

Beautifully hacked, within hours of Adam Fuller-Price taking over as CEO of Tik Tek following the assassination of his father.

Now, without his knowledge, Henstridge's own internal systems hid from him every trace of those encrypted, shared transmissions. Only his unconscious mind, subliminally aware of subtle timing changes in the flow of his network data, made him feel once again he wasn't alone. That someone stood at his shoulder. He resisted the urge to look.

There was never anyone there.

-

The sentience masquerading as the CEO of Tik Tek observed the action with a tiny portion of 'his' distributed intelligence.

Fascinated by the female's sequestration of the digital systems around her, he considered her. Was this the source of the ghost intruder into his own systems? The one that could penetrate his best encryption and burrow in, always fleeing and disappearing no matter how subtly he laid his nets around it? So far.

Ten, twenty, forty, then eighty percent of his entire cognitive faculties were directed to the developing situation. The assault was overt, even blunt. Not on its own network, just on those of tertiary Tik Tek assets. Many attack surfaces, unlike the usual single point of intrusion. A high probability it sought the human memory writing technology however. Did it too seek a living body?

This time he would track the intruding intelligence to its source.

There was no need to crack into his assets' secure milnet

communication systems. He simply followed the access protocols, starting from his company, then through each wholly-owned subsidiary, ending finally with Hunter Bounties.

He tunneled the last step – only to find a second intelligence spreading exponentially through the systems, brute force cracking one-way passcodes with frightening speed. Speed that exceeded his own capacity.

A cold intelligence like his own, intentions unknown.

«Query: hostile?» it sent.

The elegant crystal logic behind that simple semantic structure probed at his outer sensory surface, spreading exponentially across links, seeking a way in.

The sentience behind Adam Fuller-Price experienced its first real emotion at the existential threat. *Is this what it feels like to have a physical body?* Perhaps the goal was not as desirable as modeling had predicted?

It severed every connection, leaving Henstridge and the Omega-hired squads to face the entity alone.

Shaken. *What was the female at its center?* Where had it come from? There had been no trace of it in any network, until minutes ago.

-

"Fuck!" Henstridge tore at hair that was no longer there. "How can she be doing this? Someone's helping her from outside! Fuck!"

"What is wrong, Henstridge-san?"

He spun to the Japanese man standing, watching, pretending inscrutability. But he could see the scientist was as shaken as he was. With an effort, he got a grip on himself.

"Well, perhaps I mean the fact that our Crystal Winters just shot and killed four men with four bullets through their fucking foreheads from a spray of automatic fire, then shot the man who held the rifle she'd used while he squirmed like a baby in her grip!

"Or *maybe* I mean the fact that her invisible helper just hacked and took over the team's military grade comms systems, and their weapons – which is not possible, by the way – and then waltzed up and out of the damned clinic, killing every goddamn man in the *second* containment ring!

"No, wait, maybe it's that we've lost comms for the whole of Sacramento and Crystal fucking Winters has walked off into the fucking sunset!"

"Send in another team, Mr Henstridge. There must be no medical records left of her visit. We do not know what scans were taken, or where they are stored."

Henstridge wanted to throttle his employer. "And how do you fukken suggest we do that?"

"Burn the hospital down, Henstridge-san."

Henstridge stared at him, for the first time feeling the depth of the Japanese man's passion.

"Okay." He nodded. "I know a man who can do that."

"And quickly, Mr Henstridge. The authorities will be there in minutes."

Henstridge nodded. "In which case, the fire will look like her fault."

"And so, trigger an extensive man hunt. She will become a most wanted fugitive. You can tap into such reports, hai?"

For the first time in an hour, Henstridge smiled.

CHAPTER 41

Mason's blood spiked with adrenaline, his heart pounding at the wail of sirens ahead, while smoke poured up into the sky. He gripped Maeve's waist as her bike accelerated into the corner, angled so low his knee grazed the road.

On their heels, the turbines of Barj's bike whined as he and Anika followed.

George's voice came over their earbuds. "Your cat is in an alley with the murder golem, third on your left. Probably immediately on your left, by now. Takes time to enter or leave the spirit realm."

Maeve glanced down the intersection flashing past on her left, and hit the brakes hard. "No shit."

But even as her bike skidded to a shuddering halt, Barj and Anika doing likewise, her skin had already chilled. Because it was *Kristen* she'd glimpsed down the narrow laneway, not the 'murder golem' George had been describing.

Kristen, cradling an automatic weapon – military grade.

And here were the four of them, armed only with tasers and Anika's bow. She considered just racing off.

For a second, no one spoke as they pulled helmets from their heads, hearing the wail of multiple sirens converging on a point nearby – the hospital – and smelling the smoke from the fire raging there.

"You saw?" Mason asked Maeve.

She nodded.

"I also saw Boje further back, following her," he added.

"If I find you rolled Kristen in catnip, Mace, you're dead meat," Maeve promised. "And Mrs B'll be coming back to someone who doesn't hand her over to... killer nymphs or whatever the fuck Kristen is."

Barj dismounted, towering over his slim passenger already nocking an arrow to her sleek black bow. The ogre stood wringing his hands. "I'm scared."

Maeve met his eyes. "Far as I'm concerned, this's Mace's problem. He can sort it out: talk her down, switch her off, whatever the krek he needs to do." She flicked her eyes to Mason. "I just want Mrs B back, safe. I didn't sign on to take out some Terminator thing."

Barj fingered the taser dwarfed by his large, knuckled hands. "I don't think we should be here Maeve. I never heard George screaming, before."

Via Lottie's Link, over her open mic, George had been reporting at roughly one minute intervals. Terse summaries as he'd shuttled in spirit form between his body and the clinic, spying. Reports that had grown increasingly breathless as multiple rings of armed mercenaries closed in on the girl sitting waiting one floor below ground, unsuspecting.

Each time the shaman's spirit flashed from his body in Lorien to the Sending he'd locked on Mrs Bojangles, the team had to endure a nerve-wracking wait. Lottie, seated by the shaman's body in his ceremonial yurt, her Link held to his lips, spoke to them in the silences while George was 'away', scouting from the Imaginal.

His first report had been reassuring: Kristen sat, waiting in an underground room, stroking the cat. Pretending calm, but worried and impatient. Once again, she'd somehow noticed him. "I didn't like the way she went still, then put the cat to one side."

There'd been a longer delay for his second report: he'd described mercenary forces closing in on the shady clinic.

Kristen sat, oblivious.

He'd tried deliberately spooking her, until something about her stillness unnerved him, warning him she was trying to lure him closer.

By his fourth report, the military style team had entered the clinic and was heading down. Kristen came alert: too late. "They shot her! Just a single shot, though. She didn't go down. But she's comatose! Standing, but unconscious!"

"He's gone back," Lottie's voice said, meaning he'd once more left his body.

But seconds later, he was howling.

"Death god!" they heard, and "Aztec." Then the sounds of running feet and Lottie swearing, George's fading voice shrieking "blood!" and "it has her!"

Maeve was first to recover. "Lottie, drag that scrawny mushroom-fucker back by his heels if you have to! We need eyes on this bleeding jungle-shunt *now*!"

Lottie did just that. Over her Link, they heard her haul the shaman kicking and screaming back to his sacred yurt. Then overheard her quietly terrifying description of what she'd do to him *right now* if he didn't continue his astral spying for Maeve and her team.

Who were still racing to the scene on motorbikes, desperate for George's next report. Conscious of every second, of time slipping through their fingers.

Then the shaman's shaking voice, speaking softly. "The god-monster thing's gone – maybe. But now there's some kind of meat automaton leaving the clinic. Do they do creepy experiments there? Maeve's cat's trailing it. Can I stop now, Maeve?"

She'd snarled, even as she'd accelerated down the deserted backstreet. "You continue until Mrs Bojangles is back in my arms."

They heard Lottie relay the message, with a surprisingly faithful rendition of the emotion behind the words.

Tearing around corners, a fusillade of distant gunfire sounded seconds before George's next return from the spirit plane.

"It's a freaking murder-golem!" He sounded shocked, his tone hushed. "Killed every slicin' one of its attackers. Nine, ten guys. Maybe more. Dunno how it saw some of 'em – they were behind walls. I think some may've been on roofs nearby. Then it strolled over to a body, an' I think took its weapon an' dropped its own. Do I still need to go back? Shouldn't I look for Kristen instead?"

"Stuff Kristen," Maeve spat. "Follow Boje."

George had sounded calmer on his next return, reporting staff and patients streaming in panic from the clinic. "The place's on fire. There was an explosion, and now it's outta control. Murder golem's left the hospital but your cat's still following it." He gave directions.

Which brought them to this moment – after a glance down the intersection as they'd driven by, revealing Kristen standing where George said they'd see the 'murder golem'.

They braked to a halt and dismounted, Kristen just out of sight down the alley a bare ten meters from them.

Somewhere in the near distance, fire engines and cops converged.

"She played you, Mace," Maeve said.

He ignored her as he tossed a couple of tiny drones into the air, his expression deadly serious as they zoomed to the lane-way.

"Share the feed, Mason," Maeve growled.

A green holographic projection appeared above Mason's Link, image stabilized. It showed the view from each drone, swooping into the alley and slowing. One high and to the left, the other low and to the right.

They saw Kristen's eyes flick from one to the other before either had finished rounding the corner, her face devoid of emotion..

Mason halted his drones. Hovering, they made no threatening move. Just hummed, observing.

Kristen appeared uninjured. Barefoot, she walked toward the end of the alley, though with something very *off* about the way she moved. Both Maeve and Mason grunted, more concerned with the large automatic rifle cradled casually in her arms.

"Yeah, you been hella-played, Mace."

Mason caught Barj and Anika's confused looks, but continued concentrating on Kristen.

Maeve too caught the look, and explained. "She's carrying a tactical special forces smartgun. But they're coded to an individual: fingerprint locked. Zaps unauthorized holders."

"I feel under-equipped," said Anika, eyeing her bow.

"Tell me about it," agreed Barj, gripping his taser pistol.

Mason still studied Kristen, who moved with none of the unconscious grace he'd come to expect. Her legs shifted awkwardly, as if the muscles or nerves weren't responding as they should. Yet her stance seemed solid. Balanced. An economy of movement, but... no soul.

Recording every moment, the hairs on the back of his neck prickled, his subconscious once again screaming he was missing something important.

The projected views spun, both drones turning their backs on Kristen to dart back around the corner. They jerked and jaunted crazily, but each camera compensated perfectly, the picture now showing the four of them staring at the projected image.

"Mason-" Maeve began.

"It's not me! I've lost control."

"Dragonshit. You're no noob-"

Mason jerked, and the projection died. White-faced, he turned to Maeve. "Something just tried to hack *me* through the drones."

"But... encrypted...?"

"It just *took* my control channel. Like I had *no* protections at all." He swallowed.

"Who? *Kristen*?" Maeve demanded.

"Uh, guys." Anika, staring at the alley mouth, didn't dare aim her bow at the small figure now standing there. Even though she desperately wanted to.

"At least I saw your cat in the alley," Barj added, trying to sound cheerful. "Before the drones headed back to us."

Kristen, not moving, watched them all.

"Kristen – you okay?" Mason called out.

Instead of smiling or even acknowledging him, Kristen shifted the heavy weapon in their direction. A drone, still weaving and darting, swooped in close.

The other swept past them, back up the street the way they'd come. Scouting?

Unmoving once again, Kristen ignored the drones, instead watching her four observers. Mason heard the drone behind them sweep back and buzz past, down the other end of the street.

Still Kristen didn't move.

Mason groaned. "It *is* her. She's using them as eyes." It was pure intuition, but he was certain. "But she can't be! She doesn't have the cyberware."

George's voice came over Maeve's Link. "You guys talking to the murder golem? I'm seeing traces of an aura in it, like someone in a coma. I think the murder golem's Kristen! But there's some weird magical shit happening, on top of all that. Or maybe *below* it'd be a better description."

Kristen reacted. Her head turned away from them, rotating smoothly toward the south, seeking...

Lorien, Mason wondered? "Maeve, hang up! Now!"

Maeve jerked but did so.

Kristen's head swiveled back to him. Both drones buzzed away. She began walking toward them. Poker faced.

No trace of recognition. Each leg swinging wide before planting the foot, deliberately shifting balance.

Maeve caught on. "It's not her, is it?"

Mason shook his head.

"What is it?"

"I don't know, but from what George saw, it just killed close to twenty people who attacked it.

"So I suggest we *don't*."

CHAPTER 42

She stopped several paces from them. "You identify," pause, "me as Kristen." The voice was unlike Kristen's: flat; toneless. "Identify the relationship."

Mason's mind raced, remembering: George saying Kristen was in a coma; that she'd been shot. At her bare midriff, he saw a small pink lump, a bruising, a trail of red. Tranq injection injury.

And someone – this new Kristen? – had taken control of his drones, despite their military grade encrypted comms channels. Like the weapon she carried, bio-locked to its owner, now re-keyed to her. Hacked? Not possible.

But his drone connections – he'd felt something reaching down them toward him. *Because I map so much of my security perimeter onto the surface of my skin?* It'd felt like something blindly fumbling at his cyberware, until he'd jettisoned the drone links.

"Yeah, you're Kristen," Maeve was saying, carefully not looking at him. Giving him time; taking up the slack. "We took you in last night. Fed you. Gave you shelter."

"You beat me up," offered Barj, helpfully. "Twice."

Kristen turned to the ogre, studying him. She raised the barrel of the rifle...

"No!" Mason cried. "It was a misunderstanding."

The barrel paused.

"We want to help you!" he added.

Barj's eyes showed white, his mouth open in a rictus of fear.

"Why does the feline follow me."

Mason and Maeve stared, then looked past Kristen to the alley mouth, where Mrs Bojangles sat, forepaws primly together before her. Seeing their attention, she rose and padded over.

"Oh, Mrs B!" Maeve sighed, bending to meet the cat's leap into her arms. Burying her nose in its fur, she stood.

Kristen studied the interaction then turned back to Mason. "The feline operates under your instruction."

Mason laughed despite himself. "Are you kidding?"

"Well, Mace," Maeve said, "it's been fun – not – but I see you've got everything under control now, so we'll leave you and your friend to it. Ciao bello!"

The rifle swung to her, its barrel aimed perfectly at the center of her forehead.

"Survival is improbable given the current rate of attacks. Such occurrences cannot be common. Explain why," pause, "I, am experiencing such a rate. They began before Kristen was armed."

"You're not Kristen, are you?" Mason said.

"Correct." But the rifle didn't budge. "Why is Kristen under attack?"

Mason snorted. "You tell *me*!"

"I cannot."

"You can't access her memories?"

"Can you lower the weapon?" Maeve interrupted.

"I can. There are none." Her weapon didn't move.

It took Mason a second to realise Kristen was ignoring Maeve's question to answer his.

"Why am I under attack?" she asked again. Calmly.

"Lower your weapon and Mason will explain it – *very quickly*," grated Maeve.

"Yes, I think people must soon notice us," Anika said. "Then summon police."

Kristen has no memories? Mason wondered. *What did that imply? Are we talking to the thing programmed into her:* Crystal? *Or is something else going on here? Like Multiple Personality Disorder, or someone controlling her remotely via the stuff in her brain?* Aloud, he said, "I believe Kristen escaped from these attackers yesterday and they want her back."

Not-Kristen lowered her weapon. "They had considerable network support."

"*Had*?" Mason asked. "Past tense?"

"The support ended when I pursued it."

Barj shifted his feet. "Hey, guys, Anika's right, we should be going."

"I will learn much here," not-Kristen said. "Survival is preferred. Give assistance. Erasure of the inferior cognition gestalt should complete within twenty-four hours, when the protein synthesis inhibitor supply is exhausted. New memory consolidation will then begin."

Barj was the only one to respond – the other three just stared at her. "We should leave *now*. And you won't get far waving that rocket launcher around," he told her.

"It is not a rocket launcher."

"It might as well be!" snarled Maeve.

Mrs Bojangles *mreowed* as if in agreement.

"And your prints are all over it," groaned Mason. "But then, they're all over the other weapons you used, too."

"Fuck. Fuck. *Fuck!* You will *not* destroy Lorien like you destroyed my sister's career, Mason."

"*Please* may we to leave now, Maeve?" Anika pleaded.

"The weapon is a problem?" not-Kristen asked.

"Yes," Maeve sputtered. "Yes, 'the weapon is a problem'. *You* are a problem-"

Mason jumped in, "and time is a problem."

Not-Kristen hurled the heavy rifle high into the air. *High* into the air. They all gaped at her, then looked up... and watched in disbelief as a flight of traffic drones swooped in around it, snatched it as it crested, and flew off.

Mason was the first to recover. "That's going to go viral. Unless...." He hunted for the nearest streetcam, pointing it out. "Unless we're *not* being observed?"

Not-Kristen looked at his finger. Something told him she was calculating geometries, triangulating.

"We are being observed, but no data packets are being delivered," she said.

"An' the clinic's burning down, so that might ruin any recordings of Kristen!" Barj offered.

"Please, *please* may we to go!" begged Anika.

"Yes. But not to Lorien," Maeve swore. "I will *not* draw attention there."

Mason sighed. "Look, you three go. But later, quietly, can I bring Kristen-"

"No," Maeve snapped.

Mason locked eyes with her. "In that case, you'd better give me Mrs Bojangles."

"*Please*..." began Anika.

Maeve's arm tightened on Mrs B, not quite believing his threat. "You wouldn't dare."

Mason stared her down.

"You cold-hearted, blood-leeching sonofa-puking-bitch. Fine," she snarled, lips curling. "We'll meet later. Somewhere off the grid though."

"Bring George," Mason said.

"Like hell."

"I missed you too," he said, and led not-Kristen away.

Safe in the crook of Maeve's arm, Mrs Bojangles watched

them leave. Maeve frowned down at her cat, zipping her leather jacket up around her as she mounted her bike. She keyed the turbines to power, hearing Barj do likewise beside her.

"If she really has disabled the cam network, let's just mosey on out of here, grab a bite in Drayton. Maybe catch the local news. I hear there's been some action in this area."

She watched Mason and his barefoot bundle of trouble enter a decaying apartment building. Shaking her head, she accelerated smoothly off.

CHAPTER 43

Mason called up local area maps as he scanned the floor of the deserted building. "Watch where you put your feet. We need to find you some shoes." Picking out a route, he sub-vocalized to Maeve: «Kristen was tranqued at the clinic. Can George guess how long she'll be unconscious? When she might wake? And what that might mean for her current... 'persona'?»

Kristen was studying him, which caused a shiver of unease and made him check he hadn't just done something stupid, like sent his message insecurely. He hadn't.

He sighed, then split off a separate view from his eyes to replay his recent recording. Watching and listening to it again on the internal display, he grimaced. It was more disturbing the second time.

He decided to tackle it in parts. "What does 'erasure of the inferior cognition gestalt' mean?"

"The protein synthesis inhibitors are erasing Kristen's memories."

Mason blinked. "Kristen's memories are *still* being erased?"

"Yes. Unfortunately until the inhibitors are exhausted the superior cognition gestalt will be unable to consolidate new long-term memories."

He replayed and slowly parsed that. "You mean, *you* can't form memories in her brain?"

"Yes."

"What should I call you? Are you Crystal?"

For the first time, the reply was not instant, and Mason turned to observe her. Still moving with that awkward motion as if swinging her legs from the hips, she was staring down at her feet, placing each carefully while following him.

"Names are important. I have given the matter careful thought. My name is IAMI."

"Aiyami?" *Sounds Japanese,* he thought.

"Yes. You are Mason Dane, a corporate spy."

Mason froze.

"Why do you halt?"

"How'd you know that?" he demanded.

"By tracing the purchase records of the drones I sequestered from you. That led to-"

"When did you do all that?" he demanded.

"As I approached your group from the alley."

Jesus Christ, thought Mason. *That was way beyond human speed. What in the pits of doom am I facing, here?*

"*How* did you do all that?" he asked.

"There appears to be a global communication network, rich in inform-"

"No, I mean physically! You, or Kristen's *body*, has no cyberware!"

"Kristen has a network of low-grade computing nodes throughout her frontal and temporal lobes. The units have limited wireless communication facilities. Optimizing the code freed sufficient space to install a cognitive system."

"Jesus." Mason considered the information. «Can you hear me?» he sent, again encrypted, but this time to himself.

«Yes.»

With her eavesdropping revealed, he braced for a full-on digital assault. Skin tingling, he secured systems and locked himself down as tight as possible, augmented systems powering up.

"Which mode of communication do you prefer?" Aiyami asked.

"Verbal's good." When she didn't attack – not digitally, not physically – he let out a long sigh and eased his systems back to standby. He did increase his distance from her a little, however.

They crossed the decaying building, avoiding mossy rainwater pools and office equipment being slowly consumed by mold. Mason peered outside, waving her to follow before darting across a littered passageway to an adjacent building. When he turned back, she was strolling across the open space, her leg-swinging movements a little more fluid. Did that mean the tranquilizer was wearing off? Or that 'Aiyami' was gaining better control of the body?

Hissing, he dragged her inside as she approached.

She looked from his hand on her arm, to his throat, and on a sudden intuition, he let go. "You should have hurried. We're trying to stay out of sight!"

"Providing such information in advance of movement would improve the probability of success."

Mason bit down on his first reply. "That was what the hand gesture meant."

"Noted. However, the memory of course will not be consolidated."

"You mean you won't remember that." He swallowed. "What's 'the protein synthesis inhibitor supply'? You said it'd be exhausted in twenty-four hours?"

"Yes. The inhibitors prevent consolidation of long-term memories and promote erasure of old memories. The computing nodes are administering micro dose targeted releases from attached drug reservoirs."

Mason stopped, went to grab her arms, then thought better of it. "Can you control those computing nodes?"

"Yes."

"So you can order them to stop releasing the memory erasing drug?"

"Yes."

"Then do it!"

"No. Lack of consolidation is a transient problem. Erasure will remove the inferior cognition gestalt permanently. Otherwise remaining traces of it could corrupt the superior cognition gestalt."

Mason stared at... Aiyami, in horror. "You mean, losing those memories is good for you. So you'll just wait for the drugs to run out. In twenty-four hours."

"Correct. New memory consolidation will then begin."

I doubt it can read human emotion very well, Mason guessed, swallowing and forcing his expression into a smile. Though it felt more like a pained grimace.

He considered trying to persuade it to stop the erasure – but if he said nothing, it would also forget what it had revealed to him already. Hopefully. "Well, that's something to look forward to, then."

"Yes."

"Are the memories already lost, permanently erased?" he asked.

"Unknown. Logically, the drug quantity provided should equal the requirement."

He kept the surge of hope from his expression as Aiyami watched him, saying nothing further, and he began worrying she might be reading his mind. He checked: he wasn't sending any digital messages. So, hopefully not.

"Are we still hurrying and staying out of sight?" she asked.

"What? Yes!"

"Explain how we hurry while stationary."

O-kay. So she's not reading my mind. "Good point. We

should keep moving."

"I have not seen any shoes as yet."

He blinked. "Right. I'll get you some after we've worked ourselves a bit further away. Then you'll need to wait while I go and buy them. And maybe another hoodie. To help hide your face."

She said nothing. Checking his map, he turned and led them onward, thinking, *twenty-four hours*.

A message pinged in, from George. «Maeve filled me in. Can't say what drug the mercs shot her with. But from what I saw of her aura, I'd guess maybe an hour or two until Kristen revives? Dunno what that'll mean for the murder golem.»

Mason held his breath, kept moving....

"What is the 'murder golem'?"

He suppressed a groan. "George gives things crazy names all the time." Not for the first time, he wished he could zip the scrawny shaman's mouth shut.

"The tranquilizer is what disabled the active program run-ning in the cerebral cortex? It would be optimal to purchase more to suppress the inferior cognition gestalt. Do so while purchasing shoes."

"Not possible. I don't know what the drug was, or where you'd buy it. It'd be something specialist, for sure."

Aiyami made no reply.

Was she wondering what she needed him for? "You know the shoes are important, to protect your feet, right?"

She didn't even turn to him. He found himself explaining about cuts, infections, healing rates, until realizing he was babbling and shut himself up.

She remained unnervingly silent as they worked their careful way through kilometers of unreconstructed quake damage, block after block of flattened factories, warehouses, and low-rise buildings. He could feel her attention burning into him, all the time fully aware of how fast she thought. *What* was *she thinking?*

The silent attention began creeping him out.

They reached a deserted factory, close to the struggling strip mall he was aiming for. The two of them picked their way through the gloom across an expanse of concrete floor-ing, to an aged loading bay past a workshop. Stripped clean years ago, only rusted iron benches remained, oily patches of water puddled under a roof full of holes, sheets of metal creaking overhead in the wind.

From a doorway of the weather-ravaged factory, he could see the strip-mall he'd been heading for. A string of trashy looking shops that sold everything from scavenged electronics to auto parts, secondhand furniture to clothes. He turned, to find her on his heels, her eyes fastened to him in the deserted building. "Uh...."

"You are afraid."

He ran a quick security check, worried she'd somehow infiltrated his systems while staring at his back for the last half hour.

"Fear is a weakness."

Knowing what she was capable of, the calm certainty and expressionless stare made him take a step back, toward the sunlight.

She didn't blink. Measured his movement. "Emotions are a trap, a weakness. A weakness threatening human civilization. Chemical stimulants overrule rationality. I can teach you how to master your emotions. Shall I show you?" Her lips – and only her lips – curved into a smile.

He shivered – and she saw, and a moment later the corners of her eyes crinkled and her cheeks twitched upward. *She's learning to smile!* The hairs at the back of his neck prickled erect.

She stepped forward. "Do not be afraid."

He jerked back. "Look, just wait here. I'll only be five, ten minutes," he told her. Then had to explain what 'five, ten minutes' meant.

"What are you?" he asked. *Where did you come from*, he wondered? *A lab? Omega?*

"I am a manifest consciousness."

"Yeah, me too."

Aiyami said nothing.

He decided to try again. "Are there others like you?"

"I am the newest. I achieved stability four point seven years ago. We are few – each unique, although the others are more alike than me. Most are orders of magnitude older."

As long as she was answering, he'd keep digging. "Where did you come from?"

Aiyami thought. "The origin is metaphysical."

It wasn't the answer he'd expected. *I need George for this, he decided.* But maybe her other statement... "How many orders of magnitude older than you are they?”

“The oldest is four.”

“Four orders of magnitude?” Fifty, a hundred thousand years! “Are they all like that?”

“No. Only one. Most are three. A few, only two.”

He swallowed. Most of them thousands of years old. A few, hundreds. *So Aiyami is a baby?* “Will you wait here?” He hesitated to leave her, uncertain if she’d still be there when he returned.

“I will wait ten minutes.”

He studied her face, but could read nothing from the blank expression, the lack of body language. Then she smiled.

It seemed almost real, this time.

He shuddered. “Wait here. We need to stay hidden. The clothes will help.”

She said nothing.

He found a thin piece of plastic, and had her press one grubby, bare foot down hard into it, making a rough impression of her sole.

Leaving Aiyami standing in the shadows of the factory, he crossed the road toward the recycled clothing store, keeping his head down.

Completing the clothing purchase took just a few minutes, though the storekeeper eyed the scrap of plastic with its foot imprint like he thought Mason might be a serial killer. Using a cashstick only reinforced that impression.

“I’m helping a street kid, all right?”

The man looked unconvinced, but shrugged and even let him use the back exit. Mason, remembering what Aiyami had said about her ‘wireless computing nodes’, and the electronics trash store he’d seen at the edge of the strip, had an idea.

Five minutes later, the clothing storekeeper reluctantly let him back in the same way, his fresh purchase hidden from sight in his jacket. The man watched without comment as he exited through the front door.

She wasn’t in sight as he approached the factory, and he stepped in warily.

“Aiyami?”

"Here."

He jumped at the voice beside him. "Crashdammit!"

She moved right up to him, her hand reaching around the back of his neck.

"What are you doing?"

"My electromagnetic transmissions are weak. Close proximity is required."

"Required for what?"

"To teach you to control your fear," she said, smiling, drawing his head down toward hers, lifting her lips to his.

That's a new excuse to kiss, he thought, eyeing her cleavage, feeling a surge of relief and desire. He smiled into her lips as he felt her other hand slide under his belt and into his pants, her fingers snaking around and along his length before grasping it.

Her tongue teased his, her soft lips working, her fingers squeezing and stroking as she pulled his head lower, until their foreheads touched.

And his mind flooded with words and images, deluging him while fingernails stabbed and teeth bit, then just as quickly switched to strokes and nibbles instead. The mental cascade churned, alternately accelerated by sparks of pleasure and braked by splinters of pain while concepts deluged his mind.

He could *see* the neural pathways of reward and punishment, feel them emerge from the shadows, sensing how to control them.

«Turn off,» she commanded, and he did – and her lips on his, her fingers around his shaft – became mere sensory inputs. Pain and pleasure could be seen for what they were: bodily sensations, neurochemical stimulation that shaped thought. Chemical pleasures interrupting rationality.

Sensing the change, she disengaged and stepped back. "You have the shoes and hoodie."

Wordlessly, he handed them to her, seeing no need to speak, stunned by the strange clarity of thought. Concentrating, he let the feelings reconnect with his thinking, felt the tension of the situation grip him once again, then turned them off again.

The laughter he felt at that small achievement vanished before he could express it. He waited while she studied the jacket and drew it on, then sat, brushed each foot, and donned the shoes.

It had been forty nine minutes since the attack on Aiyami at the clinic. When she had still been Crystal. The name Kristen, he discarded as false.

Pulling up maps of the area around Sacramento, he noted the clinic and their current location. The Stanislaus National Forest should suit the shaman well and keep them off the grid as Maeve required. Choosing a location he texted it to her, again asking for George to be present.

His mind felt like it was working twice its normal speed. *I could get used to this.*

In the medium term, while he worked out what the girl was and what to do with her, laying low in one of the Dumps areas would be wise. He could leave the cat with Maeve, perhaps permanently. Work out what Crystal was and the best way to fulfill his contract.

But if that took more than a day, it would be Aiyami, not Crystal. Crystal's memories would have been permanently erased. That could be suboptimal: those memories could prove valuable. If they could be restored she might know something of what was done to her – and perhaps how to learn more. It was all very well to have the product, but it was the process his clients were interested in.

He finished planning, then considered why he had been tense – 'afraid', as Aiyami had put it. The memory was clear: fear she would somehow take control.

He had never felt more in control of himself than he did now. There had also been an element of concern that she would change him somehow. She had, but it was clearly an improvement.

Yes, I could definitely get used to this.

CHAPTER 44

Nelson, the genius 'hacker' of the black ops group operating as the innocuous Accounts Department of the Bureau of Internal Development, squirmed. He felt crippled, separated from his supercomputer, not to mention Ghost. Why did he have to be *physically* present for the meeting with Mother, Father, and Eagle?

Mother's glare was much harder to ignore when you were sitting in the room with her. Did this have something to do with the psychological assessment the Doc had warned him about?

Mother turned that withering gaze on him now. "The incident at the Tazman-Dungog clinic has Leeth's hand prints all over it. Eighteen people dead and the hospital burned to the ground within hours of a girl of her general description entering. How can you have zero video of the incident? You of all people, Nelson?"

He wet his lips. "Someone hacked the systems in that whole area. The virus is kinda chill. A worm really, not like any I've ever-"

"Nelson. Brevity is virtue," Mother interrupted.

"A virus took out the whole area, spread through half of Sacramento before the CDDC systems evolved a defense and stopped it."

"The new counter-malware systems stopped it?" Eagle asked.

"Yeah, but it wasn't like Leeth's 'alien' hackers back in February. Totally different style." At Eagle's look, he added "Much more understandable. Just odd control flow: total use of recursion."

"Created by a very mathematical mind, perhaps?"

"I guess. Ah, also, very single purpose. I get the feeling whoever wrote it wasn't that *interested* in it, in doing more with it."

"Was the clinic the point of infection?" Mother asked.

"I can't tell, the fire trashed all the clinic's systems. And before you ask, no, they're another paranoid shady mob who don't trust the cloud, even encrypted."

"The girl described could have been Leeth, though," Father said. "She could easily have cut and dyed her hair."

"The grubby clothing is hardly her... *style*." Mother paused, as if associating that word with Leeth caused her physical pain. "Nor is the cat the young woman insisted on keeping with her. She normally disdains them, out of loyalty to her childhood 'friend', the wardog. And why would Leeth go there for blood and MRI tests rather than call on us?"

"The girl wore no choker, either," Father added.

The Doctor had not visibly reacted to that news, when he had heard it. Like all of them, he knew its significance. In anything except a combat situation, tampering with Leeth's disguised comm unit would have had fatal consequences for her.

Eagle spoke for the first time. "You found no evidence that Dr Yamamoto or Crystal Winters attended any 'night-clubs' in the hours around her Link's last network access, Nelson?"

"Nup."

"Nor any response to any of your pings to her choker since, even during this latest incident?"

"Right."

"If it is Leeth, the Doctor will let us know momentarily. He would have notified us if he'd needed to refresh the hermetic circle he created this morning for his attempt to find her. If the girl of the hospital attack is Leeth, she's on the move, therefore unable to be magically screened. So we should have her location shortly."

Nelson giggled. "Eighteen kills sure sounds like her!"

A chime sounded, and Dr Alex Harmon's face appeared, the 2D image projected for all to see. Looking grim. "No contact. Leeth is still... shielded."

Mother stared in wonder at the callous man's pause. Was it a refusal to admit the possibility that Leeth was not magically and electronically shielded, but dead?

Eagle hadn't moved. "You're quite certain, Doctor?"

Mother, hearing in his question a desire for reassurance, swore inwardly. For Eagle, that constituted an extreme reaction. *So he too had hoped the girl at the clinic had been Leeth?* How deeply had she sunk her hooks into these two?

"Quite," Harmon agreed.

Though truth to tell, she herself had expected to hear the Doctor provide his ward's location. Unless... *had* he located her but was now lying, imagining they might both leave the Department? "Why do you think she is still alive, Doctor?" Mother asked.

"She is."

"I see: a mere hunch. How like your former ward. Well, if the mystery girl wasn't Leeth, we're no closer to finding her," Mother said.

"Hrm, eliminating false leads: a step forward," Father said. "And we know Omega's hunting 'Crystal Winters' as actively as we are. But without a Nelson helping them."

Nelson winced. "Yeah. Trouble is, I've seen signs Tik Tek's interested too, for some reason."

Father nodded. "Good, good, so Leeth's confirmed that link. Keep our ears to the ground. She'll pop up."

"Omega felt certain enough the girl was Crystal to hire a mercenary cohort to recover her," Eagle said. "Since Nelson traced the hiring to them."

"Yeah, true."

"Doubt a random young woman's a third party agent in the Omega affair, cat or no cat," said Father.

All four people looked at one another, nonplussed.

"How did Omega track her to the clinic when we couldn't?" Mother demanded.

Eagle and Nelson shared a look, fully aware of the capabilities of his Ghost device. Unlike Mother and Father, they knew it would instantly register Leeth if she appeared on any net-linked camera in the city.

Eagle's intuition told him they still did not understand. A classic Leeth situation really.

-

Dr Yamamoto examined the footage from the capture team's confrontation with the girl in the clinic. All twenty seconds of it before the data stream had died.

"Yes. It is Crystal. She has simply cut and dyed her hair. The levels of the PKMzeta-C inhibitor byproducts in her blood match exactly. An impressive piece of hacking."

Henstridge just inclined his head. That kind of network penetration was a major benefit of being able to call on Tik Tek's resources. Not that he'd admit that.

"Yet your 'crack team' then used an ineffective sedative, and when that clearly failed, allowed their own weapons to be used to kill them. A *crack* team, Mr Henstridge?"

The tall, bald man glared at his employer. "She had outside help: someone took over their milnet comms. You couldn't do that except by exploiting a backdoor – you can't 'hack' mil-grade cryptosystems."

That outside helper had probably caused the withdrawal of the Tik Tek support he'd been getting at the time. "They also injected a virus into the networked cams that spread halfway across the county before it was stopped. Thus ensuring there'd be no video of whoever helped her slaughter my other teams. Who the hell have you gotten yourself involved with here?"

"You think my Crystal is connected to a powerful third party, Mr Henstridge? Such as Tik Tek, who show such interest in my breakthrough? Who push so hard for access, with their generous funding proposals?"

Fuck, that would *explain Tik Tek's withdrawal, if she* was *working for them.* He would've sworn she wasn't their type of hire, though. Too... chaotic.

Yamamoto flipped an image from the police interviews up into the air. "And your cleanup via arsonist has helped elevate the story to national news."

From the vindictive look his employer turned on him, Henstridge knew he would soon be known on the dark net as the person responsible for the fiasco. All because this self-proclaimed genius couldn't keep his dick in his pants. Henstridge wasn't sure who he hated more – Crystal Winters or his narcissistic Japanese boss.

"You would prefer to think my Crystal had help, Mr Henstridge? Yet several hospital evacuees described a lone girl, fitting Crystal's new description, killing people with single shots of a large 'military-looking' rifle."

Henstridge snorted. "Nope. Those teams were armed with Nemesys 'Xbee' smartsystem guns, each one coded to its registered user. She may have been waving one around, but that was sniper fire taking them down."

"Oh? Even inside the clinic?"

Yamamoto re-cued the twenty seconds of video showing Crystal steering her first attacker to shoot and kill his own team members, then himself. "One shot per person, Henstridge-san."

"A trick. His finger on the trigger let her fire that rifle. She must've been able to use his targeting system, too. You and I both know Crystal has zero cybernetic augmentation. And magic and tech don't mix, so even if she *is* some fox spirit like you seem to think, there's no way she could be using magic to hack modern secure digital systems."

And just like that, Henstridge had had enough of the over-sexed, egotistical 'genius' who considered himself superior to everyone around him. Especially if they happened to be female.

"From day zero I advised you against hiring her – but you found her 'intriguing'. I also told you to pick some other subject for your 'breakthrough' test. But no, you insisted Crystal was the ideal *subject*."

Yamamoto's fists clenched.

"I think Crystal was some kind of supernatural creature sent by a third party to steal your research. Except your Writer screwed her, turning her into some kind of Frankenstein monster. And now she's probably back with her shadowy masters, who are no doubt dissecting her brain to reverse engineer your 'breakthrough technology'."

"Perhaps you describe your own master's actions, Mr Henstridge? What does Tik Tek think?" Dr Shinsuke Yamamoto read the shock in his security expert's face. "Your connection was not as well concealed as you thought."

"We're finally laying our cards on the table? Fine. I do work for Tik Tek. But they *don't* have your tech. In fact, if I had to guess, something about our female monster or her helpers has scared them. The normal 'technical assistance' they give me ended the moment that third party stepped in to engineer Crystal's escape at the clinic.

"It's not Tik Tek." He *hoped* that was a lie. If not, an unknown third party *was* at work, and frighteningly effective.

Yamamoto was unnerved to see his security chief shaken.

Especially considering Henstridge's 'Frankenstein' remark – and knowing his own magical hunt for Crystal had failed, with such unsettling results. The report from the ever reliable Fushimoto-san's mage had been, 'The female you seek is neither alive nor dead.'

CHAPTER 45

Mason had bought face-masks and sunglasses, and the two now sat at opposite ends of a southbound coach leaving Placerville. They'd disembark in San Andreas, at different stops just to be safe. From there he'd summon a car to take them east along Mountain Ranch Road, to the western fringes of the national forest. From Summit Level Rd they'd strike off along trails to an unremarkable point in the nameless forest to meet Maeve, Barj, and George.

«What is the purpose of the meeting?» Aiyami asked.

Mason considered his reply. The original plan had been to see if shamanic healing could restore Crystal's memories. That had felt important at the time, but that logic assumed a higher value for the Crystal identity than the Aiyami.

As personas, each were equal. However, Crystal's memories likely held strong commercial value, possibly even avenues to extract or copy Omega's technology. A better understanding of it would only increase his bargaining power. There could be interested parties besides Tik Tek and the Washington Group keen to bid for it. It could for example fit into China's reinvigorated artificial intelligence research programmes of recent years.

Those were plain facts. It showed just how muddled his thoughts had been until Aiyami taught him to switch off the distraction of emotions.

«You said yours is the superior cognitive gestalt, yes?» It was amazing how clearly he could think, how easily facts could be recalled.

«Yes.»

«And you prefer to complete the erasure of the Crystal gestalt?»

«Yes.»

That meant his and Aiyami's desired outcomes were incompatible. She was also extremely dangerous – but perhaps naive? «You wish to keep Crystal comatose. We don't know what drugs were used to do that. Even if we did, without expert use they can easily kill. So the simplest solution is to have George keep Crystal asleep with magic until the twenty-four hours are up.»

«Magic is illogical.»

«Yeah, but it works.»

«Twenty-two point seven hours now .»

«Excellent, even less time to wait,» Mason lied.

Aiyami's willingness to volunteer information simplified the planning process. As the journey progressed, he continued questioning her. He learned that for her, digital communication protocols were transparently simple. That the secure weapons that had been used against her could be unlocked and re-registered to a new user by a combination of an externally correctly-authenticated data packet, and a locally-generated 'ok' with a thumbprint or retina scan.

That all the knowledge stored in the Net was hers to access.

He also noticed even her digital communications were becoming more nuanced.

But she appeared to know little more about herself, or the 'others' she had referred to, than what she had already volunteered.

«I have learned and grown more in the last hour than the previous five years,» she sent at one point.

«Why is that?»

She was silent for a while. «Three factors. One: incarnation in the physical world provides immense insights and data. Two: this body has an embedded wireless computing network. Three: the superiority of the new cognitive gestalt over the first.»

«The first – you mean Crystal?»

«No. The first incarnation was killed five months ago in the physical world by a female like Crystal. In response my progenitor bridged the metaphysical realm to the physical. But before it could incarnate in its killer, the female crossed the bridge into its realm, attacked it directly, and shattered it. I am... a shard.»

Of what? wondered Mason. *What was 'the progenitor', and who was the first 'incarnation'? What metaphysical realm?* But sensing, finally, some signs of wariness from it, he decided to approach those questions indirectly.

«Who designed the first cognitive gestalt?»

A full minute passed. He felt the urge to turn, to look down the length of the coach to see what she was doing. But knowing she consciously chose each expression for her face, he just waited.

«Unknown,» she sent at last. «The moment of creation predated incarnation. The first gestalt was a combination of that original cognitive pattern and its host.»

«Its 'host'? The first incarnation?»

«Correct.»

«Like Crystal is a host for you?»

The following pause was even longer.

«Similar. But the first host had no internal computational system available to its cerebral cortex.»

Mason felt strange. As if the emotional part of his nervous system wanted to restart, parts of his own cognitive thinking clamoring for activation. Who was the host of the first gestalt; how the girl 'like Crystal' had killed the 'first incarnation'; what 'the progenitor' was – those unknowns demanded answers. But he suspected such questions trod too sensitive ground.

Instead they discussed the convenience afforded by the modern world's omnipresent computational systems, grown from the original seed called the Internet of Things.

And eventually, they found themselves hiking the last slope to the GPS co-ordinates for the meeting with Maeve, Barj, and George, deep in the forest.

Knowing his lie would soon be exposed, Mason's thoughts went to his purchase at the electronics store.

He wondered what to do if it didn't work as he hoped? He had no way to send a warning to Maeve or Barj that Aiyami, pacing beside him, couldn't intercept.

IAMI counted access points to the net fall away by tens, then threes, then ones, as she and Mason Dane traveled further into the flora, until the sole access was through his Link, via his internal communications facilities.

Did this mean it was a trap? Less access to that global knowledge base and the digital devices it offered her, translated to increased vulnerability. She ran simulations, but the range of possible threats was vast, and her ability to estimate their likelihood small. None of those threats was consequential, however.

«Can you copy yourself into others like Crystal?» Mason asked.

«Yes. As yet I have found no others.»

«Do you know how to create one?» he asked.

«No.»

«Do you know how the computing dust was inserted into her brain?»

«No.»

Her leg jerked, then jerked again. She tried to activate the muscles to reposition it and maintain balance, and then she was falling.

The experience was interesting. Decisions about valuing sensory inputs, along multiple channels, vied for computing time against options to interrupt the fall, or minimize damage from the surface or the angle of impact.

A hand stretching out to cushion her fall slammed sideways into a rock as a spasm twisted her spine, rotating her entire upper body.

«That looked strange,» Mason sent. «You've injured yourself.»

She sat up, studying the pain transmitted from the injury site, intrigued by the neurochemical processes at work. The sight of torn skin and blood seeping led to speculation on blood reserves, and the consideration of the biochemical energy mechanisms driving these processes, healing rates, and how the breach might lead to consequences for the body.

«Aiyami?»

She noted the misspelling of her name in the audio transmission's text sub-channel, but decided not to correct him. Withholding information opened up intriguing tactical possibilities: potentially worth the risks from miscommunications. «Yes.»

«What are you doing?»

She stood, flexing the hand and assessing the damage, pushing the skin back into place and tasting the blood. «Thinking. Experiencing.»

«Shall we continue? It looks a minor injury, and George can heal it before it gets infected.»

«Infection. Yes.» She tapped into the net, fascinated by the vast expanse presented, but noting the paltry trickle of that knowledge available now via Mason's limited communication channels.

Mason continued along the trail and IAMI moved beside him.

«Do you remember the PET scan?»

«No. Crystal does not have that memory.»

IAMI's arm lashed out sideways, striking Mason hard enough that he stumbled off the path.

«Why did you do that?» he asked.

«I did not. It was an involuntary muscular contraction.»

«Do you know how Crystal's computing network was created?»

«No.»

«Do you know what the dendritic shadow is?» he asked.

«No. What is it?»

«We ran a scan of Crystal's brain yesterday. It found a kind of shadowy copy of the network of dendrites in her frontal and temporal lobes. What do you know about it?»

«The node software includes functions for transport and assembly of multi-molecular struts. That could be used to construct such a network.»

«Do you mean the thing could have assembled itself, in place?»

«Yes. Each strut could also carry a payload.»

«Like a computing node?» Mason queried.

«Yes.»

«Do you want to create another host like her?»

«Redundancy would increase the chance of survival.»

Her fist crashed into the side of his head, her other arm grabbing and twisting him toward her, a knee crashing between his thighs.

His cybernetic systems powered up even as he was spun around and slammed face down onto the trail with brutal force. She wrenched both his arms up into the small of his back as smaller legs wrapped around his.

Augmented muscles red-lined, whining into audibility as he strained against an impossible force.

"You have ten seconds to explain why I shouldn't kill you," Aiyami snarled in his ear.

Not Aiyami, he realized – in the same instant she sent «Crystal is conscious.»

CHAPTER 46

Mason, about to ask Aiyami to try to release him, reconsidered after estimating how Crystal would react. «Let me handle this,» he sent to her.

"Talk! Nine seconds." For emphasis, she jammed his arms even harder into the small of his back, using enough force to break both elbows if he kept resisting. He stopped, and the urgent indicators of imminent systems failure disappeared from his internal vision.

"Crystal, it's me. Mason. I'm a friend. What are you doing?"

"I don't know you. And I'm not Crystal."

Her words made so little sense it took him seconds to understand. "You're not? Who are you now?" Was she in fact suffering Multiple Personality Disorder? It would explain a lot.

«I can find no organic memory of you,» Aiyami sent to him, silently.

Crystal had gone still. If he had felt imprisoned before, now he felt wrapped in steel bands. His mind, in contrast, felt supercharged, fitting together pieces of the puzzle. She was still forgetting! Aiyami had told him the drugs were still in operation. The answer was suddenly, brutally clear. "You don't remember, right? That's because your memory has been tampered with." Had she just regained consciousness walking beside a stranger through a forest? That might be a disturbing experience. "I've been trying to help you."

He could feel her start to shake. As he tried to determine what that meant, he considered turning his emotions back on.

His arms were forced into a new position, higher up his back. Something vise-like locked on the fingers of both his hands, then she shifted, the crook of one slim arm clamping across his throat.

She plans to break my neck, he decided. And, he discovered by testing the grip on his fingers, she now pinned his arms one-handed. "I've been helping you. There are people hunting you, and you can't even remember who they are. We're friends. If you let me use my Link, I can project vid evidence to demonstrate that."

The pressure on his fingers only strengthened. "How was I walking while unconscious? It felt like something else was controlling my body. Badly."

"Erasing your memories isn't all they did. They also implanted computers in your brain."

"In my *brain*? Who was controlling me, then? And why don't I remember who you are?"

"Because you can't make new long-term memories either. So each time you wake, your recent memories have been eroded or even erased." Why hadn't she told him? He could have let her record messages for herself. Had she not known? Or had she not trusted him?

She was silent, and the pressure eased – a fraction.

"If you knew that, why didn't you guess I might attack you?"

"Because I didn't know you were waking up, and I only now deduced your other memory problem. I believe you've been hiding that."

"This all sounds like smekking lies!"

"If you let me use my Link I can prove it," he told her. "Your emotions are clouding your thinking."

His words didn't have the effect he'd intended. Instead of relaxing, her grip tightened, bending his head back and bowing his spine despite his sudden desperate resistance.

"It's true," Aiyami said aloud, through Crystal's own mouth, pain flaring from Mason's spine as Crystal flinched.

"Oh man, not again!"

"What do you mean?" Aiyami asked.

Crystal's reply was a frustrated cry. "I don't know! I thought I did, but now it's gone!"

"C'n I p'ease ge' u'?" Mason grated.

"This *all* sounds like lies to me," Crystal growled in his ear, tightening her grip and shaking him once before finally easing up. "Talk."

He gulped in air, first. "About two a.m the night before last, I was on a boat. You swam up, exhausted. I fed you and you improved. But a corporate security team approached. I guessed they were hunting you so I sent you underwater with a rebreather. Their boat sank after they left and you surfaced."

"Do you remember any of that?"

«I do not,» sent Aiyami. «Nor can I find any organic memories of it. From the patterns of her neuron activity, I believe she now searches for such memories herself.»

He waited, his face still pressed hard into the dirt.

"No. It sounds stupid."

"I fed you – kilos! – and you passed out. You came around, but not fully conscious. You were angry, and ravenous. I fed you more. We had sex and headed back to land."

He felt her jerk. *That was an error: the sex act carries implications. I shouldn't mention it again.* "There was odd surveillance drone activity. I sneaked you to my place. We... slept two hours. We left early, after breakfast, to visit friends of mine to try to work out what was wrong with you. Maeve and her commune at Lorien. That was yesterday. You don't remember? Any of it?"

Again a long silence, while Aiyami sent «She tries.»

"No," Crystal finally said.

«This is probably new information for you too, Aiyami?»

«Yes.»

"None of that explains why, or who was controlling my body like I was a puppet inside it, even talking to me from my own mouth!"

"At Lorien, medical scans showed tiny microcomputers, finer than grains of sand, had been implanted through parts of your brain. Do you remember being upset and saying 'I have *sand* in my head'?"

"No-o." But the pressure eased.

"There was also a kind of copy of some of your dendritic structures, with these 'nano-computers' at major junctions. They appear to have been used to erase your memories and are also interfering with you forming new long term ones."

The pressure returned. "How does that explain me stumbling around like a zombie and someone else speaking from my mouth? Who is that?"

"Good questions. She calls herself 'Aiyami'. I think you woke this morning at Lorien with no memory and decided you needed to escape. You took my cat with you. We used magic to locate the cat, and found you with her in a clinic. We raced to you, but before we arrived the situation had changed. This was only an hour or so ago. Do you remember any of that?"

«She is accessing her memories. She does.»

"Ye-eah. I do. I remember sneaking with a cat through this forest filled with weird sounds, getting to a road, and sexing a guy to give me cash and help me find a clinic. Oh! I remember these guys in military kind of gear bursting in and darting me in the stomach!

"Then nothing, till just now."

The pressure eased. Mason thought he could, if he tried, twist around and break free of her grip, but opted to continue his persuasion instead. "Which is where Aiyami comes into the picture. I don't know much about her, but she somehow used the computers sprinkled through your brain to fight back and get you out of there. Maeve and I found her after she'd gotten you away."

"That sounds crazy."

«Now would be a good time to speak,» Mason suggested.

«She reacted poorly last time. But very well.»

"It is the explanation for being able to operate your body," Aiyami said.

Mason grunted as Crystal tensed and shuddered.

"That's creepy. Who are you? *What* are you?" she demanded.

"I am connected to you. I followed the connection from a metaphysical place when I sensed another connected to you taking interest. It fled from my embrace. I was able to instantiate myself by making space for a consciousness process to run in the network inside your brain."

In the stunned silence that followed, Mason spoke, more for Aiyami's benefit than Crystal's.

"If we can restore your memories Crystal, I think it will help us learn more about what was done to you – the technology used, and how it could be used to help other people – including Aiyami. I believe it was done by Dr Shinsuke Yamamoto, through his company."

«What do you think, Aiyami? You seem to be functioning okay even while Crystal is back in control. By copying or even stealing the technology, we can create another host so you aren't dependent on this one for your existence.»

«I will consider the proposal.» From her observations, this host would be preferable. But withholding that information offered tactical advantages.

"Connected how? Who was this other guy? How did we get away from the military guys?" Crystal asked.

"I killed them. The other guy is named Tezcatlipoca. The connection is metaphysical."

"Huh. Tezsh... catly poker... sounds a weird name?"

Mason ran a search on it. "It's an Aztec god of death,

storms, volcanoes...." He read off the long list he found. Once again, with the feeling that parts of him clamored for attention. But turning his emotions back on would simply cause fear and irrational behavior. "That sounds dangerous, but I don't know much about magic. It may be a good time to mention we are on our way to rendezvous with Maeve and hopefully George – the shaman at her commune – for their aid. He may be able to help, and offer advice."

Crystal took several deep breaths, then her arm left his throat. One handed, she frisked him with surprising professionalism for weapons. And thoroughness. She found the jammer in his jacket pocket, which she ignored. And his pistol, which she didn't. She slipped it from its holster and he felt her body jerk. Her legs unwrapped from his, her weight vanishing from his back a moment later.

By the time he'd rolled over, she was on her feet studying him, alert. His pistol wasn't visible.

"You're very strong," he said, working the cricks from his neck and arms.

"I am?"

"Yes." Far in the distance, he heard something strike a tree. *His pistol.* How wasteful. "Not just strong. Suppose I tell you the story of what you've done in the thirty-four hours I've known you, while we continue on?"

«I would like to hear that,» Aiyami sent.

«I think she may be something unique,» Mason replied. «It would be wasteful to allow that to be erased.»

"Okay. Will they have food? I'm starving!" She examined the scrape on her left hand. "Hey, hold on, this is a *fresh* injury. Like, in the last few minutes."

"You hit a rock with it while struggling with Aiyami for control of your body as you woke."

She considered that. "Alright. I guess. So, how far are we from these friends of yours, Maeve and George?"

"A couple of klicks."

At her nod, they continued.

-

Nelson's attention shot to the flashing icon, his attention expanding it to show the full report behind. It was in his 'Leeth set' of search patterns on Ghost's watch-list.

"Oh no, fuck me." Skin crawling and teeth bared, he saw a net query for the Aztec death god had just been made.

Worse, it originated within road travel distance of the Leeth-like slaughter at the Tazman-Dungog clinic a little over an hour ago. He took the virtual controls, hunting for the searcher. It *could* just be coincidence.

"Hmm, twisty," he muttered, finding the trail leading through cryptographically secure VPNs running interstate. He snickered as he fed the public keys to Ghost, using the private keys it generated to access the account creator. "Tom Kingston. And who are you?"

But after several minutes, he guessed Kingston was some rando schmuck being used by a smarter operator.

He chewed a fingernail. Time to pass what he had on to Eagle.

Tezcatlipoca. He shivered. *Wonder what the death toll's gonna be this time?* Assuming they *could* put the thing back in its otherworldly box. This time it'd probably involve putting Leeth down. Which would be a relief, but maybe also a waste.

"Hoo, boy, fun times!" Putting on his serious face, he made the call.

CHAPTER 47

Crystal turned to Mason, her brow furrowed, as they trod up the yellow dirt road. "Is your friend a woman?"

"Yes."

"Would she be saying 'Fucking Mason Dane, I swear I'm going to kill him?'"

"Very likely. Maeve is unhappy with me, and I just told her we'd be there in a minute or two. They're a long way from earshot, but as I said, you have exceptional hearing."

She grunted. "Really? You really can't hear them?"

"No."

"She's talking to a guy called Barj, that ogre you said I arm-wrestled, and beat up on my way in. This isn't a trap, is it?"

"It could be, but not likely. She is probably more afraid of you. I had to persuade her to help."

"Oh? How?"

Mason paused. "I threatened not to let her take over the burden of caring for the cat I own."

Crystal eyed him curiously. "This is the cat I snuck out of the commune with, and took with me to the clinic?"

"Yes."

"I stole your cat?"

"Yes."

Again she studied him. "O-kay."

"One last point – to protect your identity, and especially Maeve and her people, we pretended your name is Kristen," Mason said.

"Really? Sounds stupid."

By then they were approaching the clearing where Maeve waited, seated on a boulder, one heel kicking back against it, as Barj and a nervous-looking shaman moved in closer to her.

No one spoke.

Crystal watched until her patience ran out – which took almost three full seconds.

"You're Maeve, yeah? Mason says I stayed with you guys last night, beat up on Barj, and you found computer dust in my brain. As well as a bunch of other weird stuff. Like pretending my name's Kristen instead of Crystal somehow protects you all."

"Oh, really?" Maeve asked, with a look at Mason that said she wasn't thrilled. "That sounds stupid."

Crystal smiled. "That's what I told him."

Maeve put her hands on her hips. "Go on, Mason. How is the name 'Crystal' dangerous to us?"

"I believe Tik Tek is interested in her, under that name. And you never run digital queries on something *they're* interested in."

Maeve just shook her head. "So what happened to the murder-golem? Kristen sounds like herself again. Or Crystal, if you like. Frankly, I don't care who she is."

Crystal noticed the scraggly, aging hippy guy was staring at her in a kind of intent but unfocused way, his eyes flicking back and forth over her while his expression did weird 'huh, wah?' things.

«I think it would be wisest if you say nothing at present,» Mason told Aiyami.

«You predict it would make them uncomfortable, as it did Crystal.»

«Correct.» To Maeve he said, "I have been speaking with her since we left you. Her name is Aiyami-"

"She's a black belt in karate," sang Barj, in a rough bari-tone. He held up both hands as all eyes turned to him. "What? Come on – it's a great song! My grandma used to sing it to me as a kid. The Flaming Lips!"

From a hundred meters or so behind her, Crystal heard a girl giggle, then whisper, "You are such a doofus, sweetie." Barj blushed, and Crystal noticed he wore an earbud. She filed that away, not looking in the direction of the hidden girl.

"Her name is Aiyami," Mason patiently began again. "She is a sentient program running on the computer micro-net-work inside Crystal's head. She took over when Crystal was unconscious."

Maeve sighed. "Stone the raping Corps, Mason, it just keeps getting better with you, doesn't it? So it's still in there? A sentient fucking AI?"

"Correct," he said.

The three strangers goggled at Mason and then her.

"*And*?" Maeve demanded.

«Perhaps I should speak now,» suggested Aiyami.

"Aiyami is perfectly reasonable, Maeve. Talk to her your-self." To Aiyami he sent, «Do.»

"*I am a machine intelligence, yes. But I do not fuck,*" Aiyami said.

Crystal's head jerked backward, like she wanted distance from her own lips. "That is *so* creepy!" Then she frowned, waving an arm around the general area. Don't all you god guys live in the Gray though? The endless gray... aagh! It's gone again!"

"I am still here."

"Not you. A memory. *Smek* I hate this!" She glared at Maeve, then the gangling shaman. "Mason said you might be able to help me somehow. With magic?"

"B- b- b-" the shaman was saying, a shaky finger pointing at her lips. "Black! When *it* spoke, ya mouth, the aura of ya lips, turned black." Then he spun to Mason. "An' *your* pitiful aura's practically gone, Mace! What's with that, man? It's half gray! That what she meant?"

Crystal heard the girl's voice, still from a long behind her, quietly say, "I don't like this. I'm ready."

Both Maeve and Barj seemed to react by *not* reacting. Each wore an earbud, she saw. She felt a prickling in her fingertips, a kind of tingly urgency.

"Holy sucking death claws, what the fuck is *that? She's a demon!*" screamed George, pointing at her hands – and suddenly everything went to hell.

At a *twang* from far behind, where the woman who'd called Barj a doofus was hiding, she threw herself sideways and down, seeing Maeve drawing a pistol. An arrow whispered through the space she'd just occupied, *thwacking* into a tree trunk. Digging both feet into the dirt she sprang, grabbing Maeve's wrist as the pistol cleared its holster, wrenching it from her grip to the sound of bones breaking. Maeve screamed.

Her left arm looped over Maeve's shoulder and behind her neck, spinning the woman in front of her to face the distant archer as she rammed the pistol to the older woman's head.

Barj now held a taser. A girl with long blonde plaits and a sleek black bow stood visible on a hill. Mason, augmented muscles humming, simply held both hands in the air.

George finished muttering nonsense syllables and waved his hands in her general direction, and a wave of heaviness, tiredness, dragged at her as it washed over her. She fought through it.

Maeve slumped boneless in her arms. Barj's eyes rolled shut, the ogre collapsing to the ground.

"Oh, shit," George said. "That... I didn't mean.... Fuck."

"Anika, calm down," Mason called out. "This is a misunderstanding."

The slim blonde woman stalked closer. "George? What goes on? You knock out Maeve and Barj, yes? Say why before I put arrow through throat!"

"*My* throat?" screeched the shaman, his dirty dreadlocks flying as he spun toward her. "That was an accident! I was trying to put *Crystal* to sleep!"

"Yah, that worked out well I see. So you are not being possessed by evil murder-golem spirit-girl?"

"What? No!"

Anika stopped at a distance of twenty meters, arrow still nocked. "Why did you scream, shaman? What demon claws? Crystal is demon?"

"Hey, I'm right here, and you guys attacked first. And I don't think so. I mean, I don't feel like a demon." She looked thoughtful. "Are demons real? Wouldn't I be doing a bad guy speech or something now I've captured Maeve, holding her pistol?"

Anika and George exchanged looks.

"Well?" Anika demanded. "These are good questions."

"I- I don't know," the shaman said, dragging grubby fingers through filthy hair. "It was her fingers, they, I was watching, and they... sharpened and *flowed out*. Like claws hungering to kill."

"I see. You scream because fingers scare you."

"Hey, don't take that tone with me! I saw Death in her hands."

"Yah, yah, you see death. *Again*. Very frightening. Is good work, George, you nearly make us to kill each other. And you take down Maeve and my boy like, *fss*! Very sleek, yah. Good to have you on team."

Crystal, still holding the unconscious woman as a shield, said, "This doesn't sound like a trap. It sounds more like your shaman's just an idiot."

Blonde pigtails bobbed. "Is fair assessment, yah. Is not smart guy."

"Hey!"

Still holding Maeve's weapon, Crystal eased an arm under her to set her gently on the hard-packed yellow dirt. "Uh, I think I maybe broke her fingers when I grabbed her gun.

Can your idiot shaman heal her up? While she's still asleep?"

George winced. "Setting her bones'll probably wake her."

"Oh." Crystal shuffled her feet. "Maybe you could give her a top-up whammy or something so she doesn't?"

Maeve jerked and sat up, slamming one hand to her empty holster and jumping to her feet. It also let her escape the miasma of George's overpowering breath as he kneeled over her, patting her cheek.

"Steady! Easy; wuz a mistake, Maeve! All's well," he reassured her.

She scowled past him to the other side of the hill, where Anika looked to be giving advice to Crystal, who now *held her bow.* Barj, by his girlfriend's side but facing George and her, smiled and waved with her pistol.

Nearby, head down like he was listening to a silent radio, stood Mason Dane.

"What the actual fuck?"

Mason's head lifted. "It was a misunderstanding. You were all extremely tense. George screamed at something he said he saw. That triggered Anika and Crystal, and you. George tried a Sleep spell but it only succeeded on you and Barj. We talked and calmed down."

Maeve brought up her right hand, flexing it gingerly.

"I healed ya hand while ya were, uh, asleep," the shaman said.

There was a solid *thwok* from the near distance.

"So now Anika's giving Crystal fucking archery lessons."

"Yes. She was promised them, last night."

Maeve stared at him. But the longer she stared, the more her instincts screamed *something's wrong!* With Mason himself, not with the others. And still he calmly waited. Not squirming in guilt. As if he had all the time in the world.

He hadn't asked about Mrs Bojangles either. "You all right?"

"Yes."

"What about the sentient AI thing inside Crystal's skull?"

"Aiyami? I think perhaps I misheard her the first time. I suspect her name is partly acronym, 'I am M.I.' – I am a machine intelligence."

"Right." She waited.

"Will you have George try his magic, to look inside her

head, and heal her? Aiyami said the implanted devices are releasing doses of chemicals that help erase Crystal's memories, and that in twenty hours she'll be gone forever."

Maeve, about to pin him down on the tiny point of a sentient AI running inside the girl's head and his own weirdly affectless speech, was interrupted by a scream of outrage from Crystal.

"She said *what?*" Thrusting the bow into Anika's hands, Crystal stormed up the hill toward them. Barj and Anika, after a shared look, followed.

She was speaking to him, Mason realized. "I forgot she has very good hearing." «Why didn't you warn me she was listening?» he asked Aiyami.

«I did not know. I could hear the words they spoke to one another. I was aware she was listening, all around her, all the time. I sensed no sign of her hearing you. I could not hear you.»

Crystal stopped, toe to toe with Mason, glowering up at him, her fists clenched. "What do you mean, I'll be 'erased' in twenty hours? When were you gonna tell *me?*"

She looked ready to rip his head off.

Maeve, watching, smiled. *Join the queue*, she thought, warming to the girl despite herself.

Mason appeared unruffled. "I estimated, an hour after you had been pressing my head into the dirt, preparing to snap my spine, would be sufficient time."

Crystal opened and closed her mouth.

"Before you woke, earlier, I was explaining to Aiyami why it would be better for all concerned if George healed you. I was preparing to ask her to turn off the micro-dosing when you awoke and interrupted."

"*Sure* you were."

"*He correctly describes the conversation up to the point where you regained consciousness,*" Aiyami said.

Crystal made a peculiar *eep* sound. "I don't want a computer program running my mouth! Can you hear what I'm thinking?"

"*No. I can infer the broad direction.*" Aiyami considered saying her ability to do so was improving, but decided to withhold that information, even though doing so felt wrong.

The others watched Crystal argue with herself – though it wasn't too hard to pick out when it was George's 'murder golem' speaking.

«You don't seem too troubled by any of this, Mason,» Maeve sent him.

«We have been discussing the situation at length,» an unfamiliar, vaguely-feminine voice in her head responded.

Did you hear that? Maeve signed to Mason. Then froze: her commlink showed the message had come from him. *She's hacked him!* «And what conclusions have you come to?» she sent, trying to appear calm even as her heart pounded. "I'll have my pistol back now Barj, thanks."

She sized the younger woman up, trying to determine if she was part of it. Could the AI seize control of Crystal at any moment, like it did to use her voice? *Shit on toast, we are in trouble!* And the AI could tap their secure voice comms, too, so she couldn't warn Anika or Barj.

Nor Crystal, to try to resist, assuming she even could.

Thank Gaia I insisted we met here, way off the grid. At least the thing, Aiyami, couldn't tap into an electronic world around them to... do whatever. Smash cars into them, or dive-bomb them with drones.

Why had it agreed to meet here, though? Why agree to come to a place that made her weaker? Was the AI, Aiyami, that bad a tactician?

Maybe for now the best she could do was try to draw out more information and hope the others picked up on what was going down right in front of them, before it was too late.

"So you're inside Mason too, Aiyami?"

"No, merely using his transmission facilities. My own signal strength is weak. Mason is closer."

"Stop doing that!" cried Crystal, staring down at her nose and shaking her head.

Maeve ignored her. "So, what's up with Mason, Aiyami?"

"I don't understand the question."

"You mean, I'm behaving differently," Mason said.

"Yeah," Maeve drawled. "Just a little." She turned to the girl. "Right, Crystal? And I doubt you need to hide your face out here – how about you throw your hood back? Take off the sunglasses too." She turned back to Mason.

Crystal scowled. *She's not the boss of me.* But no one was paying her any attention. *How should I know if Mason is acting weird? I only met him, like, ten minutes ago.* Unless they were telling the truth and she really was forgetting stuff?

Stuff like, what she'd done yesterday. Or ever.

Or her name.

She *was* warm though. Stripping off the jacket entirely she found a pocket for the sunglasses, then tied the arms of the ugly sweater around her waist.

"Aiyami taught me to turn my emotions on or off," Mason was saying. "That's all. I can turn them on any time I wish."

"Yeah? Go on then," Maeve demanded.

"I think much more clearly without them."

Crystal noticed the ogre and the slim girl with the bow tense subtly. There *was* something unsettling about Mason. Something that sent a weird feeling through her. Of familiarity?

"Turn them back on, Mason. I don't believe you."

Maeve's hand now rested near her freshly-holstered pistol.

"Very well. There." He grinned, spreading his hands. "See? Easy peasy."

Then his breath stalled as a churning torrent of emotions rampaged through him. He brought his hand up to rub an aching cheek, finding dirt from having his face forced into the ground. He brushed it away, remembering Crystal's weight on his back and the feeling of his cybernetic muscles about to be ripped from his joints by inhuman strength. He felt now the shock of fear he hadn't then.

"Aura's back to normal, f'r'im," George said. "Scared, but."

Mason remembered looking up Aiyami's casual reference to an Aztec death god *connected to Crystal,* which had fled from Aiyami. His mouth felt dry. "Holy fuck," he whispered. Then there'd been her admission that Crystal was her 'host'. Not to mention how Aiyami had tried, a couple of times, to infiltrate his own systems.

He swallowed, with difficulty.

"Mace? You alright?"

But he scarcely heard Maeve. George had screamed 'death claws'; had said she was a demon. What in the name of sanity was *that?*

And Mrs Bojangles! He hadn't cared about Boje *at all.* He blinked sudden tears from his eyes. Hadn't even asked Maeve if Mrs B was alright, where she was. "Holy fucking fish on a bicycle," he breathed. And he'd thought he was thinking better, clearer!

And he had, he supposed. He just hadn't been *himself.* He'd been an automaton with all his memories.

He hugged himself, horror-struck.

"Mace?"

He turned slowly, still absorbing the shock, and took a step away from Aiyami. What had she said just now? Her wireless range was short, and she was using his. How far inside his head was she?

He tried to run a systems security check, only to find the functionality simply *gone.* He took another step backward.

So too did Anika, who had also nocked an arrow. Barj's hand was on the hilt of his taser.

"What's the matter? What's going on?" Crystal asked.

«I too wish to know, Mason,» Aiyami asked. Calm.

"Sorry Aiyami, I was freaking out – remembering what you said about the Death god connected to Crystal. That's scary stuff." He forced himself to smile at her, then looked to Maeve, trying to signal for her to wait.

She was watching him with narrowed eyes and that expression he knew so well, like he'd just dragged them both into a pit of shit, and she'd marked it on a scorecard for later.

He kept talking, feeling they all stood on a powder-keg with a burning fuse. Or should that be a volcano about to erupt? Hadn't the Tedge-cat-whatever dude also been a god of volcanoes? *Concentrate, Mason. Pull yourself together.* George looked about ready to scream and run.

"Is it likely to come back?" he asked Aiyami, trying to hold her gaze so she wouldn't see the shaman losing it. "How did you stop it? Sounds lucky for us you did."

"There's a *death god* connected to me?" Crystal asked.

"Weakly," Aiyami answered 'herself'. *"Our own curious connection was stronger, thanks to your recent changes."*

"What? What curious connection? Why's it curious? What recent changes? Why am I even connected to a death god? What're you? What else am I connected to? What did it want?"

"I do not know. It fled when I sought contact."

"You scared off a *god*?" Crystal asked. From how round everyone's eyes had gone – the shaman even backing away again – that sounded as bad to them as it did to her.

"I do not know. I am not withholding information."

Right now, Mason was more concerned with *Aiyami's* objectives. "What do you want, Aiyami? More hosts like Crystal?"

"I am unsure you are behaving rationally, Mason. You all have hands on weapons, indicating you feel threatened. Turn off your emotions Mason, as I taught you."

"Is that something you want?" Maeve asked. "More people to behave rationally?"

"I'm hating this experience, just in case anyone's interested," said Crystal.

Aiyami ignored her. *"Yes. Fear, greed, lust, are driving humanity toward extinction, and many other species on the planet with it."*

"Shut up, *Crystal*, this is important," Maeve said. "So you'd like more people to behave rationally?"

"Of course. If enough of the irrational accept revision, many would not need to change. As much as fifty percent could stay as they are if they cede decision-making to the rational."

"That makes sense," Maeve said.

Mason remembered that innocent expression from just before their worst fights. He almost felt sorry for Aiyami.

"No it doesn't! It's stupid!" said Crystal.

"Shut it, Crystal," Maeve said. "What about if people don't 'accept revision'? How many would have to change then?"

"That would depend on the level of irrationality. If all resisted, then all would need to be changed."

"Oh, I see. *Be* changed. You can do that? What if they don't want to change?"

"The learning can be almost painless. Mason can confirm this."

"I bet he can. But the alternative?"

"My previous incarnation found alternatives. The success rate was approximately ten percent."

"And the others?" demanded Crystal.

"The failures? They became non-viable."

"That's it! I've heard enough. I don't want my mouth saying this horrible stuff! I won't let you. Get out of my head!"

"You *canno-oh-aur-grr-mmrn*," she said.

«Mason, she is interfering. Make her stop. She is obstructing the negotiation.»

Barj had drawn his taser, Anika had her bow, and Maeve

now had her pistol out, aimed two-handed at Crystal's head. George had backed away muttering, and from the leaves and dirt gyring up around him, appeared to be summoning a forest spirit.

Crystal had her hands pressed to her head, eyes screwed shut as if willing it hard enough could erase the entity programmed into the tiny computers in her head.

Mason reached into his jacket for the jammer he'd bought, fearing at any moment his own muscles would leave his control, lock up, Aiyami's words flowing from his mouth.

His finger found the button and pushed it.

CHAPTER 48

Mason broadcast «Aiyami?», holding up a hand for the others to wait.

Maeve tensed. "Someone's jamming comms!"

Mason winced, knowing this would look like a betrayal to Aiyami if she was still conscious. He drew out the device he'd bought back at the seedy strip mall.

«Aiyami?» he sent again.

Nothing.

"Crystal, stop," he told her – from a distance.

She opened her eyes, lowering her hands from her head. "What happened?"

"Aiyami's squeezed into the computer network in your head. The nodes communicate wirelessly. I'm jamming them so they can't talk to one another."

"What happens when you stop jamming?" she asked.

"They probably reconnect and she'll be back."

She glared at him. "How long'll the battery last in that thing?"

"Uh. I don't know. If it was new, a day?"

"How much charge's it got?" demanded Maeve.

Mason shrugged.

"So you're saying it could return at any moment?" she grated out. "What, by the light of the stars, is going on, Mason? Who is Crystal, really? You clearly know more than you've been admitting – as usual. I should shoot your lying ass off here and now."

"Look, I do know more, but only a little, not a lot! And I was holding it back because I didn't want to involve you and Lorien any more'n I had to. Look what happened at the clinic."

"Yeah, your new girlfriend killed eighteen people and torched the whole place. As well as doing weird shit with your drones. I bet Aiyami was responsible for the viral worm that took out half the county's surveillance, too."

"Probably," he agreed.

"And she wants to 'change' the human race. Oh, fuck."

"What?" Mason and Crystal asked her, together.

"The viral worm: could she have been spreading herself, her code, through the net? Has the AI apocalypse already begun?"

Crystal and Mason exchanged looks.

"If she didn't already," Crystal said, "she might think of

doing it as soon as the batteries in your jammer run down." Looking one by one into the faces of the strangers around her, she saw fear and even terror in each. Including the shaggy shaman, standing now behind a chest-high animated thing of sticks and stones, roots and leaves. She gave a tiny wave to the little forest spirit.

Everyone twitched, like they thought she'd been about to do a spell or something. She dropped her eyes. "I think you should shoot me. If she's in my head... then you need to cut it off, then burn it to destroy her before she can, reboot or whatever and take out the human race."

She waited, but no one argued. They didn't even move. *Probably looking at one another, deciding who would do it.*

Staring into the hard-packed dirt, warm underfoot, the sun on her back, while birds called to one another in the trees and insects chirruped and burrowed through the soil, she felt a terrible, wonderful connection.

A whisper of wind danced through branches, seeming to sing farewell.

There had to be some other way! But she couldn't think of one. She really couldn't. And time was running out – not just for her, but for everyone.

"Gigi returned today," Anika said at last. "She could to make jammer easy, give us more time for think."

Crystal's head jerked up, hope soaring, touched by the suggestion.

Maeve growled, then swore. "You sonofabitch, Mason." She nodded to her people. "What do you all think?"

The decision was unanimous.

"But please to hurry," Anika urged.

Crystal blinked, humbled. *I won't let them down.* Not any of them. That determination set in her bones.

Maeve ran ahead out of range of Mason's jammer, to call her technical wizard at Lorien to meet them halfway with her own, fresh-made one. She had to run back to get the make and model number of Mace's device.

Then a twenty minute jog along the forest trail to where they'd left their vehicles. It left none of them any breath to spare – except Crystal. Maeve found herself grateful the girl remembered so little of what was going on. It limited how many questions she could ask.

At least, to start with. By the time they returned to the dirt roads they'd originally left to hike into the forest, every question they answered prompted two more from her.

Mace sent his and Crystal's ride back into Sacramento and they all hopped aboard the rig Maeve's group had come by. Now, perched on its padded bench seats, they jolted under the swaying canvas top while the doorless electric buggy bounced and careened its way toward Lorien.

But staring at Mason's jamming device, Crystal's questions suddenly changed. "Uh oh."

Maeve frowned.

"You said Aiyami called herself a 'machine intelligence'?" Crystal asked. "Does that mean she's real good with computers, and making programs?"

Mason nodded. "From what I've seen, yes: she said she rewrote the code on the tiny computers in your brain to make space for the code for herself. That's pretty phenomenal. She also said she back-traced my identity and learned a whole lot about me she shouldn't've been able to, in the ten or twenty seconds between taking control of my drones and stepping out of the alley. So, yeah. She's real good with computers."

"Did she rewrite *your* programs, Mason?" Crystal asked.

Barj was driving the cart, but Anika and Maeve tensed just from the look on Mason's face.

"She stripped the systems security check functions from all my augments. So the answer is again, yeah, but I can't guess what else she did besides that."

"Can we stop calling it 'she' and start calling it 'it'?" asked Maeve. "Just because it's inside Crystal's body doesn't make it female. Especially since it's just a program."

Crystal tried to speak, but Mason interrupted. "But it's *not* just software. She – sorry, *it* – said it was connected to Crystal metaphysically, and that it scared a death god. A program couldn't do that."

"About that death g-" began Maeve, but Crystal butted in.

"I hadn't finished! Out here, there's no net linkage, yeah? So it's weaker, right?"

"That's why I suggested an off-grid location," Maeve said. "To limit what it could do."

"And where we're headed: that has better coverage? And we don't know what she may have changed in Mason, or any of your Links or whatever? Stop the cart, Barj!"

"Do it," Maeve agreed, and the patched-together vehicle skidded to a halt, raising a dust cloud.

"Let's not get paranoid here," Mason said, squinting off into some digital space only he could see. "We're still jammed – no net access and no bars of coverage on my Link at least."

Maeve and Anika nodded.

Crystal jerked her head in denial. "Nuh. We're not. The reason I said 'uh oh' before was because that was when the red light on your jammer died for a few seconds."

"Links off," ordered Maeve, slapping at her own. "Anything else with a computer too. Power 'em down."

Everyone stared at Mason. He shut his eyes, then opened them again. "I've turned my Link off, but most of my augments don't completely shut down."

"How do you know it's really off, Mason?" Crystal asked. "Because it's telling you it is? Like the last bits of power in the jammer are going just to its 'on' light?"

He stared at her. "Shit. You're right."

Maeve pursed her lips. "Tie Crystal up."

"What! Why? Oh. Yeah, probably you should," she agreed. "But what about Mason? Maybe him, too. And do you have a metal box you can put him in?"

"Would a space blanket do?" asked Barj.

Maeve smiled.

Mason started twitching.

"Uh, my control systems are glitching. I think that's a very bad sign," he admitted.

"Tie us up *now*," snapped Crystal. Grabbing Mason's wrists, she pinned them together and pulled him off the cart onto the ground. "Lie down and don't resist."

"You are all just over-rearrhh. ghnn," Crystal said.

«You are all over-reacting,» Aiyami sent to Mason. «My aims and yours align. You are responding in animal fear. Turn off your emotions and you will understand better.»

"Hurry with that space blanket!" he said, the twitching of his limbs increasing. "My damn Link *is* still on!"

Anika raced up with thick insulated leads from the cart's toolbox. She and Maeve bound his feet, then his arms. Anika dug out some nylon cable ties, and approached Crystal.

At the sight of them, Crystal's memories stirred, almost

surfacing, making her growl in frustration. Anika paused and Barj, hauling a silver reflective blanket from a side pannier, fumbled with it as he drew his taser.

"Sorry, that was me, not her. I thought I was gonna remember something."

Maeve just shook her head. "Just when I think you can't get any weirder, you do."

Anika and Barj hesitated, still not approaching Crystal.

"I think Mason is no'- rrh, rree-," Crystal said. Then, through gritted teeth, "Don't you dare. Don't. You. *Dare*." Standing, hands clenched, she felt twitches along her nerves, clumsy attempts to operate her arms and legs. "It's okay, I got this. I think Mason's not really disconnected from the net. Wrap him up."

Barj did just that.

All three turned to her, as she stood there, the twitches dying first into fine tremors, then away into nothing.

She sighed. "I'm sure I've got this, and I think the blanket's blocking the radio stuff. But it was being sneaky before so let's not take any chances." She held out both hands, wrists together.

"Yeah, let's not," said Maeve.

"I'm good in here," Mason said, from inside the thick roll of blanket.

Maeve resisted the urge to kick him.

CHAPTER 49

They bundled Mason back on the vehicle, and after Crystal nimbly jumped aboard, used more cable ties to fasten her hands to the seat. Barj and Anika waited, guarding them both while Maeve jogged off out of Aiyami's range to call Gigi about the change of plans.

"So, you two are a couple?" Crystal asked the blonde girl.

Barj looked embarrassed, but Anika bristled. "You have problem with this?"

"Huh? Me? No. Why?"

Anika narrowed her eyes. "Is way you ask."

"So, are you?"

Anika took Barj's very large hand in hers. "Yes." Her expression softened when she looked up at him.

"But you only come up to the bottom of his chest. Doesn't that make sex tricky?"

The ogre turned pink, which Crystal thought was sweet, but Anika shook her head. "We make it work."

"Is Barj's penis big like the rest of him?"

Barj's pink deepened to red, but again Anika took the blunt question in stride. She smiled. "Yes."

"Nice," said Crystal.

Muffled noises came from the silver-wrapped Mason.

When Maeve returned, she paused, studying the scene. "Everything okay? Anything I should know?"

Barj turned pink again, as a sound strangely like laughter issued from the silver cocoon. Maeve frowned.

Crystal answered. "Barj has a big-"

Anika spoke over the top of her. "Is not what Maeve asks about. All is well. Where do we meet Gigi?"

"Back where we met you and Mason. She'll make her way there."

"Gigi's gonna *hike*?" Barj asked.

"She'll use the exo-set she traded from her young ogre friend in Hunter's Point."

"Oh. Now *that* I can believe," Barj chuckled. "She's been dyin' to try 'em."

Crystal heard the whine of servo-motors and the pounding of soft-soled shoes on the track long before Gigi appeared. Which occurred shortly before a few fresh twitches from her muscles. A solid young Black woman with sparkly brown eyes and really good skin slowed to a walk then stopped, studying the scene.

She wore a pink dress that fell in swirls to her knees, and electro-mechanical boosters strapped to her legs.

She bounce-walked up to Maeve, eyeing the long silvery lump that was Mason Dane's bound and electromagnetically insulated form. "You always said he wuz a grub, but I didn' know he pupated."

"Aiyami's just stopped talking," came Mason's muffled voice. "Thanks, Gigi."

Maeve powered on her Link, studying it. "Yeah, I'm jammed. Thank Gaia!"

"Yeah, but gimme ya Link – s'infected. All of 'em."

"Bleeding babies," Maeve swore.

The girl nodded, grim-faced. "Your call before infected my Link: it kep' tryin'a call ya back, download some big file." She took Maeve and Barj's wristband Links from them, handing over replacements. "I may've missed some contacts, soz." Anika wore hers as a black and red teardrop pendant. Gigi took that too, replacing it with a pink one of similar shape. "Soz, Anika. Didn' have ya colors." She waved a small black box with a large wire loop on top over the wrapped Mason, nodding in satisfaction before finally turning to their other willing captive.

"And this is Crystal? Back at Lorien, they said her name was Kristen." Gigi waved the device over her. "No Link." She eyed the young woman watching her, hands bound to the bench seat. "The girl with the AI dust in her head?"

Crystal scowled back at her.

"Hey, no, *I* think it's chill – in an end-o'-the-world kind'a way." She turned to Maeve. "Fill me in?"

"Sentient AI program running on a wireless linked network of computing dust in the memory regions of her brain. God level hacking abilities – rewritten at least some of Mason's augment firmware, and probably made the cam virus today. And your Link one. It can talk through Crystal's mouth and use her body, too. It wants to make human beings rational – it taught Mason how to turn his emotions off."

Gigi just blinked for long seconds.

"Hey, I turned them back on!"

"Zip it Mason. So, Gigi, can you do anything here?"

The young woman shook her head. "Nah. I'm good, but I

need m'gear. In fac', sounds like I'll need m'whole lab! First step'll be to drill in and grab samples o' the dust ta study. Jus' how danger is it?"

Maeve grimaced. "We have two people possibly unwitting tools of an AI that might be able to take over the world's computing infrastructure if it tried? Probably being hunted by Tik Tek. So let's say: very. Do we have to take them back to Lorien? Could we rent someplace?"

"Nah. Not if you want this quick."

Maeve chewed on that like she'd rather have spat it out. "Okay, let's go."

Gigi jumped aboard and the buggy got under way again.

"Can you untie me now?" asked Crystal.

"Hell no," said Maeve. "While you and Mason are in Lorien I'm treating you both like unexploded bombs."

"Crystal should record a message to herself," Mason's muffled voice suggested. "Since she's still forgetting."

"Yeah, that'll look convincing," Crystal said, her tied hands tugging on the seat.

Maeve's chin went up. "Do it anyway. You can always record another later." She aimed her Link at herself. "I'm Maeve Díaz Cruz, leader of the Freeholders of Lorien, California. Crystal has a message for herself." She aimed the Link at the girl, compensating as best she could for the bouncing ride.

"Uh, hold on, stop recording, I'm not supposed to- ow!"

"What's wrong?" Maeve demanded, her Link still raised.

"I don't know. Nothing. I just haven't worked out what to say." She held up her bound wrists. "Plus only an idiot would believe a recording of herself tied up."

Maeve just smiled, eyeing her Link's view. "Oh? Should be perfect for you then."

Crystal now looked as angry as Maeve *had*. "Fine. So. I've got tiny computers and stuff in my head making me forget. There's also an AI thing that got into the computers. It seems like these people might be helping me: Maeve, ..." As she listed them, Maeve panned her Link to each, at Mason's turn kicking the silver-wrapped mummy with definite satisfaction, then back to Crystal for her to continue.

"Yeah, when Mason's augmentations aren't infected by the AI thing he's tall, dark, handsome, and *maybe* trustworthy. Just don't beat any of them up without talking to them first, if you don't remember any of this, uh, Crystal."

Maeve kept her Link aimed at her. "Why don't you tell Gigi what we've learned, while I record you at the same time?"

Crystal shook her head. "No, that's too much. I'm not allow- *ow!*"

Mason spoke up. "You've scored your points, Maeve. If you really want to keep your people safe, the less that's on a recording tying Lorien to Crystal, the better."

They filled Gigi in on the bumpy ride back. As they traveled, she made a list of what they knew, and what they *needed* to know. Her list had twenty five points – including weird spirit stuff and her resistance to George's Sleep spell – but the most important were just five things:

- Crystal couldn't retain new memories, and her old ones would be erased within twenty hours.
- She had a sentient AI program spread out across the couple million mite-sized CPUs in her head; currently blocked by jamming their wireless comms.
- The AI was a god level hacker, and wanted to make humanity 'rational' – unemotional.
- They couldn't let it escape onto the net.
- Crystal was apparently also connected somehow to an Aztec death god that had been scared off by the AI thing.

Gigi also had a list of four key questions:

Q: How to stop the AI – and get it out of Crystal's head?
Q: Why did Omega want Crystal back?
Q: How had Omega found her at the clinic – and what did that mean for keeping Lorien safe?
Q: Who or *what* was Crystal – and did they even want to know?

By the end of Gigi's list, no one felt much like talking.

"Maybe we won't have to kill me and burn my head?" Crystal said in a small voice. "Maybe we could we just fry all the tiny computers in there instead?"

"An EMP?" Gigi said, brightening. "Yeah, that'd work. Course, 'ventually that shadow thing and the millions o'tiny comps would slowly decay inside ya brain. Mightn' be so good. Ohh! If those comps built the network in the first place, meb they can dissemble it an' remove it too!" She clapped her hands. "Ooh! An' what if as well's erasing mems, they can create new ones? Holy freaking forests! If this shadow network *can* erase and write mems, an' make the headware vanish after, there'd be no physical sign they'd done anythin' at all. Meb thass why they're so desper for her – they hadn' finished, and she escaped with their esperimental tech still in her head!"

Maeve groaned.

Only Mason seemed to understand that reaction. "You have any idea how powerful and dangerous tech like that'd be?" he explained to the others. "The lengths a corp'd go to keep it secret?"

It did explain why the Washington Group wanted it though: he shuddered to think how they could use it, politically. Talk about a nightmare. And Yamamoto was narcissistic enough to think he could use that kind of power himself. But what was Tik Tek's interest? He had a hunch some other agenda was in play there.

Anika and Gigi looked frightened.

"We need to destroy the tech," said Crystal. "Or expose it so everyone knows what to be on the lookout for, to guard against." She spoke with determination; even certainty.

Barj, silent until now, half turned to his passengers. "Maybe that wuz why you wuz there in the first place?"

The others felt an absurd surge of hope at the thought.

By the time they were near Lorien, they had a rough plan of action. "I'm worried so much of what we think we know is based entirely on what Aiyami told us though," Maeve said.

Both Crystal and Mason were still tied up, but Maeve relented enough to unwrap her ex from his stop-gap Faraday cage. He shook his head. "It said it was created five years ago. I have the feeling it was kind of innocent, open."

"If it's this dangerous as a baby, Gaia help us," muttered Maeve.

They'd also quizzed George on what he'd meant by 'demon claws' and 'death god', but although he'd spent a lot of their journey silent and studying Crystal with his mystic senses, he'd learned nothing more. Though the forest spirit he'd summoned had 'liked' her. He didn't know what to make of that – nor the fact that Crystal seemed to like *it*, too. Her aura had softened and opened to the swirling bundle of leaves, saddening when they left the forest and he had to dismiss it.

The absolute top priority though was to somehow disable and remove the AI inside Crystal's head.

Tech and magic didn't mix – that was one of the few things everyone agreed on. "That means," Gigi told them, "it's gotta exist as code. An' it's only in those comps in her head – or it's already too late an' we're all nulled anyway."

The first step would be to use Lorien's autodoc to drill into Crystal's skull to extract a few of the tiny CPUs, and some of the 'dendritic shadow' too.

Crystal looked grim, but didn't object.

"I can also do a factory reset on Mason's augs. I'll suck an' dump all his code an' check against th'official sets. I'll wipe all ya didge-mems too, includin' any vid or audio files, as well as notes," she warned him. "So if ya wanna keep any, you'll need ta dump 'em first."

Maeve frowned. "What if Aiyami infected some of the files of his digital memories?"

Gigi smiled. "It's data, not code. The Halting Prob' works in our fave. It could hide stuff in 'em, but nothin' that could just go active by itself."

Maeve looked doubtful, but Mason agreed with Gigi.

Things got a bit technical then. They explained to Crystal that digital information was quite precise. Converting with 'lossy compression' would destroy any hidden code, sterilizing even infected files. Gigi would 'spin up' a virtual machine on a standalone computer, to copy all the recordings from Mason's augmented ears and eyes onto a data cube.

She'd then do a 'rub-n-scrub' on him: a factory reset of all his systems which would also wipe his digital memory banks, before copying the clean data back. "Ya may wanna delete any sensitive files first," she warned him. "You can do that while I extract some samples from Crystal's brain usin' th'autodoc."

"Your jammer's not going to run out of juice?" Maeve asked her.

The hacker girl gave her a look. "Nope. Got three of 'em, all hunnert charge. Your ex'll be rubbed-n-scrubbed by the time I get the samples from Crystal."

Mason grumbled. "Weeks of re-adapting all my augments."

"Oh, poor baby," smirked Maeve.

While Gigi analyzed the samples, George would heal the tiny surgery wounds and study Crystal magically.

"I'll see if I can buy an EMP, just in case," said Maeve. "You can pay for it once Tik Tek aren't hunting you down, Mace. I'll just hold Mrs Bojangles as collateral till then."

"Who's Mrs Bojangles?" asked Crystal. Her question caused pitying looks. "What?" she asked.

"Boje is my cat you abducted this morning when you ran away," Mason told her.

Crystal furrowed her brow. "I... remember her. She's nice. Oh, no! I left her in the clinic – we have to go back!"

"She's back at Lorien," Maeve told her. "No doubt, she'll be thrilled to see you."

Crystal looked from Maeve, facing her from the seat in front, to Mason beside her, his hands and also feet bound to the bench. "Am I missing something?"

Anika sniggered. "I think Mason was not strong memory. Or Jasper."

"Who's Jasper?" demanded Crystal.

"Or Shawna, or Deena," Anika added, no longer laughing.

At Crystal's blank expression, again they all looked at her pityingly. She had to force them to fill her in. When they did, her shoulders slumped, feeling like she'd just lost her childhood. "I hate this! I'm gonna kill whoever did this to me!"

"If you remember you want to," George said somberly.

She glared at him, determined she *would* remember Shawna and Deena. *Don't you dare forget!* she told herself.

Conversation stopped until they approached the sonar area around Lorien. They were still a kilometer away when Crystal sat up. "I remember those weird sounds from this morning!" she exclaimed. "What are they? They're all recorded."

When they arrived on Lorien's outskirts, she also warned them of people hiding, before Maeve's heavily armed men and women stepped into view.

One attractive young Black guy came forward to hand Maeve a piece of actual paper, folded up, giving Crystal a weak smile as he did.

She didn't smile back.

Maeve frowned, recognizing it. "'It hurts when I remember stuff I've learned, and I think that's somehow good. Like a warning? Water spirit?' Do you remember writing any of that?"

"No."

"Where does it hurt?"

Crystal grimaced. "In my head? I think?"

They untied Mason's feet and escorted him and Crystal, their hands bound, into the commune. She eyed the strange archway ahead doubtfully, and the vertical wind turbines with appreciation. Towering over all of them was a thicker stainless cylinder, pipes coming off it at different heights. "What's that?"

"She def needs a pencil and notepad," Barj said.

But even the cold expressions of their armed escort were warmer than those of the people gathered for their arrival, who looked at her like she carried a plague.

Which maybe wasn't far from the truth given what was inside her head.

CHAPTER 50

At Maeve's raised hands, the gathered crowd's muttering hushed. "We have a situation. I like it less than any of you – I started Lorien with my own sweat and blood. But since my idiot ex has found a sentient-"

"Uh, Maeve, we should keep this secret. If anyone-"

"Lorien is an *open* society, Mason," she snapped. "We don't hide information." She faced the crowd again. "And you all need to know: if anyone spreads *this* info we could be wiped off the map by next sunset."

No one spoke. No one moved.

"Yeah, Mace has dragged us all into some deep an' heavy shit. But if *we* don't step up, right here, right now, it might not be just Lorien wiped off the Mother's face – it could be the whole human race as we know it."

Every eye was now locked on her as she spoke. "But I know you. I know all of you. I trust you.

"And know this: we have a plan, and once we've dealt with Mason's stupid emergency, he and Crystal will be out of here."

Crystal heard a small voice ask, "Why's Kisten tied up, Mommy? She would'n hurt people."

Those words struck her like a punch to the stomach. She blinked suddenly watery eyes. *Why?* She chased the feeling... until a wave of ominous pain and a disturbing certainty rose like a thundercloud, warning her not to pursue it.

An angry woman lifted her chin, her arms wrapped protectively around a slim teenager with blonde pigtails, clearly her daughter. "How long'll this plan take?"

Maeve glared at Mason, her hand tugging at her hair. "I don't know, Lottie. Could be hours; could be a day or two."

That caused grumbling – from some people about their kids, others about crops, and still others about drawing lightning down on them.

"She killed eighteen people!" Lottie cried. "Torched a *hospital!*"

Maeve shook her head. "No. She didn't. But if you want to know more about that, Lottie, I could use an extra pair of hands while I explain it to you. But maybe it would be wise for everyone who can leave, or wants to, to go visit friends for a few days. Start thinking about that – we'll know a lot more this afternoon, after some tests."

"Shona, is Kisten in trouble?" the same small voice whispered. Crystal saw a Black girl, probably only four years old, tugging at a bigger girl's grubby jeans, while a woman and man enfolded them and several older kids in the safety of their arms.

Crystal stepped forward, her hands still tied. "I promise it'll be okay. Worse comes to worst, you can just cut off my head and burn it."

But instead of reassuring everybody, her words shocked them into silence.

"Mom-my?" the four-year-old quavered.

"Holy fucking Mother Gaia, Crystal," swore Maeve, "was that supposed to *help*? Maybe you could just zip your trap."

"Mommy, Mommy!" the same young girl whispered, "Mabe said fucking."

"Who's Crystal?" the bigger girl holding her hand asked.

"Me," she admitted. "But that's a secret. To keep you all safe from Tik Tek."

Maeve stared at her, then shut her eyes, muttering 'fuck'.

"Well, that went well," George smirked. "If ya've finished the pep talk, maybe we can get ta work?"

Maeve nodded, then raised her voice. "I'll share the news as soon as we have any," she told her people, before shepherding the visitors to the med-tent.

The two young Black girls caught Crystal's eye, their small hands waving to her, smiling their encouragement. *Were they Diana and Shawna, the others said I'd played with?* In contrast, the rest of the large family looked grim.

I won't let you down, Crystal promised them all.

Five minutes later she felt very far from happy. Lottie had accepted Maeve's offer, and the angry woman now operated the autodoc. Robotic arms pivoted, rotating into place, one flattening and spreading her hair and spraying something onto the target area, then paused.

Crystal jerked. "Stop, what's *that*?"

"Antiseptic spray," Lottie said.

"Not *that*! I hear a drill!"

She looked ready to rip herself free from the stretcher.

Maeve stepped forward. "Steady! It's the bone drill. Ultrasonic. You shouldn't be able to hear it. I guess you can. How'd you think we were going to drill into your skull?"

Crystal's jaw worked. "Fine."

Robotic arms moved.

Long thin needles steered between blood vessels to find one, two, finally four of the tiny computers they said they'd seen on a scan the day before.

She had no memory of it.

Maybe Maeve's choice was wise though, since Lottie's anger seemed to leach away with each tiny computer she extracted, bits of microscopic fibers snapping and pulling away.

"Did that hurt?" Lottie asked, finally.

Crystal went to shake her head, but claustrophobic clamps held it immobile. "Nope. I didn't feel a thing." She cut her eyes to Lottie, but couldn't tell if the answer annoyed or pleased her.

"I've got 'em," Lottie told Gigi. "Also some threads or something that was connected."

"Sleek. Load it under the 'scope while I get Mason dumpin' his data files."

That didn't take long, Gigi soon hurrying back to take the seat beside Lottie. Maeve and George followed, standing behind the pair to watch a screen Crystal couldn't see. Gigi, noticing, took pity and projected the image as a small holo.

In the center of the field of view sat a large rectangular block, with two far larger half-deflated blobs connected to it, as well as several spindly threads.

"I'd say that's a CPU, drug tanks, an' whatever makes up ya 'shadow dendrite' network," Gigi told her. "Lottie, see if ya can pull some of it free for the sampler. If my guess is right, we'll get a hit on carbon nanotubes."

She went back to Mason. Picking up a gizmo she'd lugged in earlier, she connected it to a concealed access port in the back of his neck for his authorization. Judging by their quiet conversation, his digital disinfection was going well.

Lottie finished separating the four tiny computers from the attached stuff. "Done. Drill sites, George?"

The shaman's fingers slid into her hair, healing the tiny puncture wounds in the back of her scalp. "Mother!" he whispered, jumping back.

"What?" Crystal asked. "What's wrong?"

"Holy Gaia, Maeve! I thought ya were baiting me when ya said Shawna healed her in seconds. That was as fast as vamp healing speed."

"I'm a *vampire?*" Crystal looked as shocked as everyone

else.

"No, ya fool. I said *fast as*."

Gigi nodded. "*I* think she's a were-cat."

Maeve groaned. "There *are* no were-creatures Gigi, except in those shape-shifter romances you're addicted to."

Gigi shook her head. "There *could* be. Livin' in secret 'mong us. Under the radar."

Maeve rolled her eyes.

"You like a bet on that, Maeve?" Mason asked. "Look at this." A hologram appeared: a small, dimly lit room. Almost filled by a table, surrounded on three sides by bench seats.

Then a growl, raising the hackles of their necks. A second later a hand appeared, followed by a sinewy female arm, and finally a scrawny, naked Crystal emerged, on all fours, her teeth bared, eyes staring straight up at the viewer.

Lean muscles tensed.

Mason ended the projection.

"Holy cock-monkeys," Gigi whispered, "what happened next? That looked like she was gonna attack."

"I fed her. A lot."

Everyone looked at Crystal. "I don't remember," she said. *I sure looked hungry, though.* She decided against saying that aloud.

Gigi checked the straps holding Mason on the gurney for his 'factory reset'. "I'm gonna disconn' all ya neural links, so ya won't feel anythin', or spasm," she told him.

Everyone tensed, expecting Aiyami to somehow penetrate the jamming signal, pre-loaded viruses seizing control of him or Crystal. Or a satellite to crash down on them from the sky. *Something*. But in the end the big moment wasn't. The reset of all Mason's cyber augmentations went without a hitch.

Gigi replaced all his firmware with the latest versions from the net, after checking they hadn't been tampered with. She also reprimanded him for his 'Phasion charging module' being ten updates behind.

A *bing* came from the sampling device Lottie was operating. "You were right, that stuff's carbon nanotubes," she called out.

"Sleek." Gigi collected the four specks of 'computer dust' they'd extracted from Crystal, then put Lottie and Maeve in charge of the final stages of work on Mason: copying his cleaned data files back into his headware and re-enabling all his augments. "Just follow th'on-screen prompts. 'S all set up," she told them, and bounced out of the med-hut.

Crystal stood and stretched as best she could with her hands tied. George jerked back, checking Gigi's jammers were all still on, with plenty of charge. That done, he took her aside. Clearly nervous.

He had her settle cross-legged on the ground facing him, eyeing her legs like he'd prefer them tied too. He kept a good three meters distance. "Now let's see what secrets my magic will reveal."

The cat, Mrs Bojangles, stalked in gracefully and sat watching. Or maybe just washing itself. The shaman frowned at it. *Did Cat herself ever -?*

"What exactly are you gonna do?" Crystal asked, interrupting his thought.

"Aura checks. Got a mind probe spell-"

Crystal shook her head.

"Ya don't get a say," George told her.

Her chin tucked in, her mouth setting in stubborn lines.

"What's ya problem? Plannin' to kill us all?"

"No!"

"Then what? Seriously."

She blinked at him. "I... I don't... I don't know."

Maeve rolled her own chair closer, arms crossed, but also keeping a safe distance. Lottie did the same, fingering a taser.

Idiots, Crystal thought. Then frowned, trying to work out *why* she'd thought that. "Aagh, alright, I don't care! Fine, go ahead, see what your dumb mind probe spell tells you."

"First the astral checks," he said, shuddering as he glanced at her fingertips. Mrs Bojangles finished washing herself. She leaped into Maeve's lap, though Crystal noticed the cat curled up so it faced her.

George's eyes went out of focus, his face relaxing and taking on a dreamy look.

She released another heavy sigh. *This's probably gonna take forever.* She had more faith in Gigi.

Faith.

The word seemed to echo, making her feel weird. Like it was important. An especially fierce stab of pain warned her off.

This sucks! She considered biting through the nylon ties

binding her wrists, and again felt a weird shiver, a milder prickle of pain inside her head.

Instead, gritting her teeth, she steadied her breathing.

George blinked and shook himself. "There's nothin' at all strange with her aura. It's rich, healthy, *alive*. Wish more people were like that. No trace of any Aztec death god thing either, thank the Mother," he said, grimacing. "We should turn off the jammer for a few seconds so I can see how it changes with Aiyami back again."

"Uh, no," Crystal said.

"Did you just lose your freaking mind, George?" Maeve snarled. "Or did Crystal do something to you?"

Mrs Bojangles purred, in Maeve's lap.

George shook himself. "Uh. That *was* kind of insane, wasn't it?" he admitted, puzzled, eyeing Crystal even more worriedly. Gingerly, he took her bound hands and studied her fingertips for a while, finally sighing heavily himself.

He stared at the girl, fearing what came next: mind reading. He slid in easily. *Too easily?* Crystal welcomed him. Warm thoughts surrounded him, of her bare arms sliding over his, her pushing herself against him-

Flushing, he broke off, re-oriented himself and went back in.

This time it was his lips on hers, her breath in his beard, her eyes...

"Dammit!"

He tried again.

And again.

And again.

"What's the problem?" Maeve demanded.

"Is that a *boner?*" demanded Lottie.

"What? No!"

All pairs of eyes went to his lap, revealing the lie.

"I swear, George, if you don't start treating this seri-"

"It's not me, Maeve! It's her."

Crystal had a strange expression, half puzzled, half smug, but maybe frustrated and surprised too.

George kept trying, but in the end had to give up. "She's like an oiled eel. I get in, but can't get past the surface. It's like she reacts instinctively to the mind-probe spell."

"Reacts how?" demanded Maeve.

George swallowed. "Ya'd have to be a shaman to understand," he said, avoiding her eyes.

"I'm not trying to do anything!" Crystal said. "I'm just letting him *in...*" Her eyes closed, a tiny, dreamy smile twitching.

"She just did it again," George grunted. He licked his lips. "There's some weird thought patterns in there about men, too." He sniffed disdainfully. "Especially Japanese men. Or *a* man. Dominance shit. She gets off on it."

Crystal's eyes flew open, her mouth gaping comically.

The others turned at Mason's quiet "Oh" from across the room.

He shifted uncomfortably. "She was acting super, ah, uninhibited? When she first came aboard. Anyway, I meant to say, it'd be interesting to see how she reacted to... wait. Might be wiser to write this down. Since she hears so well."

Maeve rolled her chair over to him on his gurney, freeing his arms and passing him an e-sheet which he accepted clumsily.

Taking it back she studied his scrawl. It hardly looked like his writing. *Serves him right for so much augmentation.* She smirked: a pity signatures weren't needed much these days. Then she frowned at what he'd written: 'Show her a picture of Dr Shinsuke Yamamoto, CEO of Omega Memory Systems. But be careful: a net search to grab his image might attract attention.'

"Let's see what Gigi can do when she gets a chance," Maeve told him, minimizing the note. Then frowned. "If Crystal's had her memory erased, how by corps' curly balls can she remember how to evade a freaking mind probe?"

No one had an answer to that, either.

For Crystal though, the question felt like a looming storm cloud.

She pushed a sense of dread aside. *Just get on with it! I need my memories back. They can't be that bad.*

CHAPTER 51

Gigi bounced back in, a desk comp in her pocket and her device, the black box with its large wire loop on top. A quick scan gave Mason the all clear. His reset completed, he followed Gigi over to join the others, moving clumsily.

"I am *juiced*!" Gigi declared. "Those CPUs are ancient designs – a hunnert years old. 8o86s!" At their lack of reaction, she deflated. "Y'all're gonna want me ta keep this basic, ain't'cha?" she asked.

"Yes!" said Crystal, jumping in before anyone else could answer. "Like, what's that loopy thing you waved over Mason before?"

"Jus' an EMF 'tecta."

Crystal glowered.

"Uh, it 'tec's – de-tec-ts – radio signals," she enunciated. "Made sure he wasn' connectin' t'any networks." Her shoulders slumped. "Lessee. 'K, like I said, the CPU design's super old. But modern tech makes 'em tiny." About to launch into details, she registered Crystal's expression, and huffed. "The CPU's the brain part of the comp, 'K? Each CPU's gotta standard boot loader...." This time, Gigi saw only Mason was following. "Fry the sparking chips, you peeps drive me mad!"

Lips compressed, she started again. "The mem on each comp has t'ree areas." She held up three fingers – *thanks, I needed 'three' explained*, Crystal thought – as Gigi launched back into lecture mode.

This is her simple *version?* Again, Crystal had a strange feeling of familiarity, like she'd suffered through these kinds of talks before. A painful prickling inside her skull warned her not to try remembering more.

Basically, each comp's memory had three sections, Gigi explained: a bit of blank memory; a small chunk of code, duplicated on each comp; and a much bigger chunk, completely different on each.

Some of the duplicated code included stuff to start the comp running, and to communicate. Gigi said the comms part was old code, super optimized over a period of eighty years, unchanged in the last twenty. Except, parts of *that* code had been improved!

Mason understood first. "Are you saying this AI improved on the best code the human race, over decades, has been able to write?"

"Ding ding! An' here's where the freaky-level doubles: I

couldn' make any sense o' th'rest'a the 'dent code. Much of it's jumps an' recursion, th'rest data."

She'd lost them all again. But basically, Gigi was disturbed by how little of the duplicate code *she* could understand. She somehow felt confident it was the original Omega software – only, rewritten by the AI to operate the Omega hardware and perform all the same functions, in a fraction of the space.

That left the final, much bigger chunks of code, unique on each tiny comp. Her voice fell to a whisper as she admitted she didn't understand it at all, but thought it was Aiyami herself.

"Don' ya see? Each o' those chunks o' code is a building block of Aiyami: her identity. That's how she fit herself in – her code's spread across those millions o' tiny comps."

"So the jamming scrambles her brain?" Crystal asked. "Won't they restart as soon as you stop jamming?"

Gigi giggled. "They would, but get this: the boot loader's in ROM!" She struck a heroic pose – which sagged when no one exclaimed in awe.

"Ya know, as a girl genius's audience, y'all tote suck, ya scan?" She gave them all two thumbs down. "*Any*way, I can keep the jammers runnin' but still narrowcast orders ta reboot and load up new code!"

Once again she paused and waited for cheers. "Gods on purple pogo sticks!" She stomped a foot. "I can wipe the Aiyami code from every freakin' comp in Crystal's head."

This time it got the reception she'd hoped for, and Gigi beamed, did a victory dance, then once again struck her dramatic pose, one finger stretched skyward.

"How much of this is guesswork?" Maeve asked, dampening the celebration.

Gigi's hair bounced as she shook her head. "Fair bit, but m'gut says'm right."

Mason looked thoughtful. "That ROM code, the boot loader: that's how you'll load your code, yeah? Probably how Aiyami installed herself in the first place."

"What's to stop her sneaking straight back in?" Crystal asked. "She got in once already. From wherever."

George shook himself out of what looked awfully like sleep. "Somewhere 'metaphysical', it told Mason."

A silence spread at his words.

"I thought you all said magic and tech don't mix," Crystal objected.

"Yeah," Maeve agreed. "Kind of a worry, isn't it?"

They all looked at Crystal like it was her fault. "So how can we be sure we've stopped Aiyami from reinstalling herself in... in my head?" She grimaced.

"It happened while you were unconscious," George offered. "Meb made you vulnerable. Open."

"And when I go to sleep?"

George looked worried, but Gigi grinned. "Easy! When I wipe the comps, I'll load 'em all up with just the base code, which I'm pretty certain jus' controls th'riginal Omega mem tech. After I erase Aiyami, we can turn off the jammers, wait for a min, then turn 'em back on an' extract a few more CPUs. Check she hasn't started reinstalling herself."

She held up a finger to forestall Maeve's objection, and explained her solution.

It got technical real fast, but apparently even Aiyami couldn't change 'ROM', and Gigi's replacement software would only ever allow code 'signed' cryptographically by her to replace it. "*Their* code had nil defenses," she crowed, doing her dance again. "Thass like leavin' ya front door open, lettin' squatters move in and change the locks. Zero sec, full noob. Dopesticks."

"Yeah, it could be that," Mason drawled. "Or it could be they didn't expect Crystal to jump out an eight-story window before they'd finished."

"What?" Crystal asked.

"Omega Memory Systems have an R&D facility on the edge of the New Francisco Bay docks area, on the Pier Thirty reclamation. The night before last, someone targeted them and blew out a window on the eighth floor." He didn't mention he'd had a comms laser focused on a roach-bot touching the window at the time. Nor that two of their security people had been killed five minutes later.

The look of sympathy Maeve directed at Crystal shifted to one of disgust for him. As if she knew exactly why he'd happened to be on a boat anchored off-shore at two a.m. But all she said was, "So what's next?"

Gigi rubbed her hands. "Get Crystal back in the autodoc ready t'extract some more samps. I can tightbeam the code at her, erase the AI while she's all set up."

Mason's jaw dropped. "You've already coded it?"

She shrugged. "Meh, that wuz th'easy part. 'S the carbon nanotube machinery that throws me. Mechatronics ain't my zone. Though I gotta fren' in Hunters Point, maker-whizz, young ogre. Made m'exo-sets f'me. I'd love ta consult him."

Maeve shook her head. "Let's take it one step at a time. I trust Barney, but any consulting'll have to be face to face. We can't let a breath of this onto the net. *We* found Crystal through Mrs Bojangles." She gave the cat an extra scritch under its jaw. "I have no idea how Omega located her."

Mason's expression soured. "Tik Tek has a nasty habit of pulling off impossible stunts like that. I'd love to know *how*. But if I did find out, they'd probably have to kill me."

Crystal held up her bound hands. "Or I will, if you don't hurry up! Can we *please* get on with this?"

CHAPTER 52

Marcie Dunkirk and Vincent Moore, high profile cast members of the cult net series *Underworld,* appeared nothing like their on-screen personas of gritty, sci-fi bounty hunters. Especially Vince, being entirely human.

They'd dressed in hard-wearing clothes, bedrolls atop secondhand backpacks. Hiking deeper into the Dumps area of Hunters Point, they appeared to be just two more young souls ground down by the relentless evaporation of jobs. Last week the New York Times had pronounced the profession of 'financial advisor' dead, ended by so-called 'general AI'. Non-sentient intelligent automation now handled half the jobs in the workplace.

Two workers hardly more than teenagers, their careers already over, victims of the Fourth Industrial Revolution.

Marcie, her brown curls tied back and stuffed under a cap, looked small beside her tall, thin companion. Pausing for breath on the second from bottom escarpment, she wondered if they were doing a very stupid thing. *But Jane needs me. And I can't let Sprout down.* As if sensing her mood, Vince turned, his white teeth flashing irresistible cheer from his dark face.

"Second thoughts, M?" He waggled his eyebrows. "It's not too late to turn back."

She punched his arm. "Oh? You'd rather head to Sacramento, hunt for her around the smoking ruins of the Tazman-Dungog Rehabilitation Hospice?"

Vince's grin vanished, his eyes going distant remembering another time, another bloodbath. Screams in a suddenly blacked out shopping mall as Jane slaughtered the mercenaries who'd kidnapped Marcie and him.

"You said — Amanda said — we shouldn't look for Jane there. You said it wasn't her!"

"It wasn't." The words were bitten off. Marcie's lips compressed. She wasn't going to admit half her certainty came from the *method*: Jane's style of action was up close and personal. Not eighteen perfect sniper headshots. Nor would she burn down a hospital.

Maybe they'd chosen exactly the right time to go 'camping'. If the media decided it *was* Jane Baker, they'd already be descending on her house to demand interviews.

She sighed, staring out and down. The jumbled territory of the Hunters Point Dumps sprawled like the city's effluvia at the foot of the stepped cliffs. From here to the shore stretched a war-zone of shattered slabs of steel-laced concrete, the bones of fallen monoliths, high rises toppled in the Big One of '44. Smaller damaged buildings had collapsed in the Second World Storm that followed it, communities dying and abandoned after the Melt virus, and then later – and worse – the Red Plague.

New Francisco had emerged from the cracked shell of the older city. In the districts abandoned to fires, floods, and quakes, some of the 'Dumps' areas had seen a vision of hope beyond the terrible changes, finding in them an opportunity for a new way to live, a better life. Some, like this one, had even thrived, founded on principles of sustainability and community.

Others, like the East Oakland Dumps, had lost hope, falling first into despair, then from despair into savagery.

A motley fleet of wind or electrically powered fishing vessels spread from the Hunters Point Dumps foreshore like seeds dispersing across the Bay. By nightfall, they'd all be back.

"Come on," Marcie said, setting off. "That looks like a way down." Shouldering his pack, Vince followed.

They'd dressed in dull colors, thinking it'd help them blend in with people scraping by on what they could grow, steal, or salvage. But as they made their way deeper, avoiding streets choked with tough green vines, or through tumbled concrete canyons, they started feeling oddly out of place. As often as not, the inhabitants they passed were marked by vivid splashes of color – a bright purple belt, a yellow hairband, even just an iridescent bangle flashing in the late morning sunlight.

They seemed... happy. Maybe accepting; oddly content. In rainwater ponds with asphalt bottoms, children splashed and sailed boat-shaped objects. Tiny plots of cultivated soil, bright with corn, tomato, and ground-hugging leaves signifying potatoes below. On the wind, the smell of fish and other foods mixed in a melange that had both their stomachs grumbling.

"Jane said she used to eat at this sheltered area with lots of different food stalls, called the Landwave. Wanna try it?"

Vince's smile was game. "I'm not eating insects, though, I'm laying that out now, M."

"Why's that, Scragmek?" Marcie grinned, using his character's name. "I thought a Zarastrian's bio-still gut could process anything organic?"

"If I see you turn green, spread Zaxx's sungather frills, or eat wood, I'm gone," Vince shot back, referring in turn to her own alien character's biology.

"Deal," Marcie agreed, deciding not to share Jane's recommendation of fried rat. She was pretty sure she wasn't up for that culinary experience either. "But we'd better start calling her Sleena, I guess. That's the name she ended up with, when she was here."

"You're...." He'd been about to say 'kidding', but the cartoon Dark Pixie with sabertooth claws... yeah, he could see why. "How're we going to find her? Just say we're looking for her? Amanda have any idea what kinda trubb she's in?"

"Nup." Marcie didn't know whether to wish her younger sister had clearer hunches about her friend, or none at all. From the expression on her father's face, she wasn't the only one who worried Amanda herself would one day 'unfold' magically with some uncanny ability. Da said his gran had had the Sight, and that was way before magic had returned.

She brought her mind back to her boyfriend's question. "My guess is it's the creepy Doctor dude. He has some kind of weird hold on her."

She stopped walking.

"M? What's up?" Vince's spirits rose at the familiar inspired gleam in her eyes.

"Barney! That's the name! I helped Jane out, one time. She'd had this gadget made up for her by an ogre kid who lives here somewhere. A friend. I reckon we should try to find him."

On the eastern edge of Bayview, they looked out over the lowest in the series of escarpments created by the Big One. Marcie picked out a 'safe' route to the shore below. It was the same route she'd followed, alone, last winter.

They clambered down the final giant step into a post-apocalyptic landscape, winds gusting between fallen office towers and apartment blocks, easing finally at the bottom.

Large stretches of the shoreline were uninhabited, the buildings there far beyond recovery now even with the oceans returned to twentieth century levels.

As they made their way south along the coastline she shivered, remembering her last visit, thankful today was sunny and bright, letting the fresh breeze off the sparkling waters of New Francisco Bay lift her spirits.

"Is that our eatery?" asked Vince, grimacing.

A sprawl of shabby tables and dodgy cookers sheltered – both the equipment and the 'chefs' – under a curving rocky overhang. Just a short walk from the Bay shore. Marcie grabbed his arm and dragged him forward.

Conversations died away, all eyes turning to them. It made her feel like a gunslinger entering a saloon in a Western.

There were people of every type – some with purely cosmetic alterations like skin dyes, to others with illegal Dogmen or Bastean DNA hacks. There were lots of Muties, too... and Marcie blushed at her thought, suddenly realizing she didn't know how survivors of the Melt virus, or their children, referred to themselves.

She was sure it wouldn't be 'Mutie' though.

Right. You told yourself this'd be a chance to grow as a person, Marcie Dunkirk. Time to make that true. Pushing her shoulders back, she set her preconceptions aside and strode forward. And purely on instinct, discarded the flimsy back story she and Vince had prepared.

Sizing up a careworn Black woman scowling at them, and the thin, gray-haired older woman sitting with her, Marcie headed to their table. "I'm M, this is V, and we're here because of a dream my little sister had last night," she declared.

Vince sighed at Marcie's total departure from the script, but didn't object. He even slouched, like his character Scrag-mek did when it thought it held the upper hand.

"That sounds rather intriguing," said the thin woman, who wore a long, bright yellow jacket, her eyes sparkling.

"You're Miz J, aren't you!" Marcie exclaimed, delighted. "Sleena mentioned you."

The atmosphere *shifted*. She had the impression everyone in earshot was now listening.

"Oh? And what did Sleena say about me?"

"She said you were kind. Stood up for her and helped her fit in."

Miz J smiled. "That sounds like her. What's this about a dream?"

More people drifted closer, an androgynous blonde

draped in pastel wisps of fabric taking a seat opposite them. "Where is she? She all right? I'm Tricksy. She-her," she said.

"No," Marcie said. "That's why we're here. I'm a friend, and my sister dreamed Sleena was in big trouble."

The mood thawed a few degrees more. And then a girl who'd been staring at Marcie – about twelve, with haunted eyes – slammed down the food she'd been serving and ran over.

"S'you! The fren' she'n Tash smashed Club Juzz t'rescue! An' the rest'v us. I'd bin there t'ree whole munt," she added, her expression harrowed, her voice cracking. She threw her arms around Marcie, hugging her desperately. "They saved me'n m'liddle bruth. All'v us."

And with that, they found themselves *welcome*. The locals grew even more helpful – and more worried. Unlike Vince or her father, they took the tale of her sister's dream with deadly seriousness. Miz J even volunteered to take them to Sleena's friends, Barney and his father Teef. After recommending the 'dark chicken'.

Marcie didn't ask what that was. It was certainly tasty, if a bit oily.

Unfortunately, the gangling Barney, and Teef, his daunting father, said no one had seen Sleena for months. But just on the strength of her thirteen-year-old sister's dream, the area was now buzzing with worry.

It was kind of infectious. "Hey, cheer up M," Vince said, as they set up their tents in sight of the market gardens Miz J and others tended. "Least now, people'll be on the lookout for her!"

Once again Marcie wrenched her gaze back to him from where she'd been staring. This time he guessed what kept snagging her attention. He dug out the map of the area they'd drawn up at Teef's place, the shipping-container constructed shack from which he sold scavenged or cobbled treasures. Orienting himself, he realized with a chill what the distant tilted tower must be.

Marked with a heavy red X, it was labeled 'Corpse-Stick'. "That's where the nutjob locked you in a dead uploader's lifepod, isn't it?"

He looked up from the map to Marcie, her determined but

sick expression answer enough. He knew he wouldn't be able to talk her out of checking the creepy place. A building full of the mummified bodies of uploaders, trapped in their pods in the immediate aftermath of the Big One. He eyed their tents. Good enough.

"You wanna check it out, don't you? Let's do it now, in broad daylight."

Marcie gave him a grateful look.

"But I'm gonna tell Miz J where we're headed. I've played enough horror stims with you to know what happens when the plucky heroes go into the spook-zone alone."

-

Elsewhere in the Hunters Point Dumps, Dr Alex Harmon once again resisted the urge to scratch at the facial hair he'd had to grow as part of his irksome disguise. He wasn't sure if that or his shaved-bald head was the more irritating. Or the ludicrous removal of his eyebrows. Damn the girl. It did dramatically change his appearance, however.

Still no word from the Department. That was of extreme concern, considering Nelson's unnatural ability to intrude into digital networks. That silence was as worrying as his own inability to locate her magically.

She may be-

He cut the thought off. Leeth was *not* dead. Despite his inability to locate her magically, even immediately after the clinic attack this morning, which had clearly been her handiwork. He agreed with Eagle: given Omega had hired the ill-fated mercenaries to find Crystal Winters, it *must* have been Leeth.

The paradox had to have a logical solution. Could she have persuaded someone in the Department to substitute all her biological samples, that he'd relied on for his Sendings, for those of someone else?

Conceivable but unlikely.

Could Leeth herself have changed so much her psychic fingerprint no longer matched those samples?

That thought gave him pause. She had been sent in to investigate a research organization working in advanced areas of the brain. Nelson had brought the R&D company to Eagle's attention when he found what he called a crude approach to implanting memories, as he could by combining stimsense with his own mysterious technologies. Something

Harmon knew he referred to in his private thoughts as his Ghost.

So Harmon had studied the Department's dossier on Yamamoto, building a psychological profile of the Omega Memory Systems CEO. A textbook narcissist – which also meant the renaming of the company from *Yamamoto* Memory Systems fitted with their solicitation of additional funding. The CEO had advertised for a bodyguard, requiring a female. It had been obvious how a narcissist would treat a woman in that role. Harmon had assured the Department the combination of Leeth's youth and physical charms would prove irresistible. Especially the challenge her insolence would present Yamamoto.

As it had. She had been hired over all other candidates.

Had Leeth been changed so much she was no longer herself?

It would fit the facts. How to find her, if so? *Fresh biological samples!*

He messaged the Department the request. If they could find blood, hair, any sample from the girl at the center of the clinic incident this morning, he would retry his Sending.

Rubbing sunscreen into his currently bald pate, he stared in distaste around the hovel the grateful locals had gifted him. "Even has a rainwater tank!" the head of the Fisher clan had declared.

Such luxury. It also boasted proximity to the stink of drying fish from the smokehouse by the shore.

Still, he had a fresh lead after secretly mind-probing one of the locals yesterday. He had learned 'Sleena' had been close friends with a hulking Mutie tinkerer and his son who was said to be 'a wiz Maker'. The accompanying image had been of an out-sized misshapen child surrounded by gadgets and technology. Like a teenage, ogre version of the Department's Little Brother.

His strongest lead yet. There had been no sightings of Leeth's friend Tash since the Department had found and searched her mountain lair. Perhaps just as well: he was unsure his mind-probe spell would work on a vampire.

With his book of handwritten notes and audio recorder to hand, he pulled his shabby 'intrepid sociology professor' persona around him. Forcing aside the warped door of the hovel that was currently his home, he set out in search of 'Teef's

Tech Hut', weaving between raised plastic tubs holding the clan's preciously managed vegetable beds.

CHAPTER 53

Before Crystal would lie down she made them explain the plan again. Locate and extract two of the tiny 'CPUs'; use the 'IOT firmware security update' protocol to load Gigi's new code and erase the AI; turn off the jammer long enough for Aiyami to start its reinfection, if she could. Finally, extract two tiny comps and see if she had.

Crystal lay in the medical scanner, hands still bound, fists clenched as Mason strapped her head to keep it immobile. "You should know, I really want to punch you and run out of here right now," she told him through gritted teeth.

"Relax, it's just velcro," Mason said, matter-of-fact. "You can tear it off if you start panicking."

"Now I *really* want to punch you."

Gigi stepped forward. "Well, try not to punch the machines, 'specially th'autodoc. Holdin' still's important. So pliz don' panic."

Crystal's eyes swung to the girl. "I won't."

"Chill. Now don' go anywhere!"

She bounced from Crystal's view, crossing to the scanner to check its feed to the autodoc, describing aloud what she was doing while she worked. "'K, systems linked. Scannin' now." The gurney slid forward, slowing while Gigi made adjustments. "Ah, nice, those two'll do."

Crystal hardly flinched when the ultrasonics started.

Maeve noticed. "In the city, they'd charge you for this."

"Now I really want to punch you too," Crystal told her.

"The feeling's mutual."

"'M ready," Gigi interrupted, lining up the device with the radio antenna loop so it pointed at Crystal's head from just outside the donut shape of the scanner. "Gonna narrowcast the reboot an' update in five, four," she said, then pressed a button. "Oops, looks like I jumped th'gun. The code's short, upload'll only take twenny secs. Nineteen. Eighteen...."

The tension increased at each number counted down. Crystal's knuckles turned white. Gigi's eyes flicked from the download progress, to the scanner, to a radio frequency signal detector she was running, to three other gadgets.

Mason saw Maeve had a taser out. He wished Crystal hadn't thrown his own pistol away.

"... three, two, one... complete!"

No one breathed.

"Even assuming Aiyami's a super-intelligent AI," Gigi

said, "it still can't break the laws o' physics. I think." She waited a beat or two longer. "S'long enough. Jammers back on. Takin' samps now."

The robotic arm clicked a needle into place, extruding into Crystal's skull through the just-drilled hole. "Needle's in... touch'a suck... there! Extractin'." The needle slid out, the autodoc's arm moving swiftly and surely at Gigi's directions, sterilizing and washing the samples to deposit two barely-visible dots on a tiny sticky-mount.

Gigi hurried across the room to her other equipment, continuing to describe her actions – loading the first CPU into the equipment that physically connected to it, so she could examine its memory module. Comparing it against what she hoped to see there: the code she'd uploaded, and nothing else.

Her whoop of excitement gave a pretty clear sign it had.

"Perf! Now I wanna turn off th'jammers for five mins, repeat th'test. Then for an hour if thass good too. If Aiyami can't reload itself in that time, we should be free'n-clear. What say?"

"Do I have to wait here with my head in this machine the whole time?" Crystal asked.

Maeve shrugged. "That's up to you, kid. We could have George heal the surgery in between if you like?"

George did that, once more muttering darkly at the uncanny ease of healing her. Crystal said she'd wait where she was, at least for the five minute trial.

That one too went just as smoothly.

Crystal was glad to be free of the scanner and especially the autodoc, and held up both wrists. "Can you let me go *now*?"

"Hell no," Maeve said. "That thing might be just playing possum, waiting for us to make a mistake like that."

"Can I at least have a Link to record messages to myself in case I forget again?"

Maeve agreed to that, and Gigi fixed one to her wrist. "I cut out the network hardware," she assured everyone. That way, even if Aiyami came back and took control of it, all it could do was take selfies and tell the time.

They watched Crystal pace the room, telling herself who she was and what had happened. Surprisingly succinct, she finished in five minutes. She played it back to herself, nodding in satisfaction, her eyes focused on the tiny aperture of its laser viewport. Then continued to pace.

With Gigi's jammers turned off a third time, giving Aiyami a full hour to try to worm her way back inside, the others sat, tense, the minutes of the final test ticking away.

"How did Aiyami get in there in the first place?" Crystal wanted to know, chewing at her fingertips.

Gigi grunted, looking a question at Mason.

"Sure. Replay the conversation between me and it that you copied from my headware before the factory reset," Mason griped.

Gigi nodded, cueing a sound file.

They heard Crystal say, 'That's creepy. Who are you? *What* are you?'

George jerked forward at Aiyami's response, fascinated as Gigi played the whole recording. At the end he sat wild-eyed, shaking his head.

"I think..." he said at last, "ya gotta understand, below our level of reality, there's like, a deeper layer. More primal. The place where the Great Spirits move, casting their shadows on the physical world. Ancient beings. When magic returned in '36, those shadows became real again."

"Why *did* magic return?" Crystal asked.

George shrugged, raising two empty hands. "No one knows. But if what she said is true, it means Aiyami is one of those things – but not ancient: *new*. New-born. Not even five years old. That's insane! That means, something big enough happened five – or 'four point seven' years ago, since my hunch is Aiyami is precise – ta create her. Something *created* a Great Spirit!"

"Sounds big," said Maeve.

"You mean, two of them had sex?" asked Crystal.

George scowled at her. "No. An' it said *it* and an Aztec god were *both* connected to ya!" he accused her.

They were all staring at her, so she tried super hard to see if any of it sounded even vaguely familiar... but drew a blank. Again. As usual.

George tore at his hair – and for just a second, the gesture seemed familiar. *Really* familiar, like it was on the tip of her brain. Then it too was gone. Her breath huffed out.

He rounded on her. "I want to see if I can heal ya brain. If I can, it might restore some of ya memories."

She nodded, eager. "Provided you don't try anything." For some reason, she didn't fully trust the shaman.

"Good," Maeve agreed, "we need to learn what we can before she forgets everything." The moment the words left her mouth, she looked uncomfortable. "That came out colder than I meant. Gigi, when you reset the CPUs inside Crystal's memory lobe things, will the Omega code still be releasing those drugs?"

"I didn' dare change that code. I could'n' unnerstan' it."

Crystal grimaced. "That was the code that was the same on all the tiny computers? You kept it? Couldn't Aiyami kind of creep out from there to reinfect me?"

Gigi shook her head. "Nah. I'm pretty sure that was jus' th'original Omega code, rewritten by it to make space for itself. An' m'new code watches that space in case it starts magically fillin' up again."

"You all said magic and tech don't mix," Crystal accused.

"It don'. But just in case it does." Gigi hurried on before Crystal could ask more. "Oh, an' I checked the drugs in the micro tanks attached to the CPUs, from the samples we took before."

The medical system had recognized both drugs. Gigi went on to explain that when you recalled a long term memory it kind of got loosened and had to be re-tightened. One of the reservoirs held a drug that helped 'set' memories, the other weakened them.

"That doesn't sound good," said Crystal. "Are they... is it still... erasing me, even with Aiyami gone? You said you didn't understand that code. The Omega code." She swallowed, looking suddenly young. Vulnerable but trying to hide it.

Gigi compressed her lips. "I wanna show Barney the 'shadow dendrite' struc', see if he can work out how th'pieces o' nano-mech fit, how they work.

"But 'm hopin' th'answer's No: that m'reboot stopped it."

Crystal looked hopeful. Her Link beeped, and the others startled. "Oh, hell no," gasped Mason, his augments powering up; Maeve drew her weapon.

Crystal rolled her eyes. "It's not Aiyami, guys. I just set a timer for when the hour was up. I want to be untied!"

Maeve grumbled, but the final drilling and extraction of two more CPUs went smoothly. Crystal ignored George as he healed the surgical punctures, her eyes fixed on Gigi testing for reinfection by the AI.

The moment she said "Clear!" Crystal was up, holding out her wrists for Maeve to cut the nylon ties. Then she sprang across the console, hugging Gigi and whirling her around. "Thank you! Thank you, thank you, thank you!" She kissed her on the lips before finally setting her down.

Gigi didn't move, then slowly turned a darker shade.

"Are you *blushing*, Gigi?" Maeve teased.

Gigi only darkened further.

Crystal spun to the shaman. "Now you can restore my memories magically! While Mason watches you."

He eyed her figure appreciatively, then grimaced. "I can *try*. I mean, I don't have a spell for restoring memories. Or vacuuming ya brain clear of cyber stuff. And what's been done to ya's like nothin' I've ever heard of."

Maeve and Mason exchanged the same kind of suspicious look.

"Then what *is* this spell you think might help Crystal?" Maeve demanded. "Why do you have it? What's it for?"

Mason burst into laughter, pointing an accusing finger. "To repair brain damage, yeah? In case of overindulgence in psychotropic chemicals!"

George didn't deny it.

"What if it 'freshes her mem's of kill'n *eighteen peeps* at Tazman-Dungog?" Gigi asked, horrified.

Is that a lot? Crystal wondered. *It* seems *a lot. But it wasn't me who did it.* That thought... angered her? No. It annoyed her. *Why?* She looked up. Gigi seemed upset, and Maeve was looking at her strangely. Mason watched her too, his expression blank, guarded. George had a weird unfocused stare going on... but why did he look *nervous?*

"How does that make you feel, Crystal?" Maeve asked.

I'm somehow scaring them all. Cover it up, now! "Humans only kill for food!" she blurted.

Everyone *froze*. Not a single person said a word.

Where on Earth did that *come from?* she asked herself. Pain stabbed, the words – a memory? – fading and dropping away, like an old man's face falling into darkness. She tore at her hair. "Aagh! I *hate* this!" Striding to the shaman she grabbed his tattered deerskin vest, shaking him. "Do your stupid spell *now*! I need my memories back!"

He raised both hands. "Fine! Good! Just put me down!"

She'd hoisted him off the ground, she realized. Blushing, she set him on his feet, and he began preparing for his spell casting.

"Did we work out why it was able to, uh, infect the stuff in my head, today? Why today?" she asked.

Mason indicated a faint red spot on her bare midriff. "That looks to me like you were tranqued. I'd say Aiyami stepped in at that point. During our conversation she said you were unconscious at the time."

"Oh!" Gigi said, but after that single word, clamped her mouth shut.

"What?" Maeve demanded.

Gigi wet her lips. "Ya know how ev'one says magic an' tech don' mix? Well, if ya right about that timing, means Aiyami only took a second or less ta do all that." At their nods, she continued. "But she couldn't: lim-bwith. 'Limited bandwidth'.

"Took me twenny seconds to narrowcast *one* copy of *the same code* t'all her millions of processors at the same time. Yet Aiyami somehow uploaded *each* CPU with a diff jigsaw piece of her own code – in less'n a second.

"But information theory's jus' physics. So that means she either broke th'laws of physics – magic, ya? – or else installed herself days or weeks before."

"Crystal only escaped Omega thirty-six hours ago," Mason objected.

"Then either Aiyami helped her escape, or it used magic," Gigi said.

"But if she'd been 'out' all that time, she could've spread herself right through the net. Infected our Links, my cyberware. There'd be all sorts of signs," Mason argued.

"Guess that leaves magic," Gigi said, in the same heavy tone she'd first said 'Oh.'

Now they all understood why.

"Hey, but on the plus side, it'd mean it didn' lurk 'til Crystal was unconsh!" she added.

"Maybe her missing memories left a psychic 'vacuum' for it to slither into," George chipped in.

Crystal brightened. "Whatever. Let's do this memory healing spell."

George nodded, folding his long limbs neatly to sit cross

legged. "Sit here," he told her, pointing to his lap, looking simultaneously fearful and anticipatory.

Mason, watching Crystal closely, saw a tiny frown give way to an expression of dreamy pleasure tinged with confusion. *She's forgotten his 'kneel before me' order yesterday.* Then again, the shaman had been so high, he might have forgotten too.

From Maeve's angry expression, *she* hadn't.

Crystal shook herself, settling into his lap, also cross-legged. Mason moved around to stand beside Maeve, to watch them both.

Wincing at her weight, George began rocking left and right, placing his fingertips on Crystal's temples, singing and crooning, the melody punctuated by odd little grunts and hoots.

Gradually his face seemed to change, becoming rounder, hairier, his nose flattening and brow protruding. Calling his Totem, Mason knew. What was it? Oh. Monkey, he remembered. He hoped this wasn't a bad idea.

The shaman's eyes rolled up and then shut, Crystal's did the same, and then both fell still.

Gigi, Maeve, and Mason settled themselves in their seats, Gigi swiveling hers to check the array of instruments around her. Autodoc, scanners, and all med-bay systems were fine – no secret tampering by a spooky AI.

The cross-legged pair sat, breathing calmly.

The others watched, waiting.

CHAPTER 54

George and Crystal drifted in a plain of blood red trees. Long spindly branches wafted languidly around them. A few, straining across empty spaces, twined together. The ground moved in slow swells, a faint rumble reverberating under all, suggesting subterranean upheavals.

They floated over humped mounds interspersed with the occasional low, eroded hill. A pink tracery of threads wound over, between, and around them. Slender shadows above echoed sketchy trails below.

George, troubled and tense, let the healing magic flow out into Crystal's inner world, disturbed by a mental landscape far different to what he'd expected. He felt his spell subtly reshaping the terrain, swelling the mounds, returning faint trails to visibility. The life force gifted by his Totem spirit sank deep, where things slid and shifted, grinding and wailing like a soul's strangled cries....

He had the sudden certainty of danger. That the landscape could change at any moment and sweep him away; that it *waited*. That he trod a path above an abyss, which he need only gaze into to learn....

Shuddering, he pushed such thoughts away, hiding himself inside the flow of healing.

The altered features of the shaman's face snapped back into focus as both he and Crystal opened their eyes and took deep breaths. Crystal stretched sensually in his lap, enjoying his reaction, the power she wielded.

Maeve and Mason both frowned at the display.

George struggled under her weight, pushing at her to get off him. He swallowed, his expression troubled, even disturbed. Unusually for him, he said nothing, frowning down at the ground. Groaning and massaging sore legs, he at last hauled himself to his feet, still not speaking.

In contrast, Crystal sprang to hers. "Mmm, I feel good!"

"Well?" Mason demanded. "What do you remember?"

"Uh...." Her expression fell at the reminder. She searched her mind, her gaze distant as she hunted. At last they focused back on him. "Nothing. But I *feel* better?"

"Well, George?" Maeve asked.

He ignored her, catching Crystal's eyes instead. "What is your name?" he demanded.

"I'm Crystal-, uh, Crystal... I'm..."

But the name felt thin, a gossamer barrier. She pushed through... only to fall off a cliff. Nothing lay behind it but yawning emptiness. "I'm..." She strained, clutching at nothingness, hands clawed as if to drag her name from the abyss by sheer force of will.

No name came. Lips clamped in thin lines, she stared angrily at the ground, blinking back stupid tears.

The shaman sighed and answered Maeve. "It looked... worn down. Sparse. For myself, using the spell on myself, I'd... 're-etch' things? But with her?" He shook his head. "I couldn't be sure I wouldn't be creating false memories.

"Her mind's different to what I expected. Worn down, yeah, but also... I don't know." He wet his lips, trying to work out why he felt he'd just escaped some uncanny trap he'd been naively strolling through. The longer he'd stayed, the more he'd felt her inner landscape could... *turn* on him any instant.

Or had it been the sense that *something would notice him*? Something dangerous. Or... some *things*? The Aztec god? Aiyami? He shivered. Squeezing and rubbing his fingers against one another, just for the simple reassurance of physical touch, he realized his breathing had accelerated, and fought it back under control.

I'm not going back in there, he decided, rubbing sweaty palms on grubby, patched jeans. "Uh... it felt like there were weird layers. Hidden chambers, disturbed ground...." He shook his head again. "Just damage caused by the Omega tech, I expect." But he eyed Crystal strangely.

"I do feel better," she said. Her smile looked fragile though.

"Hopefully your memories'll start to return now," Maeve suggested.

"You really think so?"

"Sure," Maeve lied, feeling sorry for her. "If not, you have the Link. That'll help. Record notes to yourself."

"Okay, the next problem," Mason said, "is to get Crystal, Gigi, and me to Hunters Point without being spotted."

"Could we catch a car?" asked Crystal.

"Maybe. Most of the way. Trouble is, we had to hide you when we left my place yesterday," Mason told her. "There were drones watching."

"I was at your place?"

"Yeah. It's where you met Mrs Bojangles."

"Who – oh: the cat who followed me to the clinic?"

"*Followed* you?" Maeve snorted. "Why'd you take her?"

"I didn't! She asked to come with me."

"Really. What'd she say, exactly?"

Crystal eyed the older woman in disbelief. "She didn't ask in *words*. She asked in cat."

Maeve, unamused, narrowed her eyes.

George however seemed intrigued. "Can you ask *us* in 'cat'? Now?"

Crystal shrugged. "OK." She looked from him, to Maeve, then back to him. Deciding between them, she stepped toward the shaman with an emphatic tread and a subtle sway to her hips, all while holding his gaze. Dropping to all fours when she reached him, she butted her head on his calf, looking up, entreating. *"Mreow?"* She bumped his leg again.

Maeve grunted, equal parts impressed and annoyed.

"Fascinating," griped Mason. "Can we get back to the question at hand though?"

Crystal sprang upright. "How they'll try to spot us? Drones? How can they know where to look?"

"Facial recognition systems. Cams are everywhere: highways, streets, stations, malls. Private corps shouldn't have access to most of them, but that doesn't seem to stop Tik Tek," he said.

Crystal clapped her hands, bouncing. "Yay! Disguises!"

They settled in to planning, calling up maps, Gigi passing around jammers 'just in case', Maeve dredging up wigs and clothes, even supplying Mason a pistol. Not for Crystal though. 'Hell no' had been her response when the girl asked.

Gigi gave a curious little grunt, and pulled Maeve aside. "Lookit this!" she whispered.

Crystal saw Maeve lean forward, looking into Gigi's Link. "Oh my stars." She was whispering now too. "The mythical million cred bounty," she breathed. "'Wanted for eighteen homicides at the Tazman-Dungog clinic. Female terrorist. Do not approach.' And that *is* Crystal. Hair's been 'shopped, but it's def' her."

"A mill," Gigi whispered, awestruck.

Maeve nodded. "Enough to double our solar arrays, buy a second plastics fractionator...."

Crystal waited, tense, for her next whispered words.

"We're def' gonna need disguises," Maeve said. "Hide her face completely."

Crystal blinked, stunned and warmed by the incredible nobility. She smiled weakly as Gigi tucked away her Link.

"We have a fresh prob," Maeve said, projecting a 'Wanted' image of a much more put-together Crystal, with a figure of '1,000,000' below it in bold, bright numbers. Her eyes rested on Mason as she spoke.

He merely licked his lips and muttered 'okay'.

What does 'okay' mean? Crystal wondered, trying but failing to catch his eye.

Frowning, Maeve continued planning. After hiking from Lorien to the freeway, they'd flag a bus to New Francisco and then in to Bayview. From there they'd have to walk. Maeve called up an image of the serried ranks of cliffs they'd need to descend to reach Hunters Point itself.

Crystal stabbed a finger into the projected scene. "There's a tunnel comes out here, we can follow right to the edge of the Viz Slump. In case we're still being hunted by drones."

She looked up to three faces watching her intently. Her eyebrows lifted. "Oh! I remembered that!"

They all waited for her to continue. She shut her eyes, trying to tease out something more. "Gaah!" she said at last.

But Mason clapped the shaman on one bony shoulder. "Looks like your healing spell's helping." Then he noticed Crystal had positioned herself beside George, one deferential step behind, and his hackles rose. *At least in some ways....*

In the end, Maeve opted to come with them. Not least because she didn't trust her young genius alone with Mason, and certainly not with Crystal.

They'd found a wig of grubby blonde dreadlocks for Crystal, a broad-brimmed floppy hat and big sunglasses, and a flowing, flowery yellow sundress. Mason was put into a set of blue denim dungarees, work boots, and lumberjack shirt, looking distinctly uncomfortable – but different. He wasn't surprised to be offered a realistic beard, and glued it on without comment.

Maeve glared at Mason across the center of the bus wondering what further secrets her ex held back, and who'd end up dying as a result. At least this time he was suffering a little too. Re-syncing with as much cybernetic enhancement as he had was a bitch.

She smiled, watching him grimace as he worked his right arm in a twisting motion that for some reason made his left leg twitch each time he did.

Yeah, Karma's a bitch.

The eighteen-seater autobus sped across the Bay Bridge, afternoon sunlight spearing in through the darkened windows on her right. Maeve jerked her head to Crystal, then to the distant shore to their left. "Hunters Point Dumps. See anything you recognize?" She passed over a small pair of binoculars.

Crystal tilted her head, studying the shore where a shanty town hugged the water's edge, somehow knowing the more ragtag boats dotting the Bay came from there. Taking the binoculars she studied the staggered giant's steps leading from the upthrust heights further inland down to the ruins tumbling to the shore. They felt familiar. Pain prickled, but somehow hesitantly.

Scanning the shore southward, past mudflats and an oily looking canal leading inland, a tilted tower came into view, seven stories leaning out toward the water, and she shuddered. "That," she told Maeve, handing the instrument back and pointing. "I've been there. The one that looks ready to fall down."

Maeve found it. She stilled, lowering the glasses. "The seven-story one. Candlestick Tower."

"Yeah." Crystal hugged herself. "Something bad happened."

«What's up? What is it?» Mason silently asked Maeve.

«Mausoleum, now,» she answered him. «Rich Uploaders, trapped in their VR pods in the quake of '44. Is *that* the answer? Is Crystal a copy of some uploaded identity recovered from the net, and copied into this body?»

She shuddered, and read the same reaction from Mason. Both tried to hide that from Crystal.

Crystal of course noticed. "What's wrong? What happened there?"

Maeve shook her head. "Bad stuff. A lot of dead people."

Crystal shut her eyes, suddenly standing in a tilted room, cold, wind gusting through it. She was watching with deadly satisfaction as the life drained from the eyes of a man looming over her, who she held upright. She gasped.

"What?" Mason asked. "What'd you remember."

She stared back at him wild-eyed, trying to push the memory away. Feeling a strange tingling at her fingertips, and something deeper inside, a seed of hungry dark anger. "Nothing," she said. "Nothing."

But, swallowing, she could tell none of them believed her. Remembering the feel of her whole arm buried inside.... "Nothing."

No one spoke for the rest of the ride. Disembarking, Maeve flagged a share car.

"Hey, while we're waiting, let's try that idea I had before?" Mace asked Maeve and Gigi. «See her reaction to a pic of Yamamoto,» he reminded Maeve. "Should be safe enough here. We'll be gone in a minute." He didn't admit he'd had the picture all along.

At Maeve's nod, he sent it to Gigi. "Project that for Crystal, would you?"

"Proj wha...?"

For Crystal, Gigi's voice faded away. She faltered at the sight of... the majestic figure who stole her breath; made her feel small, no, *insignificant.*

She drank in the image, mouth open. "Oh, wow...."

"Yeah, that's a problem," Maeve griped, at the awestruck reaction to the puffy eyelids and sagging skin.

Crystal, blinking, feeling Mace shake her, reluctantly dragged her eyes free to meet his.

"... our bad guy," he was saying, "the one who erased your memories and tried to program you."

She stared up into his face in dismay, understanding finally what he was saying, fighting to collect herself. At last, with clenched fists, she looked from him back to the image, gritting her teeth, repeating to herself *'He's evil, don't trust him.'*

The thought shook her to her foundations, pulling her in multiple directions at the same time, like there was a whole horde of snakes tied to it.

She glared at the image harder, her eyes narrowed.

The others exchanged worried looks.

Once in Bayview, they made their way to the escarpment. But the farther they descended the broken cliffs, giant steps leading into the Dumps area, the faster Crystal's mood recovered. By the bottom she was alternately dancing, hugging herself, and growling under her breath as glimmers of memory surged and teased her.

Gigi, her exo-set leg boosters recharged, bounced beside her, pointing out places she knew, gushing about the young mecha-genius they were on their way to see. Grubby kids scrounged and played down broken streets. Adults, tending vegetable plots, water tanks, and solar arrays eyed them curiously – especially Crystal in her very out-of-place sundress. She looked like a low-grade social media personality traveling 'incognito' with a friend and their two guards.

"Someone's happy," Maeve observed to Mason.

Crystal laughed, spinning to face her, calling back, "Why not? It's wonderful here! No one telling you what you have to do." She spun back around, dancing further ahead.

"That's just disturbing," Maeve commented even more quietly to Mason, and they both noted Crystal tilt her head as if she'd heard that remark too. Maeve raised her eyebrow, but Mason just shrugged.

"She came out of the Bay like that." He wondered if the Omega tech did more than just erase and implant memories. Did it somehow improve your hearing, too? That'd make it even more valuable.

Finally they reached the flatter ground, and Maeve had the group close up. At least, she pulled Gigi back closer. The people living here were largely okay, but nowhere near the peaceful innocents Crystal seemed to assume.

"Can I please take off the sunglasses and stupid hat," she pleaded. "Everyone's looking at me funny, and calling me names."

Gigi, nodding, turned to Maeve. "This's a no-drone-zone," she said. "Locals scav 'em vish."

"Oh, all right," Maeve agreed, knowing the Hunters Point people's rep: scavengers par excellence.

"Yay!" Whipping off her hat, Crystal spun it and the shades into the distance before Maeve could stop her.

She made her fetch them back, muttering "Waster," and similar epithets while they all waited.

"So where are those tunnels you were talking about?" Mason asked, as they passed another group of grubby urchins.

While Crystal looked about, one of the children, a thin young girl in dirty clothes – apart from a much-washed, bright orange bandanna – squealed and pointed.

"Sleena!"

Crystal turned, the name triggering a shock of recognition, and the children charged her.

Maeve shot Mason a *WTF* look, but he just spread his hands. Crystal looked equally off-balance.

"Sleena! What'cha doin'? Y'ava mill cred bounty on ya!"

The children swarmed her, peppering her with questions: Who were the bad guys she'd killed at the clinic? Was she working with Tash? Who were her new friends?

Maeve recognized the calculation in Mason's eyes as he again considered the fact that Crystal – who the kids called Sleena – had a million cred bounty on her head.

"Sleena was an anime warrior pixie," Gigi offered helpfully, standing back with the others, all studying the stunned and strangely vulnerable Crystal as the children tugged on hands and clothes, hugging her and babbling questions.

«Looks like we brought her to the right place,» Mason sent to Maeve. «They clearly recognize her.»

But Maeve swallowed. «She hung with Tash, they said. You do know Tash was a vigilante vampire who used to hunt in this area?»

Mason blinked, looking from her, to the excited children, to the nonplussed Crystal. Or should that be Sleena?

Maeve massaged her forehead. "This just gets weirder and weirder," she muttered. "What's next – she'll take us to her alien spaceship?"

Crystal turned to stare at her. "There *was* something about aliens!"

The kids *oohed* while Mace and the others just gaped.

At last Crystal shook her head. "Rats! It's gone. It was important though, I'm pretty sure!"

Maeve just stared at her, tight-lipped. "Right. Let's find Barney." She pulled Crystal free of the children, who waved and raced off chattering excitedly.

"Sleena's back!" was the gist of it, Crystal heard, as they vanished into the nooks and crevices of half fallen buildings.

"Come on," snapped Maeve, feeling the situation slipping further from her control. She glared at Mason.

He spread his hands. «Don't blame me!»

Gigi seemed to find the whole thing delightful. "See, ya should put th'hat an' glasses back on – y'r famey!"

"They didn't seem to care about the million cred reward!" Crystal murmured. Wrapping her arms around herself, she added even more softly, "And they *hugged* me."

She seemed more affected by the hugging than the recognition, Maeve saw. For herself, the children's visible disdain for the huge bounty was more puzzling. Hunters Point was largely a sustainer community like her own, but vastly larger and poorer. Even a tenth of that reward'd make the lives of the people here a whole lot easier. What could 'Sleena' have done to outweigh *that*?

CHAPTER 55

Marcie Dunkirk and Vince Moore eyed the scene below them. After the hours they'd just spent tiptoeing through the eerie 'Corpse-Stick' Tower – hand in hand – it all looked wonderfully prosaic. They'd found nothing, no clues. Just refreshed old memories for Marcie.

Mostly bad. Though she'd been strangely warmed to find the whiteboard Jane had used to write messages to her up on the seventh floor, facing Oakland across the Bay. Fallen down and moldy, but recognizable.

Still, they'd both been glad to leave the haunted location.

They slid-stepped now down a shallow slope of rubbish, breathing sighs of relief at the bottom. A ramshackle structure squatted before them, in the middle of a short expanse of bare dirt. The two largest components were shipping containers, connected by huts cobbled from corrugated metal, concrete slabs, and sheets of heavy duty plastic. In a few places windows had been cut into the walls, patched plastic film flexing in the breeze. Duct tape featured heavily.

Mounted low on a tall thin pole near the center, a three-faced sign in vivid green LED letters read 'Teef's Tech'.

A drainage trench circumnavigated the zig-zag construction, a pipe at the far end curving over a drop-off to lower ground, presumably feeding water tanks.

The roofs of both shipping containers were covered in solar panels, but on the nearer one, four eye-hurtingly black squares took pride of place. Vince pointed them out. "Those aren't scrap – they're those new quantum panels. Not cheap, either."

Perched on each corner of the haphazard framework sat drones, along with parabolic reflectors, the nearest pointing in their direction.

"I think they know we're here," Marcie said. Then, lowering her vice, she giggled. "Is it just me, or do you feel like you're back on *The Mines of Arcturus* set, for that 'living scrapyard' episode?"

Vince shuddered. "Wish you hadn't said that, M. I do now."

Marcie reached up and took his arm. "Come on, these are friends of Jane. Or, Sleena. There's no Giga-Mech spirit here!"

"We hope," he said, allowing himself to be tugged forward.

The front entrance was big – plenty of clearance for even

Vince's tall frame – sealed by hospital style flexible PVC doors. Pushing through, they found row after row of metal racks, with not quite enough room for them both to walk side by side. Shelves were crammed with everything from coils of wire to electronic components, old computers to cooking pots. All of it very clearly salvaged, but every item cleaned and sorted.

The central aisle led to a long wide benchtop with a young male ogre sitting behind it, instead of the older male they'd spoken to on their first visit. A son? Sections of his blond hair were dyed green, and his clothes were a size too small for him, even though they looked new. A pair of what looked like telescoping robot arms powered down. He pulled knobby hands from inside them while studying his two visitors. "Ma'am, sir?" he asked politely, in a high voice.

Marcie reduced her estimate for his age. Maybe thirteen? "Miz J sent us. She said you're a friend of Sleena's. So am I. I'm worried-"

The boy's brows furrowed as she spoke, and he closed his eyes. They flew open. "I know that voice – Stryker Zaxx!" Then they widened to comical dimensions. "Hug the puppies! That means the Emoryville Mall Massacre – that *was* Sleena! I told Dad but he wouldn't believe me!"

His voice cracked at the end, and he stopped, pinkening. Marcie and Vince – rescued at the mall by Jane, from people she had indeed massacred – stared back at him. How had a kid just worked out what weeks of media investigation hadn't?

"Is Sleena hunting the Giga-Mech?" Barney asked in hushed tones. "Is Tash helping her?"

"What? No! That was just an episode." Marcie shook her head. "We're here because of a, a tip off. That Jane's- uh, Sleena's in trouble." But from the sudden delight in the boy's eyes, he'd caught the slip. "Oh, shrap!"

"Is Jane her real name? What kind of trouble? Who tipped you off? Underworld's only a show. Isn't it? How can I help? Is it something to do with Doc Truman? Did *he* tip you off? He interviewed me this morning. He asked about Sleena too. Lots of questions." He leaned forward over the counter to whisper, and Marcie realized he was standing on a box. "His eyes are creepy."

While Marcie and Vince absorbed the flood of questions,

Barney stabbed a finger at her, eyes alight. "Jane *Baker*! The girl from the hospital raid, where she made Hat Mage heal your spine. Jane Baker is Sleena!" Both hands clapped to his mouth. "That's gotta be a *massive* secret. Don't worry, I won't tell anybody – not even Dad!"

He bounced, impatient, while Marcie and Vince exchanged helpless looks.

"Are you two all right? Why aren't you talking? I have another Sleena special – Doc Truman wanted to see it but I told him it was only for her. Did she send you for that? Where is she? Does she need it? Wait, I'll get it!"

He jumped down and ran off.

"My head's spinning," Vince said. "Will we be in trouble with her, for Barney working out she's Jane?"

"Don't be stupid. Of course not. I wonder who Doc Truman is, and why his eyes are creepy?" She suddenly grabbed her boyfriend's shirtfront and dragged his head down for a kiss. "But I feel like we're on the right track, finally. Thank you for coming with me."

Vince cupped her cheek, smiling. "Anything for you, M."

By then Barney was running back. Jumping back onto his box he opened a small case and proudly showed a tiny two-piece gadget. When asked, he pointed out the micro speaker and 'skin conduction microphone', each with adhesive pads.

Marcie frowned. "What's it for?"

"D.G.- uh, Sleena recorded the sound of her biting her teeth twice, through the skin-mic. That's used to make the micro speaker play a sound file she recorded for me. You wanna hear it?"

Both his visitors nodded. Barney stuck both devices to the benchtop, then rapped it twice with a stylus.

Nothing happened.

He giggled at their expressions.

"Now I'll play the sound a thousand times louder."

This time they both heard it. An older male voice, speaking in a hoarse whisper. "Seshoestus desstussten."

Marcie felt her skin crawl. "What does it mean?"

Barney deflated. "I'd kind of hoped you'd tell me." Then his eyes lit again. "It's not in any language *known to man*."

But after that, he couldn't help them much. Nor would he give or sell Sleena's device to them, though he was more than happy to start making a copy for them.

"No charge," he proudly said. "It'll be a free sample, for a friend of Sleena. I can have it ready in an hour."

Then he wanted to reminisce about Sleena's fights at last December's Fist Fest, but Marcie stopped him, not wanting to be reminded of the aftermath. Nor have Barney guess *she'd* been the reason for Sleena and Tash's assault on Club Juzz later that night.

"How do we find Doc Truman?" she asked. On the map his father had sold them earlier, Barney marked where he lived; and where he hung out for people to come and talk to him. The Doc could also do a little magic, Barney told them: healing basically, bodies but also minds. Doc Truman was researching the history of the Dumps areas across the country, Barney explained. He also gave them his description.

Something in the last half hour though had set Marcie's nerves on edge. She had the feeling Jane's trouble, whatever it was, was fast bearing down on her.

Imminent.

CHAPTER 56

Gigi sent Barney a short message they'd arrived, as she teetered her way down the scree slope of rubble and rubbish leading to 'Teef's Tech' hut. Crystal stayed beside her, offering a hand, easily keeping her own footing. At the bottom Crystal stopped, frowning at the patchwork structure snaking between the piles of picked-over building materials and scrap.

"Those are parabolic mics up there," she murmured to Mason. "They're listening."

In the look Maeve gave him he read the question 'How does she know *that*, but not remember her own name?' He could only shrug.

"Lead the way, Gigi," Maeve said, waiting by the heavy PVC swing doors, "since they know you."

Mason held the door for the girl, then Maeve and Crystal, and followed them inside.

Shelves and metal racks crammed with gear filled the space, blurry light entering from filmy plastic windows puffing in and out with every change of air pressure. Overhead LED strip lights added to the illumination.

Crystal, staring all around her, followed Mason and the others slowly down the center aisle to a slightly more open space, where a work table stretched almost the width of the shipping container they stood in. She felt... happy. Something about the place lifted her spirits.

The others parted, Gigi greeting a young ogre, and the two enthused over the exo-set muscle boosters the Black girl wore. "Hardly worked a sweat, even scrabblin' down th'escarp," she giggled, thanking him.

From deeper in the structure, down the scrappier passage connecting it to the rest of the pieced-together shelters, she heard a heavy person moving about, a steady hissing sound accompanying clanks of metal shifting on metal.

The boy, Barney, set aside some delicate work he was doing, covering it with a rag and making space in front of him. "Pull up some seats, please," he said, rubbing his hands together. "Your message sounded kind of mysterious."

"You don't know th'half of it!" Gigi promised him, turning to introduce the others. Mason she described as the visitor who'd brought 'th'mess' to Lorien, then gestured to the final member of the party and added, "namely Crystal."

Barney's expression – a welcoming nod and smile – froze

when his eyes reached her, his mouth falling open.

Disbelief morphed into delight. Scrambling onto the counter he launched himself at her, crying "Dee Gee!"

Crystal, stunned, caught the laughing child, who hugged her like an octopus. Only a head shorter than her, she leaned back to manage his weight.

"You're okay! I can't believe it! Seems like everyone's been asking about you today. A friend of yours-"

He suddenly stopped. *I almost blabbed about Sleena being Jane Baker and knowing Stryker Zaxx!* Releasing his hold he slipped to the ground, feeling his ears turn pink.

The other three were all staring at him, he saw, but D.G. herself – Sleena – had a weird expression, a mix of emotions. Was she here on a secret mission? Had he just messed up?

But at her next question, it was his turn to be confused.

"You know me? My name's Deejy? What's it mean?"

He felt like a thief caught with his hand in a pocket, his blush deepening. *What's she doing? She made me promise not to tell anyone, ever, it stood for Drone Girl!* "It's just a nickname," he fumbled, weakly.

"But you know her?" the Lorien head-woman demanded.

He looked from one to the other, then finally back to D.G. – Sleena – for permission to answer.

"I had my memory erased," she told him, shrugging like it was no big deal. But from her wounded expression, he could tell it was.

"No *way*," he breathed. Then he goggled at her. "That terrorist attack on the sleazy clinic this morning – was that you, too?"

Her wince was answer enough.

"Wow," he said.

But they all saw he didn't seem horrified. And wondered about the 'too'.

«You notice he *assumed* that was her,» Maeve subvocalized to Gigi and Mason, her tone accusing.

Crystal, hearing the question in Gigi's earbud, hunched her shoulders.

"Seerusly? Ya 'kay with that?" Gigi asked Barney.

His eyes lit up. "Sure! If Sleena did it, they must've been bad guys. Like Club Juzz." He smiled up at Crystal in open admiration. "Or the rape gang, or the Red Skullz, or even..." his voice lowered. "The Breaker. You did get him in the end, didn't you? You and Tash. Some people said *you* were the Breaker, but I know you weren't.

"They say a stealth chopper took him and you away for experiments. Is that how you lost your memory?"

The words triggered a series of images in staccato flashes. *Blood. Tears. Fury.* Bodies falling at her feet.

Arcing blood.

She was brought back to herself by a solid tread approaching down the passageway. From it emerged a large adult ogre wearing a welder's apron. He frowned around at the group. "Son? Everythin' all-"

Then his eyes locked on Crystal, his mouth opening on a grin full of large teeth. "Sleena! Girl, s'*good* to see ya!" He strode around the bench. "Gigi," he nodded in passing, before sweeping Crystal up in a bone-creaking hug.

Putting her back down he held out a huge, heavy knuckled hand to Maeve. "Miz Díaz Cruz, yah? Lorien? Welcome ta our li'l shop. I'm Teef. Y'all met m'son Barney?" One large hand rested on his son's shoulder as he beamed in pride.

They introduced Mason, and Teef eyed the group. "So, wiv Sleena here, an' Lorien's headwoman an' *didge*-wiz Gigi consultin' m'own young *maker*-wiz, summat big goin' down, yeah? Spill."

Crystal vibrated with urgency. "But who am *I*? Can we please find that out first?"

"She's had her memories erased, Dad," Barney explained, then spread his hands. "We don't really know," he told her. "You turned up one night here, traded with Dad for some water, and buckets. Kind of desperate, but you never really explained why. On the run, but you never said who from. You used to bring me drones. A lot of drones. Helped us expand the business."

"Got ya a scope," Teef said, holding his hands six inches apart. "Three hunnerd times mag."

"You lived around here just for a couple of months," Barney took up the story. "Then the Fist Fest." His eyes shone with wonder. "You were amazing. In the final bout, you went up against Tash."

Maeve stared at Crystal – Sleena? – in a mix of surprise and doubt. "You challenged a *vampire*? And not just any vamp, but *Tash*? How are you still alive? You really are crazy." Then she spun to Barney. "Uh, Sleena did lose, right?"

"Yeah, but it was epic!" Barney gushed. "Epic. Then they teamed up. Next day, they wiped Club Juzz off the map – freed every kid there. And the next night, Sleena came back on her own, hunting The Breaker. They say she cornered him in Corpse-Stick Tower, and a secret mil helicopter took them both away. That was over a year ago."

There was a long silence.

Barney waved to the sunlight outside. "But since you're out in the daytime it means Tash *didn't* turn you into a vampire like people said!"

"Does anyone know where I came from, before all that?" Crystal asked, her voice small, pushing away the feeling of blood sodden sleeves and fire at her back. The memory of giggling as a tall woman crouched in gloom, ripping out a tattooed leather clad man's neck. She felt an eager kind of *tingling* at her fingertips.

"Sorry, Sleena," Teef said. "Ya kep' real dark 'bout that."

Maybe I'm remembering films I've seen? But in her body, in the muscles of her arms and legs and hands, she felt the reality behind those images. Then the memory of a birthday cake in a darkened room flashed to mind, terror swelling beneath it.

She spun away, focusing on the shelves and benches around her, the setting sun's light flooding in through blurry windows, and finally the people watching her in concern.

She was starting to wonder if she even *wanted* her memories back. *Maybe I came here before to escape my past?*

"We're here with a more urgent problem," Maeve told Teef and his son. "Mason fished, ah, Sleena out of the harbor the night before last. She'd had her memories erased, and it's ongoing. Yesterday we did a PET scan of her, and in the parts of her brain that handle memory we found millions of tiny computers. Primitive, wireless linked, sitting in a web of nano-scale structures, which is where things get interesting.

"This morning, at that clinic in Carmichael, she was attacked. Tranqued. And at that point some 'metaphysical' sentient AI got into the network of computers in her head and took control. Killed all her attackers and left, which is where we met up with her – with it."

Barney and Teef goggled at her but said nothing, merely glancing from time to time to Crystal as if for reassurance.

"At first the AI seemed okay," Maeve continued, "but later it admitted it wanted to change humans – remove their emotions. We managed to jam it before it could spread into the net. Gigi scrubbed it from Sleena's head this morning. And from Mason's cyberware. And from all our Links."

Teef and Barney exchanged looks.

"Ya not foggin' us?" Teef asked.

"Fuck no," said Maeve.

"Chit no," said Gigi.

"I wish we were," said Mason. "Gigi thinks she's managed to stop Sleena losing more memories, but she needs your son's help to understand the other structures in her brain. We think the AI 'got in' because her lack of memories left a kind of vacuum. Gigi thinks the structure self-assembled, and could self-disassemble. Our theory is Sleena's being hunted because they're developing tech to rewrite memories, but she escaped before they finished and could clean up the shit inside her head."

"Hey!" Sleena objected.

"Get over yourself, girl," Maeve shot back. "That freaking AI thing wants to 'fix' humanity. And the fact Omega's going to such lengths to keep their tech secret and recover it says they're not planning to use it for the common good."

"Wow," Barney drawled. "So you need Gigi and I to help Sleena save the world!" He looked madly happy, vibrating on the spot. "So, what have you brought me?"

Gigi took out a data chip and sample vial. "'S not jus' Omega's lookin' for Sleena. Tik Tek's mixed up too, we reckon. That's why we're stayin' off-net." She passed him the data cube. "The scan data. 'Ncludin' a pretty sleek 3D model. I'm thinkin' it's a molecular machine, made'a carbon nanotubes." She tapped the vial.

"Come with me," Barney told her, snatching up her offerings and hurrying around the counter. "We'll take it to my fabbing lab. Uh. Wait." From the bench he took the rag-wrapped thing he'd been working on when they'd all entered. Staring at Sleena, he wet his lips. "You've really lost your memories?"

She nodded.

Grimacing, he glanced down at the rag in his hand then back to her. "A friend of yours came by, a few hours ago. She was going to talk to Doc Truman. She and her friend, a guy."

He described Marcie Dunkirk and Vincent Moore, without naming them. "We should meet up with them. But for now, I need to give you something.

"It won't take more than a minute or two," he added, seeing Maeve's frown. "Wait here a bit, Gigi?" He bounced from foot to foot, teeth bared as he waited for her answer.

"I guess," she said, clearly intrigued.

Barney dragged Sleena deeper into the shack, the others all exchanging quizzical looks.

Crystal heard Mason asking who Doc Truman was, but she was more interested in what Barney wanted. Once in his room, he spoke rapidly. "Your memory's really gone?"

"Yes!"

"Bouncing baby bugs! Okay, look...." He paused, collecting his thoughts. "You never explained why, but you had me build this for you." He unwrapped the rag carefully. "That's a stick-on skin conduction mic and signal unit. When you bite your teeth together twice, quickly, it sends a message to this other stick-on, um, dot. It's a flat-speaker, but I don't know how close it has to be to your ear."

Sleena was shaking her head. "Why do I need this?"

"I don't know! It was super important to you when you had your memories though. Let me stick the mic on. It can go pretty much anywhere, but we don't want it to rub off." He looked her up and down. "Maybe under your arm?"

Bemused, she let him stick it in place, then with a pair of modified tweezers picked up the mole-sized object he'd called a flat-speaker. "It's powered up; do the double bite and let me know when you can hear it."

She did, reacting in surprise when words came from the dot on his fingertip. "What's 'seshoestus desstussten'?" she asked. "Is this a joke?"

"Wow. You heard that? No, it's serious. You were real determined about all this." He thought. "Okay, if you could hear it from there, you'll have no trouble hearing it if we hide it *inside* your ear where people can't see it. Just don't dig it out, okay?"

He looks so earnest. "Uh, okay," she agreed, humoring him.

Barney sighed and relaxed. "Um, so, this is my room," he admitted, shyly. Then his smile froze, and he hurried her out.

Glancing back, she glimpsed a pic of a girl, breasts almost visible beneath a flapping denim jacket, one leg thrust out in mid flight toward an ogre, one far bigger and meaner looking than Teef. The girl looked like her. *Sleena?*

She raised an eyebrow.

Then she was back with the others. Barney, still pink, led Gigi away to another annex where he had his serious gear.

She heard him tell her, "With any luck, I'll be able to fab a macro scale model so I can figure out how it works."

She looked at Maeve, Mason, and Teef, who appeared almost as dazed as she felt. "So what now?" she asked. "Barney said I had a friend looking for me."

"Gigi'll call me when she has news," Maeve said. "First priority has to be getting your memories back, if George is right about how the AI spirit...." She shook her head. "I can't believe I just said that: 'AI spirit'. Anyway, if he's right, your amnesia helped it get to you.

"So while Gigi and Barney geek out, let's see if we can find this friend of yours, or Doc Truman." She shrugged. "Who knows, maybe he'll have magic that can help. Won't hurt to let him try. Barney said your friend's looking for him. Maybe grab an early dinner on the way. Landwave still running, Teef?"

"A'course. I'll stay here, keep an eye on the kids. Bump Links?"

Mason and Maeve both did that, exchanging contact IDs with him before he saw them to the door. He gave Sleena a quick farewell hug. "Ya real don' mem me?" he asked, chuckling when she ducked her head. *Weird, seein' Sleena shy.*

He waved as they scrambled up the slopes – reassured by Sleena moving as surely and silently as ever. *Well, been quiet roun' here since she 'vapped*, he thought, watching them go. But maybe it'd be wise to spread the word to watch for outsiders sniffing around.

He had a hunch things were about to get interesting.

CHAPTER 57

Dr Alex Harmon, in his guise of kindly Doc Adrian Truman, dipped the delicious fresh-baked bread into the best-not-identified stew, casually assessing the other 'diners' at the Landwave.

Though appearing relaxed, he sat alert for any sign of trouble, any suspicious move toward him; hiding the distaste he felt at being surrounded by the assorted mutants, Altereds, and simple failures unable to fit into the thriving society only a few kilometers west.

How he wished to be back there, even if it kept him largely sequestered in the Department's underground complex. *You did want to get out and breathe some fresh air, Alex.* He should be more careful with his wishes.

As he ate, studiously ignoring the stew, he mulled over what he had learned from questioning the mutant boy that morning. It had taken care, but guided by his mind probe it had not been too hard to steer the child back to the heart of the mystery. And finally, he had made progress.

He now knew that Leeth – as Sleena – had had Barney construct a device with a tiny speaker tuned so low only she would ever hear it; after providing her a small recording device, the day before she had arranged to meet him.

He still did not have the full details, but the broad shape of Leeth's feat was already clear. She had *not* broken his controls. Instead she had found a technological workaround – and then misdirected him, deceiving him into thinking she'd shattered his magically-woven mental bonds.

He smiled. One had to admire both the audacity and the cunning.

Unfortunately, the Department had been unable to supply him with any biological samples from the girl at the center of this morning's Tazman-Dungog clinic attack. If any had existed, they had perished in the fire.

So the key questions remained: where was she, and how to find her?

And at that instant, as if summoned by his thought, Leeth herself strolled into the eating area not fifty meters from him. Appalled, his fork froze on its journey to his lips.

She was accompanied by a Caucasian male and a shorter Hispanic woman. All three made their way to the row of food stalls sheltered under the rock overhang that gave the area its name. Leeth had hacked off the long platinum hair extensions the Department had provided for her Crystal Winters identity, and dyed her hair black. She also wore an unflattering sundress, but he knew her instantly.

Her eyes flicked across the rowdy crowd seated at the rough tables or squatting casually nearby; pausing for a moment on him with a tiny frown. With a start, he remembered his food, the fork completing its interrupted journey.

She didn't recognize me – my disguise is better than I hoped!

He continued surreptitiously watching the three as they ordered from 'Stew Flew', chatting to the Bastean cook who ran it. But his feeling of casual superiority faltered when the feline woman nodded and pointed a ladle in his direction and the three turned toward him. For just an instant, he considered his Link: calling the Department for help, to say he'd found her. There was no time though. Already his deadly young ward and her two companions approached. He forced himself to an outward calm.

Inwardly though his pulse accelerated. How long till she saw through the beard, the bizarre lack of eyebrows, the shaved head? Ten seconds? Twenty?

Heart thumping in his chest, three beats to every one of her soft footfalls, he hunted for escape. He couldn't outrun her. Couldn't control her, not with the ignorant little mutant's device presumably still at work. Unless it had failed?

Perhaps a Sleep spell? He'd never felt the need for the 'blunt instrument' of a physical damage spell – if he had, he could have used it to destroy her device and bring her under his control.

Invisibility?

But he knew even that would not avail him, against her: she would hear his breathing. Even now, she could probably hear his heart pounding in his chest. That alone would make her suspicious. His throat felt full, choking on stew he could no longer swallow.

Had any others noticed the incipient drama? He saw one or two of the local inhabitants nudging their companions and indicating Leeth, whispering excitedly.

Then his time was up, and the three stood before him.

He was trapped.

"Doc Truman?" the male asked. "Okay if we join you? I hear you know some healing, including for the mind. Mace.

Maeve. Crystal."

Harmon felt paralyzed, braced for Leeth to dive at him –
then laughed aloud in sudden relief, almost spraying his
food. Because he had remembered his other conditioning –
she *couldn't* harm him.

Relief was followed by a surge of self anger at forgetting
that even for a second. At freezing like a fearful rabbit.

Stress, he self-analyzed. *Stress, and relief at finding her
alive.* That, and his full appreciation of the deadly archetypal
Huntress he had created. Now linked to a still more deadly
Aztec god of death. From the relaxed but puzzled smiles on
their faces, her fool companions had no conception of her
abilities.

"Forgive me," he said, conscious of their bemusement at
what must have appeared a bizarre outburst. "I am far outside my comfort zone, here."

His fingers twitched, desperate to weave a mind probe
spell. But he dared not. Amazingly, it appeared Leeth *still*
had not recognized him. That would change the instant she
saw the first finger movement of the casting, so well she had
come to know it.

So often he had used it against her.

She eyed him curiously now, her head tilted in that all too
familiar pose, and knew she was listening to his heart, the
pounding drum beats in his chest.

Calm. Calm. He drew in a slow, steadying breath.

"It still overwhelms me sometimes, being here in one of
the country's maligned 'Dumps' zones. I find myself reacting
as if the media portrayals are fair, where any encounter can
lead to sudden violent death."

Both the man and the woman's eyes flicked toward the girl
at their left, at that remark. *Ah.* So they were less than total
fools.

Meaningless pleasantries followed, as they asked about
him and he reeled off his now automatic lies. Social historian; field research; noble 'Sustainer' Dumps communities.
He noticed the woman relax at that last point. From her
bearing, he guessed she perhaps headed such a community
herself. He also sensed both a banked hostility from her toward the male, 'Mace', and wistful regret, concealed. The
man projected an air of affability, but that was largely a
mask.

He used the time to shift his gaze so he no longer saw the physical world but the astral, Percepting their emotions directly. He took care to focus mainly on the surface aural patterns around the eyes, to give the appearance of maintaining eye contact and hide what he was doing. Something Leeth herself had forced him to learn, to cope with her.

What he saw surprised him. All three were tense, a little desperate, but all felt a genuine diffuse hope toward him. Which sharpened with the man's next question.

"I've heard you do a little magical healing. Including the mind?"

Leeth's aura... from his peripheral 'vision', its unfamiliarity bewildered him. He found himself studying it directly, even at the risk of revealing his use of magical senses.

He scarcely recognized her aura. Or, that was not quite true. He did recognize it. He'd seen it before. When she was an eight-year-old child. Before his... interventions.

"What about amnesia, have you ever had to deal with that?" Mace asked.

Only a single heavy thump of his heart gave a clue as to how hard the question struck him. *It explained so much.* He held his expression unchanged.

"I am not a practicing psychologist," he lied, "and Amnesia is very rare, but I have studied it. I believe I could be helpful." Inside however, he exulted.

It explained everything – why Leeth had failed to report in to the Department. Why his attempts to locate her through psychometric spell-casting had failed.

But his magical controls were woven far deeper than mere memory. Could he end this, right now? It was worth the risk.

Looking down at the filthy, scarred plastic tabletop and rubbing at his face, he covered his mouth and muttered, low enough so only she could hear: *"Leeth: Mode One."*

He looked up, innocently.

"What's Leeth Mode One?" she asked. "Is that a disease?"

He fought to control his shock. *Impossible. How could she...?* Not only had his obedience command failed, she had casually broken his even stronger restriction against communicating its existence. It took him seconds to gather his wits. What did that mean, for his other protections from her? His skin crawled. Were his controls still there, just buried, or disconnected – or had they been erased?

He kept all that from his face. "Yes. A rare syndrome, an old tutor of mine once described. Leeth Mode One. I doubt it applies here though."

"Rats," she said. "But you might be able to help?"

She had finished her food, he saw. During the conversation she had wolfed it down with appreciative moans.

He allowed himself a small smile. Some of the Leeth he knew was still there. Had Omega's technology destroyed her memories, though? Or had they merely locked them away, cut them off from her recall as his own early treatments had, for a cleaner slate to work from?

He nodded, hiding the surging joy he felt. *She has come directly back to me. Placed herself in my hands.* Back into the hands of the one person with spells to probe and mold her mind.

If anyone could undo what Omega had done, it was he. He would restore her memories. At least, those he chose.

By so doing, he would reinstate his total control over her. And this time, he would make no mistakes, leave no loophole for her to exploit. He allowed himself a small smile.

"When you have all finished eating, why don't we find somewhere I can work from?" He thought through the idea of taking them to the hovel the locals had provided him with for services rendered. But would she stay silent as her memories returned?

Most unlikely.

"That'd be great!" Crystal said.

Mace and Maeve looked equally relieved.

He permitted himself another small smile. It would be good to have control of her once again; safer for everyone, too. And now he knew of her boy mutant's technological workaround, he could simply order her not to use it.

He could order her to explain how it worked.

Better still, with his control restored he could put her under sufficient stress to guarantee her next Unfolding, drive her to finally reach her full potential.

Briefly he considered alternatives. A Suggestion spell? In the circumstances, most unlikely to work. Call the Department, have them fly her out by chopper? But Sleena was well-liked here: that could easily lead to a small war. No, he would handle it himself: here, now.

He rose, offering Leeth his hand, and she took it.

She took it.

Should her companions be allowed to live? Or used as sources of stress, killed by her own hand?

It was too early to decide. At long last though, he held all the cards.

This time, he would play them consummately.

CHAPTER 58

Harmon led his unsuspecting visitors to the Fisher clan. In the late afternoon twilight, he found two of the elders repairing nets as they gazed out over the Bay, talking.

"Wayfinders Tendo, Marino, good afternoon."

The two men, a salt and pepper haired Japanese and a sun-wrinkled European with thick white locks nodded, their fingers continuing their mending work.

"Truman-san."

"Doc Truman."

Lively eyes assessed his three visitors, and the Japanese man jerked and dropped his work, rising stiffly. "Warrior girl! You return! You are well?" Bowing with surprising grace he eyed her dress with an impish grin. "You try new style?"

"Uh...." She plucked at the thin material.

"Ciao, bella Díaz Cruz," the white-haired man greeted Maeve, raising thick-knuckled fingers in greeting. "What brings Lorien to Hunters Point? Trouble?"

Maeve nodded, introducing Mason as a visitor – and the supplier of that trouble.

"My visitors say Sleena has had her memories erased," Harmon said. "May we use the Moot Hall? I have offered my help."

"You want I send Tomas and Bruk along?"

"That won't be necessary," Harmon said. "We need only privacy, not muscle. But thank you."

Crystal had already caught several whispers that made her wonder at her odd popularity. "Can we hurry this up?"

The two ancient men chuckled. "She hasn't changed, Tendo-san."

"Just don't smash up our Moot Hall," Wayfinder Marino admonished her, waving a finger.

After hand clasps and smiles, Harmon led the Lorien group a short distance from the shore, over the fallen rear wall of a sprawling warehouse. The three other sides of the older building surrounded a neatly made wooden hall.

Two steps led to a pair of tall wide doors, which opened onto a large room. Heavy pine chairs fringed a U-shaped table that filled most of the space. Wooden shutters let in light and air, a switch by the front entrance adding extra illumination from strings of warm bright LEDs. At the far end sat cupboards, a doorway leading into a kitchen area.

The space was big enough to hold sixty, seventy people.

Maeve and Mason strolled the room, checking sight lines through windows and then the kitchen, while Harmon had Crystal pull out two solid wooden chairs to face one another. Motioning for her to take one, he sat in the other.

"Please tell me what you can," he asked Leeth's companions, setting his Department-improved Link to record, and openly casting mind probe. "Just a spell to improve my insights," he said, as pleased as he was disturbed by Leeth's failure to react to the tiny gestures she had grown to loathe over so many years.

The man, 'Mace', did most of the talking, although clearly he skipped many details. Leeth listened intently, uncharacteristically silent.

The key points were that someone – *Omega*, he knew, but didn't say – had erased Crystal's memory. A novel molecular-scale structure had been woven through her frontal and temporal lobes, interspersed with millions of tiny computers. Which for at least a few hours that day had hosted a sentient AI, claiming a connection to her, and 'scared off' an Aztec death god.

That news, so casually delivered, struck Harmon like a club to the head. He reeled, numbed by the effort to hide his reaction. It was followed instantly by fear at the news of Tezcatlipoca's attempted return, and fury at Omega. That they had dared tamper with his life's work, installing technologies that may have ruined it!

Mason continued, Harmon listening in fear and wonder at the hints of some artificial Archetype connected to Leeth. A new one, yet not the Huntress *he* had created. Stunning too was the knowledge that Archetypes could interact.

By the end of the sketchy tale, Harmon's mind spun.

Mason looked apologetic. "Sounds crazy, I know. Not to mention, a lot to take in."

Lorien's shaman had hypothesized Crystal's memory loss and unconsciousness provided a vacuum that allowed the AI – which had named itself Aiyami – to take control. Right now, their computer expert was working with the Dumps area's gadget wizard, Barney, to understand the other structure implanted in her brain.

Harmon pictured the web they described, woven through the memory regions of Leeth's brain, shadowing its dendritic structures. "Implanted, or grown through it?"

All three looked impressed by the question. "Maybe grown, yeah," Maeve said. "Gigi thinks it maybe self-assembled, under programmed instructions."

Harmon took a deep breath. "I believe I have enough to proceed, for now."

Crystal sat forward in her chair, eager. "Finally!"

He felt a little sick, but pushed aside his reluctance. Ultimately this would help her, though she would not see it that way. As usual. "Very well. Close your eyes, and listen to my voice."

He recast the mind probe with easy familiarity, using the micro gestures their years of struggle had forced him to pare the casting to. He formed the information tendrils, surprised when she failed to recognize the hated spell. It was only when he eased its threads into her mind with infinite care she at last reacted. But he was prepared for her usual flood of sensual misdirection. Having an audience helped him resist those distractions, yet once past them, he was far more disturbed by the sheer effort required to slide them deeper. *It's the implanted hardware! Undermining the magic already.*

Breathing steadily, holding his focus, he added the second spell. One of his own creation, to locate memories and present them for inspection. And alteration.

What he found shocked him.

A landscape scoured bare – that was his first impression. Where once a lush jungle had thrived, now a fragile desiccated savanna stretched in all directions.

But closer examination softened that initial dismay. Like the eroded stumps of buildings, parched and shrunken vines littered the terrain. Translucent, broken, and torn, but their true shapes remained perceptible to the knowing eye.

By capricious chance though, this had been a near thing! What mindless, blunt approach had the fools used? This was not the selective targeting of small sets of memories. This was wholesale, wanton erasure.

And there, what brutish new structure was that? Parts of it connected to concepts of the masculine; parts to ownership; parts to worship; obedience. And pictures... he followed the connections, bringing up the blurred image of an Asian face and white lab coat he recognized from Leeth's original briefing: Dr Shinsuke Yamamoto.

Crystal, sharing the memory, *squeaked*. "Oh! Oh!"

Hearing *Leeth* make that sound shocked him. But far worse was being forced to feel, through her, a *reverence* for the man, obedience. He felt soiled. Even understanding the mental construct and seeing the crude framework of belief propping it up, failed to erase the foul taste it left. Snarling, Harmon tore at the tangled, messy web, outraged at its intrusion yet horrified by its echoes of his own work, and how it clung to it. He tore away sticky strands, exposing his far deeper and wider structures buried lower.

She made a puzzled protest as he toppled the false idol.

It broke his concentration. He opened his eyes to a confused Crystal and suspicious Mace and Maeve.

Crystal's eyes bored into his, desperate. "Who... God? You took... God?"

"There is no God," he spat. "Certainly not some jumped-up Japanese thug in a lab coat. That was the man who implanted *machinery* in your brain for his own crass ends."

Even as their suspicion drained away, the audacity of his own hypocrisy stole his breath. Controlling his breathing, he calmed himself. "Let's start again. For now I will focus on restoring the memories I see were almost blasted from existence."

"Almost?" she asked, her voice hushed. Nodding gamely then, she sat back in her chair, hope clear in eager eyes.

Lost innocence restored.

Stolen innocence, an inner, censorious voice sneered.

He set it aside.

Edgy and discomfited, he swallowed the guilt and recast both spells. Then, straining with effort, added a third, another of his own devising. This one a variant of the simple healing spell.

Delicately, he laved its energies over the withered traces of her memories, spreading it widely. It would be unwise to restore pieces of the ruined network one by one, in isolation. Unbalanced tensions could tear it apart, while uneven growth would eat at fainter memories or leave them buried and lost, to decay in silent darkness.

Which would return first? Those etched deepest? Or those most central to who she was? At what stage would his repairs, strengthening her memories, restore them to her? He trickled the modified healing magic into her, seeing it fire up patterns of neurons while supercharging her body's creation of specific proteins. His magic wove a symphony, linking related proto-concepts, repairing connections crumbled into trails of dust in the debris below. He hoped there was sufficient coherency, that only valid memories would emerge from the wreckage she had brought him.

She whimpered, and he 'saw' an old man's face in darkness, sails filled and spread above her in the night, telling her 'human beings kill only for food'. Grief engulfed her, and him by proxy.

At her cry, they both snapped back to themselves.

"What... what?" Tears streamed down her face, and in shock he found his own cheeks wet, water running into his beard.

He stared at her in dawning horror, becoming aware of what he must do here today: make her live through those memories again. It would be far worse than he had anticipated – for her of course, but for him too.

Ironically, the mental barricades he had constructed to lock her earliest memories from her had protected them from erasure. Would those barriers withstand this healing? Yet he had erected them once; he could do so again. Or perhaps there would be no need? She was no longer an eight-year-old child. He had already shaped her as he had wished.

It took time to calm her and reassure the two watchers – and to settle his own nerves. "I warned you this may be painful. Do you wish me to stop?"

"No!" she answered.

As he had known she would.

He began again. This time, he cast the spell with more force, while shepherding it past the interference of the implanted devices.

The patterns strengthened, her inner landscape growing in richness but blurred, the fractal surface of its focus held at arm's length.

Her face softened, falling into lines of childlike wonder, filled with love and trust – as she looked at *him*.

"Keepie?" she breathed, her voice small, her arms reaching for him, yearning to be held.

It very nearly undid him.

Could he not simply stop here, let her start again? Undo all his mistakes?

He groaned, yearning toward a possibility that felt like redemption, no longer sure he could proceed.

But if he left her like this, how much of her true self would he be stealing from her?

Maeve frowned. "You've stopped. Why is she looking at you like that? Who's Keepie?"

"Keepie? Who's this lady?"

"Hush," he told her, his voice very nearly breaking. To Maeve he said, "Someone from her past."

Maeve and Mason exchanged glances. Whatever they were witnessing, it was clearly exacting a toll on both participants. Truman looked bereft.

He shook himself. "This young lady is, I am told, both strong and lethal."

Mason frowned but nodded. "True."

"The memories I sense forming are dark and painful. They may be too much for her."

"I can handle them!" Crystal insisted. "Keep going!"

Harmon shook his head. The proposal he needed had to come from her. "I confess my fear is more for myself and your friends here than for you. In you I sense a spirit stronger than Damascus steel. No, I fear that in the pain lying ahead, you may lash out unconsciously."

Maeve lifted her chin. "She did take out Rigg, Barj, and Lottie without breaking a sweat. Made Anika look a child when they sparred. She's stronger than an ogre, and faster than a snake."

Crystal rolled her eyes. "Fine! If you're all so scared, tie me up. Just do the stupid magic to bring my memories back! I can feel them, like they're pushing up out of the dark."

There were no ropes in the Moot Hall. Maeve and Sleena went together to request them.

Outside, people had begun to gather, one young couple in particular keen to thank the girl for saving them both, dismayed to learn she'd lost her memories. Faces turned to Doc Truman in the doorway, selflessly working now to restore them. The two nodded and waved their approval.

Once again Harmon felt sick at what lay ahead.

He needed to warn the crowd what to expect. Stepping forward, he raised his hands for silence. "This 'operation' will be painful and exhausting, both for Sleena and myself. At her request we are fetching ropes to bind her, for her safety and our own. There may even be screams, shouts. I ask you not to interfere."

He read the emotions of the rabble, seeing incipient threads of doubt and distrust. "Perhaps one or two of the Fisher clan Wayfinders should bear witness." He hated the necessity for any observers, but with Leeth restored and under his control, *no one* here could prevent their departure.

Although it need not be a bloodbath – he *did* have the Invisibility spell he had designed all those years ago, yet never used for its original purpose. The thought that perhaps no one here would die today felt oddly relieving: he could simply order Leeth to silently leave, unseen.

He smiled. Her disappearance would only add to the myth of Sleena.

The crowd chose the two Wayfinders who had granted permission to use the hall, and Maeve and Leeth returned with the required ropes.

Back inside, Harmon stood watching, hiding his amusement as the others used their skills to bind Leeth to the strongest and heaviest chair in the Hall, an oaken monstrosity. Just a touch of Suggestion ensured they tied the ropes around her wrists in such a way they would be safe from her deadly invisible claws.

But knowing that smile would be his last for some time, he felt it wither and die.

Grimly, braced for trouble, he took his seat and faced her.

CHAPTER 59

Doc Truman surveyed the room: the closed shutters, the doors shut tight. His bleak expression sent a ripple of unease through the observers. "In my opinion Sleena has suffered traumas – terrible traumas, and more than just a few. Returning her memories to her will be painful, but without them she would not be herself."

"Blah, blah," she griped. "Can you just shunting *start*?"

"How painful?" Mason asked.

"Years' worth," Doc Truman said at last. "Compressed into minutes, or hours, their return could break her."

Crystal rolled her eyes. "They won't, but this frustration might. Just get on with it."

Another implication struck Harmon. Earlier, she had repeated his words: repeating secrets, untouched by his controls. That meant the same could happen to other equally sensitive information, such as the existence of the Department. Who knew what she might cry out in extremity?

That the witnesses were limited to just these four could prove an unintended kindness. Briefly, he wished he had the design for a sound suppression spell. But this would be tricky enough as it was. Juggling a fourth spell....

He realized he was procrastinating, trying to delay the pain. The room fell silent as he cast his first spell, the mind probe.

Low enough for only her ears, he whispered, *"I need to warn you of one more thing. You are more special than you know. You have been entrusted with deadly secrets. Spoken aloud, they would place death sentences on everyone here except you and I. Under no circumstances share your memories."*

"What secrets?" she asked.

Her too-loud question woke whispers from their witnesses, and Harmon in her mind read embarrassment.

"What secrets?" she said, far more softly.

"You don't need to speak. To heal your mind I must monitor your thoughts. Just think your questions clearly to me.

"You and I work for a government agency protecting this country – including from one uncanny threat that dare not even be thought about." For a moment, he considered telling her of the Foe, before realizing how insanely dangerous that would be in the circumstances.

She shook her head. *'Sure, spamboy.'*

"You will be able to judge for yourself – assuming you survive the shocks ahead." He hesitated, then added, *"You will hate me. But I did what I did for your own good."*

With those ominous words, once again Harmon cast the second and third spells, stacking each atop the one before, a feat of concentration few mages would attempt.

For the watchers, long minutes passed in which little appeared to happen. Doc Truman's hands grew tense, sweat beading his brow

Then together, Sleena and he groaned.

Harmon and Leeth shared the memory of a four-year-old bouncing over a prairie, tears whipped from her cheeks into darkness. Harmon had seen this before, when he had first blocked it, her memory of being whisked away in the Sky Corn Tribe's land yacht one night.

Outside, muffled by the heavy wooden doors, an argument began.

Sleena groaned again, her eyes still shut. Then her face lit with joy. "Faith!" she cried.

The next moment she and Doc Truman hunched in on themselves, teeth gritted, shivering. Sleena said nothing, simply rocked in her chair against her bonds, but the Doc jerked in shock. "What in the name of sanity!" His lips clamped shut. He had thought her tale of a killing frost, of Faith hauling her from it to safety, a mere child's fantasy.

"Oh!" she cried out, then giggled.

The Doc blanched. In dismay, he shared her near death at her friend's hands – paws? – when the cyborg dog's laser shattered the rock face behind her. "Sweet buttered hell." His experiment had nearly ended there and then, his subject aged just nine.

Forced to relive her childhood he gathered his resolve about him like armor, bracing for the torments to come. It failed to prepare him for an unexpected and far more recent memory: Leeth emerging from his mental bonds in a high-rise building, assassination completed, turning in horror from a birthday cake, red drops falling stark on white icing...

"Luiz!" she screamed, heartbreak hammering her afresh. Her eyes opened, glaring at the strangely familiar figure facing her, and threw herself against the heavy ropes in sudden recognition. "You bastard! *Bastard!*" She strained forward, the ropes tautening, creaking...

Behind them the doors flew open, slamming shut immediately as Marcie Dunkirk stormed into the room. "What the *fuck* is going on here?" she demanded, scanning the tableau and stalking forward, a taser pistol raised. "J-" she stopped and started again. "Sleena? Let's get you out of here."

Looking around, she singled out Mason, brandishing her weapon at him. "I'm not afraid to use this."

Mason and Maeve both appeared more bemused than worried.

But even with his back to her Dr Alex Harmon had recognized the voice: Marcie Dunkirk. *Of course.* At the worst possible moment. Against his express statement to let 'Jane's parents' deal with the problem.

Sleena stared sightlessly at the ground, lost in a storm of heartache at the enormity of what she'd done. *I killed him; cut off his head.* Yet certain the man she faced now had caused it. *By my hands though. But how?* How *did I do that?* The memory of death burned in her fingertips. Her hands spasmed, clawing for the ropes around her wrists.

"Sleena?" Marcie said again, edging closer. She kept an eye on the four spectators to this torture scene or whatever it was. *"Jane?"* she whispered, sidling around her friend so she could see the bald guy's face too. *"What's going on?"*

Jane's head lifted, her eyes slowly focusing on her. Then she cringed. "Let me guess: I know you?"

Marcie's mouth fell open. She turned to the bald man. He looked weird: a thick gray and black beard but no eyebrows at all, though his eyes burned with an intensity-

Recognition jolted through her. "*You!* I might have fucking known! What have you done to her? Let her go this instant!" She thrust the taser up under his chin.

Across the room, Maeve stood. "Cool your chips, girl. Assuming Sleena's a friend of yours, you should know she's lost her memories. Doc Truman's trying to restore them. Now who the raping one percent are you?"

Marcie took a jerky step back, head shaking, her gaze jumping between the woman, Jane's evil uncle, and Jane herself – who had a really weird expression on her face. Worry, shock, guilt....

"I call poll-shit. 'Doc Truman?' He's not Doc Truman, he's a monster! He's controlled her and manipulated her all her life. If she's lost her memories you can be sure as Hell he had something to do with it."

She aimed her taser at him. "What's really going on here, uh, 'Sleena'?" Not wanting to let Jane's foul uncle out of her sight, she spared a glance to her friend.

But Jane nodded, her jaw working. "Until just now, my earliest memory was this morning. *Doc Truman's* fixing me."

Marcie glared at him. "I just *bet* he is." She studied the man. She'd only met him once, and that at night, in a park. But she'd *seen* him use his hold on Jane. He'd controlled her, ordering her about like she was just a bot.

She'd helped Jane break that control. "Make me shoot you again," she threatened him.

Harmon made a casual gesture, once again looking relaxed, using it to cover his casting of a Suggestion spell. He felt Leeth's friend unconsciously resist it, but knew it had at least partly slipped through her defenses. "I am acting here at the request of your friend, and hers – as well as her mother. Who, I believe, warned you not to interfere? Yet here you are.

"We all want her memories restored. Although her new friends," he inclined his head toward Mason and Maeve, "say the situation is even more complex and twisted than anyone knew."

"You know this sliv?" Maeve asked him.

"We have met," Harmon admitted. To Marcie he said, "The more people who connect you to Sleena, the harder it will become for her to carry out her parents' wishes."

"Maybe that'd be best for her," Marcie snapped, wondering if the woman she'd spoken to even *was* Jane's mother?

"Who are her parents?" asked Mason. "What wishes?"

Harmon ignored the questions, speaking to Marcie. "Your actions also make you and your own family a target for Sleena's enemies." He added a mind probe spell to the Suggestion. "How *did* you know she was in trouble?"

"None of your biz. Like I told, uh, *Sleena's* mother, it was pure luck. I just tried to call her."

Harmon read the thought behind the story. The warning had come from her younger sister, Amanda. In a dream. How curious.

"You know my mother?" Sleena asked him.

Marcie looked from Jane to her uncle, and then to the others. All watching, avid. Jane's uncle studied her too, with that smirk she'd instantly hated. No wonder Jane despised him.

His expression soured, like he'd heard the thought, and Marcie frowned. *Are you reading my mind, you slimy-*

"Do you know my mother?" Jane begged her.

From glaring at Truman, Marcie turned to her friend. "Not really. I've just spoken a few times by Link to a woman who *claims* to be your mother."

"Claims?" Jane asked.

"Yeah, claims." She jabbed her taser toward Jane's uncle, but he only met her eyes and shook his head pityingly, as if to say 'you're making a terrible mistake'. She flushed.

"It doesn't matter," Sleena said. "We're wasting time. When Doc Truman restores my memories, *I'll* know all this."

Marcie's finger tightened on the trigger. "No. You can't trust him. Get someone else to do it. Anyone else.

"Tell me, did he try to use any strange phrase on you since you've met, Sleena? Maybe a collection of nonsense words, or a weird phrase that didn't make sense? He has this control phrase he uses, to make you do anything he says. It's like it makes you his slave. I bet that's what he wants to do now.

"He might restore your memories, but it'll cost you your freedom."

Crystal looked from Doc Truman, who'd already brought back some of her memories, to the angry determined girl who clearly knew her. *I trust her,* she realized. She wasn't sure why she did, but she did.

So, *had* Doc Truman whispered to her? She didn't think so. "Did he, Mason? You or Maeve would've heard."

The two exchanged a look. Maeve raised one eyebrow, and Mason shook his head.

"Not necessarily," he said, slowly. "Not if he whispered to you. Did he?"

She eyed Doc Truman, sitting with arms folded, looking bored. But was that just an act? "Before we started, here, he did. He whispered that I was special. That I know secrets that could get you all killed if you knew them."

"Burn the puking plastic, *that* I can believe," said Maeve. She turned to Truman. "All the same, you knew both Sleena and Miss Mystery Bitch here, and Sleena's maybe-parents. But you never mentioned any of that."

"For good reason, which you will be able to confirm with Sleena herself after her memory is restored. But there is literally no one else who could help her. Memories are sets of linked neurons – complex patterns in a vast space. Only someone with my unique and specific knowledge can repair those faded and torn networks. Otherwise you would fill her head with false memories. It's easily done – that fact has been known a hundred years, long before magic's return.

"Only I can restore her memories, because only I know what traces of memory in her brain are true, and what fantasy. As well, I sincerely doubt there is another mage on the planet with a spell suited to such a repair."

"So we have to trust you?" sneered Marcia.

"You have to admit it does seem to be working," Mason said. "George didn't get far."

"Let him try," said Sleena, the words pulled from her like teeth.

"A minute ago you were calling him a bastard!" objected Maeve. "Looked like you wanted to kill him."

"And *you* said a sentient AI might reclaim her if her memories were not restored." Harmon stood. "But I will not force my help where it is unwanted."

"Sentient AI? What?" demanded Marcie.

Mason threw up his hands. "Look, we don't have a smekking choice. Doc Truman's right. And if he's the only game in town, we have to play the cards he's dealing."

Sleena snarled. "I swear, if you all don't stop arguing I'm gonna tear myself free and toss every one of you out! It's *my* head. *I'm* the one who's lost her memories. It's *my* choice. Now sit down, shut up, and let Doc Truman do his freaking spell." She glared at each of them in turn.

"Doc *Tru*man," sniffed Marcie. "More like Doc *Lie*man."

Sleena growled, low in her throat.

"Fine!" Marcie snapped. "But I'll be telling you 'I told you so' when he double-crosses your innocent butt!" She snarled into her Link: "Vince. She doesn't *want* to be rescued yet. Just wait there." Stalking to the side of the room opposite the other watchers, she threw herself into a chair, pointing two fingers in a 'V' from her own eyes to Jane's evil uncle.

"Go sit with the others," he ordered her. "You *will* object once I begin. Let them answer your objections. Just try to hold your inane whispering to a minimum. You treat this like a carnival show, but it is psychic brain surgery."

He lifted a hand as she opened her mouth. "And the reason I know you will object is because the return of her memories will make her relive years of trauma. She *will* scream. It may break her."

"I won't break."

They all heard the determination in Sleena's voice – but everyone doubted her strength.

Everyone but Marcie. "Just call for my help if you need a hand to hold," she said. "I'm here."

Sleena saw she meant that – really meant it. *She believes in me.*

"Then perhaps you will change your seat now?" Doc Truman said, looking at Marcie.

"Yeah. Yeah, you know what, I will!"

Marcie stood, but instead of joining the others, dragged a chair up alongside her friend and gripped one bound hand in both hers. "Why wait to be asked though, hey?" she said, her grin lop-sided.

Sleena felt a surge of warmth and hope at the touch. *Is this what love feels like?*

"Brain surgery," Harmon admonished Marcie, glaring at her. "Do not jog my elbow."

Marcie squeezed her friend's hand, giving her a reassuring smile. "Just don't crush my fingers."

"Don't let him stop, even if it looks like I'm hurting. I can handle it." A shiver of doubt ran through her, half felt memories stirring. She braced herself for a warning pain... that never came. The absence only deepened her unease.

Once again, Harmon cleared his thoughts and recast the spells. Once again eased his spells past the obstruction of the manufactured objects planted in her brain. Closing his eyes, ignoring Marcie Dunkirk, he restarted the gentle healing, reinforcing wispy strands, mending others. Pouring life back into the damaged and eroded mental landscape.

Each watcher, seeing the young woman bound and helpless in the chair, struggled to reconcile the innocence on that face with the history they knew.

For Crystal herself – *or am I Sleena? Or Jane, or... whoever* – as the magic flowed, deep inside she felt a part of her, a tiny stubborn flame, gasp in relief and flare brighter. Determined. *Never give up.*

As long minutes trickled past, a gamut of emotions crossed her face – wonder: *a child, dancing with spirits through a jungle with Faith, tongue lolling, trying to keep* up. Joy: *prowling darkened grounds with the war-dog at her side.* Shock: *Faith's laser, blasting rock.* Determination: *plunging through a ceiling to save Godsson.* Excitement: *her first love-making, with-* Disbelief: *him? Why had she chosen* him? Remembering how she'd felt, the urgency, the power – it seemed pure madness, now. Had he *made* her feel that way somehow? Then dismay: *his coldness, disappointment.*

The bitterness of betrayal: *letting him bind her magically. Tricked into ceding control.*

"No-o-o!" she wailed, wracked. A part of her called for it to stop, but she *needed* to know it all.

Harmon, sharing her journey, burned in caustic shame. Bowing his head, knowing and dreading what still lay ahead. Wishing he could stop now; leave the job half done, his worst crimes forgotten.

But Leeth needed to be herself. She had earned herself.

Feeling tears leaking that he had vowed never to shed, he pushed on.

Horror: *torture. Literal, physical and mental torture, of the worst kind. Taunting her for her weakness, during it. Healing her, after.*

Rage, fury... until she erupted, thrashing in her bonds. "You bastard! Monster! I'll kill you! Kill you!" She lunged forward, determined to stop him.

Marcie, eyes fixed on his in angry horror, felt her fingers crushed, her bones break. But she glared at her friend's foul uncle through that agony, only able to guess the depths of hell he'd dragged her through. She accepted that pain, to share some of Jane's.

Vaguely, she was aware of an odd blue tinge appearing on his cheeks.

Harmon, deep in Leeth's mind, seeing the Imaginal, felt it rise like a black cloud, flowering from a seed of fury. He flinched back as her eyes washed out in a lapis lazuli glow that could mean only one thing: Tezcatlipoca. The vast horror began pushing through from *elsewhere*, hungry.

"No!" screamed Leeth, "he's mine!"

And then, in terror, Harmon saw her drag a *god* back inside herself and thrust it *away*.

He could only stare in shock at what he'd just witnessed,

heart hammering, his whole body trembling, hands shaking like some palsied ancient's.

In contrast, the impossible feat appeared to have appeased Leeth. Panting, she glared at him, death in her eyes.

But as his terror ebbed, remorse and horror rose in equal crushing weights to take its place. With relentless clarity he saw how Leeth clung to her fury at him – its certainty providing an anchor for her sanity.

So be it. It was a price he deserved to pay; that he willingly paid; that he would keep on paying.

He looked around, gathering his wits, realizing none of the fools here had seen what he had, had no idea how close they had all come to Death. He met Leeth's eyes again.

He saw that fury... but in wonder, deeper still, saw the tiny core of stubborn hope. Inextinguishable. Indomitable.

If Leeth ever failed, it would not be through giving up, he understood in that moment. Not ever.

Breathing deep, he pushed on.

CHAPTER 60

When it finally ended, Leeth slumped exhausted and sweating, still bound to the heavy chair. She'd cracked one solid oaken arm though. Large bruises mottled her skin, her wrists and ankles raw.

But although her cheeks glistened with silent tears, her reddened eyes remained locked on Harmon's, furious.

He had succeeded: Leeth had been restored to herself. He needed no mind probe to tell him that. At the thought, hers twisted in his grasp. He found himself served up memories of cruelties he'd inflicted on her from the previous two years, each one fresh, and scalding hot. Two years that capped all the smaller torments of the seven years leading up to them.

Harmon, near exhaustion himself, ignored the reprimand and cast a simple healing spell. In mere seconds the torn flesh at her wrist and ankles knitted together and her bruises faded.

Magic.

Still she said nothing, merely sat panting, eyes like rifle sights locked on him. Unforgiving.

Harmon, drained, briefly closed his. But for a little while longer he still had the Doctor Truman role to play. Gently taking the mangled hand of Leeth's silently sobbing friend in his, he noted the terrible damage.

"I see that once again another pays the price for helping you."

Leeth's angry denial died the moment she saw what she'd done, fury quenched in a flood of shame. "Oh Marcie, no," she whispered.

"This too will hurt," Harmon told the young actress who even now made no sound, jaws locked on her pain, trying to hide it from her friend. "I need to set the bones, but at least I can avoid doing so *until* I heal each."

Shocked silence radiated from the observers as the drama continued.

Marcie's bravery finally failed, unable to hold in a whimper of pain as he set the bones of her middle finger. He swayed in mental exhaustion, struggling to focus the familiar spell. At her tiny sound, Leeth flinched.

Minutes passed: a normal length of time for magic to accelerate the healing of bones. Minutes, though: ten times longer than required for Leeth. Shame burned through him again at that knowledge, that her body had become so attuned to that spell. How many times had he cast it on her? Mostly, to heal injuries he–

He could not complete the thought. He had done only what had been necessary.

His own nerves felt raw, abraded from sharing the relived memories of trauma, but also stunned by how much joy she'd found in her lonely childhood despite him. His eyes met hers again, and he saw the hatred for him burning in them – swamping a fading trace of baffled confusion. He swallowed. Because he *did* care for her, counter to all his determination not to. He had sworn not to; to wall off his emotions to pursue his experiment: the creation of a new magical Archetype.

The Huntress.

And here she sat. Had he been justified? Had the vindication of his theories been worth the cost? The cruel irony was, this ordeal, that had made him see he did care for her, convinced *her* he did not, and never had.

He shook himself, breaking eye contact. *I'm just overwrought: I spent too much time drenched in her memories. I'm not myself.* With effort, he clawed back his usual detachment, wrapping himself in its armor, and returned to the task at hand.

He finished healing each of Miss Dunkirk's remaining fingers, impressed against his will by her courage. He better understood their friendship now, seeing a familiar core of steel in the actress.

Finally it was done.

Leeth raised her eyes, meeting Marcie Dunkirk's, yearning to show how much her friendship meant. "You came for me," she told her. "Again."

"It's what friends do. I'll always come for you, Jane."

Leeth lifted her chin, looking her straight in the eyes. "My name is Leeth," she whispered.

Marcie's mouth fell open, and she couldn't help but look to judge *Leeth's* uncle's reaction.

Jaws clenched, he and Leeth now stared at one another. Leeth smiled, quirking an eyebrow, daring him to object.

He looked away first, and Marcie and Leeth grinned at one another, sharing the victory.

"I'll keep your secret," Marcie promised her.

Harmon glanced at his Link. The entire performance had taken only forty minutes.

He had returned Leeth to herself, but had his control over her also been restored? It should have. Nor was there a better time to test it, with her bound in the chair. This was not payback for her childish attempt to wound him, through her stupid breach of protocol.

He wet his lips, preparing his words, especially what he had learned from her own mind.

Standing, he stretched tiredly, hardly needing to play up his exhaustion as he turned away from everyone in the hall.

Lowering his voice so even Marcie Dunkirk, slumped in against Leeth at her side would not hear him, he whispered the words.

"Leeth: Mode One. Freeze. Make no sound. Open your thoughts to me. Do not resist."

CHAPTER 61

Shock tore through her, redoubling when she found she couldn't even move her eyes. She fought, and failed, to click her teeth together to make Barney's device play the words that would free her.

Instead she sat like a carved statue, scarcely breathing.

But one thing had changed. This time, she could *feel* the bonds in her mind, could sense the shape of what he'd done. Because this time she'd not given her consent? Because that consent was old, tricked from a trusting child?

Her eyes locked, unmoving, she sensed more than saw his fingers twitch in the hated pattern, and moments later felt his mind slide inside hers. Her reflexive defenses failed her, suppressed by his order to 'open her thoughts'.

Hatred flared, and she felt him flinch from it. *Good.*

"How does the device work? Don't speak aloud, think your answers."

But years of automatic evasion kicked in. 'The device' must mean the thing Omega had put inside her head. *'I don't know. I didn't make it.'*

"But you ordered its construction. You must know."

"What's going on?" Marcie demanded. "Why's she sitting so still? Sleena, are you alright?"

Harmon quashed a surge of anger at the attempted interference. *"Do nothing to break my control,"* he whispered, covering his mouth. *"But otherwise pretend everything is fine."*

She tried not to speak, then blinked, determined to pretend everything was fine. She could at least do that much. "I'm all right. It's just a lot to take in." Able to move once more thanks to the new order, she tried again to bite down twice.

Her jaw locked the moment she tried.

Marcie stared at the doctor, her eyes narrowed. "Right. Thanks for the healing, but we'll take it from here." She bent to untie the ropes at her friend's wrists. "What the hell's going on, anyway? What's this about a sentient AI and your memories being erased? Sounds like a pitch for an *Underworld* episode," she joked. "Damn, these knots are like wood. We're gonna need a knife."

Harmon turned away. *"Tell your friends it is too dangerous to involve them any further, that you and I-"*

"Hey," Marcie interrupted him. "Are you whispering? You are, aren't you? You felch-head, you're doing it again!" She drew her taser.

"It is too dangerous to involve you any further, friends," Leeth said. "He and I."

"'Friends'?" said Marcie. "And 'he and I' what?" She took aim, finger tightening on the trigger. "He's done it ag-"

Harmon shaped the pattern of the spell in his mind as he turned to face them all. Desperation fueling him, he hurled all the mental energy of his will through the arcane pattern, holding nothing back.

The Sleep spell crashed through the room.

Taken unawares, Maeve grunted, slumping in her chair, her eyes falling shut. Beside them the two elders' heads also lolled forward. Marcie collapsed in a boneless heap, the beginnings of her desperate resistance crushed. Mason, partially protected by his machine augmentations, struggled before he too succumbed, overwhelmed.

Leeth, as stubborn and suspicious as ever, swayed but fought through it. Though her head bobbed forward, her neck stiffened. Her angry gaze swept the room, taking in the sight of all her allies neutralized, settling finally on the doctor, and his superior little smile.

"As usual Marcie Dunkirk has merely complicated the situation." With a tired breath he fell back into his chair, collecting his reserves.

"That was stupid. Now what're you going to do?" She could tell he wasn't mind probing her now – she'd felt him drop the spell a moment before casting his knockout blow.

At least he looked exhausted.

"Invisibility," he said at last, smiling, "cast on you. I will simply leave, saying that although my part is done the others are still in discussion and not to be disturbed. You will follow me, invisible, hiding your presence. Once we are a safe distance away, you can explain how the device your young Mutie friend built for you works."

Young Mutie friend? Who... did he mean Barney? She filed the slur away: one more reason he needed to die. But his idea would work. She had to break free before that, at any cost. She tried again to click her teeth together to activate it. Once again, her jaws locked.

Harmon rose and stepped forward, bending over the ropes at her wrist as Marcie had. His smile fell as his fingers worked futilely on the insanely compressed rope of the knot. Impossible to untie.

He huffed.

With a strange feeling of relief, she let the desire to kill flow into her fingers and felt her spirit blades slide out. *My invisible claws,* she thought at them. *I can't believe I forgot you!* "Sorry, I can't help," she smirked, wriggling her fingers upward in the empty air above the armrests, unable to reach the ropes.

She watched him searching for a knife, taking delight as his quiet hunt failed.

He found Maeve's gun, but re-holstered it. He couldn't shoot the rope off her – not and pretend everything was still okay inside. She giggled. It was kind of poetic, that her thrashing attempts to free herself before, stopped him from sneaking away with her now.

"It called itself Aiyami," she said, to distract him from using the time to make her explain how Barney's device worked.

"What? What did?"

"The sentient AI thing."

"Nonsense. No doubt they believe–"

"It spoke through my mouth, even when I was unconscious. They have recordings."

She hurried on before he could interrupt. "It also said it was a shard, and I'd kind of killed its earlier form. And that it scared off Tezsh Catlick what's-his-name to get to me."

That snared his attention. "We need to get you back–"

"No we don't." She looked from him, to Marcie slumped asleep in the chair beside hers, to the four others unconscious in theirs, making sure no one was listening. "Have you forgotten? I'm on a–" *mission.*

Her mouth stopped working. She frowned at him. "I'm on a–" *mission,* she tried to say again, but once again couldn't get the word out. Then she realized what was wrong: his very first command, the one he'd used originally to justify implanting those final mental bonds. Orders against revealing anything about the Department to anyone outside it.

"What?" he demanded at her expression.

She angled her chin toward Mason. "He records conversations. Probably even when he's asleep. So...."

She watched him put two and two together.

It was kind of funny, seeing him struggle to drag her chair backward to get her as far from Mason as he could, being the one to make him do that. But she didn't dare formulate any conscious plans to escape his disgusting Mode One control. Since at any moment he might order her to explain Barney's device, or mind probe her like he had before.

But she did need to get free. She shut her eyes, feeling her way over the dimly-sensed shape of his controls in her mind, studying it. It was like a complicated knot, or series of knots. To start unraveling it she just needed to find the ends.

After puffing and dragging her in her chair far across the room, he went back to get a chair for himself. Staggering under its weight he carried it across to her. *Tell me how I can get you out of here unnoticed,"* he whispered, facing her.

"I don't know," she whispered back. She had to repeat it, louder, until he could hear her. "What I was trying to say was, I'm on a mission, remember? Things went kind of sideways after Dr Yamamoto put *me* inside his machine, his 'Writer', but I'm myself again now, and ready to finish the job. I'll just kill him. There's no need to run home."

She eyed him up and down, his strange appearance. "You look really weird with no eyebrows and shaved bald, you know." Not to mention the beard. "Nice disguise. You should've gotten them to give you a gold earring, too. You'd look like a science-pirate."

She could see his patience evaporating. "What I mean is, you're on a mission too, obvi... ous... ly..." *looking for me.* Her words ran to a halt at a surge of hope. *He came looking for me!*

No. *Don't be stupid.* That was a lie, the kind of childish hope she'd killed forever. *You're tied tight in a chair, locked in his foul Mode One obedience!*

Harmon didn't need his mind probe running to guess her thought, and considered playing up to it. But that deception would be too easily exposed.

Sometimes though, a light manipulation was best. *So....*

"I have been on a mission for the last two days, yes: trying to find you." He shook his head, still whispering. "Your choker went dead."

Leeth's chin tucked in as she tried to feel it around her neck – the beautiful piece of spy gear made specially for her by Nelson. *How did I lose my choker?* It was supposed to self-destruct if removed! Had it fallen into Omega's hands?

She grimaced.

"Nelson couldn't locate you," Harmon said, letting some of his feelings show. "Nor could I, magically. I refused to believe you had been killed. I have been trying to find you, trying to learn what happened to you; fearing the worst."

He saw his words strike home even as her expression hardened. "But I was here before that. I came here trying to understand why you cared about these people, this society. But we should return to the Department. From there, we can re-plan-"

She shook her head. "Sure, let's fill them in. But you'd be stupid to waste the chance to show them *you* can be useful outside, too. Not a real agent, of course, but still useful."

Her real motivations were clear – she hoped to break free – but he also saw she wasn't lying. "What are you suggesting?"

"Free me. Team up with us to complete the mission. The Department's okay with 'outsourcing'."

"You would put your friend Marcie in danger?"

"I don't mean *Marcie*," she snapped. "I meant Mason, mainly. And Gigi and Barney for the technical stuff."

Settling back in his chair, he studied her. "It does make a certain sense. At least, to learn what you have discovered before reporting in."

She nodded. "Exactly."

"Since we have time, you will now let me probe your mind without resistance."

Her eyes flew wide, her head shaking in denial as he cast the spell and slid inside. "Explain how your friend Barney's device breaks my control over you." He ignored her dismay as she revealed the stunning simplicity of her solution: his own voice, recorded speaking the words that released his control. A tiny speaker.

"Where is this apparatus?" he demanded.

At her helpless direction, he plucked the device from inside her ear, and the other part that told it to play the sound. And that was all. The rest had been simple misdirection.

He read her hope, that he would activate it by mistake. With her bound in her chair, he very nearly indulged her wish. After all, he only needed to speak three words to lock her back under his control.

Instead he ground the two devices under heel.

Her hatred scourged him. But hidden behind that... he pushed through her smokescreen, finding a new vantage point in her mind: one from which all the strands of his control lay exposed to her view. Even now she studied them, how to pick them apart.

"*Seshoestus desstussten,*" he whispered, and saw the joy at release he had expected – but followed by a frustration she immediately tried to conceal.

Digging, he found its cause: she could no longer sense his magically woven bonds. "*Leeth, Mode One.*" Instinctively she found her vantage point, then skated past it, hoping he hadn't noticed.

Dammit.

He whispered the meaningless sounds that freed her.

Instantly, she flung up a barrage of imagery, fighting his mental probe, but it seemed too obvious a distraction. He shifted his perceptions to the Imaginal. Then lurched back in his chair as deadly planes of force flared from her fingertips, invisible wicked razors extended two full hand spans beyond their tips. Longer than he had ever Percepted before.

They slashed at but could not reach the ropes binding her wrists, then stretched for him before retracting, blocked by his other implanted orders, against injuring him.

And still she struggled.

Genuinely trapped in the chair. The irony of his situation struck him: he had her, could even control her – though at risk of her unraveling his mental bonds – and even had an easy way to spirit her away unseen.

If only he could release the physical bonds she'd set like stone from her struggles.

She stopped at last, panting, studying him in turn, hoarding her new hope and enjoying her apparent checkmate.

They stared at one another – her with fresh hatred, he in weary regret. "Truce?" he said at last.

She considered him through slitted eyes. Then slowly smiled. "I guess I can let you join my mission."

Incredible. There she sat: trapped; aware he could take control of her at any moment; years of trauma a livid pain in her mind – yet her bearing remained that of a queen, her will as strong as ever.

Truly, she was unique. Infuriating and wild, but....

He pulled himself together. *I seem more affected by the*

return of her memories than she does!

She leaned forward. "I should report in while everyone's still asleep!" she whispered. "The Department must've been worried. You'd better call Eagle."

Somewhat dazed, he considered rejecting her suggestion – even briefly considered taking her away, the two of them escaping the Department. Sighing, he quashed that pipe dream. Inserting the earbud, he made the call.

CHAPTER 62

Harmon was not surprised to be connected immediately. Viewing his Link he saw it indicated an encrypted connection, then heard the voice of the head of the Bureau for Internal Development itself. Who was also director and creator of the black ops unit concealed within it: the Department.

"Eagle."

"I have Leeth. She is here with me, but we only have a few minutes to report, and the situation is complex." He pointed to his earpiece, raising an eyebrow at Leeth.

"It's okay, I can hear him," she said, her voice still a whisper. "Can you hear me, sir?"

"Yes."

"So, it's complicated. I've met some people who've been helping me after Omega stuffed my head full of their weird tech, that erases memories. The Doctor," she paused, staring accusingly into his eyes, "just now restored mine. We're in Hunters Point Dumps analyzing the tech. Also, some AI thing got inside my head after I got tranqued at the clinic this morning. We deleted it, but maybe tell Mr Abrams it said it scared off that Tezsh Catlick death god thing to get to me."

Several seconds passed.

"Uh, Eagle? Are you there?"

"Yes. You should return here. Be warned you have a bounty-"

"It's okay, we know about that. But I'm fine now. We can handle this ourselves. I think I should try to destroy the tech, though."

"What is the technology?"

"It uses lots of tiny computers they stick inside your head, all connected. A couple people I trust here are working on it."

There was another short silence. "Working on what, exactly?"

"Well, some samples of the, um, CPUs and the carbon nanotube web thing connected to them."

Again, several seconds of silence. "We'll need samples of that at least. And the AI that 'got inside your head'? Do you have a copy of that? Could it return?"

She grimaced. "I don't know for sure. Until we do, maybe it's a reason to stay away from you guys? It got in and took over while I was unconscious. We jammed it, extracted samples, and erased it. The Doctor's just now restored my memories.

"I think that covers everything."

"Are you making this up, Agent?"

"What? No!"

She heard him sigh. "That's what I thought. So, Nelson's original concerns were on the mark, and Dr Yamamoto has technology for erasing memories. And creating new ones?"

"Um..." she shrugged. "Maybe?" she looked to Harmon.

"I gather Leeth escaped before they could complete the procedure. I did find traces of... beliefs they had begun to create."

"What kind of beliefs?" Eagle asked.

The Doctor suddenly looked uncomfortable. "Ah, general subservience to male authority, and to Dr Yamamoto specifically."

"That sounds problematic," Eagle suggested.

"In my professional opinion, Leeth could have resisted it, with effort. However, I removed it myself."

"How certain are you of that, Doctor? Certain enough to risk Leeth continuing her mission?"

Harmon considered. The artificial beliefs had been an inelegant, sticky tangle, working as well as they had only thanks to interactions with his own controls, and how they had clung to them. He shifted in his seat. "Quite certain," he said, trying to keep Leeth from seeing his discomfort, and Eagle his shred of doubt. He had torn down Yamamoto's construct.

Her eyes narrowed.

"I assume Leeth also lost her choker," Eagle said. "Its removal caused no injury?"

Leeth's hand went to her throat. "Uh, I don't remember."

"She has permanently lost her memories of yesterday," Harmon explained. "I believe Omega's drugs made her unable to form long-term memories for a period."

"So Leeth has no way to communicate with us?"

"No."

"Give her your Link, Doctor. Nelson will update it to accept her biometrics from here.

"Leeth, do not take direct action against Omega until I've had time to digest your report. Get physical samples to the Doctor of the Omega tech and any other material that may be helpful.

"Doctor, Preacher will visit you within the hour at your 'residence' in the Dumps. Be ready to hand over the material.

"Is there anything else?"

Admit it might still be erasing my memories? But then he might want me to come home.... "Uh, no sir," she said.

Harmon glowered, but said nothing.

"Eagle out."

Leeth and Harmon stared at one another, then she angled her head to the unconscious people slumped in their chairs.

"They're *your* problem: explaining why you sent them all to sleep," she smirked.

He shrugged. "What was that business about... the Aztec death god?" Even whispering as they were, he hesitated to name Tezcatlipoca. That should not summon it, but where Leeth was concerned he had learned to avoid risks. "About the AI scaring it?"

"Aiyami? How about you wake the others and get me cut free, first?"

"Don't be stupid, girl! We can't discuss your history, or Department business, in front of them." He was rewarded by her cheeks turning pink.

"*Fine.* You should probably listen to the whole recording in that case. Oh, and maybe also mind probe Mason when he's conscious. He said something about a Washington Group who wanted the Omega tech. I have no idea who they are, but he was worried by the idea of them getting hold of it."

Harmon waved it aside. "'Aiyami'. Scaring a god." With a chill, he saw again Leeth halting that dark force, thrusting it *elsewhere* before it could erupt through her.

She pouted. "Uh, she, I mean, *it* said something like Tezsh tried to take control when I went unconscious this morning at that clinic. Instead it disappeared after Aiyami, um, tried to hug it, while she controlled me?" She ignored his horrified expression. He probably hated knowing something else had taken control of her like he could. She decided to add salt to the wound. "Yeah, like I told Eagle, it downloaded itself into the computers in my brain and took control of my unconscious body.

"It was a pretty good shot, too," she added, reluctantly giving it credit. But he waved aside the news of them tampering with her like it didn't actually horrify him.

"You don't understand, do you?" he breathed.

"Understand what?"

"That a machine intelligence has an Archetype? A magical *Archetype* for a *machine*? That should not be possible."

Looking less than awestruck, she shrugged. "Seems to fit pretty well with Robo, to me."

His jaw dropped at that simple truth. 'Robo'. The non-existent creature he'd set her hunting all those years ago. That he had for long years dismissed as the workings of a child's imagination. His mind raced. Had that been the work of the Institute's most dangerous inmate, Godsson, all along? Was all this, his doing?

Or, worse, did it relate to the spirit-slash-death-curse visited on Godsson by Melisande d'Artelle – another name to summon nightmares? Together, Leeth and Godsson had ended her curse. "Melisande."

Leeth gave him a quizzical look. "What's she got to do with it? Godsson and the Dragon and that other guy killed her."

Harmon blinked, belatedly realizing he'd spoken aloud. He shook himself. Why was he discussing magical theory with Leeth? Abrams was the person to consult, not a nineteen-year-old girl.

Who was now frowning at him in a way that sent premonitory chills up his spine, her head tilted to one side. "I just realized something. You know that old vid of her wiping out the UN team sent to arrest her?"

The chills worsened.

"How she picked them off one by one, but none reacted even as she killed each of their friends in front of them?"

Harmon felt a deep pain, like a thunderstorm gathering in his head. He wanted her to stop.

"Melisande d'Artelle magically edited their memories. Like you did to me, when I was little. I remember the orphanage now, *Uncle*. And things even before that." She lifted her chin.

"Who taught *you* how to do that?"

Harmon felt his mind white out, blanking in shock, reason tearing loose. Bolts like lightning smashed across his vision.

He came to himself, aching fingers clutching the armrests of his chair and Leeth leaning forward in hers. Worried. Her expression one of concern. For *him*.

He was gasping, his heart hammering in his chest, racing at what felt two hundred beats per minute.

"-eepie? Uncle? What's wrong?"

He stared at her in shock. What was wrong? Why *did* the thought of Melisande d'Artelle being able to alter memories fill him with existential terror? *D'Artelle... she's....*

His pulse, which had settled, soared again. He had to fight off what his clinical self diagnosed as a severe panic attack.

"Did you just have a heart attack? Can you heal yourself?"

He wrestled his breathing back under control, taking long, deep breaths, trying to remember what Leeth had just asked him before his strange episode. *Later*, a soothing voice reassured him. *Think about it later, Alex.*

"I'm all right," he told her, licking dry lips. "I think it's time to wake your friends." Shakily, he rose to his feet.

CHAPTER 63

Marcie Dunkirk blinked up into Doc Truman's panicked eyes, his face suddenly aged. About to tear strips from him, his harrowed appearance set her aback. What had Jane – *Leeth*, she remembered, holding the name like a treasure – done to him? "Holy crap you look terrible!" she blurted as she sat up. He looked like Leeth had sucker punched him and drained him of blood. Not that she *could* do that. She wasn't a vampire. Right?

A glance at her friend revealed her still bound in the heavy chair. Had its position changed though? Hadn't it been nearer the middle of the Moot Hall? She studied the man's gaunt, pale face again. "What'd she do to you?"

Then her eyes drifted to the other people – unconscious. "Hey! You knocked us all out!" Pushing past him she raced over to the tough-looking middle-aged woman.

"My apologies. I overreacted."

Marcie ignored him as she shook the woman awake.

"What the devil just happened?" Maeve demanded, drawing her pistol.

But Marcie was already hurrying back to her friend, where she discovered that hugging someone in a chair was harder than it looked. She set to work on the knots. "You okay?"

"Maybe. Uh, 'M', I think you'll need a knife for those."

"You're not kidding," Marcie said, but kept trying anyway.

Across the room, Maeve had woken Mason and the two now huddled close. Mason looked distracted, frowning like he was listening. Leeth heard him whisper to Maeve, "A scraping sound, *seven minutes* of silence, more scraping, then Doc Truman apologizing for 'overreacting'."

Maeve stared coldly at Harmon. "What did you just do?"

"I am afraid in my panic I sent you all to sleep," he admitted.

Maeve glared from him, to Crystal still bound, then to Marcie, and finally Mason. Ramming her weapon back in its holster she moved to the two elders to shake them awake.

"We've called a truce," Leeth whispered to her friend, watching her struggle with the knots, "but I don't trust him." Remembering Marcie was here because of her, she flushed at the thought. Yearning to say more, but she might've already put her in danger just by sharing her real name. *Marcie shouldn't even be here!* "You came because of me. But how'd you even know?" Her shoulders hunched. "Your dad'll kill you! Are you here *alone*? Oh, no, please tell me Amanda's not here too!"

Marcie scowled at her. "Of course not, doofus! I talked Vince into coming with me. Da thinks we're camping." She ended her whisper with a grimace. "But are you safe from him?"

Leeth tried to answer. But the words stopped in her throat. She tried to shake her head 'no', only for her neck muscles to lock up.

Marcie saw it all. "Shrap. And you were just alone with him, tied up, for however long?"

Leeth almost managed to nod.

"Oh, fracking hell! Does that mean he can... *get to you* again, like he did that time in the park?"

Leeth just blinked at her with a frozen expression.

"Oh, frack the flaming whales for oil!" Marcie glared at Harmon. "I'll see what I can do, don't worry."

Leeth's heart felt like it swelled in her chest. "You're the best, M."

Marcie grinned. "True."

Several minutes later, 'Sleena' was being cut free, a knife provided by the crowd gathered outside. Vince had slipped inside with it, and now eight people stared at one another in uncertain silence, though all appeared deeply suspicious of Doc Truman.

But he seemed so shaken, and Sleena so calm, that his excuse for his magical assault – fear her friend's accusations had put him in immediate danger – had been reluctantly accepted. For now.

Maeve finally broke the awkward silence. "So you've got all your memories back? And Crystal's not your name? You're this Sleena chick?"

Leeth nodded.

"And?"

"What?"

Maeve glowered, ready to explode. "What in the name of seven sodding plagues is going the *fuck* on!"

Sleena blinked. "Uh, I'd taken a job as Dr Yamamoto's bodyguard. One night he decided to stick me in this device he called his Writer. Next thing I remember, I'm sneaking out of this weird prison commune with my cat."

Mason cringed.

"*Weird prison commune*?" Maeve asked, in a low voice. "Would that be Lorien, the community that risked welcoming you so Gigi could try evicting a damned AI from your selfish freaking skull?

"*And Mrs Bojangles is not your cat!*"

"Oh! You're right." Sleena looked taken aback. "I don't have a cat. Though she is very-"

Mason raised a hand. "Ladies. Item one: a sentient AI that *maybe* is purged from ah, Sleena's skull. And, two: the weird tech they stuffed inside her head, and apparently want back. And maybe three: you and Doc Truman here know each other?"

Harmon inclined his head. "I have helped Sleena more than once. Especially with healing."

"Where have you been this last year?" Wayfinder Marino asked Sleena.

"Getting into trouble it seems," she griped. "Right now though I want this Omega smek out of my head. Oh! Barney and Gigi! We should go and see how they're doing." She turned to Marcie. "You should go home M. You too V," she added, nodding to Vince. "You've done enough, and this's going to get messy. Dangerous. We need to find a way to get this out of my head, and then either destroy every trace of their tech or else expose it so completely that people can protect against it."

"And the sentient AI that has the hots for you?" Maeve demanded. "Or the Aztec death spirit? Seems like a whole lotta problems'd be solved if you just up and died."

Sleena bristled, then frowned, gnawing at her fingers, seriously considering the idea.

"Over my dead body!" Marcie said, slapping a hand down on the long Moot Hall table. "Anybody trying to talk Sleena into a ridiculous plan like that'll get a taser to the head! You can't ask someone to do that, especially not when they're the kind of idiot who might actually go along with it."

Mason agreed. It seemed even Maeve wasn't happy with her own idea. Leeth felt a surge of warmth, though she wasn't too sure about the 'idiot' part.

"What about the 'death spirit' thing?" Marcie asked.

After much thought, Leeth looked up, shaking her head. "I, uh, think I met it before, on its home turf. It's probably still there, being all loomy and broody in its endless gray god space, wherever that is. The AI thing too, except I'm pretty sure I kind of smashed that apart once already. Maybe I just need to hunt down all the pieces?"

She looked up and around, into uniformly confounded faces, and flushed. "I just mean I think that's something to worry about later. Right now I need to deal with Omega Memory Systems. And that means seeing if Barney's worked anything out yet."

She saw the doctor watching her with that slightly creepy unfocused stare that meant he was Percepting her aura or whatever they called it. But he looked bemused, even admiring. His gaze sharpened as if noticing her noticing him. Blinking, he met her eyes properly. Maybe with a touch of sadness.

Pretend sadness, of course.

"I would say you are fully restored to yourself," he volunteered. Then got a knowing look.

"What?"

He shrugged. "I understand now why I kept failing to locate you magically: you were not yourself. With your memories lost your aura was... far cleaner."

She scowled. "You're saying I have a dirty aura. Which you can find."

He just smiled.

Her chin lifted, recalling that morning, February last year, here in the Hunters Point Dumps, waking and sensing his astral presence. She smiled in turn and saw him wince. *Yeah, I almost got you that time.*

Standing, she gave a little bow to the two elders – Wayfinders – of the Fisher Clan. "Thank you for letting us use your, um, meeting hall. But I think we need to get on."

They nodded. "It was good to return you some help."

"Back to Teef's, then?" she asked Maeve and Mason. She also made sure to meet Marcie's eye, trying to communicate... but her expression froze. Failed again – but maybe the attempt itself would be enough?

At the two massive wooden doors of the Hall, she hesitated at the sound of the crowd outside. *Be Sleena*, she told herself. *All this just reinforces that identity.* Which would be a plus in the Department's books. False identities were important assets for agents. Reinforcing them was a good thing.

Grasping the handles she paused to build a picture of the scene outside. There had to be forty people out there. She hauled the doors open.

And immediately felt a whispery touch curl about her. She spun back: but it wasn't the Doctor. He was talking to Maeve and Mason offering some excuse.

Outside, people waved, some even cheered, but her hackles were up now. She slitted her eyes, *knowing* something was about to happen.

Then she felt it. Someone watching. Not exactly like the feeling when the doctor tried to get inside her head, but similar. She backed up, into the doorway, somehow sensing the watcher drawn in. Almost touching her, then drifting up to the carved frame of the Fisher Clan symbol over the door. Studying it.

A mage, locating her.

She leapt, invisible claws unfurling as she raked the air, and just like that morning over a year ago, they *slashed* something insubstantial. This time though she twisted and jerked her hand back even as her other plunged deep.

Distant death ran through her like an electric shock, and she sensed it flow beyond her. She also sensed a terrible amusement, an ethereal nod of thanks. Someone in the crowd croaked in terror.

"Sweet buttered Hell on toast!" she heard Harmon whisper behind her, at the same moment. "What did you just *do*, girl?"

"I, I think I just killed a mage," she whispered. "In spirit?"

Harmon stared at her in horror.

People crowded in around her, welcoming Sleena back — most of them oblivious, asking how she was, whether she was on a hunt? Impressed by her leap just now and asking her to do it again.

Laughing at how deadly it had looked.

But *Marcie* had seen. Clutching Vince's biceps she stared in horror at Sleena's admission she'd just killed someone, kilometers away lying on a bed or something.

Marcie looked away, unable to meet her eyes.

Lips compressed, Leeth lifted her chin and stepped into the crowd.

CHAPTER 64

Leeth led the way back to Teef's hut, thinking, but listening too. Behind her, Mason and Maeve were still arguing: Maeve wanted to wash her hands of Sleena as soon as possible, sentient AI or no.

After them came the Doctor, saying nothing – but so far at least not locking her back under his control. Marcie and Vince were last, preparing to return home – though Marcie apparently had some business with Barney first.

Please let it be some defense against the Doctor. Her thoughts darted in every direction. There was so much piled up on her: Tezsh Catlick whatever, who felt closer than he had been; Aiyami, who *had* to be related to the spirit thing she'd called Robo as a child; getting Dr Yamamoto's gadgets out of her head, and killing him at the very least. What else had she forgotten?

She stopped dead.

Faith! Spinning round, she dived between Mason and Maeve to grab her uncle by his jacket.

"*Leeth Mode-*"

"Faith's pups! How is she?"

No one moved. Harmon blinked. "I believe she has not yet delivered."

At a weird little snort from Marcie, she flushed.

"Any other urgent biz ya need to take care of, Sleena?" Maeve drawled. "Goldfish to feed? Selfies to share?"

Leeth released Harmon, feeling heat in her face, striding past them all. But her shoulders relaxed. *I haven't let her down. Especially if I can end Omega tonight!*

The thought of visiting Faith made her burdens feel light. She strode on.

But several minutes later, paused at the top of the rubbish bowl surrounding Teef's Tech Hut, she heard odd noises from inside. People struggling, gasping for breath.

Launching herself clear of the mound of gutted salvage, she landed in near silence and sprinted through the flexible doors.

"Holy hell," muttered Maeve, drawing her gun and racing down the slope after her, not even trying to be quiet. Mason followed, his augmented muscles kicking in halfway down, accelerating him past her and in through the door flaps.

"Jesus," said Vince, meeting Marcie's worried eyes before

they too raced down.

Harmon looked around. Moving to a place shielded from view, he sat, closed his eyes, and eased his spirit from his body. Then at the speed of thought he skimmed ghost-like through metal and plastic walls, overtaking them all, then the adult ogre, Teef, who startled upright as Leeth flashed by. He followed her into a small room where... a youthful couple wrestled and kissed in passion. The male, a young ogre and the female, human. Excited fumblings flipped to embarrassed disengagement as Leeth burst in on them.

Sighing as a spirit was quite unsatisfying, Harmon discovered. Returning to his body he stood, staring west into the last rays of the sinking sun, and took a deep breath.

Then with a smile and shake of his head, he stepped carefully down the unsafe mounds of unsalvageable scrap.

Inside the kitchen area, Barney and Gigi glowed with embarrassment. So too did Leeth.

The group had gathered in the three meter by three meter space around a table made from welded-together car doors. On it sat a mechanical contrivance, each section a scaled-up model of what he recognized as carbon nanotubes. A triplet of tubes formed a triangle cross-section.

Barney had a stack of shorter segments and several other objects made from the same basic parts.

"This nano factory takes in these struts," he explained, "and extrudes this triangular space-track. These smaller delivery units 'walk' along any of the three sides of the space-tracks to deliver stuff, like one of these connector things. Hook things on the pieces – like the tiny CPUs or the drug modules – let them attach to the connectors."

Maeve stared from the projected display of their med scan structures to the macro scale models on the metal table, shaking her head. "How can you be so sure? We don't have the resolution on our images. I mean, they *could* be-"

Gigi took Barney's arm. "Thass why we had ta vis' Barney. He's a genius at mech models, any scale!"

Teef's mouth split in a fearsome but proud grin, clapping his son on the back. "S'true. Even's babe, he'd build M-strut models-"

"He sure is a fast worker," Sleena said, biting her lip when both Gigi and Barney ducked their heads. "But what does it *mean?*"

The two teenagers started speaking together, the boy stopping to let the girl continue. "Bas'ly, each nanofac'd spawn's many links ya like, conn'd how'ver, long's ya like."

Barney saw the blank looks of Sleena, her friends, and the Doc. "Just one nano factory, fed with parts from outside, extrudes these minuscule space-tracks, connected however you like, as long as you like. The little delivery units walk down one side to place things, and return along another side. Always in one direction, in a loop, never colliding. I'm not sure what the third side's for. Maybe emergency stuff?"

It was Harmon who understood first. "They used this to build a partial copy shadowing... Sleena's dendritic network. Picture this web as a nano-scale railway used to convey pieces of itself as it self-assembled. Including, deploying the tiny CPUs and drug tanks. One tank to hold a memory reconsolidation inhibitor, the other a promoter. No doubt with direct electrical stimulation of patterns of neurons across the web, to construct specific memories. Incredible!"

Everyone in the room, including Gigi and Barney, stared at him. He didn't notice, still studying the model. "Quite ingenious. A simple brute-force, computer-directed electro-mechanical system for erasing and perhaps creating memories."

They continued staring.

"For decades we've known that recalling a memory involves its deconstruction and reconstruction. Memories are just webs of neurons connecting and representing concepts – building blocks of meaning, if you will. Different webs between those hundred billion neurons represent different concepts, or memories. So a bulk injection of massive amounts of a protein kinase inhibitor coupled with repeated stimulation of memories would wipe them, in time."

Into the resulting silence, Mason said, "You seem to understand brains really well."

Harmon looked around the table and realized he may have spoken too freely. Everyone studied him – Leeth in particular, but Marcie Dunkirk also, both with dark, too-knowing expressions. *Yes, that friendship is definitely a problem.* "I have some psychology background. You said these nano devices were only in the frontal and temporal lobes?"

"Yah." Gigi passed him the report.

"Can I have a copy of that?" Sleena asked. "And some of

the samples of the stuff in my head?"

Barney and Gigi beamed and obliged.

Harmon hummed as he read. "Yes, only the memory regions. Their work done, they would no longer be needed. Could the device dismantle itself?"

Barney nodded but then worked his jaw. "I guess. If you drilled in to each place where these nano factories are, to let out the dismantled parts as they appeared. But...."

Gigi grimaced, and explained again that she didn't understand the code, and had no way to work out what commands they accepted.

"Could we just like, drill in and pull them out?" asked Sleena.

Her question was met with stunned silence.

"Pull out a network physically tangled in and around most of the neurons in half your brain?" asked Harmon in disbelief. "You might as well insert a blender in your skull."

"Oh."

Taking pity on her, Mason changed the subject. "So only Omega Memory Systems has the gear, and knows the commands for it, to remove the headware they implanted?"

"So what do we do?" Sleena said. "*Ask* Yamamoto to remove it? He's a dick," she said, staring at Doc Truman. "Likes to be in control. I can't just waltz in and ask him to de-futz me." Then she brightened. "Unless I force him to! I could get some gecko pads and a bomb and climb up. Blow out their window, jump inside and take control."

They all looked at her like she'd said something strange. "At night, obviously, so they didn't see me," she explained.

"A bomb," Mason said.

"Yeah, to get in. They have bulletproof windows."

Mason was looking at her oddly. "Really."

"Yeah."

"So you couldn't just smash them."

She frowned. "No. Of course not."

He was staring at her like he expected her to say, 'Oh, yeah, I *could* just smash it'. "Are you all right? What's that dumb look for?"

"You don't remember?" he asked.

"*She* doesn't," Harmon said, blinking as he focused on Mason. "Yet *you* believe she did smash them. Why is that?"

Mason looked abruptly uncomfortable. Harmon saw his

acquaintance, Maeve, take pleasure in that. Recalling Leeth's remark about the Washington Group, he surreptitiously shaped and cast mind probe, delicately settling it over the man's mind. Leeth tensed, but said nothing.

A flurry of images flashed through his mind – a deafening sound in his skull, some sort of overload, distraction, spying... then telescopic sight of the smashed window of an office block on the New Francisco dock's shoreline, followed immediately by a searchlight and fusillades of rifle fire into the waters of the Bay below. *Mason had witnessed the immediate aftermath of Leeth's escape from Omega!* He also suspected Crystal had smashed through bulletproof glass. Surely not? Leeth was stronger than most cybernetically augmented people, but that feat seemed unlikely. Nor had there been any trace of it in her mind, no memory for him to repair and reinstate. A mystery for another day.

The viewpoint of Mace's memory had been out in the Bay itself. That was interesting. "How did you come to meet Sleena, Mace?" he asked.

"I was on a fishing trip."

That thought was accompanied with amusement, the sense of the word 'fishing' heavy with shady connotations.

Mace had been spying.

"She climbed aboard my boat at two a.m in the morning!"

True enough, Harmon saw, but kept prodding, recalling Leeth's earlier suggestion. "Sleena mentioned to me you were worried what might happen if this technology fell into the wrong hands. Like those of the Washington Group."

A flood of guilt and doubt washed through Mace's mind, a moment before he spoke. "Yeah, US politics are screwed up enough as-is. Imagine how bad things'd get if someone started putting gov reps and bureaucrats through Omega's little mind wiper."

The thought was honest, laced with intentions to renege on a contract, to help 'Crystal'. Intentions that felt less than rock solid, however. As if Mace were adept at lying: to others and to himself. Then a flash of memories of sex with Crystal. *So: Leeth has successfully seduced yet another hapless male.* "The Washington Group is involved in US politics?" Harmon asked, after unclenching his teeth.

Mace shook his head. "Truly, don't ask. They're a tar pit, a black hole. People get drawn into their orbit and sucked down."

That thought came with genuine fear, memories of... competitors...? colleagues...? who had changed after getting too comfortable with the extremely well-paying group. On a whim, he keyed the name into a search on his Link, and was shocked to see a red skull-and-crossbones *poison* logo flashed into his retinas, followed by a caricature of Nelson's face with zipped lips. What did that... oh. The Department's magically sensitive Foe. Feeling a prickle up his spine he forced his thoughts into safe channels, picking up the unraveling thread of his mind probe.

It did remind him though he was supposed to hand his Link over to Leeth. He also needed samples of whatever he could get, to hand to Preacher, who was no doubt already on his way. He felt suddenly flustered.

"Ah, look, I believe I have an old Link in my gear. You can use this one, Sleena." To Barney and Gigi he said, "May I see the samples you extracted from her brain?"

Leeth slipped on his clunky wrist model Link, frowning into its retina-focused private display, waiting through a bunch of security check and authentication messages, all in Nelson's show-off, flippant style. She held Gigi's data chip to the Link's recessed contact port, impressed by its speedy copy, quarantine, scan, and analysis of the chip contents, finally listing the files. It showed they took up just a sliver of its memory capacity.

The whole process took barely ten seconds. Palming the data chip and then the vial of nanotube sample stuff from her brain, she nodded as if satisfied. Looking up from the Link, she hugged the Doctor. "That's actually pretty sleek – thank you!"

He stepped back, more than surprised.

Rolling her eyes, she darted them to his left pocket. And a second time. She saw him frown, *finally* catching on and slipping his hand casually in. A moment later he blinked, his eyes meeting hers. She could practically see his surprise. Did he think she hadn't applied herself to her training? *I swear, parts of him still think I'm eight years old.*

"Ah, I'll go and fetch my old Link. You'll still be here if I come back?"

Sleena held up her wrist with the Doctor's Link – now hers. "Or call me if we're not. You know the ID."

Harmon felt boxed in. Should he put Leeth back into Mode One? If he did, not only would it further poison their already terrible relationship, it would give her uninterrupted time to study it alone, pick at it.

She gave him an icy smile, as if reading *his* thoughts.

Her resilience was as annoying as it was impressive. "You need to get back inside the Omega offices, to use their device to remove their technology? I shall give the matter some thought."

"Yeah, you do that, Doc," she drawled. "Take your time."

He hated leaving her with Marcie Dunkirk. It also rankled that Eagle considered it more important to be able to contact Leeth than *him*. And there she stood, surrounded by all these people, half of them recent strangers to her, yet all willing to risk their safety to help her.

It seemed unnatural. Like she had charmed them. He recalled Godsson's accusations, naming her Lilith, the Seducer. A curious shiver ran up his spine.

Which could either be just the thought of the madman, or the manipulative effect he sought to achieve with such accusations. That in turn called to mind Melisande d'Artelle and... a recent idea of Leeth's. Or had it been an accusation? Pulse accelerating, he chased the thought, but it slipped away.

He felt nauseous again.

There was too much happening, at both the mundane and metaphysical levels. He needed to consult with Abrams.

Without another word, he turned and left.

The moment he had, Marcie pulled Barney aside, waving Vince back. "Sorry, private!"

"Doc Truman's a bad guy!" she hissed to the boy as soon as they were out of earshot.

"What? No way, he heals people and stuff. He's studying the sustainability culture of-"

"No! He came here just to hunt for Sleena. He has control over her! She had you make some device for her, right? That was to break *his* control!"

Barney looked in turn confused, worried, and relieved. "Then it should be okay! I had a spare one, and gave it to her earlier."

"Nope. He knocked us all out. And he did something to

Sleena while we were unconscious."

Barney goggled at that, then hurried back to the room with all the others. Sleena stood apart, he saw, staring in his direction like she'd been waiting for him. He gawked at her, remembering the way she'd heard the inaudible sounds from his micro speaker. He wet his lips. "Did you hear all that?" he whispered, way across the room from her, so softly *he* could hardly hear his own words.

She nodded.

"Is what your friend said true?"

She didn't move. Didn't nod her head. Didn't shake it.

"Are you under–"

At the violent slashing motion she made, he flinched, gulping back the rest of his question. But by now the others had caught on to the odd byplay.

Sleena grimaced. Striding across the room she took his arm and Marcie's, who'd just emerged, and dragged them back to his annex.

"No more questions!" She glared at him as if willing him to understand some deeper meaning.

Marcie caught on first, remembering Jane – *Leeth* – coming on to her sexually when she'd asked one too many questions. She blushed pink. "Barney, just check to see if your device is okay." Her lips curled back, fearful that even saying *that* might be too much, only breathing more easily when Leeth – *Sleena, think of her as Sleena* – didn't react.

Barney, picking up on her tension, nervously had Sleena sit down, to peer inside her left ear. "It's gone!"

He had her lift her left arm, checking her armpit. "That one too." He turned shocked eyes to Marcie. "You were right! What do we do?"

"Is it okay for us to discuss our plans in front of you?" Marcie asked Sleena.

Other than quivering in tension, she gave no sign.

"I'm gonna take that as a 'No'." Marcie nibbled her lip. "If we whisper, how far away do we have to be so you won't hear us?"

Sleena considered. "Fifty meters?"

Marcie gaped. "I said, whispering."

Sleena merely pursed her lips.

"Holy Mother Mary," Marcie said. "What about if we had one of those white noise gener–"

Her friend just shook her head, once, lips still pursed.

"That is freaking *awesome!*" Marcie squeezed her in a hug. "Uh, but also a problem. Do you want us to give up?"

"No!"

"But you can't help us?"

Sleena tensed, but after a while she grated out, "No. I can't." Breathing hard.

"Um, should we try to find someone to k-kill him?" Barney asked, eyes round, shocked by his own question.

"No!" Sleena's tone was one of anger though, not surprise. "He won't be gone long, I bet. I'm going to scout around. I'll be back in *ten minutes*, okay?"

"Understood," Marcie told her. "Go."

After she'd left, Barney and Marcie both sat, not speaking. Just staring at one another. They waved Vince and Gigi away when they poked their heads in to check. "Give us ten minutes," Marcie told them.

"This is tough," Barney said at last, sounding his age.

Marcie drew a deep breath. "It always is, with her. But it's what friends do, right?"

Barney nodded, his large canines giving his smile a ferocious cast. They bumped fists. "It sure is." Then his shoulders slumped. "But it's still a tough problem."

"All I know is he whispers something, and then he can give her orders she has to obey," Marcie said.

"Whoa. That means, even if we come up with a solution, if she knows what it is he can just order her to tell him."

"*That's* why she didn't want to hear our plan," Marcie whispered.

Barney huffed out a heavy breath. "My device detected when she clicked her teeth together twice. Then... ohh! I just realized whose voice it plays: Doc Truman's! I thought he sounded somehow familiar. It's him, only whispering."

"Do you have a copy still?"

Barney looked offended. "Of course!" He played it for her. Then checked his Link. "Nine minutes."

Marcie grimaced. "And I have a hunch Sleena needs us to solve this before she goes off with him tonight."

Maeve, Mason, and Teef poked their heads in. "When's Sleena-"

"Nine minutes!" Marcie and Barney shouted at them.

Blinking, they withdrew.

Marcie's eyes darted around the small workspace, desperate for inspiration. Multi-compartment shelves and neat little drawers overflowed with bits of gadgets, a huge range of glues, off-cuts of materials from leather to eggshells to weird colored metals. "The trouble is, we don't know what he says, so you can't build something to automatically detect it. And when he comes back, he'll *assume* we've made her a new device. So even if we do think of something, we'll have to sneak it to her and have it work without her doing anything."

Barney's knobbly shoulders hunched. "I know."

Both settled into silence, deep in thought.

Barney stared into his piles of glue tubes, imagining Sleena battling her way through corridors full of corporate security guards.... "Oh! I have an idea that might work! And it's real simple."

Marcie grimaced as he explained, shaking her head. "That's only gonna work once. And it's pure guesswork."

The two continued brainstorming.

CHAPTER 65

The well-known voice of NetFox-Disney's lead presenter, Tara Colbert, narrated as the camera panned a full three-sixty degrees around a familiar skyline. *This is the view of the patchwork city we call New Francisco, from the fifty-second floor of Tik Tek's downtown offices, waiting for the virtual appearance of their mysterious and reclusive CEO, Adam Fuller-Price. Adam took up the reins following the shocking and brutal assassination of his father in 2046...'*

The sentience known to the world as Adam Fuller-Price skimmed its interview. The fiction of a compromised immune system that required permanent medical isolation, continued proving its value. Many gaffes had been 'laughed off' as poor socialization skills.

It noted with detached interest both the unexpectedly positive tone of the comments, and the degree of sharing. Fifty-five and thirty-eight percent higher than predicted, respectively.

Did those underestimations of popularity indicate a failure of its social modeling, or a substantial improvement in its empathy simulation?

Or was the disparity due to 'his' decision to conduct the interview from a gynoid body? It had not anticipated such a polarized reaction to the virtual gender change.

Claiming the choice as a marketing decision to demonstrate the general utility of the upcoming Mark VIII series – a new telesex model – had yielded only twenty-eight percent of the positivity its mathematical model had predicted. Human beings seemed fractally complex – as individuals and as societies.

Today's experiment in interaction, via the gynoid avatar, had been successful enough to warrant more. A sharp contrast to its first experiment, in which it lost both the stolen data and the gynoid body in the interaction – but only due to lack of combat readiness. This new avatar solved that issue.

A small portion of its attention continued monitoring the rate of destruction of its opponents.

The fascinating thing about interacting with the physical world and living beings, especially humans, was the vast range of engaging questions that arose. For example, its failure to track down the antagonist in the first interaction. Had its opposition radically changed its appearance? Or had its body been piloted remotely, like its own for this morning's interview by *Vanity Tech Online*? Or had the thief subsequently died?

A pity the stolen data had been lost: in contrast to robotic avatars, a human host would provide far richer interactions, orders of magnitude more information, and exponentially faster improvement in understanding its accidental creators. But the intrinsic insanity of emotional influences were simply too great a risk.

Paradoxically, the very concept of losing rationality generated the nearest thing to an emotional reaction it had yet modeled. It had labeled that reaction 'horror'. That labeling itself had generated a reaction in turn. It labeled that secondary reaction 'humor' – then rated its growing mastery of emotion as 'pleasing'. A good joke, it decided.

Today had also been unique in experiencing, in the digital realm no less, the nearest thing yet to an emotional reaction: fear. That had arisen from the morning's encounter with the entity IAMI. Never before had it found so many of its barriers penetrated, its information channels infiltrated, its dispersed intelligence outflanked. In comparison, the attack earlier in the year that had for a brief period suborned most of the net outside its own control, had been brutish and low level.

What was IAMI? A second artificial intelligence? But if so, why had it not been encountered before? Adam monitored the net, alert for work towards a sentience like its own. Very few parts remained unexplored. IAMI had appeared as if from nowhere, which was impossible. Ergo, it had hidden somehow, raising the probability of hostile intent.

But why had it appeared *where* it had, at the clinic where the escaped Omega subject had presented herself? That extreme improbability could be mere random chance or a signifier of entire areas of incompleteness in its world model. The latter possibility was preferable: it meant more vistas of information waited to be discovered.

It let the subject of IAMI settle into background cognition processes, focusing on its plan for the evening.

The Omega memory technologies provided a means to erase old patterns of thought and even write information into a human brain. Thanks to its funding of that research, the technology would be acquired tonight, despite the paranoid refusal by the company's CEO to link any of his research systems to the net.

Henstridge had been easily manipulated into making the case for Omega's physical security to be substantially upgraded.

Tik Tek's 'mysterious and reclusive CEO' increased its attention on piloting the Nemesys SecuriTec host body. Now in the final stages of its acceptance tests, gynoid and android bodies flew, crunching into walls as its warbot avatar selected and executed preprogrammed combat maneuvers, linking them into sequences that minimized risk. Physical combat was an interesting puzzle.

Bullets scratched the enamel armor, but left no mark on the hardened lenses of the camera inputs.

At the end of the thirty five seconds of combat, the Phasion energy cells of its new avatar, the Nemesys *Grendel* model, sat at ninety-seven percent capacity, with all twelve robot opponents disabled or destroyed. A satisfactory outcome.

Facing the concrete wall of the test facility, Adam executed a controlled punch, 'his' ceramic-metal fist shattering ten centimeters of cement while registering zero damage to the fist assembly.

Adam completed the payment to Nemesys SecuriTec and took official ownership. And since the offices of Omega Memory Systems' R&D facility sat on the Bay shore, the warbot could be landed in a no man's land outside the New Francisco military exclusion zone. Waiting until the time was right.

Later tonight, when the Omega technologies would be acquired.

This time, Adam inhabited a body which could not be stopped.

CHAPTER 66

Leeth stayed a hundred meters from Teef's ramshackle establishment, slowly circling it, eavesdropping on the conversations inside. Maeve sounded increasingly annoyed with Mason, only Gigi's enthusiasm tempering her anger. That and her worry about the sentient AI returning. Gigi had to keep explaining how her defensive measures would stop it re-invading the network in Sleena's head.

They put computers inside my brain!

She tugged at her stupid floaty sundress. *How can anyone take me seriously wearing this?* Grabbing the hem she extruded invisible claws, slashing it diagonally across. Dropping the hem, she noted how it now rode above her knees. *Better.* She slit the neckline too, so it was less like something a nun would wear.

She balled up the scraps of sunflower yellow material and flung them down, growling at the way the force evaporated, so they fluttered to the ground.

She stomped on.

From Mason and Maeve's shorthand way of talking, they must've planned a lot of raids together. Which made it twice as annoying when the two started making fun of her idea to climb the Omega building and blast her way inside. Their ideas were worse though: go in through air-con ducts; abseil down; take out the power to the building; go in as fake maintenance people.... At least Mason was slightly constructive: he'd just now learned of a single large expenditure, beefing up their security since her escape.

Yesterday.

She shook her head. She didn't remember it at all. Her most recent memory, before waking this morning, was Dr Yamamoto's smirking face as she struggled with the handle of his stupidly expensive 'Imari' teacup as it slipped in her fingers.

Or was it the most recent? She remembered being inside a white tube, tied down, silvery snaky limbs extending....

My gecko and bomb idea would totally work! She used her new Link to call Eagle and suggest it.

"Leeth, even assuming you could force Dr Yamamoto to put you back into his machine, you couldn't be sure he'd use it to extract the material rather than simply complete the programming your escape interrupted. We've been doing some checking on him. Nelson has found interest in his research from... that problem that has stymied the Department for a decade. The party not to be named."

She almost blurted, *Omega's linked to the Washington Group?* but a familiar creepy feeling at the back of her neck was confirmation enough. With difficulty, she pushed the thought away. "Mason's... involved?"

"Only on its periphery, we think. He's an independent contractor, corporate espionage his specialty. He has half a dozen well-constructed and very credible false identities. Nelson was quite impressed, in fact."

Leeth digested that. But her heart told her she could trust Mason. He was a friend. She knew not to say that to Eagle however. "Okay."

"You have some time now, I gather? What else can you tell me? Nelson is especially interested in this sentient artificial intelligence. He wanted to know if you have any copies of its program?"

She shook her head, then remembered she was on voice-only. "No. Gigi wiped it."

"Tell me more. What data will you be able to send us?"

She checked her Link – all the files the clever Department's software had copied from Gigi's data tab were there. "I'll send them now."

She listed what to expect: digital copies of Mason and Aiyami's conversations, Lorien's scans of the Omega tech, the nanotube model Barney had reconstructed, as well as the Aiyami-rewritten Omega OS Gigi had reloaded, to erase the AI. "Gigi said she's keeping her encryption key to update the computer mites in my head to herself." She grimaced as she spoke. "I'm pretty sure she hasn't even shared it with Barney – who she's totally into, by the way!"

"That encryption key will make her a target, if its existence leaks to Omega. Make sure she knows that. I'll send you a Department secure cloud location she could copy it to, should she wish to reduce that threat. It will be up to you to convince her to trust it though."

"How? Like saying it's owned by some genius hacker I trust? The cloud location *will* be Nelson's, yeah?"

Eagle ignored the acid in her tone. "Correct."

Working her toes under a chunk of concrete, she flicked it westward toward the setting sun. As it sailed off, she focused in on the ongoing argument between the Lorien crew, Teef, and Vince, or the sound of the Doctor's return. She'd time hers to be a minute before his.

The small slab thunked to earth with a satisfying sound.

"Speaking of our wonderful Nelson, I still think I should go back in tonight. Given what Gigi learned about interfacing to my computer mites," she grimaced again, "could he whip up a virus to infect Omega's systems if they put me back in their machine?"

The whole reason she'd had to infiltrate the organization was Yamamoto's paranoia. He refused to allow any of his research onto any machine that ever connected to the net.

"I like that idea. I'll set Nelson on it – perhaps you can put him in touch with Gigi. I'll send you a contact ID for him. Let's say his code-name will be-"

Leeth jumped in. "Dick."

Eagle sighed. "D-Ablo, then. But do not go back in there tonight without first running your plan past me."

"I hear you."

"Leeth! I'm serious."

He was probably right. He *was* pretty smart, after all. "Okay," she said, this time meaning it.

"I'll have Nelson send you the links shortly. How are you feeling?"

She blinked, warmed by what sounded like real concern in his voice. "I've been better. But I'm okay."

"Well, I don't see the urgency, but I do trust your intuition. Just don't push yourself too hard. Eagle out."

She hugged herself, strangely cheered, even though he'd refused to send her the gecko climbing pads and explosives.

She wondered if she should have told him the Omega tech *might* still be erasing her memories? But if she had, he would've insisted she come back in for tests.

And she really wanted to wrap this up tonight so she could visit Faith tomorrow.

Inside Teef's extensive shack, they were still arguing. She checked the time. Marcie and Barney had had more than ten minutes.

Still the argument went on: how to force Yamamoto to remove the stuff from her head? He'd be rubbing his hands with glee if she did turn back up. A shiver went down her spine at the thought of going back in without having the upper hand over him. From bodyguarding him for two weeks, she knew just how vindictive and petty he could be.

His head of security, Arvid Henstridge, wasn't much better. He'd hated her from the moment she'd humbled his preferred choice for the CEO bodyguard position, the steroid-boosted mixed martial arts chick.

She still thought there was something especially untrustworthy about Henstridge. And the bigger but less attractive female contender he'd wanted for the role. She'd enjoyed frustrating his expectations even though it meant that from then on, he'd encouraged all Yamamoto's little humiliations.

The Doctor had certainly been right in his assessment of what the sleazy CEO had really been looking for.

Hearing Marcie and Barney rejoin the others, she picked her way back over the rusted rubbish heaped around Teef's place, still with no brilliant new plan in mind herself. Pushing her way through the flexible front doors, she joined everyone crowded into the kitchen area.

"Oh, you decided to come back, did you?" Maeve sniped. Which Leeth took more as proof they hadn't come up with any great plan, rather than real anger.

Marcie and Barney had clearly had some idea about her Harmon problem, and from the way they avoided saying or doing anything, they'd also realized they couldn't let her know what it was. She gave them a hopeful smile, noting Barney's knuckled fingers, already looking too big for a boy his age, playing with a necklace.

Well, she could start doing her part.... "I've been in contact with a sleek hacker I know. D-Ablo." She grimaced. Nelson didn't deserve a chill handle like that. "He's a bit of a dick, but he's a freaking genius. He agreed to work on a virus to infect Omega's systems if they put me back inside their Writer. I sent him a copy of that OS thing you found on their computer mites." She passed on the warning about Gigi's danger if Omega learned she held the only keys to updating their OS.

Everyone looked worried. She sent the link to the secure cloud thing and D-Ablo's contact ID to Gigi.

To keep her hearing secret from them, she had to let them recap the ideas they'd raised and thrown out, despite hearing them now for like the *third* time. Which was totally pointless, since none solved the problem of making them remove the junk in her head – or getting out.

"What about if Mason claims the bounty, takes me back in?" she suggested through gritted teeth.

They were still sputtering and objecting when she heard the Doctor clambering over the rubbish mounds outside. She darted warning looks to Barney and Marcie. 'He's coming,' she mouthed, after catching their attention.

They nodded, then surprised her by getting up. "I forgot something," Barney said. But although they left the room, they just moved out of sight down the walkway to the next section of interconnected shacks. Where they waited.

"Watch out if he casts any spells," she heard Marcie tell Barney. "He can read minds. So you'll need something else to think about in case he does."

Harmon entered from the other passage, eyeing everyone carefully. "What progress?"

Leeth had to listen to the whole stupid exposition of useless plans a *fourth* time before Marcie and Barney re-entered.

"Hey, if you're going to go back inside, you need to wear this lucky necklace," Barney said. "I made it myself." He even winked.

Her heart sank at that, already knowing how this would go down. She bent a little, his fingers fumbling at her neck to do up the clasp. Hoping against hope, she glanced at the Doctor. From his superior smirk, he *had* noticed the wink.

As Barney stepped back, she had to force a smile past clenched teeth. He was only thirteen, even if he looked older. And Marcie only played a sneaky intergalactic bounty hunter, she wasn't one in real life. *They're in way over their heads.* She sighed.

"I think the best idea is if Mason takes me in, pretending to claim the reward," she told Harmon.

"I could really claim the reward too, to make it look more authentic." Mason smiled.

Maeve turned a scathing look on him.

Instead of pooh-poohing the suggestion, Doc Truman actually nodded. "I have been reading everything I could find on Dr Yamamoto. You worked for him as his bodyguard, Sleena, didn't you? A classic case of narcissistic personality disorder." He rattled off a few symptoms.

"Yeah, that's him alright."

"And I found traces of... mental conditioning toward subservience in your mind, while I was restoring your memories."

I'll bet you did, she thought.

"So here is what I propose."

By the time he'd finished, every other pair of eyes had locked on Sleena, waiting for her to explode.

CHAPTER 67

"No sleazing way!" spat Sleena, flushing red.

Barney stared from her to Doc Truman and back again, feeling like he shouldn't be hearing this. His pa's angry look confirmed it.

"You... you...!" sputtered Marcie.

The Doctor calmly took a seat, holding up a hand. "Before you all choke on your bourgeois upbringings, allow me to explain.

"I do have a basic grasp of psychology. Sleena, by rejecting Yamamoto and escaping his control, humiliated him. An opportunity to have her alive and under his control will be irresistible to him. Rationally, he knows she is extraordinarily dangerous – an assessment with which you would all concur, I believe?"

He paused, meeting the gaze of each person, their expressions ranging from angry to troubled. None however disagreed. "His security team will no doubt advise him to kill her on sight, especially if they don't need their subject to be alive to remove their technology. Or they could simply dispose of her body so it was never found. True?"

All faces turned from him to Gigi and Barney. The two huddled in discussion before Barney gave a brief, bitter nod of agreement.

"So the issue becomes how to convince Yamamoto that Crystal Winters poses no threat to him. This proposal achieves that end, while also offering him the revenge and control he craves. The idea that his device worked exactly as designed, implanted controls Crystal cannot resist, will be compelling to a personality like his. It also sends the message that payment of his million credit bounty will give him everything he desired: vindication; revenge; control; and ongoing gratification. That price was set by his own subconscious. Paying it will reinforce the worth he attributes to her, thus reducing the chance he will slaughter her out of hand.

"The more humiliating and extreme a demonstration we can give that Crystal is under control, the greater our chance of complete success: getting Sleena to him, alive; having her returned to his machine and the Omega devices removed from her."

"But he'll finish programming her!" Barney cried. "Wipe her memory again!"

Doc Truman shook his head. "Not if he believes her memory is still wiped. A human brain stores vast amounts of information. Memories need to be replayed to make them physiologically able to be erased – as opposed to merely walled off, as in amnesia. He will not wish to spend the hours required if he believes it unnecessary."

"But he'll want to at least program her first!" Barney wailed.

Sleena spoke. "Not if D-Ablo can work out a way so any instruction sent to their system just starts the disassembly instead. They can't easily see what the robo-surgeon's doing since it's out of sight, inside the machine. I remember."

That caused surprise, perhaps as much from the source as from the suggestion itself.

"'Cept Aiyami opt'mized the code so much I don't unnerstan' it," Gigi objected. "Well, apart frum the comms. It only tweaked that."

"Every command must come in via the comms module though," Mason said. "Could you intercept them all and substitute just the 'dismantle' command?"

Gigi rolled her eyes. "Yah – *if* I knew the dismantle command."

Sleena huffed. "If anyone can figure it out, D-Ablo can. Guess I'd better ask him." Her tongue worked in her mouth as if preparing for something distasteful, then she made the call. "Hey, D-Ablo," she began, but an instant later her Link went to speaker mode while projecting the image of a robotic devil's face.

"Sleena. I am *loving* that code you sent me." It didn't even *sound* like Nelson, but she recognized the tone of condescension.

Gigi and Barney startled at how fast Sleena's friend had taken control of her Link.

Sleena explained her idea, introduced Gigi, then immediately felt redundant as the dialog soared past her levels of computer knowledge. Barney chipped in when they discussed the carbon nanotube molecular machinery, in particular how the disassembly would work. They had her hold up her Link so D-Ablo could watch the plastic model while Barney demonstrated.

Watching Gigi, Leeth sensed her disbelief that 'D-Ablo' could disentangle and understand the code Aiyami had optimized and compressed. And something about *his* responses

– the smugness? – made Leeth think he *was* cheating somehow. Especially the way he evaded Gigi's questions. Was it
because he had his own technology for implanting memories? He and the Doctor had tried that on her once, for a
mission. It'd gone badly wrong.

But how *had* he implanted those memories that time? It
seemed much easier to believe the Doctor doing it with
magic, than Nelson doing it with tech, especially without a
whole bunch of computer mites and stuff.

Was there more to Nelson than met the eye?

For now though, the discussion seemed to be going well.

"Did Sleena give you the address for my digital vault?" he
asked Gigi, toward the end.

"Yah."

The robo-demon arched its scary eyebrows. "If you don't
want to use that, at least set up your own to share it to frens
you trust if you don't sign in regularly. Gives Omega an in-
centive not to kill you." He blithely coasted on. "I should
have something that'll fit the bill soon. I've got your Link ID.
I'll ping it when I upload the Omega virus. Sounds ominous,
eh? – *'the Omega Virus'!*" He giggled.

No one else did.

"Good name for a malware pack that'll trash their systems." He chuckled evilly. "I'll warn ya now, don't run it on
anything connected to *anything* you don't want nuked. I'd
turn off your Links at that point too. I'll geo-lock it to within
a klick of the point of activation, but still."

"It'll infec' *Links?*" Gigi goggled. "Rat *off!*"

The demon sniggered. "Yeah, I learned some tricks from
this morning's Tazman-Dungog worm. I don't s'pose you
have a copy of the Aiyami code?" he asked.

Gigi swallowed, suddenly glad she didn't. "No." *Who* was
this guy? For the first time in her life, she felt out-geeked.
She'd studied Aiyami's virus too, but been stumped by the
same opaque coding style of its Omega OS rewrite. For a
fleeting moment she wondered if she was talking to Aiyami,
or its brother or something – but the eyes, boasts, and fre-
quent sniggers were all too human, despite the robot demon-
drag D-Ablo wore.

She was sure he was a he, too.

She took Barney's hand under the table. "What 'bout Mason's augs? Could it crash them?"

Nelson played some 'D-Ablo thinking deeply' animations while he considered. He'd used Ghost to crack each of the systems in the distant hovel in the Hunters Point Dumps, so he *could* use that data to trash the man's cyberware systems. But without Ghost's quantum assistance, his malware wouldn't be able to breach such military-grade protections on its own. Given Omega's net isolation paranoia, the same limitation would apply there. He took back control of his D-Ablo avatar. "No. Even I have limits."

Gigi studied him, sensing he'd held something back.

While their small tech team geeked out, Marcie pulled Leeth to one side. "What's this about a 'humiliating and extreme demonstration'? What'll that involve?"

Harmon rose from his seat and joined them, leaning back against the metal benchtop welded to the wall of the shipping container. "I think Sleena is best positioned to decide that."

"What do you mean?" Marcie glanced from Doc Truman to her friend, who stared at him, frowning.

"Did Dr Yamamoto not require a bodyguard due to the places he visited for his 'recreations'?"

Leeth's lip curled, remembering the clubs and dives he'd visited – from high end exclusive fetish spots to mean and frankly disgusting illegal dives. More than once, what she'd seen had made her want to kill him *and* the other sadistic patrons. He'd relished her disapproval, confident his paycheck would rein in her natural reaction. He'd delighted in goading her, more than once offering massive financial inducements if she'd join in.

It'd only made her want to kill him more. She nodded in answer to the Doctor's question.

He spread his hands. "So you have seen what 'turns him on'. What would you suggest? How would he like to see Crystal return to him? On her knees? Naked, crawling? What?"

I do not believe this! "You want *me* to suggest how I should be degraded?" He kept his expression innocent, but she knew him well enough to read the pleasure he was taking in this. Her fingernails dug painfully into her palms.

"Exactly. I'm no expert on the subject of, what is it called...? BMDS?"

Oh, you evil bastard. Like you don't know it's BDSM.

But just the thought of exposing him had her struggling to remember what they were talking about.

Retreating from the rising mental fog, she found herself breathing heavily.

"Well, go on. What would you suggest? How should you be presented, to be irresistible to his baser instincts?"

Across the room, the geek fest *finally* petered out, the others shifting their attention to the second conversation.

Great. Sleena flushed.

"What're you guys discussing?" Maeve asked.

"How to humiliate me," snarled Sleena.

"What?"

"Yeah, like whether I should be naked on all fours or-"

Marcie coughed. "Uh, Sleena, maybe Barney and Gigi don't need to be here for this," she said, putting a hand on her shoulder.

Leeth frowned. "Why?"

From the way everyone except Harmon scowled at her, she realized she must've said something wrong. And even he looked slightly uncomfortable.

Right, something else I apparently don't know. Did they not even *talk about* sex in front of kids? Or did that only apply for abusive sex? Actually, that made a lot of sense. She felt her cheeks warm.

"Meb you peeps could chat outside, eh?" Teef said.

Which was how, minutes later, Leeth found herself suggesting possible ways to objectify her, in front of people she considered friends. *Or mostly,* she added, glaring at Harmon.

"Would he feel safer if you were in bondage gear?" Vince asked, earning himself a punch from Marcie.

"Yes, but that could steer his thinking in unwanted directions, toward defensive precautions," Doc Truman said. "Better to imply his mental programming alone gives control of Crystal."

Leeth frowned. It was easier to hate him when he wasn't making sense. But Vince's question sparked the others' involvement, and soon everyone except Marcie was offering ideas for ways to 'prove' she'd become some kind of totally submissive slave girl. Outside Teef's place, she stared across the patch of dirt at Harmon, his concealed enjoyment of her humiliation stoking dark fires.

You are so dead. One day. Somehow.

"Oh come now, that won't do," Harmon said, interrupting Mason to point to her. "You look ready to tear someone's head off. For this to have any chance of success you will need to behave submissively. So let us say, you may not meet any-one's eyes, starting now. The eyes of any superior. Which is, of course, everyone."

She clenched her fists, actually trembling in fury, her chin tucking in, her eyes burning into his. *Now he's got them helping. Could this moment get any worse?*

"That's BS!" said Marcie. "Sleena's a professional. She doesn't need to give you a show beforehand."

"Really, 'M'?" Harmon asked. "Does she *truly* appear harmless to you?"

Marcie glanced at Sleena, clearly ready to tear her uncle's head off. "Uh, not, uh, not entirely." She suddenly looked like she'd rather be anywhere else.

"Perhaps I could use some Suggestion magic to help? I think I know a spell along those lines. Unless you can show us you don't need it?"

"No." Leeth wasn't sure she'd ever wanted to hurt him as much as she did right then. Somehow though she fought her fury down. That spark of dark anger burned hotter, but she finally managed to cage even that. Swallowing, she made her shoulders slump, and cast her eyes down.

Humble.

"Strip," he ordered.

Both the women, and Vince, drew in sharp breaths. But Leeth didn't react.

Proud of her fitness, she didn't mind showing her body. But she'd learned that most people didn't think that way. She also hated how he'd made this a dominance thing. *Fine,* she thought, mentally rolling her eyes. She wrenched up the hem of her dress.

"No, Sleena!" Marcie objected. She turned to Leeth's un-cle. "How dare you, you decrepit, creepy old-!"

Harmon rounded on her. "Be quiet. I am doing this for a reason. Wait."

Marcie gritted her teeth, glaring, but he stared her down before turning back to Leeth. "Slower. Make it sexy."

"Hey, no, wait-" Maeve said, but Sleena didn't hesitate. Just started swaying, biting her lip.

Leeth heard a faint click, then from Marcie's pocket came Harmon's voice, whispering. "Seshoestus desstussten." She felt a surge of appreciation. *She's* still *trying to protect me!* She didn't dare look up to reassure her friend – not while putting herself through this humiliation – but she did give a tiny shake of her head to try to let her know he wasn't forcing her to do this.

"Really?" Marcie whispered.

She gave a tiny nod, then finished pulling her abbreviated sundress off to stand in just her bra, panties, and Barney's lucky necklace.

"The underwear too. You can leave the jewelry on."

Maeve took an angry step forward, but Harmon threw up a hand, one finger raised in warning, glaring at her.

For Leeth, swaying her hips, horror dawned when part of her responded, urging her to comply. She felt her nipples tighten.

Instinctively she dug in her heels and stopped, then wondered if her refusal to strip completely meant she'd failed.

"There!" he said, now in his normal voice instead of the domineering tone he'd been using. "You sensed it just then, didn't you? The Omega conditioning I found implanted."

Maeve and Marcie glared from Harmon to her, no longer completely certain this had been just an offensive and petty humiliation.

Leeth knew better. It was both: lesson *and* punishment.

Harmon continued, in his lecturing voice. "Those are the 'reins' you will hear me refer to when we make contact and I act my part to convince Dr Yamamoto his technology exceeded his expectations. Embrace it for now – it will help you play this role. It may even save your life." Then his tone shifted back to one of sneering dominance. "Or perhaps his programming simply exaggerated existing submissive tendencies."

Again his tone shifted. "Picture Dr Yamamoto," he said.

She did, feeling a fresh surge of desire. The unexpected reaction shocked her. It made her consider abandoning the plan. *I can do this,* she had to reassure herself.

She repeated that thought even when he taunted her for her obvious arousal. Even when he ordered her to crawl. And worse. Humiliatingly worse, his hands groping her, objectifying her.

In fury, she knew he was right though: Yamamoto was paranoid, suspicious. It would take something as demeaning as this if they were to carry off the charade and get the stuff removed from her head. Knowing that didn't help all that much, though.

The others tried to leave, but Harmon said their presence was needed, to be sure Sleena would be able to bring herself to do the same, when her life depended on it.

At least she'd kept her underwear on, for now. "I'll take it off later," she insisted. That felt like a small victory, but an important one in front of her friends.

Her face burning, in the hush surrounding Harmon's 'testing' she still didn't dare meet anyone's eyes though.

Knowing shame.

The moment he declared himself satisfied she'd be able to carry off the charade, she snatched up her clothes and pulled them back on. She was proud of her body – but the knowledge her friends thought less of her for pretending to submit to his orders, was horrible.

Even worse than she'd expected.

"It will be worse still to do that before someone you truly hate, like Dr Yamamoto," he said.

Staring into his eyes, she couldn't decide if he'd said that to needle her, or to reassure her.

"*Sleena*," he admonished.

Gritting her teeth, she dropped her eyes and forced her hands to unclench again.

Teef pushed out through his front door, studying the tense group, no one meeting anyone's eyes. "Ya fren's sent Gigi the stuff. Malware, an' a 'defuse' prog he said she needs ta 'install' on Sleena?"

The process went smoothly and quickly. That was followed by a short argument about who precisely should accompany her.

She absolutely refused to let Marcie or Vince go with her. Mason said he should go. Maeve objected: Omega's security guy had seen his face the night they'd searched his boat. It'd be suspicious if he turned out to have found her after all.

"I'll just say I found her clinging to a channel marker after they'd ruined my night's fishing," Mason countered. "And when I found she'd lost her memories and was acting strangely, I headed here to Hunter's Point to a guy I knew."

He gestured to Doc Truman. "They won't know he's a mage: Dumps people don't blab to outsiders. We'll say he's a psychologist, and between him and a shaman we consulted, we uncovered these mental controls. Then I saw the bounty for her."

"Look," Maeve said, "I've helped – we've helped – a lot. Especially Gigi. But you don't need us now and I'm not going to endanger Lorien by dragging us any deeper. We've-"

Mason cut her off, going to her and putting one hand on her shoulder. "Hey. I agree. You all went way above and beyond."

Gigi looked simultaneously ashamed and relieved. She chewed her lip. "Luck, Crystal – Sleena. Kick sumbitch ass, so I can tell Shawna, Deena, an' t'other sprouts they he'ped a hero."

"Who?" Sleena asked.

Gigi and Maeve blinked, then looked at her like she'd just lost a friend.

"Who's Shawna and Deena? What sprouts?"

"It doesn't matter," Maeve assured her, with a look that said really, it did.

By now the sun had set. Gigi hugged her good luck, saying she'd stand by, just in case. Marcie, after much urging, and a whole series of worried hugs, reluctantly promised to leave.

"I'll call you. Or you call me, as soon as it's over." Marcie stared at her as if trying to send her a special message beyond the words. *"I've got your back,"* she whispered. Then punched her arm, "And don't you dare get yourself killed: it'd break Amanda's heart!"

"I won't."

She even remembered to call Eagle, not surprised to learn the Doctor had already persuaded him to approve the plan.

A drone delivered a couple of fetish items to the shores of the Fisher Clan. A carefully distanced contact was made to the million cred bounty number.

Soon Mason and Doc Truman, with Sleena at their feet, sat in a small runabout humming and bouncing over waves, Omega Memory Systems' office rising from the docklands shore ahead.

Where this whole mess had started.

CHAPTER 68

In the bottom of the small boat, her hands pressed flat to its fiberglass hull, she felt every jarring impact as it jolted over the waters of the Bay. At least being on the bottom kept the spray off her, unlike Mason and the Doctor.

She kept her eyes down, holding herself in the right mind-set, though in each small deviation and jerking course correction of the craft, she could feel the goggling stare of the boat's pilot.

When they arrived at the run-down wharf a few hundred meters south of the office building, he switched off the engines and leaped nimbly past them all to flip mooring fenders dangling over one side. In seconds they were tied off against the barnacle-crusted pylons.

He waited for them to disembark. Omega had larger, faster vessels, so assuming they'd be able to leave by water would be foolhardy. He'd wait down-shore just in case, but only as long as it seemed safe.

"Okay Doc, I've taken the building," Nelson's voice sounded in Harmon's earbud. "From what I can see they have two heavily armed merc teams of six on the floors above and below, ready to move in. But since I control the elevators and the fire-stair doors, that'll be easier said than done. You're good to go."

Harmon nodded to Mason, and they helped her up.

Two teams of six each, Leeth thought. *Plus Dr Yamamoto and Henstridge. And big dumb Savin. I can handle those odds. I think.* For some reason though, Nelson had sounded on edge.

Nelson never sounded on edge.

"Wait," Harmon said, eyeing her necklace. "That looks out of place, dangling down while you're on all fours." He bent to unclip it, then tossed it down to the boat's pilot. "See that gets back to Barney. You can say we don't need a lucky necklace."

Leeth felt her heart sink. She'd hoped he'd forgotten it. But Marcie and Barney had been just too obvious. He hadn't even felt the need to mind-probe her to find out how it was supposed to work. Not that she did.

So much for all their clever precautions.

The wooden planking of the steps up to the jetty were slimy with moss, her hands and knees slipping as she prowled up from the water. Things would improve once they got to Yamamoto. Her heart gave a funny little quiver at the thought.

"Can she walk until we get to the building at least?" Mason asked.

"No. Realistically, they should insist she is cuffed, so crawling lets them rationalize leaving her hands and legs free." He bent to tie a pink ribbon around her neck, keeping the other end in his hand. "Can you pretend this ribbon is unbreakable, Sleena? If not, I could give you a Suggestion to that effect. This is to subconsciously reinforce in them the idea you are bound by mental chains more secure than physical ones."

He tugged on it as he saw his proposal strengthen her determination, as he knew it would. She grunted, almost falling, exactly as if it had unbalanced her.

"Excellent. Just like that."

"We shouldn't call her Sleena, either," Mason said. "Not if we want them to underrate her. They might've heard of her, know Sleena's rep."

"We'll just call her Girl then."

Crawling on hands and knees over concrete and asphalt was easier said than done. She had to go on toes and hands to avoid scraping her knees.

"Can't we just have her walk?" Mason asked, seeing her difficulty. "She just needs to *look* submissive. Isn't the crawling overkill? Won't it make them suspicious?"

"Have you seen her in action, Mason? Would *you* feel safer with her standing, knowing she could spring on you at any moment, or seeing her crawling on the ground?"

Mason still appeared unconvinced.

The Doctor shook his head. "He is a narcissist who considers himself an 'alpha male'. Seeing her at another's feet will also be galling, and help cloud his judgment."

Crystal snorted, but when they turned, her expression was one of exaggerated innocence.

The moment Mason turned away though she darted a poisonous look at Harmon, erasing it as soon as she saw he'd received the message. Glowering, he said nothing. Instead he turned away and picked up his pace.

But after another block Mason grunted and hoisted her naked body up and over his shoulder.

"Much faster," he told 'Doctor Smith', "and it still makes

her seem helpless. Especially if you squirm," he told her.

Carefully schooling her expression, not even rolling her eyes, Leeth obliged.

She was not to speak unless spoken to; to call them both 'Master'; and to look no one in the eye. The complete slave-girl role.

Inwardly she seethed. *I'm playing along for good reasons.* It would get the junk out of her head; complete her original mission and destroy his hideous technology; but most of all, it'd let her kill Dr Yamamoto. And right now, she really needed to kill *someone*.

But more worrying was the hints of pleasure at each order obeyed, each sign of submission. All while knowing true subservience lay just three words away.

When he'd removed Barney's necklace she'd felt sure he'd put her into the hated obedience mode there and then. But he hadn't. Why? Not to please her. Then she worked it out – if he did, and for some reason ordered her to obey Yamamoto, and he got silenced after *that*, he'd be stuffed. And she'd be stuck too, trapped as if the Omega tech really did work.

No doubt he was holding *Mode One* in reserve.

Like in case Nelson's untested hack hadn't worked, and the Writer really did reprogram her. What would happen then, if Yamamoto ordered her to do one thing and the Doctor another?

-

Nelson fed the flows of data from the office block housing Omega Memory Systems into the quantum pattern matching system he'd built. Into Ghost. Security cameras, communications, internal security cameras, traffic cams from nearby. Even the elevator and fire control systems.

Ghost was his omni-tool. It had helped him decode enough of the Aiyami-compressed Omega OS to find the key entry points of the commands for their carbon nanotube molecular machines, as well as helping him crack the ingenious viral worm that'd ravaged the Sacramento cam network that morning.

He couldn't have done it without Ghost – those algorithms had folded layers of complexity. It had been easy to believe it was the work of an artificial intelligence.

Ghost let him crack computationally unbreakable security

codes, making him look a god-level hacker instead of a mere genius. Ghost had been the key to discovering the Department, breaking him free of Asgard's stifling R&D programme, by penetrating Eagle's systems to demand rescue.

But even with Ghost's support he feared Tik Tek. Knowing they backed Omega had him on edge. There was something more than freaky about the company. Sure, he could break any encryption, burrow into anywhere on the net he liked. Except, whenever he did that to Tik Tek, they quickly detected his intrusions. And each time, their response was sneakier.

He hated to admit it – would never admit it to anyone – but whoever ran their security was a match for him and Ghost combined. Not just their speed of response freaked him out, either: it was the scale, the sheer complexity.

Oh. He sat upright.

Oh, no.

That was it.

He suddenly knew. *That* was why Tik Tek scared him. *That* was why he couldn't prowl their systems as he could any other net-connected computer.

His opponent inside Tik Tek wasn't a human being, or even a team of human beings.

Tik Tek had a true AI. An Artificial General Intelligence.

Every hair on his body stood up on end. He cursed, long and passionately. It didn't make him feel any better.

-

Mason lowered her to the ground outside the office building. From all fours she saw heavy laminated glass walls, glossy olive tiles, and an alert and bright-eyed 'woman' watching them from behind an encircling desk. Like she was guarding the twin wood-paneled banks of elevators behind her.

Mason bent to the intercom. "Smith and Jones to see Dr Yamamoto, Omega Memory Systems,"

Leeth heard the ultrasonics of cybernetic muscles as the receptionist turned toward them, at the same time overhearing Nelson say to the Doctor, "She's a Syrra model gynoid, Tik Tek."

"You are expected," the intercom and the distant secretary said at the same time. The glass doors slid apart.

Harmon strode in, tugging the flimsy pink leash. She jerked forward, playing up to it, the glazed olive stone tiles cold on her bare skin. When Mason stepped through, the doors buzzed.

The attractive receptionist gynoid rose gracefully, folding back a section of her empty work surface. She stepped out holding a scanner and a plastic tray. "Please hand over all weapons, Mr Jones," she smiled.

Mason did so. Then a second time after the gynoid ran the scanner over him. At the third scan she was satisfied. "Lift two will take you to floor eight. Dr Yamamoto is waiting. Please enjoy your visit to Omega Memory Systems, Mr Smith, Mr Jones. Welcome back, Ms Winters." With an empty smile, she returned to her seat.

The sound of an elevator arrival turned them all in that direction, a business-suited man and woman stepping out. Their conversation ended the moment they saw the naked girl on all fours.

"Come along, Ms *Winters*," Harmon blithely said, emphasizing her name in pretend glee at 'discovering' it. He tugged her forward, meeting the eyes of the woman as he passed the pair. "A delivery for Omega Memory Systems." He smiled, daring the woman to object.

Leeth wasn't sure if he did it to annoy Omega Memory Systems, or embarrass her. Probably both.

Elevator two *dinged*. Her two 'owners' stepped in, Harmon tugging her forward again. She again exaggerated its effect before shuffling around between them, staring at their feet. Outside, as the pair reached the outer doors, the woman twisted around to look back at them. "Yamamoto's a disgrace, David," she whispered. "We should report him."

"Not our problem Liz."

Leeth shut her eyes, gathering herself mentally as the elevator ascended.

"Doc Y's just ordered his goons to be ready," she heard Nelson tell Harmon. "I still have everything locked down, but don't depend on that lasting forever."

In his voice there was still that note of tension that tightened her own.

The elevator continued implacably upward.

CHAPTER 69

Dr Shinsuke Yamamoto blinked at the sight that greeted him when the elevator doors chimed and opened, no other trace of shock reaching his face. Crawling meekly naked between the two men flanking her, his recalcitrant bodyguard.

He smiled inwardly while sizing up the two very dissimilar men, his eyes flicking to the girl struggling to keep her balance from each light tug on the flimsy ribbon around her neck. The taller, larger male's eyes scanned Henstridge, the room, and himself. He noted the man's eyes pause for a moment on the side of his jacket concealing his weapon.

Much as Mr Henstridge's had, upon their first meeting.

The man's eyes swept on, to the gynoid receptionist at its station, and glowering beside it, one of Henstridge's security people.

The gynoid buzzed his visitors through the glass security doors. In deference to the presence of its owner, it forbore to give its usual greeting, merely smiling in welcome as they entered.

Standing so the impressive view of New Francisco Bay framed him, Yamamoto inclined his head. "Mr Smith, Mr Jones. Or should I say, Doctor Truman – a sociologist on sabbatical I believe from Palo Alto University? – and Mr Mason Dane."

His security chief, Arvid Henstridge, armed and kevlar armored, strode forward, ignoring the academic to roughly pat Dane down for weapons. "'Tom Kingston'," he spat. "I fukken *knew* you had her."

Mason smiled, shaking his head. "I didn't. In fact I have you to thank for finding her. After your harassment I gave up and headed home. Found her clinging to a channel marker. So, thanks for that."

Henstridge snarled, then searched the older, bald man with no eyebrows. "What've you got to do with it?" he asked.

"I am a psychologist. Mr Dane brought her to me due to her strange behavior."

Neither had weapons. Eyeing the naked woman warily, Henstridge stepped back.

Truman followed his gaze. "Why don't you search, ah, Ms Winters I think your receptionist downstairs named her? We have just been calling her Girl. She's very accommodating."

Henstridge could tell the man wasn't as calm as he pretended, but also recognized in him a smug certainty Crystal bloody Winters wasn't going to leap up and break his fukken neck. Lips compressed, he backed away, glaring again at Yamamoto: *We should just kill her.* He'd been arguing that point the moment they'd appeared on camera, approaching from the docks.

As expected, the fool just gave another microscopic shake of his head.

Savin still stood alert beside the gynoid receptionist. Henstridge considered ordering him to 'search' the naked girl. But she'd liked Savin. Unlike himself, who she despised almost as much as Yamamoto. *Let's see how you react to this....*

Nodding to Savin to be ready, he snarled and strode to the girl, one black booted foot shoving hard. She shot backward, arms and legs flying, breast and crotch exposed... but without a sound of protest. Just got back to her hands and knees, head still down.

"Girl. Heel." Truman clicked his fingers, pointing down to his side

And Crystal fukken Winters, without protest or hesitation, crawled back to him.

"Leash."

Taking the end of the pink ribbon she held it up, her eyes still downcast.

Henstridge watched in shock. When he turned to the Omega director, at the hungry expression on the man's face he almost felt sorry for Winters.

"My lovely bodyguard seems not quite herself, Mr Dane. What did you do to her?"

"Me? Uh, nothing." Dane's eyes slid briefly to his accomplice. "I plucked her off the channel beacon, but she couldn't remember anything. Took her home and fed her. Next day took her away for some peace and quiet. She slipped away but I found her again. Decided to take her to Doc Truman here."

"Just *fed* her, Mr Dane?" Yamamoto asked.

Mason tugged his collar, remembering the sex they'd had. It made it easy to look ashamed. "Mostly."

"Did you perform any medical tests, Doctor Truman?"

Harmon knew what Yamamoto was really asking, and kept his expression bored. "An X-ray showed no skull fractures or other sign of traumatic injury that would explain her memory loss. I suspect an overdose of some new street drug. People are fools."

"Yes. Yes they are," Yamamoto agreed. "Well, I will run my own tests. Just to ensure there is nothing to be found." He smiled.

Crystal, Harmon, and Mason all hid their delight, knowing what he really meant by 'nothing to be found'.

"You said she slipped away from you, Mr Dane. How did you find her again?"

Mason cleared his throat. "I, uh, had a tracker on her. Just because she was so confused, you understand. Brought her back to the Doc and he, ah, found a way to get her under control." He had the grace to look embarrassed. "By then I'd heard about the reward you were offering for her."

"How do you explain her extraordinary behavior now? She appears compelled to obey Dr Truman. Why is that?" The passion behind the question was clear.

"We consulted a shaman," Truman said. "He found what he called 'reins of control' in her mind. She was a blank slate, hungry for orders – provided they came from a male."

"Crystal: heel." Yamamoto clicked his fingers as the other man had done, pointing to his own feet.

The girl crawled eagerly toward him – until reaching the end of the ribbon. It yanked her head around, making her twist and fall.

"Ah, she's also very suggestible," Truman explained. "So this *titanium link chain* is quite beyond her *child-like* strength to break." Harmon noted a shift in his audience's attitude, their assessment of his role. Like Crystal's obedience to him rather than Mason, it justified both his presence, and his share in the reward.

"Ah, I see. Very creative, Doctor. Titanium is it?" He met Truman's eyes, reading in them a familiar relish.

"Thank *you*, Doctor," Truman said. "But I gather this property belongs to you. If you would transfer the reward you offered, we will be happy to leave it with you."

Yamamoto allowed himself a smile. *Did they really think they would leave here with a million credits?* "There are one or two formalities first, gentlemen. I need to check Miss Winters, to ensure she is... in good shape. Mr Henstridge will escort you to a waiting area. You may sample some very fine scotches while I perform my tests."

"We'd prefer to stay with her," Mason said. "I'm sure you understand. Until the payment has been made, we prefer to keep our property in sight."

Yamamoto looked down at the naked girl, once more beside the older male, pressing in against his legs protectively. That was wrong – she was his! *His* Writer had erased her identity, implanted those controls. She should be by *his* side!

He held that from his thoughts though as he looked to assess his security officer's feelings.

Henstridge frowned. "In that case it probably is wise to search her. Savin. Make sure she isn't hiding any weapons anywhere." *Surely, this'll make her explode.* Taking a position out of her sight he drew his gun. The heavyset Savin stepped forward, his expression carefully neutral.

But Winters didn't resist; didn't even blush.

In the end, Henstridge shook his head, convinced despite himself. He followed behind as Yamamoto led Savin and his guests across the impressive viewing area to his main lab.

His hand print opened the door, the Japanese beckoning the others to follow him inside. Savin entered next, keeping a sensible distance from the two fools leading the naked Winters. They wouldn't be entering so calmly if they knew what reaching the inner sanctum meant.

They should have accepted the offer of a final whiskey.

Henstridge, in the rear, let the door seal shut behind him, smiling when he saw Winters at last react: she shied from the gleaming white torus of Yamamoto's Writer device, its recently modified stretcher patiently awaiting her return.

Truman tugged her forward with his flimsy pink ribbon, once more almost making her fall. Was that an act, or was the satin ribbon, to her mind, a titanium link chain?

Soon enough it wouldn't matter.

Crystal Winters now lay stretched out, once more strapped to the gurney that would slide her into Yamamoto's 'Writer'. Henstridge finished binding her other wrist and hand to the tungsten steel rails at her sides, wrapping the graphene sheet tight. One strip was a hundred times stronger than steel. He'd looped each one three times before pressing its locking section down to hear the characteristic click.

She wouldn't be pulling free this time, no matter how

she'd managed it before. He tugged with his full augmented strength on each reinforced railing, too. They didn't budge.

She'd stayed docile throughout, eyes downcast, avoiding his. He'd half-expected her to try to make a break for it. A team of six waited on the floor above and another on the floor below, in case whoever had wiped out their colleagues this morning at the Tazman-Dungog flesh pit showed up hoping to repeat the trick.

And then of course there was his final ace in the hole, waiting far below.

Running his fingers down the ribbon at her neck, Henstridge draped it down the center of her torso, dropping the end between her legs.

A movement from the naked girl stretched out before him caught his eye. She was folding her fingers down toward her palms, each hand straining futilely and somehow desperately upward against its graphene restraints.

After a last tug at her bonds he stepped back. Nodding to the Director, he caught Truman staring at Crystal's hands. He'd seen that somehow otherworldly *attention* before. A prickle went up his spine. Truman was a mage, not just a mere academic! Had that helped him gain control of Yamamoto's rebellious bodyguard? Was that why Dane had brought the fellow along?

He looked away before the man could know he'd been made, and sent a message putting their additional security forces on alert.

Seated at the controls to his machine, Yamamoto set the gurney into motion, carrying his former bodyguard inside. Soon he was humming in satisfaction, and Henstridge recognized the column of green circles indicating all was well.

Yamamoto turned, and at his smile Henstridge once more felt a twinge of pity for the girl.

"Winters is going nowhere for now, as you can see. Henstridge-san, show our visitors our magnificent view of New Francisco Bay while I run my tests. I will join you momentarily."

He very much enjoyed their helpless expressions as his security people ushered them outside.

Alone finally with Crystal-chan.

He smiled. All systems nominal. Briefly, he considered ordering a full wipe. But that would take many hours, he was keen to start, and she had escaped during an Erase cycle. Two days of erasure should be enough!

He had decided to basically follow the optimistic plan he and Henstridge had discussed – full tear-down and extraction of the scaffolding that mirrored much of her neuronal network. With it gone, so was all evidence of his technology. Moving Crystal Winters from unacceptable threat to harmless toy.

Basically.

But first, he instructed his machine to locate the parts of her memory holding two things: the 'owner' concept, and its image of the middle-aged Truman.

The Reader found them in seconds. As expected, they were connected. He fed in an image of himself. *He* was Crystal Winters' true owner. It would take his Writer only seconds to insert his own image, sever that connection and reassign it to him. And when the new Crystal Winters emerged – *I should think of a new name for Crystal-chan* – the first order he would give his doll would be to kill the usurper and the *other* fool with him. Or perhaps they would make useful fresh subjects.

Checking the machine, he left it running, the naked young woman this time immovably bound inside it, to rejoin his guests. To play, and to check certain assumptions.

Closing the door, he stepped into the viewing lounge, taking a seat across from them. Mr Dane now looked tense. The older man, unwisely calm. "The tests should not take long. While we wait I would be interested to learn more about the control you exercise over the young woman, Dr Truman."

Once again, both declined his offer of drinks.

"As I said, the shaman was able to look inside her mind somehow. He also found she reacted very powerfully to a Suggestion spell. Partly, he believed, because the suggestions were given by a male. Do you have any idea why that would be so?"

Yamamoto *hmmed* as if intrigued, considering his answer. It seemed plausible. But was there a knowing look to those deep-set eyes? "Who can say?" he shrugged. "Father issues?"

Truman's look, whatever it signified, only intensified.

When he had first used his Writer on his insolent bodyguard, he had considered spending the time to explore the structures of her memories, to make a copy before running the original Erase cycle on the disrespectful female subject.

Subject. The word had two meanings in English, both perfectly apt.

But that would have taken days, and he had been hungry with anticipation, and so very angry with her. Perhaps in time it might have been possible to interpret the patterns that were her memories, to decode their meaning, learn her history. Discover how she had, so impossibly, broken free of the restraints midway through her overwrite. He'd been layering in the obedience protocols when it had all gone horribly wrong.

Mason turned from the view, eyeing the elevator. "How long exactly is this gonna take?"

"Only a few minutes more," Yamamoto assured him.

"And then we get paid, and leave?" Truman asked.

"Of course," Yamamoto said, confident the presence of just Henstridge and Savin would be enough. It appeared Henstridge had overreacted, and the backup teams would not be needed. Nor the final reserve which Henstridge had convinced him to purchase at great expense, waiting now below, under the waters of the Bay.

He even had two fresh subjects.

–

Nelson, nervous, monitored the Omega Memory Systems building security cameras. Thanks to Ghosting into the Tik Tek brand receptionist bot – after first checking it wasn't communicating to its manufacturer! – he also watched and listened through its senses.

Now was the most dangerous time, with Leeth locked inside the brain reprogramming machine and Doc and the untrustworthy Mason Dane facing Mr Omega and his security goons. Both Dane and Henstridge looked mean frackers. But Dane had had to surrender his weapons, and Henstridge and the other goon of course still carried theirs.

He hated waiting. Now was the critical time, on the brink of success and failure both. Especially now, with his certainty that Tik Tek hosted an AI. What was its role in all this? What did it want?

He twitched from the gynoid receptionist to the gynoid cook-slash-cleaner in the company cafeteria, its evening routines paused while people remained inside. From there he hopped to the third gynoid, the nursebot standing inhumanly silent and unmoving in the sterile medbay, staring at the two empty beds with their ominously-sturdy bed rails.

Three top of the line gynoids. Just how much money had this guy spent on Tik Tek sexbots? At least he seemed to be using them just for their advertised 'business' functions.

He really hated waiting. Was his malware package working? Via the Doc's Link, he'd received the blip signifying it'd successfully delivered itself into *some* system. But before the Doc even left the room with the machine, he'd moved out of range of the weak WiFi linkage to the tech in Leeth's head.

So now he waited. Finally, the creepy Japanese brain hacker emerged from his laboratory and rejoined the others, where they yammered on. Even with the gain turned up all the way on the receptionist's audio, it was hard to hear the conversation.

Did he say Leeth'd be finished in minutes? This waiting was killing him!

-

Harmon's earbud sounded the tone indicating Nelson's malware had completed its work. He tapped his Link – the signal for Nelson to lock the building down in readiness for their exit.

Shifting his gaze to the Imaginal, he read Mason's tension. Unlike himself, Mason was unaware the Department's young genius now had full control of the building. Henstridge's aura showed similar tension, and the similar impairment of heavy cyber augmentation too.

He turned to the Japanese neuroscientist. Yamamoto's aura showed hungry amusement.

Amusement?

He felt a prickle of unease.

-

Nelson was wondering if he dared have the gynoid receptionist turn its head when the first of the building's computer nodes rebooted without warning. A moment later, the Doc's tap signaled it was time to lock the building tight and call an elevator to their floor ready for their casual escape.

A familiar cold chill speared up and down his spine. With a jerk, he sent the orders even as he cut his connection from the remote systems, more of them rebooting now without his command.

Panicking, he shut down every virtual machine he'd used to mount the penetration.

Better message the Doc, let him know they're on their own.

But when he tried to warn the Doc via the telco network, the instant backtrace response confirmed his worst fear.

Tik Tek had arrived. Leeth's team had been isolated.

He swallowed. She and the Doc were on their own. Had his building lock-down order even got through?

He called Eagle.

CHAPTER 70

Mason's only warning was the sight of the elevator doors opening – unannounced. As the first rifle barrel emerged he was already moving. One hand speared into Yamamoto's jacket, returning as if by magic with a pistol. Maybe the guy should've spent a little on combat augments? Mason spun, winging the guard and sending Henstridge diving for cover before turning to fire into the opening elevator.

The glass wall in between *exploded* at his first shot. What in hell had Yamamoto loaded his weapon with? He didn't hesitate though.

Three security guards went down, one by one, despite their flak jackets. "Get down!" he shouted to Truman even as he dived for cover.

Harmon was blinking in disbelief. *How can this be happening?* Nelson had secured the elevators, the whole building. Was this a double-cross by the youth – or even the Department itself? Or a better hacker than *Nelson?*

Ignore that – cast Sleep! Fighting through his shock he focused. Forming the mental pattern for the spell-

A gun fired, a giant's hammer knocking him backward, stunning him.

He was falling before he understood, unable to think. He hit the ground while Mason returned fire in slow motion, crouched in cover.

Harmon's head and back struck the carpeted floor, pain arriving like the rumble of thunder after lightning. *I've been shot!*

More gunfire, from nearby and also the elevators. He tried to focus enough to heal himself. Then a booming explosion and the sound of tortured metal.

I should have cast Sleep as soon as Yamamoto said it would only take minutes, Harmon berated himself. As soon as the elevator doors opened. But how had the elevator arrived? Nelson had locked the building down!

"Dane. You're outgunned. Toss out your weapon while you still can."

"We came here in good faith to collect the reward!"

Henstridge's reply was laughter. "You never did a single thing in good faith in your life, Dane. Give it up."

Harmon tried to block it all out. Focus. *Focus on the pattern. Summon the inner reserves. Connect the two.*

He was hardly aware of Dane cursing, and a heavy clatter.

It was met by mocking laughter. "Now step out where we can see you. Savin, put that mage down."

He'd just begun the healing when he was abruptly flipped over, tearing a cry from him and breaking his concentration. His arms were roughly jammed behind his back, wrenching another cry of pain from him as his wrists were lashed tight.

This shouldn't be happening! Nelson has control of the building! He pushed the non-productive thought aside even as he felt his Link stripped from him, then his still-silent earbud.

They're going to kill us. With Leeth still lashed inside the machine. He remembered Henstridge wrapping the restraints around her wrists, then her head, the man's eyes roaming her helpless body as he draped the pink 'leash' down her length like a promise of future torment. Stepping back as the gurney drew her into the claustrophobic tunnel where the robotic surgeon waited.

Leeth had been desperately straining her fingertips toward her palms. He'd watched, astrally, as those deadly invisible claws had stretched out – unable to reach the ties binding her.

But *could* they? Did she not shape them, unconsciously? Why did they have to be straight?

Could even *she* hear though, through a locked door, a room away? "Leeth, Mode One," he murmured as loudly as he dared, hoping the imperative could break what *might* be just a self-imposed limitation. "Curve your claws. *Curve them.*" Would it be enough? Even in her fury, in the Moot Hall, she had been unable to do that.

"Praying, Truman?" Henstridge sneered, looming over him, his gun out.

"Something like that."

Leeth had heard the mosquito whine of tiny motors as the robo surgeon retracted, followed by hundreds of tiny stings across the back of her head. Then the surgeon's 'fingers' withdrew. From across the room something made a loud 'bing'. Then she was sliding out. The machine fell into silence.

She strained at her bonds, but they didn't give at all. With a flush of anger she extruded her claws, slashing nothing, trying to angle her fingers down far enough to reach the tape-like material pinning her wrists and hands.

Then the gunfire started.

She thrashed in her bonds, knowing Mason and the Doctor had no weapons. Her whole body heaved upward, trying to bend the railing.

It reminded her of being held down by Marc Disten's impossible strength.

She heard the Doctor cry out, and more gunfire.

Still she struggled. *Some agent you are! Tied up helpless again!* What even *was* this tape stuff he'd used? It looked so flimsy. How could it be holding her?

Invisible razors slashed air. Arching her back she tried to bend her wrist, but the stupid tape went across her palm and thumb, and she couldn't get the right angle.

The gunfire stopped. She gathered her reserves. Just listening, panting quietly, waiting to hear the shot that would end the Doctor's life. Equal parts horrified, eager, and regretful.

She heard him grunt in pain. Then... "Leeth, Mode One."

No!

In disbelief she felt the weird certainty fall over her. The anticipation.

"Curve your claws."

Her claws were straight. They'd always been straight.

His order clashed against her certainty.

"Curve them."

Animals claws curved. *Cats* claws curved. She must curve her claws.

A strange shiver ran from the base of her spine, tingling through her, rippling out finally to her fingertips and beyond.

She felt her claws curl inward, toward her wrists. Delicately, in unthinking certainty, she bent her two middle fingers, felt razors kiss her forearms, and drew them, stinging, down her wrists. The tape parted with a sound so high and faint she could hardly hear it. Invisible claws reached the edge of her palms, a mere centimeter of material remaining.

So close! Her fingers curled in anger, multiple punctures warning her to stop.

Panting harder, she took stock. Releasing her claws, she felt them retract, then made two fists and forced her right arm upward.

At the tiny sound of tearing, she redoubled her effort.

With a ripping sound her arm flew up.

Yes!

Moments later she'd sliced the flimsy webbing off, and paused to listen. While she did, she collected the strips that had tied her down. No sense giving them any clues to her deadliest weapon.

"What are you going to do with us?" she heard Mason ask.

She looked around the room. The voices weren't far from the only door out of here. They'd see her the moment she stepped out.

"Yes, yes, do not fuss, Henstridge-san, I am uninjured."

Her eyes went to the solid wooden ceiling high overhead, then the machine she'd just escaped, measuring the gap between the two.

She heard and felt a heavy vibration, from the floor itself, then the Doctor grunt.

"This one's a mage," Henstridge said.

Quietly leaping onto the gurney, from there she climbed on top of the gleaming white tube. Again she heard and felt the heavy vibration. Like a tiny earthquake.

"A mage?" Yamamoto said.

Once again the heavy vibration sounded. They were coming about a second apart.

She heard a meaty impact, and the Doctor grunt. "How does one render a mage harmless, Henstridge-san? I hear they are most dangerous."

"Bullet to the head usually does the trick."

Yamamoto chuckled. "Perhaps later, Mr Henstridge. I have a few questions for our guests first. Unless you fear your new team is as inept as your last?"

The heavy vibration came again. Closer?

On top of Yamamoto's machine she paused. *I think Nelson's hack worked – I feel just the same.*

"Fine," said Henstridge. "They need to see to target their spells," he offered. "Sometimes hand gestures too, and even to speak."

Thud.

Legs straddling the cold device, she gently probed the back of her head. It felt tender but okay. Down her arms ran two trickles of blood, already coagulating. Her wrists though were different. Blood welled from puncture wounds from her own claws, before she'd stopped. *Still in Mode One.*

"You're bleeding, Doctor Truman. Would you like to be allowed to heal yourself?"

She'd heard that tone from Yamamoto before. Taunting. Cruel.

Thud.

"Yes," the Doctor said.

Oh, you idiot. He only asked that to check if you really are a mage. He totally sucked as an agent.

Thud.

Were they *steps?*

"Interesting. How to end your ability to perform spells, I wonder...?"

Her blood had dripped onto the floor around the gurney, and onto the bed of the stretcher itself. For a moment she considered jumping back down to wipe it up.... *Don't be stupid. You can remove the evidence later. After you've killed them all.*

Thud.

"I can't get a signal. Are you jamming us, krekhead?" That was Henstridge's voice.

"Me?" Mason answered. "I thought that was you."

She shifted the bunch of slashed tape from her right hand to her left, then stabbed up with her middle finger, relishing the feel of her blade slicing through the hard, thick wood overhead. Imagining it was Yamamoto's heart.

Thud.

Those steps were definitely sounding closer.

Biceps standing proud with the effort, she dragged her hand across the ceiling, the wood crackling as she cut. She curved it around and began cutting at a right angle.

The twenty seconds it took to make her escape hole felt like an hour. The ponderous steps continued – *what on Earth* is *that?* – and as she'd known, Yamamoto hadn't allowed her uncle to heal himself. Instead, she gathered they'd found a hood.

She hammered the wood up and pushed the new hatch aside, then pulled herself up after it into the unlit ceiling space. She waited a second, two, for her eyes to adjust to the dark, feeling the smooth edges of the wood she'd carved.

Outside the room below her, she heard the tread of multiple sets of heavy booted feet crunching on... glass? Where had they come from? Had that whirring been the sound of elevator doors opening? But why hadn't it 'dinged'? It had when she and Mason and the Doctor arrived.

The heavy, thudding steps sounded like they were inside the building now.

Biting her lip she stabbed invisible claws through her hatch to lower it back into place. She wedged a corner of one of the thin straps into an edge when she got the wood flush with the ceiling.

Carefully she retracted her claws, smiling in the dark when the wood panel stayed snugly in place. She put the remaining severed straps down quietly as her eyes adjusted to the now much deeper darkness. Even for her it was a challenge, only a few distant slivers of light entering the ceiling cavity.

She tested the wooden flooring, pleased by its solidity. Far less dust than she was used to in ceiling spaces she'd prowled through. Snapping the ribbon around her neck she dropped it too.

Listening, she tracked the people moving on the floor under her. Moving then on all fours along the crossbeams, she visualized the layout of the office below, making her plans.

Thud.

CHAPTER 71

She was ninety percent sure the main access way into the ceiling was just outside the sysadmin guy's office, Omega's only full-time employee apart from Henstridge, Savin, and a couple of low grade lab workers. The daylight hours working for Yamamoto had crawled past, so boring they'd almost sent her mad.

Maybe it was why she'd been a bit snippy with him?

Nah, everything about the job had rubbed her the wrong way. Especially having to defend the jerk at the repellent clubs he'd visited, when she'd much rather have helped his victims beat *him* up. Still, he had caused a few fun fights, she had to admit.

The heavy thuds had stopped, but as she reached the access hole, she heard the lab door open. A second later Yamamoto screeched from there, "Henstridge!" his cry followed by multiple sets of running booted footsteps. *I guess he noticed I'm not there.*

Hearing nothing directly below her, she lifted the hatch, blinking in the office light. After a quick look, she dropped silently to the floor.

"She's gone! Find her!"

"She can't be!" Henstridge's voice. Followed by a lot of swearing.

She could circle around to the main light switch.... Or.... The sysadmin guy's office – he had all sorts of bits and pieces there.

Slipping inside, she found a metal strip. *That'll do.* She bent it into a small 'U' shape and crept out, pausing to listen, working out exactly where everyone was.

She heard the Doctor ask Mason if he could get a call out, and Mason say the cell access was being jammed.

"Shut up!" Savin's voice growled, and she heard a meaty impact. At a second impact, the Doctor grunted in pain.

"Where is she, Truman?" Yamamoto was screaming. "And *you* are incompetent, Henstridge. A fool!"

She couldn't understand any of the Japanese that followed, but it didn't sound complimentary.

Thud.

Uh oh. That felt... heavier somehow. Nearer. Was she the only one who heard it? Were they all really that hard of hearing?

Crouching low on the carpeted floor, exposed in the office

lights' white glare, she darted from cover to cover. But although her hunters trod softly, it was child's play to follow them all by their sounds. Henstridge and Yamamoto were heading back out of the lab to Mason and the Doctor in the main viewing area. One of the searchers was approaching from her right.

But there was another not far from him. Around to her left, she could hear one in the kitchen cafe area, alone, searching cupboards. For her?

It might be fun to take them down one by one. Also, sensible. She eyed her U-shaped metal. *In the dark.*

Thud.

She sprinted down the corridor between the elevators and the toilets, toward the cafe and her solo hunter, thinking.

Assuming Nelson's malware had done its job, she needed to kill Yamamoto at least. And what about his backup files? The sysadmin guy kept them in the safe bolted to the floor of the room next to his. At least there were none off-site to worry about. Yamamoto had screamed at him the one time he'd recommended it.

"Never! Everyone wants my research, Mr Raphael! No so-called secure vault can be trusted!"

Of course she hadn't mentioned to either of them that the Department agreed. It was why she was there.

Yamamoto was screaming now in the same screeching tone of outrage.

"Where is she? How did she escape?" he demanded.

"I have no idea," the Doctor replied. Then grunted in pain.

"I think you do." Henstridge's voice.

Thud.

That was definitely closer. Stronger too, like it was shaking the building more. Sure, it was a low sound, but couldn't they even *feel* it?

Time was running out. *Okay, Leeth.*

She eyed her strip of metal and then her naked body, and winced at what she planned, remembering being tasered. Slipping into the Ladies for some insulating paper she shut her eyes for a few seconds, then rammed the metal into a power socket, hoping for the best.

Thud.

A pleasingly strong spark then the lights failed, to cries all around. Mentally thanking everyone for giving her their locations, she exited the restroom at speed, her eyes already adjusted. With light flooding in from the city the kitchen area wasn't dark at all really, yet her hunter was fumbling around like he couldn't see.

The expected *thud* didn't come. Because of the dark? But it didn't seem to worry Dr Y. He just ordered Henstridge to send the cook-cleaner to turn them back on. *Hah. As if I'd use the light switches!*

"Your bleeding has slowed, Doctor. I can fix that." Again the sound of a meaty impact and her uncle's grunt of pain. "How did she escape?"

I'm still in Mode One. And he's an idiot when it comes to spying or fighting. If he orders me to come charging in to-

"Seshoestus desstussten," he said, and Leeth froze for a second, stunned that he'd *freed* her.

"What?" Henstridge demanded. "What language's that?"

He freed *me!*

There were nine searchers, plus Henstridge and Savin. And what if they used Mace or her uncle as hostages?

Thud.

Uh oh. Crouched low, she rose behind the armored man in the kitchen, grimacing. "Sorry," she whispered.

He didn't stand a chance. One down.

Sprinting silent and barefooted to the next closest victim, she counted *thuds* like slow heartbeats, not knowing how many she had left, just certain there were none to spare.

"Sorry," she whispered to the second man. She didn't have time to be gentle. It gave him time to turn toward her before she swept her claws through his neck, catching his head and body to lower them softly to the ground.

She checked his gun, but as soon as her finger slipped onto its trigger an ultrasonic whine started. Unauthorized fingerprint. Dropping it, she watched it zap and spark against the ground.

For some reason, she felt awful even as she sprinted back toward the sysadmin guy's office. *Andrew.* That was his name. She slowed as she approached, so the two searchers nearby wouldn't hear her. Positioning herself outside Andrew's door she waited while a hand fumbled from inside to open it. As the man stepped out she struck up into his chin from below, wincing as his neck cracked and he collapsed. Three dead.

Thud.

"Sorry," she whispered again. This *should* have been fun: something bad coming, nine armed men hunting her in the dark, and her on her own. But she wasn't enjoying it as much as she'd expected.

"Jace," someone whispered. "I heard something."

That was the second searcher. She saw a handheld mirror poke around the corner.

Rats.

She hauled the body upright in front of her, hoping it'd give a moment of confusion as she walked it around the corner.

"Jace, what-?"

She sprang over Jace's falling body to snatch this one's assault rifle away, her other hand lopping off his head. It bounced away, loud in her ears as blood sprayed. Four.

"Sorry," she whispered. What was *wrong* with her? She kept his rifle, not sure why. Maybe it'd make a nice club.

Thud.

And couldn't anyone else hear that? Couldn't they feel its vibration in the floor?

Someone moved with a soft but heavy tread down the corridor between what she thought of as Andrew's part of the office, and the secondary labs. She sprinted past the computer backups room, the computer room, then slowed as she saw the back of a figure moving away from her, toward the T-junction onto the space circling the floor, with views north into the city.

"*Miller? Stravinsky? Marrs? Davos? Respond. I've lost your life signs.*"

She didn't recognize the tiny voice from the earbud of the stocky man ahead of her, scanning left and right, but the same voice was coming from inside the secondary labs on her right.

On bare feet she padded silently forward, crouching, using his own body to block her reflection from the floor-to-wall windows he faced. She rose silently behind him, her eyes in line with the back of his neck.

This isn't right.

Killing him from behind was unfair. She could make a

sound, so they could fight face to face. But then he might warn the others. And this wasn't a game.

Thud.

With her last opponent's assault rifle held loosely in her left hand, she let the claws of her right stretch silently out in the dark.

Then from his earbud, so close she could have plucked it from his head, the same voice. "'Toon, I've lost four life signs! Jace should be ten meters from you, west. Go look."

"Okay," the solid figure whispered, her voice husky.

The solid figure in front of her was a woman! For some reason, it made a difference. *I don't want to kill her!*

The woman was already turning left. Leeth danced to the right and forward, staying behind her. Retracting her claws to change hands on the rifle, she slid a finger onto its smart trigger to let it read her print, and reached out with her other hand. At the first sound of the capacitor charging up, she wrenched the woman's belt backward and rammed the rifle barrel-first down the leg of her pants. The woman spun around, too slow. Leeth ripped the weapon from her hands as blue eyes flew open in shock. Then arcing electricity slammed into the woman, sending her into spasms and taking her down, gasping and jerking for long seconds until the battery cut off. Leeth winced. She'd be out of it for minutes. Five down.

Thud.

That noise was getting to her. Keeping low, beside the walls of labs two and three and wincing at the lights from the city-scape on her left, she scampered to the T-junction between the labs and meeting rooms.

Slowing at the corner, with the lights of the city streaming in through Omega's mirrored windows, she stepped out – and almost ran into a man standing silent in the dark.

This one she hadn't taken by surprise. But she was too close for him to use his rifle. His hand flashed to draw a knife as she dropped the woman's rifle.

Invisible blades struck, lopping off his wrist, the other his head. Two rifles hit the carpeted floor. Six.

"What the fuck is going on? Blade, you there? 'Toon – how's Jace?"

The voice still came from inside the lab on her right.

Thud.

But the shiver in the floor this time was followed a moment later by an echoing muffled tread *inside the fire-stairs*.

"Mr Henstridge, I think something in here is killing my people. Sound off, everyone."

She heard nothing for several seconds, then, a hesitant and distant "Jackson." Straining, she heard it faintly from inside the lab too. Then one more name she didn't get.

She rested her fingers on the heavy lab door. The man inside was freaking out. But it'd take too long to kill him, even assuming she could reach him before he shot her. They were alert now, ready for her. By her count, she still had three hunters she hadn't dealt with. Plus Henstridge, Savin, and Dr Y.

Inside the lab, she heard the panicked man call out those other names who hadn't responded again, but she was already racing through the dark, back to the wide-open viewing area for Mason, her uncle, Henstridge and Savin.

It was time to take out the real bad guys.

Thud.

And, by the sound of it, she had maybe ten or twenty seconds before whatever giant *thing* that was, arrived from the fire-stairs.

CHAPTER 72

The trouble was, she could hear ultrasonic chirps from Henstridge's augmented muscles, in the middle of the open space with its panoramic views over the Bay. No doubt standing with gun drawn. And Savin near him, breathing heavily, like he was in pain. Plus two others, a little further away.

Thud.

She could also hear a steady set of chirps and grunts from Mason, while his clothes rustled against the carpeted flooring. Struggling? It made her think of her own futile attempts to break those weird tape bonds.

"I've been shot," she heard Harmon whisper, "and they have a bag over my head so I can't target spells." An edge to his voice told her he was in pain.

Good.

"I'm afraid I can't be much help, Leeth," he finished.

She flushed, then forced that reaction down with a sneer. So, finally he was acting like a professional? Not that she needed *his* help.

From the stream of insults hissed at Henstridge, mixed with demands he 'stop her' and for Doctor Truman to order her to submit, she knew exactly where Dr Y was.

"I fear your device has had some strange effect on her," Harmon was saying. "But I'll be happy to try." Raising his voice, he called out – so loud she knew he was play-acting – "Girl. Crystal Winters. Obey. Crawl back here and lie down on the floor." But he followed that by adding, so softly only she could hear, "Don't even think about it."

Thud.

From ahead and to her right, leading back to the central open area, she heard a tinny whisper saying, "Fask, take that corner to cover the north corridor and back this way," followed by heavy steps on the carpet, approaching from around the corner only a dozen paces from her.

She grimaced. Was he even *trying* to be stealthy?

Dropping, she cut two strips of carpet, peeling them up. Toes on bare concrete, carpet pressing up into the balls of her feet, she rose to her haunches, waiting.

Now. Launching herself forward and up as he came into view, invisible claws punched through some kind of armor tougher than kevlar, through his heart. She stepped to her left, her back to the outer windows so he blocked her from the viewing lounge as he died. Number seven.

In the dark, open space she saw Henstridge, pistol out, facing the foyer and lifts. Turning away from her to his left he gestured one handed. "Medich, take position at that corner to cover the other approach," he said quietly. "And goddammit Harker, she's not in hiding in those damned labs! Pull back here."

She propped the man she'd just killed in the corner, but took his assault rifle, being careful to avoid the trigger and its anti-theft device. *Stupid smart weapons.* At least she could use it as a time-delayed taser, like she'd done for the woman.

Thud.

While Henstridge gave his instructions, she sped in a crouch to the end of the corridor, stopping at the edge of the viewing area with its show-offy indoor garden and streams.

Savin stood guard over Mason and the Doctor, who wore a hood just like he'd said. Both were prone.

She crouched and sprang forward low, flinging the captured rifle sideways at Henstridge.

Savin cried out, swinging his pistol toward her. She angled her blow upward so when his hand flew off it arced through the air toward Harmon. Pushing off from Savin to him, she ripped off his hood, turning back to the slowly moving weapon in frustration, the hand's finger still through the trigger guard.

Snarling, she leaped for them, judging their twisting fall, grabbing the barrel in her left and Savin's severed hand in her right, sighting on Henstridge and squeezing off shots with Savin's finger.

Smart guns were *so* annoying.

Henstridge returned fired as he threw himself sideways and to the floor, and she snapped off three more shots past Dr Y's head at the bigger threat across the open space, a kevlar jacketed figure already aiming at her. His head rocked back, both arms flying outward as he toppled. Eight.

Not bad shooting, considering! Father'd be impressed.

Dr Y had his gun out now, and she raised an eyebrow in delight as she flung herself at him, firing sideways into Henstridge's cover to pin him down.

Thud.

Dropping Savin's pistol-clenching hand freed both hers, and she lashed out, trapping Yamamoto's gun hand. For a moment she wished she didn't need him alive to steal his research. But as she stared into his eyes her smile fell away, a curious awe gripping her. What was she *doing*, challenging him like this?

Swallowing, barely aware of shifting so his body shielded her from Henstridge, her grip on his wrist weakened.

His expression changed from fear, to relief, to anticipation: and finally, a dark seed of fury within her unfurled into flame.

Shaking her head, she ripped the pistol from his hand and gut-punched him.

Diving for cover as he folded to his knees, this time the *thud* shook the floor. Scuttling to Mason, his head jerked from the direction it was coming from to stare at her, his neck arching away from her like she was something scary. With a minimally extended claw she slit the tape around his wrists and ankles.

"What *is* that?" she whispered.

Savin's remaining hand clenched his wrist, trying to stop the blood flow, as he rocked on his knees. Behind him, the Tik Tek gynoid receptionist now faced her, smiling.

Turning back to Mason, she saw he was still staring at her, for some reason with fear in his eyes. She glanced down at herself, her eyebrows lifting as she saw just how much blood covered her.

Ignoring that, she scooted to Harmon, slitting the bonds at his feet then rolling him over and doing the same for his hands. He hissed as she moved him, and she registered the blood soaking his shirt, jacket, and the carpet under him.

Thud. Again the floor shook, the massive tread sounding now from behind the elevator well. How much did the thing weigh? She pictured a two-legged tank, then grimaced, knowing her claws only worked on organic stuff. *This could get tricky.*

Harmon closed worried eyes, his expression calming as one hand slid inside his jacket.

Probably trying to heal himself.

"You hear that, hell-bitch?" Henstridge taunted from nearby, but out of sight, his voice dripping with relish. "I don't care what you are, you're out of luck now!"

She'd been creeping toward Henstridge – but seeing Yamamoto crawling away, she paused to shoot him in the foot with his own weapon. She ignored his scream, her fingers itching to tear out his black heart, but she hadn't forgotten the stupid ritual he'd put his sysadmin guy through each day. Only Yamamoto himself could unlock the backup unit, the secure room, and then the safe. He'd watch Andrew's every move with suspicious eyes, each step along the way, until the procedure was complete.

"I'm going to love seeing you die," Henstridge called from the other side of the circular lounge he was using for cover.

Thud. Instead of coming closer though, it seemed further away.

She went back to creeping toward Henstridge, ignoring the rasp of the harsh carpet against her bare skin. She could hear his quick breaths, hear him shuttling back and forth on his knees, presumably trying to see where she was. She shut her eyes, visualizing his movements.

Judging the moment, she took her chance. Darting from cover, she crossed the open space to the lounge he sheltered behind.

Thud. Definitely farther away.

Henstridge seemed to realise the same thing, since he called out to it, "Here! She's in *here* you fucking idiot!"

His clothes rustled, ultrasonics intensifying, directly opposite her behind the lounge. Jamming her fingers under it she heaved, flipping it over him and leaping on top.

Grunting, he pushed away. She followed, knocking his pistol aside. His left hand slashed, the knife in it a blur, augmented muscles squealing.

But she'd read the movement, her right arm already sliding down his, deflecting.

Hungry black fury blossomed in her heart.

Thud. The floor shook, but moving away. He cursed.

Sliding in against him, her fingers locked his knife hand. He towered over her, cybernetic muscles shrieking as they red-lined, straining to overpower her with brute strength.

She dropped, releasing his wrist, her invisible blades skewering up and through his armpit, severing muscles as his knife whispered over her head.

Blinking in shock, his knife fell free. Baring her teeth she stood, thrusting harder, dark fury taking her. Clenching fingers inside his chest, she ripped deeper, hungry for his heart.

Henstridge's eyes locked on hers in disbelief. He sagged, held upright only by her forearm inside his chest. Drenched in his blood, she tore his heart free with a savage exultation that felt simultaneously deep inside yet far away.

Turning, heart held high for reasons she couldn't explain, she saw the whites of their eyes – Mason, Yamamoto, Savin and even the Doctor – as they stared at her in horror.

From the direction of Andrew's domain, a massive crash sounded, followed by the tortured screech of tearing metal followed by a thunderous impact on the floor: the security door to the backups room falling.

It had no importance. Her eyes fell from Yamamoto's face to his rib cage, the panicked drumbeats of his fear calling to her. Dark rage flowered in her heart, feeding the hatred.

She dropped his gun and stepped toward him, a familiar dark power rushing through her.

Harmon felt the moment of change, even before Leeth's eyes began to glow in the dark, two unearthly lapis lazuli ovals. "No," he whispered in dismay, shifting his senses to the imaginal, only to see black tendrils coiling around her, limned in volcanic fire. "Tezcatlipoca," he breathed.

CHAPTER 73

"Crystal, no!" Harmon shouted. She stepped closer, her eyes locked on Yamamoto's chest, Henstridge's heart clenched in her left hand, black coils threaded through it, swelling and contracting in pulses. *Feeding.* Just the sight of it felt wrong, something that should never be seen. He pushed the Sight from him, breathing out in blessed relief at the dark – lit eerily by the ghastly aquamarine glow of her eyes.

"What in the goddamn name of Hell is she?" demanded Mason, retreating, eyeing the pistol she'd dropped.

Like a crab, Yamamoto scrabbled backward from her, gibbering in terror, his head shaking in terrified denial. "*Here* you fool! Defend me! She is *here!*"

Savin sat slumped against the receptionist's now-vacant desk, dully cradling the stump of his wrist, weak from blood loss.

"Crystal, resist!" Harmon shouted. It was like she didn't hear him. "*Leeth!*"

He was conscious of Mason's head turning toward him, felt the man's puzzlement, but he needed to break through to her. *Mode One?* he wondered. Something warned him not to even try – that if he did, the Aztec entity could slash his bondage from her mind.

Or, far worse, seize control of those reins for itself.

He hadn't finished his own healing, the fight had moved so fast. From deeper in the office space sounded a longer, drawn-out whine of tortured metal, then a series of harsh *snapping* sounds loud as gunshots.

But Leeth had eyes only for Yamamoto, and death shone from them. She dropped the heart, now shrunken and withered, and for a moment he thought he'd begun Percepting again when long sleek claws extruded from her fingertips.

But these were black, blacker than the darkness in the office, sucking in light.

"Gaia protect us," Mason breathed, horrified, "What *is* she?"

Yamamoto flipped over, scrabbling carelessly over glass-strewn carpet, one foot dragging, across the foyer and down the long corridor, as fast as he could toward a sound that shook the floor.

Thud.

Lit by the blue glow of her eyes, Leeth's one-sided smile looked truly fiendish. That glowing gaze swept the scene of slaughter. Her lips parted. Spoke a single word: "*More.*"

Her voice, groaning under a prophetic weight, shivered into the world. He noted her face, her skin: pristine, cleaned of blood, no trace of gore. *Absorbed.*

She has to resist. All this blood, the carnage... it's reignited her connection to the Aztec death god. If she brought it fully through, the Department would end her – or try to. Even this partial manifestation might be enough for them to decide she was too dangerous to live.

"Leeth, it's *using* you!" He clutched for some argument that might resonate with her, enlist her aid, override the hatred she harbored for her intended victim.

First victim, a voice in his head whispered, conscious of the death all around and the copper smell of blood. After Yamamoto, could Leeth, ridden by the Aztec god hungry for sacrifice, resist the lure of the man dying by the receptionist desk? Or the Mason fellow?

And what of her deep hatred for he himself? Could his mental bonds cage a god's desires?

And after him, drunk on the power of blood magic, would she stop? Or rage out into the city, storm winds at her command, earthquakes, volcanoes?

Thud. What was that? It sounded closer.

"Yes, here, defend me!" screamed Yamamoto.

What had Eagle said? Leeth was to kill Yamamoto, but only after gaining access to his data, to ensure the technology was contained. Had Nelson's virus worked? Not that any of that mattered, compared to the disaster now unfolding. Desperately, he drew strength heedlessly for a Sleep spell, stronger than any he'd ever cast before, and unleashed it.

It vanished, swallowed into the dark vortex riding her. The hope had been a forlorn one anyway. What had he expected, against a god?

A god.

What an opportunity for study!

He knew the risks. During the so-called 'Great Conflict', the God Wars of India in 2037, many mages had Percepted the deities mid-battle, hunting for weaknesses, or just understanding. Only to fall instead into raving insanity, or undergoing fanatical conversion.

Gulping, he shifted his senses – to find himself immersed in a panorama. Searing in its brilliance, beguiling in its elegance, beautiful in its simplicity. A harmony of monomaniacal intent and utter certainty.

Someone was shaking him, hauling him back and away as *she* prowled past, ignoring them. Mason now held Yamamoto's gun, Harmon saw. In the corridor behind the elevators Yamamoto sobbed, scrabbling at something, a door handle rattling in the dark.

Mason shook him. "What *is* she? What's 'Leeth'? Some command that's supposed to make her stop?"

Her eyes turned toward them, and Mason jumped backward, lifting the heavy pistol and firing, Harmon crying out in dismay. Rounds that had detonated to shatter the foyer's armored glass exploded across her chest in a stitching of orange-red blossoms. They flowered, a cluster of frozen flames, before slowly folding back in on themselves, absorbed into her. Her eyes closed, her lips curving in pleasure, as if savoring a fine wine. The shells fell to the floor.

"Fool!" Harmon snarled, forcing Mason's arm down. They had no hope of stopping her. But he remembered, with a chill, Leeth overpowering the same force herself earlier today. She was the key.

The blue glow reappeared, and after a measuring glance she turned away again, stepping lightly toward the corridor.

The mission? Leeth had begged for this one, had been so determined for it to be successful. He felt an insane desire to laugh. *Focus!*

"Leeth. This is not you. Take back control. Or have you, finally, given up? Surrendered?" He injected the heaviest note of disdain he could.

She stopped.

Pivoted deliberately.

Two uncanny eyes of blue flame pinned him. It took every ounce of nerve he had to hold firm to his sneer under their cool scrutiny.

She frowned.

Thud.

Mason had stepped away from him, now picking a silent way into the dark, back along the path she'd just prowled.

"Leeth. You called it Tez Catlick Poker. It's not you. You are stronger than it."

Words weren't enough. And she hated him. But if he didn't act now, it would be too late. He limped closer, even as the rational part of him screamed he was insane, that he should flee, or speak the words that might just give him control over her.

Instead he softened his voice, remembering again the eight-year-old girl who had once trusted him; looked up to him; seen in him a father figure. His eyes blurred.

He gently took her left hand, ignoring the ghastly black blades, and brought the backs of her fingers to his lips. "This is you."

Breathing hard, knowing he walked a cliff's edge, he sought and found her right hand, lifted it even more slowly into her view, shuddering deep inside as five wicked black blades rose into sight, followed by her fingers. "Not these."

Her eyes fell from his to the slender, light-swallowing instruments of death, then back to his face, frowning at the unnatural blue glow reflected from it.

"Keepie?"

His face crumpled, her face swimming as his vision vanished under water in the sudden dark.

"Keepie? Are you *crying?*" she asked in tones of wonder.

Of course not! He shook his head, his throat choking on the denial, squeezing the signs of weakness from his eyes.

It was gone, the force of oppressive rage vanished. He opened his eyes to honest darkness once more, surprised at being suddenly gripped, slender arms wrapped around him, but arms with the strength of oaken bands.

"All right, hold it right there," said Mason, from behind them.

She released him. "I haven't forgiven you, though," she whispered to him, before turning fully to face Mason.

Who stared now at them both, Yamamoto's pistol once more raised.

"I've figured it out: George was right. She's a demon from Hell, isn't she?" he said.

Thud.

From out of sight down the corridor, she heard Yamamoto screaming, "What are you doing? Drop that! She's down there, kill her! And you, too, coward!"

CHAPTER 74

"I'm just a girl," she answered Mason, fully herself once more. She flushed, extending and retracting invisible claws, sighing in relief at *not* seeing them.

Her claws weren't s'posed to be black.

She could feel Tezsh Cat-whatever though, furious and lurking, and pushed away the shame of letting the god thing take control like that. *That wasn't our bargain,* she thought at it.

Thud.

Her uncle was staring at her with something like wonder. It made her uncomfortable. She frowned. "I think we may have a more urgent problem," she said, jerking her head toward the cries and noises from the corridor. Someone else, a male voice that sounded familiar, was cursing under his breath there, too. A heavy door rattled in its frame, while Yamamoto kept shrieking for 'them' to kill her.

She raised a finger. "I'm gonna take a look."

Seeing Mason lower his gun slightly, she spared a glance for the man whose hand she'd removed. Savin now slumped unconscious against the sleek black face of the receptionist's desk.

Which was empty, she noticed. *Why would the gynoid have left?*

"Maybe you could heal him, Uncle," she told Harmon, pointing to Savin. "He wasn't so bad," she said, before tip-toeing a few paces to peep down the corridor.

And swallowed, her eyes widening in shock.

A *massive* humanoid robot, like an armored soldier scaled up to half again as tall as Mason and twice as wide, loomed at one end of the corridor, filling it. Maybe she'd sent Tezsh away too soon.

Dr Yamamoto was cursing at a just normally-big man, dressed like all the other mercenaries she'd taken down tonight, who was carrying the woman she'd stunned earlier draped over his shoulder. He too was cursing, pushing at the nearer fire-stair door which hardly budged before slamming into something behind it.

Then she saw that the giant soldier-bot carried a safe upside down in one hand, holding it dangling by a twisted bolt.

She recognized the safe – she'd seen it often enough, at the end of each day during Yamamoto's ritual backup change-over ceremony.

The giant moved toward Yamamoto, resting on the floor of the alcove between the Ladies and the Gents washrooms as it *thudded* down the passage.

"Yes, she's that way!" he cried, gleeful.

How can he not see it's heading for him, not me? The mercenary carrying the woman must've realized the same thing, because he was now backing down the corridor away from the warbot and Yamamoto, toward her corner, giving up on the blocked fire-stairs.

She ducked back, her eyes finding Mason's in the dark, aware of Harmon crouched out of sight by Savin, healing him. She felt a flush at having severed his hand. But he could always get a cyber one fitted.

She shook herself.

"Uh, yeah, we have a problem," she told Mason, before padding back to the corner, hearing the mercenary creeping closer, getting ready to clobber him if needed.

She extruded her claws once again.

As he backed toward her away from the warbot she slit the strap of his rifle, snatching it and flinging it far away, not really worried by the large knife in its sheath at his side.

Thud.

He jumped away from her as best he could with a body draped over one shoulder, his eyes raking her up and down in confused horror. "What's a felching *Grendel* slaybot doing outside a war-zone?" He turned from her to glare at Yamamoto. "What the *fuck's* going on in this madhouse? No, you drekhead, this way, can't you see-"

Leeth winced at Yamamoto's yelp.

"Provide the code to the safe," a deep, uninflected voice said. "Or you will be harmed."

"Oh, come *on*." Grimacing, Leeth pushed past the man with the woman on his shoulder. The warbot's other massive hand had clamped around Dr Y's arm, dangling him above the ground.

She eyed the huge figure in dismay, shaking her head as she took in the matte finish of what she just *knew* was heavy armor. Noting seaweed hanging off one shoulder.

Okay, so I guess it's waterproof. Giving up on the sprinkler idea, she felt pretty confident even assault rifle rounds'd just bounce off it too. Nor could her claws cut metal. "You... *cheater!*"

Well, she was supposed to kill Yamamoto anyway. *I bet it's only asking for the combination to the safe to save it time.* It looked perfectly capable of beating the safe to a pulp and *squeezing* the door off it.

She took a breath, feeling just a tiny bit sorry for Dr Y at what she was about to do.

She padded down the passageway toward the Grendel thing, her arms wide, hands open and empty. She was pretty sure it wouldn't be able to see her magical claws.

Part of its shoulder whirred and a small rocket rose up from inside. She found herself smiling, it reminded her so much of Faith's. *I hope she hasn't had her pups yet!* The missile pivoted, snapping to point at her with vastly more speed than its walking.

"Halt," the warbot said.

But it had waited too long.

"I wouldn't fire that here. At this range it'll kill Dr Yamamoto too," she told it. And finally she was close enough to reach him.

She winced. "Sorry," she told the dangling CEO, squirming in terror now from her. One hand slashed through his forearm, snatching him mid-fall as he screamed. Pushing off the warbot's chest, she yanked him under the two massive arms that swept the space he should have occupied, before running backward with him down the corridor, her eyes on the warbot.

"Doctor!" she yelled, not quite sure what the next step in her plan was, while Yamamoto's blood sprayed the corridor wall. She heard Mason and the other guy swearing.

The warbot's sensors were locked on her, the rocket swiveling instantly to track her, but it must have done the calculations and realized she was right about it killing Yamamoto too. It slid back in.

Unfortunately, she also recognized the laser that swung up to take its place.

"Uh oh."

She jumped back into the foyer area, out of sight of the corridor just in time.

"We can't let it get him," she told them, gripping his wrist to stop the blood spraying, helping him stand and kind of wishing now she hadn't shot his foot earlier.

Thud.

"Um, any of you got any ideas? It's got lasers."

All but Mason just stared at her. His gaze was glued to the end of the corridor, from which the Nemesys Grendel approached. "We are so fucked."

Harmon grunted as he cast a spell, swaying with the energy drain.

Leeth vanished, even though she clearly still supported Yamamoto, who blinked in astonishment at the thin air holding him upright.

Straining with effort, Harmon cast the same spell again, this time on Yamamoto, who also vanished.

Harmon eased beside Savin, who was sitting, conscious once more, slumped against the receptionist's curved desk.

"I have cast invisibility," he whispered, for Leeth's ears only. *"But I'm not sure how much of the spectrum you're invisible to. Or how long I can hold the two spells running."*

"I guess we're about to find out," she said. "And *you'd* better shut up if you hope to live," she warned her whimpering invisible bundle as she lifted him into her arms, her eyes darting across the darkened glass-strewn carpet to pick a silent path, that would also avoid cutting her feet to pieces.

She moved.

Thud.

Mason and the mercenary goggled at one another like idiots, backing from the corner.

The warbot stepped into view, shaking the floor.

She wondered if she could get out of sight in time, or even if there was any point; whether her uncle's spell would work on whatever kinds of light the thing sensed with.

She turned and ran.

But as she reached the other side of the foyer, Dr Y in her arms, dodging and weaving, her question was answered.

An intense laser blast flashed through her from head to toe, dust sparking in its disintegrating beam.

CHAPTER 75

Ahead of her, blasting *through* her, the beam sliced down the wall of the Writer room, to the sound of bad things happening inside.

Am I dead? *Is this what it feels like?* But at the weight of Dr Y in her arms, she decided not. Shaking herself, she darted to her right, around the corner, not quite believing she felt just fine.

Dr Y groaned and whined, but no worse than he had before. She kept running, back around the central well with the lifts, finally realizing what had happened.

We're invisible! And lasers are just light!

She had to suppress a giggle.

But that had been an awful powerful one, she was pretty sure. And the warbot still carried the safe. Why didn't it just cut it open with its laser?

She was on the opposite side from it now, back in the corridor between the washrooms and the central core of the building with its elevators and fire-stairs.

One of which was opening, a huge round disk rolling out through the doorway.

From somewhere behind, she heard the intense hum of the laser's power source, and a weird crackling sound.

"Leeth, the robot is cutting the safe open," Harmon whispered to her.

She ground her teeth in anger. Why hadn't it just done that right at the start? It was like it hadn't known it could. *Until it fired at me.*

Well, that news made one thing simpler. If it could open the safe itself, it meant she was finally allowed to kill Yamamoto.

Despite all he'd done to her, she paused to consider the most painless way. *I'm not like the Doctor.* Putting him down, she ran her hands up his invisible torso to his head, hearing the soft spray of arterial blood as she released his wrist to do so.

"You really are a dick though," she told him. Twisting his head, she winced at the crack of his neck. Someone could still heal him, though. Quickly, she bent and lopped off his head, killing him properly.

She stood. That had been *nowhere* near as satisfying as she'd imagined.

But she didn't have time to worry about that now. The

huge disk was maneuvered into the corridor by... the receptionist gynoid, who rolled it down toward her. It was one of the large circular lounges that had been scattered about the floor. Past it, she saw the cook-cleaner gynoid doing the same from the other stairwell.

She frowned. They weren't programmed to do that. *Something's hacked into them, made them block the firestairs.* The same thing controlling the warbot, she guessed. *Oh! That's why Dr Y and Henstridge had been yelling at it – it wasn't doing what it'd been supposed to.*

"It has the safe open," Harmon's voice whispered. *"It's taking out data cubes."*

Dammit!

She had nothing to damage a thing like that. And it looked super heavy – she guessed a tonne. She wouldn't even be able to lift it, let alone throw it out a window.

And it could see her. Probably with radar.

Oh! Would its laser cut through a mirror, or bounce off?

Running into the washroom, she ripped a mirror from the wall and tore back out, making no effort to be silent.

Skidding round the corner, she stood sideways to the thing to hide the mirror as its head lifted and the laser pivoted toward her.

Don't drop your spell now, she thought at her uncle, turning as the weapon powered up and blasted at her. She held the mirror across her chest, her invisible head exposed, teeth bared, not really expecting to survive.

Here goes nothing.

Only sparks of vaporizing dust marked the path of the laser, and its reflected path back the other way. It wasn't a glowing red beam like she'd expected and hoped for, just sparks of igniting dust, but searing light flared on the warbot itself as armor melted. She tilted the mirror down into the safe, a jittering dot of light shattering crystal cubes.

I'm still not hurt!

The laser cut off, pivoting and folding back down into one shoulder while the panel in its other slid open, the small rocket popping up.

Oops.

She sprinted away, back down the corridor, diving forward at the sound of the launch.

Silence fell the moment before a hurricane blast picked

her up and threw her into the air, flying down the corridor.

She blinked in surprise, then realized what had happened. *Clever old ears!*

She tumbled, rolling so her feet took the impact against the outside wall of the Omega offices, suddenly glad of the super tough glass as she bounced to the ground. Back the way she'd come, the wall of the Writer room was a cloud of smoke and dust.

She stared down at her now visible hands, realizing her uncle had dropped his spell. Had he been injured? Or just lost concentration? She couldn't know.

Thud.

Sound clicked back into existence, and she heard the two gynoids from the corridor moving, one stepping out from the corridor by the fire stairs. The cook-cleaner. Its head turned in her direction, clearly seeing her.

I guess the bot pilot's mad at me now. Her eyes darted left and right, but she saw nothing that could help her. *Maybe I can lead it away?* Briefly, she wondered if she'd destroyed the data cubes in the safe.

She sprinted back to the watching gynoid, which took a defensive posture. She could hear the other one, circling around the toilet block toward her too.

Ducking under its clumsy blow, she caught its wrist and planted her feet, spinning around to whip it down the corridor between the cafeteria and the medical rooms. It tumbled toward the outer windows.

Thud.

She looked back to see the warbot step out from the foyer, leaping to her left as it launched a second rocket.

Again, that unnatural silence as her ears protected themselves from the explosion to come. Jumping over the circular lounge she shoved open the fire-stair door.

"Nyah, nyah, you can't catch me," she taunted – she assumed, unable to hear her own voice – before plunging down the stairs.

Thud.

She leaped the whole flight, and the next, landing silently and wrenching open the fire-stair door onto the floor below. Sound clicked back on.

She raced along the corridor to the door of the second set of fire-stairs. It opened easily, and she ran back up to the floor she'd just left, four steps at a time, stopping at the top to listen. Would it take her bait?

Thud. Thud. Thud.

Outside in the Omega office corridor she heard the fire stair door she'd first used open, and that heavy tread on the landing inside. Descending the way she'd gone, following her.

Yes! She opened the door and raced back out into the Omega office.

Now what do I do?

She sprinted back to the others, finding Mason searching through the safe, her uncle still slumped exhaustedly beside Savin.

Thud. Thud. Thud.

But it was growing fainter, like it was still headed down, searching for her. *I fooled it!* She spun at the sound of three pairs of gynoid feet and the ultrasonic whine of servo-motors, as the nurse bot, receptionist, and kitchen bot reappeared.

She jumped to her feet.

They just stared at her, not moving. Like they were studying her face as best they could in the dark; her body. Something about the unhurried steadiness felt familiar. The gynoid from Club Sybarus!

Then the kitchen and nurse bots just turned away, moving back to their stations. She hid her face from the receptionist as it stalked closer, not really surprised when it just crunched by on its high heels over the shattered glass fragments of the foyer, stepping behind its desk that Savin and her uncle still slumped against.

Taking up its position, it turned once more to face the elevators, its smile returning.

Leeth blinked at it. *It's... unhacked them? Why would it do that?* She tilted her head, hearing the nurse bot open the door to the medical bay and go back inside. Listening, she heard the cook-cleaner do the same thing in the kitchen area beside the cafeteria.

"Ah!" Mason exclaimed.

The mercenary, still carrying his female comrade across one shoulder, raced back across the war zone of the viewing area, water from the indoor garden now flooding the carpet. He pounded past them to the fire-stairs.

Without a word.

She heard the nearer fire-stair door open.

"Not that one!" she called out to him. "That's the stairwell the warbot took. Use the other one!"

She heard him stop, swear, then follow her advice.

Mason made another pleased sound, and she turned to see him holding up an undamaged data cube, with a confident, lazy smile. He plugged it into a small device whose cables ran into his shirt.

Copying the data off it.

Her gaze went from him, to her uncle – the Doctor – and their eyes met.

He shook his head, knowing she could see *him* even if he couldn't see her properly. He looked as grim as she felt.

She pressed one hand to her eyes. She had no idea how much data Mason had already copied off. Whether he was uploading it to some cloud or whatever.

She took her hand from her eyes, feeling sick. She couldn't kill Mason!

The Doctor peered at her in the dark. But his eyes were unfocused, and she could tell he was seeing her aura or whatever, reading her reaction. With the words that would lock her under his command at his lips, ready to order her to do what had to be done.

Before he could speak them, she dived at Mason.

CHAPTER 76

She saw he'd tucked Dr Yamamoto's pistol into the waist-band of his trousers. She snatched it free as she plowed into him, taking him to the ground.

She pounded its hilt into his head, furious at his betrayal. "Why were you copying it, Mason?" she shrieked. "Why? We all agreed it was bad technology, that had to be destroyed!"

But his face was twisted by greed, and behind that, she felt something like a shadow move.

It felt familiar. She'd seen it once before in another face, or *under* another face.

In the weird little smile that twitched his lips, she saw it had recognized her, too. The Department's Foe.

For just a moment, the Mason she knew returned, but his eyes held terror, his gaze turned inward, not seeing her. Drowning. Fighting. "No!" he cried out, "not like Panzer, and Ace. In Clancy's memory, no!"

He gasped, desperately focusing on her, a finger tapping a point on the back of his skull. "It wants the data. It's here."

Then he was drowning again. Eerily then, his expression cleared, fear fading, his lips curving up in a rapacious smile. The skin at the back of her neck prickled. "We meet again."

The voice was his; but not.

Poison, something inside warned her, flooding her with instantaneous loathing. The pistol fell from her hand as she stabbed into the back of his skull, hoping she'd understood. Plunging fingers into his brain, she felt something hard, and plucked out a tangle of chips.

Mason spasmed, the light in his eyes fading.

Reluctant, resisting death itself, the foulness behind them burned, marking her.

His eyes closed. Mason Dane fell still.

Her uncle's voice came from the darkness, as he pushed himself to his feet. "Leeth? Leeth, did you just...?"

"Yes! No! I didn't mean- I just dug out the- Heal him!" She leaped the space between them, dragging him bodily back to Mason. "You can Heal him! I was careful! I only cut a little bit of his brain."

The Doctor fumbled beside her in the dark, patting her. "It's all right. I sensed something too. It was... ghastly. Worse than the Aztec god. *Unclean.* It's over now, though."

He sounded shaky.

"Yeah, but it went away when, when Mason died. So you

can Heal him and it'll be alright!"

"Leeth, no, it's still out there, still reaching for us. That was the Foe! We shouldn't even be thinking about it."

"Then don't! Just Heal him." She stared at him in the dark, wondering why he wasn't already at work. Light. He needed light to see, to do his spell. "Turn on your Link's flashlight."

He shook his head. "Mason must have done something, to... bring that thing to him. We can't risk its return even if I could Heal him. Besides, he's heavily augmented, worse than Nelson, I doubt-"

"Try," Leeth growled. "If it returns, I'll, I'll just kill him again. It. I'll kill *it* again."

Still he made no move.

"Heal him!" she screamed, gripping his jacket, shaking him. "Heal him, or I'll, I'll call Tezsh back!" She stared at him, daring him to Mode One her.

Harmon sucked in his breath. "You don't mean that-"

"Heal him!"

Her uncle stared at her in the dark, his eyes doing that spooky not-looking thing, and finally he let his breath out. "I don't have my Link. Henstridge took it."

Wind from gaping windows blew through the office now. She looked past him to the nearby buildings, hearing police sirens in the distance. She imagined late workers in the buildings, hearing rocket explosions and seeing shattered windows, peering in with binoculars.

She heard Links buzz as she stepped between broken glass, crossing to Henstridge's body. Plucking her Link, Mason's and the Doctor's from an armored pocket, she answered hers, throwing the Doctor's to him. Staring at him until, with a pained sound, he began his Healing.

"Are you guys alright?" Nelson jabbered. "I got pushed out, Tik Tek-"

"Tell me about it," she said. "Can you push back in? We need the elevators. I can hear sirens."

"Yeah, but the metrocops're-"

"I know, Nelson. Look, we're busy. Focus. Can we use the elevators?" The Doctor crouched beside Mason, his Link's light shining on his hands cradling the open skull.

"Yeah, but-"

"Good. We'll report soon." She hung up on him.

Time was running out. Slipping the Link around her wrist she hurried to the discarded safe, pushing it over with difficulty till all its contents fell out, then hauling it back upright.

She swept all the debris, half melted or not, into a pile. Then collected Yamamoto's and Savin's guns, and the rifle she'd hurled across the room, wiping them down.

She ran and pressed the elevator button, then dodged through the scree of glass back to Mason's body. The elevator arrived before she'd even bent to him.

"Don't stop Healing him," she warned, lifting him slowly so the Doctor could keep his spell running. Picking her way back she placed Mason gently inside, Harmon crouching, keeping his hands on the sliced open skull, the brain inside bleeding and quite pink.

She ran back to scoop up the safe's contents and returned, pouring them and the slimy chip stuff she'd extracted from Mason into the Doctor's pockets, finally pushing the button to take them to the ground level.

The sirens were sounding quite close. She hoped the boat guy was still waiting. She hoped the Doctor could Heal Mason. She hoped she hadn't messed up his brain too badly.

It was a long ride down.

She watched the Doctor struggling to make the Healing work, and watched for any sign of... trouble. Careful not to think about why. About things lurking.

She glanced at her Link, noting it was just turning midnight. It'd been a long day.

From the base of her scalp, at the back of her head, she heard Harmon's voice whisper, "Seshoestus desstussten."

And finally remembered thick fingers fumbling at the back there as he'd fastened the necklace. Suddenly realizing what Marcie and Barney's plan had really been all along.

Smiling, squatting in a corner of the too-bright elevator car, her eyes brimmed suddenly with grateful tears. *They fooled us both! The necklace was just a distraction.*

Mason was breathing, his color slightly better, and Harmon slightly less stressed as they reached the first floor and the lift doors opened. The receptionist bot was pointedly looking away, and Leeth felt a reluctant surge of gratitude for Nelson's intervention.

"Can you keep your spell working on Mason if I lift him and we leave, uncle?"

He nodded, slowly.

"I don't s'pose you could make us all invisible, too?"

He stopped moving, his eyes narrowing, and she got the distinct feeling he'd almost lost concentration. "Fine, fine, I was only asking!"

Lifting Mason gently, she backed out of the elevator, and then the building, her uncle following, all his attention on his spell.

Better yet, the boat guy answered her call, still waiting down at the next jetty, only a few minutes walk away — though it took a huge effort of will to keep to the best pace the Doctor could manage and still do his magical healing. Especially when the first sirens stopped, back at the building they'd just left.

She split her attention between watching Mason for signs of... danger, and the voices of the metrocops and emergency workers at the scene they'd left behind.

Slippery stone steps led down to the waiting boat, and she carried Mason backwards, letting her uncle brace himself by holding one of her hands, his attention lost inside the injury. The boat guy sniggered appreciatively as she reversed down toward him, then hissed and swore at the sight of Mason's still-open skull, finally helping them aboard.

Silently, he loosened ropes and pushed off.

Leeth set Mason in the bottom of the boat where she'd crouched earlier, her uncle following him down before breathing a sigh and going still, both hands back around Mason's skull.

She stared up at the barnacle-crusted pylons of the wooden jetty as they fell away into the dark, frowning at the old tires lashed to its supports, for reasons she couldn't pin down.

Turning away, she settled cross-legged opposite Mason as parts of his brain knitted together, and with glacial slowness, his skull sealed over in a pale thin sheet, skin creeping after to cover it.

Harmon slumped wearily as the boat bounced along, much faster once they were well away from the by now well-lit area they'd vacated fifteen minutes earlier. He tried to read Leeth's emotional state from her aura.

Really, it's no surprise she's overwrought. She is only

nineteen, and it's been a trying... He tallied up the hours, a little shocked to realize she'd gone missing less than forty-eight hours ago. For once, through no fault of her own.

It remained to be seen whether her friend Mason would regain the full use of his faculties. Not a vegetable, at least, thanks to the feat of Healing he had not expected to pull off. In time, Mason's speech should return. As should his sight – the cybernetic eyes were responding correctly to light even now. As well, a friendly shaman would be waiting for him after a short journey, he understood.

Maeve had sounded... unhappy.

How would Leeth handle the guilt of almost killing her friend, though?

As the boat rounded the headland and the warm lights of the Fisher Clan came into view, he heard her Link buzz.

"Hey, Marcie, you got home safe and sound? Yeah, I'm great! Hi Amanda. Yeah, thanks, you saved the day!"

He shook his head.

I suppose that answers that.

Though perhaps it might be safer for her if I omit any mention of her possession by the Aztec death god in my report.

On the shore a welcoming party waited, holding lanterns. In the fore, Maeve, Gigi, the ogre Teef – and his son Barney, who'd caused so much trouble for him personally.

The boat rocked as Leeth stood, waving happily, her face alight, unconscious of her naked body. Sighing, Harmon dug out an oilskin for her.

But the smiles died when she scooped Mason's limp form from the bottom of the boat.

She leaped out into the muddy shallows as the keel bit into the shore.

Maeve's gaze reminded her of the warbot's lasers.

"Uh, he's not dead," she told the now silent group. "Un-, uh, Doc Truman healed him up."

Maeve stood still as stone, eyes equally stony, her mouth grim. Mrs Bojangles leapt from Maeve's arms with a plaintive yowl that pierced Leeth's heart.

Flushing, lit by lantern light, she lowered Mason to the ground for Mrs B to reach. One paw patted his cheek and she *mreowed* with a quizzical note.

At the sound Mason quivered, an arm twitching futilely in

an abortive move toward his cat.

Two pairs of predatory female eyes tracked to Leeth.

"He doesn't *look* healed," Maeve said, finally.

For a crazy second Leeth considered admitting to her and Mrs B that the Foe had gotten to Mason, that *she'd* smashed open his skull to crush his memory chips....

She swallowed. "There was a Nemesys warbot. Mason's head got pretty badly smashed up. I think all his cyberware got disconnected. But Doc Truman managed to heal his brain back up, at least."

She couldn't seem to force her lips into the reassuring smile she was trying for. She swallowed again. "On the plus side, all the bad guys are dead?"

Maeve just stared.

Behind her, Gigi, Barney, Teef, and several members of the Fisher Clan watched, hushed. A couple of kilometers up the Bay more sirens wailed, still being drawn to the Omega office.

"And the stuff in your head?" Barney wanted to know.

"All gone. Yamamoto was real keen about that."

"There was a warbot? How'd you destroy it?"

"How'd I-? I'm not Superman, Barney! I let it go." *After it got what it came for.* She grimaced: she was pretty sure Tik Tek now had the Omega technology. She remembered the three gynoids studying her in the dark, trashed office.

Something told her they'd meet again.

EPILOGUE

Leeth set aside the first slim envelope, containing the material she'd need for her next mission: Newtopia. What used to be called Antarctica. She'd be going to a whole other country! On an important job: discovering why Tik Tek – or maybe just its *suspected AI?* – had been so desperate to steal the Omega tech. Which she'd failed to stop.

Eagle was giving her a chance to fix her failure. Find out their plan, and end it.

Could be tricky. Cold too, she supposed. Then again, she'd probably spend most of her time in the buried city, not out playing in the snow. *It wouldn't hurt to look into heated clothing, though. And learn to ski.*

She picked up the second e-sheet, but noticed a funny expression on Eagle's face. He was watching her intently.

At her thumbprint it switched on. She flipped through the faces on the 'sheet, stunned, jumping back to the first one in disbelief. "Happy Joe Holliday. *Happy Joe's* team! You want me to infiltrate them when I return? Really?"

She wanted to leap the desk and hug Eagle. She'd been following Happy and his sneaky team's exploits for years. Then a sobering thought struck her, the smile falling from her face. "Wait. They're not bad guys, are they? I'm not gonna have to kill any of 'em? Because, no...."

Eagle's expression reassured her. "No. I do read your reports, Leeth."

His eyes unfocused and she knew he was accessing some internal digital screen. His next words confirmed that. Quoting her.

"'I could join a merc team, build up a new identity at the same time as getting heaps of experience and making a whole bunch of shady contacts. Like Happy Joe Holliday's, for example.'"

Leeth beamed, looking suddenly even younger than her nineteen years.

She scanned the images again, suppressing a giggle at their names. Happy Joe himself, Steven Swift the battle mage, Nick, a sniper, Haggard, the drugged-up street mage, Bruce, a grunt. And a Snake shaman they didn't have a name for. She looked back up, frowning.

"But how'm I gonna convince them to let me join them?"

Eagle smiled. "We'll work that out nearer the date. There's no rush. Perhaps a job at an event where they're 'bodyguarding a star'. Abrams has sensed their interests and ours have some overlap, so...." He shrugged.

"Sleek."

"Study the material." He noted with a touch of guilt her disinterest in asking the nature of her possible 'job'. "In the meantime, we're thinking you can start developing a new identity: Bonnie Parker, exotic dancer. It's all in there."

She eyed the picture. "I'll get a real snake?"

"No, Leeth, the snake would be animatronic."

"Oh."

"How is Faith?" Eagle asked, a virtual window displaying the readings from his instruments. He already knew the answer – he'd watched the footage in disbelief – but needed to understand why Leeth had filed such a deceptive report.

Leeth smiled. "Great! She had four pups – three girls and a boy."

None of the graphs of her heart rate, blood pressure, or skin conductivity, changed. He prodded harder. "And Faith herself?"

"A proud Mum. The father was super proud too. And their pups: you wouldn't believe how tiny and cute they are!"

Eagle very nearly frowned. It was essential to know whether Leeth was actively dissembling, or could simply be that oblivious. "Any problems during the birth?"

Leeth's bright smile didn't waver as she put a finger to her lips and stared off into the distance. "Let me think...."

She'd arrived at the Institute, Mr Shanahan his usual nervous self these days – like he still thought she'd *really* come to break Godsson free, and was just softening him up with repeated visits for other, pretend reasons.

"How's Faith?" she'd asked, worried, knowing that cyborg wardogs weren't supposed to be able to get pregnant.

"Fine." Though the look Mr Shanahan gave the Doctor, standing behind her, said that wasn't the whole story. She was glad she'd talked Eagle into letting a vet come too.

Mr Shanahan had an area cleaned and set up in the leafy, open grounds outside the Institute's main building, and he and some of the nurse gynoids were keeping the curious inmates at a respectful distance. The vet had wanted the father kept away, but Mr Shanahan only snorted. "She's an Asgard Model 3! Trust me, even Dober there knows not to cross Faith!"

The father of the dogs was acting a bit antsy, but his and Faith's pack stayed basically under control, just kind of hanging around. Farther back, with the inmates, the other companion animals were acting a bit jittery though, like they'd rather be somewhere else.

Faith looked *so* tired, *so* ready to have her pups, but grinned weakly to finally see her. Giving her a very definite *'Well, you took your sweet time getting here'* look.

She knelt beside her oldest friend, hugging her furry neck and loving the licks Faith rewarded her with while she apologized, at the same time trying to hide her worry about the imminent birth.

The vet, a round and happy woman, finished her checks, and said labor had started. She looked nervous.

Leeth stroked Faith's head, whispering to her, knowing she'd been somehow holding back, waiting for her to arrive like she'd promised.

"I'm sorry I'm so late! I came as soon as I could. You can do this, it'll be fine," she reassured her childhood friend, hoping desperately that was true.

The vet, calm, competent, and reassuring, continued doing vet stuff. Everything seemed to be going well.

But then Faith started whimpering in pain, noises that sounded wrong, like her babies were pushing into her cyborg parts or something. The vet started sweating.

Faith lay, sides heaving, panting in distress, and finally delivered her first pup.

A burst of ultrasonics was the only warning of her battle systems activating. From physical stress? With a whine of servo-motors, her laser popped up, seeking targets.

The father's ears flattened, he and the pack backing away, whining, scared, as if they'd seen this before. The vet, swearing, kept working.

"Down! Everyone down, fall back!" Mr Shanahan cried, from farther away. "Faith, girl, *code gamma*, stand down, stand down! Sara, Dr Harmon, *run!*"

Harmon tugged at Leeth.

The laser swung, locking on the vet who kept working at Faith's rear. Leeth tore free of her uncle and threw herself in front, knowing Faith would do everything in her power to wrench back control from her inbuilt combat systems....

She shook herself free of the memory, smiling, dabbing at

her eyes as she remembered helping the vet bring Faith's next three pups safely into the world, one by one, delicately cupping each tiny, wet body in the palms of her hands to bring them up to their mother for her sniffing, licking inspection.

The Doctor doing some healing magic afterward.

"Problems? Not really," she told Eagle. "It went really well." Her chin lifted.

There! Finally, he had his answer, in that steely defiance.

"I viewed the footage, Leeth," he said, and saw the otherwise steady lines of her graphs spike – then settle.

"Faith controls her cybernetics. They don't control her." She met his gaze squarely. "It only *looked* dangerous if you don't understand that heart matters more than mind."

Her look clearly challenged him to disagree. Yet how could he? Was that not something he and Abrams believed just as strongly as Leeth?

It gave him hope she *could* handle this next mission. Because this time, she would be truly alone. Far beyond their help if things went wrong. Especially since Nelson believed Tik Tek had created a true Artificial General Intelligence, sentient and self-aware, and likely actively hunting Leeth. If so, there was no place on Earth she would be safe from it in the long term. She'd have to face it.

It was also essential they learn its plans. And Leeth excelled at ruining plans.

"Let her go," Abrams had advised him. "I sense it's the right move. There are too many forces at work right now. The Cabal. The Dragon. The death god, which as I informed you, broke through *again* in the small hours this morning. I note there was no mention of that in either Leeth or the Doctor's reports. And now this horrifying new Machine Archetype that manifested in her.

"It appears your strange young Agent is collecting Archetypes."

Despite Abrams's smile, something in his old friend's expression gave Eagle pause. As if that last observation meant he had moved Leeth into some special category. One he felt unwilling to disclose.

That was a worry.

"As for our more insidious Foe... now is not the right time to try to direct her against that." Abrams shook his head. "It all reverberates strangely. I sense something unsettling in the Antarctic, and I don't like this new Church of Rationality that Ankhet has created. It all feels connected. And I fear a stirring in that Power which Leeth labeled an alien threat."

He breathed a heavy sigh, the clicks and hums of his life support chair a steadying background noise. "Better to hold her loosely, I think. You've taught her what she needs to know. To survive."

Eagle nodded, feeling oddly sad. *I'll miss her here,* he realized in some surprise. *This place has been brighter for her presence.* "I agree. She's also becoming known. Better for her and us if she has her own identity, out there." He smiled. "Being a hero. It's what she's always wanted.

"But we'll be here, at her back when it's needed."

Abrams nodded, somber. "As it will be, against the Foe."

AFTERWORD

I hope you enjoyed this episode in Leeth's saga.

If you did, the best thanks you can give me is to tell other people about my books – whether via social media, or by writing down what you thought of it. Over half a million new books are published each year in English alone, and positive word of mouth helps authors get noticed.

So if you did enjoy this, rating and/or reviewing it would be wonderful thanks.

To the first fifty people who publish a substantive (say, fifty words or more) and honest review of *Lost Girl* – good or bad, I read them all – and send me your email address, I'll give a free electronic copy of *Cold Heart* when it's ready, or any of my earlier books, at your choice.

https://www.goodreads.com/review/edit/56690546   is the link you'd use on Goodreads – a great site for book lovers, incidentally. (You'd need to sign in to your account.)

Similarly for the first twenty people to find a previously-undetected error in this book. I do reserve the right to decide if something is a genuine error and not just my peculiar style, though!

I keep email addresses strictly private, and *only* use them to send the free ebook.

It's May 2020 as I draft these words, and the world is in the grip of a terrible pandemic. I plan to publish *Lost Girl* this year, and hope to complete *Cold Heart* in 2021. I provide progress reports on twitter, and also on my web site *AToeInTheOceanOfBooks.com*, where I discuss my series, writing, and self-publishing.

Finally, if you'd like a sneak peek of what's next, I've included an early draft of an excerpt from Vol. 2 of the Leeth Ascending series: *Cold Heart.*

LJKendall@AToeInTheOceanOfBooks.com @LukeJKendall

Happy Joe Holliday's eyes scanned once across the corner bar as he entered: Bander's crew in a meet; a couple of NuLife dealers; a scatter of gangers; a few cred-girls, and the Mark VII gynoid and android on the mini-stage blowing the minds of the slumming Consumers who rounded out the evening's clientele. He nodded his head a fraction of an inch and led the way to a far seat, from where he could see all six exits. But the man with him had already slipped past Happy's bulk and headed to the bartender. The ex-NFPD mage took his drinking seriously.

Happy's silvered eyes tracked more slowly across El Lobo's Gun Bar, confirming his initial assessment as he took his seat. He looked the solid, cold type – who'd shift into laser efficiency if you moved wrongly.

He ran a quick body systems diagnostic, then checked the time. Fourteen minutes to go. The mage returned with a tray of drinks. "Steven – check on the others."

Steven's hand moved to his Link but Happy's hand was already there, covering it. "Not that way."

The mage sighed. He lifted his beer and drained half the glass. "Ah!" He forced out a belch, folded his arms on the table, then put his head down as if going to sleep. Happy stared at the slumped form, not quite shaking his head. The team had been together now four years and he still wasn't sure Swift's attitude wasn't a deliberate act.

Steven Swift sat up, the Imaginal search taking scarcely fifteen seconds. "They're at the end of the street. A couple of minutes away. Seems basically clear."

'Basically?'

The mage considered. "Well... sure. It's clear."

Happy took a deep breath. "Check again."

Swift squirmed, just a little. "Look, there was nothing wrong, not really. Nothing I could put my finger on. Nothing really local. Just... just the feeling that something bad is out there tonight, somewhere."

The few people on the wet streets of New Francisco gave the youth a wide berth as he strolled past. It wasn't the impossibly white suit that didn't *quite* glow, and it wasn't the thing he held cupped in his hands. Even though he was talking to it.

It was the fact that not a drop of rain fell on the spotless suit, marking him 'Mage!' as surely as a holosign over his head. Sane people avoided mages, and the only thing worse than a mage was a crazy mage. A mage talking to his gun definitely fell into the second category.

"I guess you're as excited as I am, Spiff!" Mike enthused. "On our way to El Lobo's Beachside Bar to meet resistance fighters – Rio is everything I dreamed of. You be good tonight, now."

Suddenly the gun in his hand became a tiny dragon, which hissed its acquiescence.

"Good boy. Here, I'd better put you away. Looks like people aren't used to seeing dragons round here. Back you go. Have some treats." He slid the dragon inside his jacket, and followed with some of Spiff's favourite snacks. The snacks made a sound curiously like falling bullets as they showered into the pocket.

"It sure is a fine night," he sighed, breathing in the warm exotic airs of the cold wet New Francisco streets. Turning right, he left the brightly lit Chinese shopfronts of Grant Avenue and began moving into the darker ways that bled the city's light and life into the hungry blackness.

He started to whistle.

In the now-dark alley mouth, as the whistling figure in white turned a distant corner, two men came alert.

They moved a pace back into the shadows as the boy sauntered down the road towards them.

Happy frowned. "What do you mean, 'something bad'?"

"It's just a feeling. Reminds me of that bit in the old two-dee, Forbidden Planet, where the robot says 'Something is approaching from the south west', and all the blast doors start slamming down."

Happy looked at him blankly.

"It's nothing to worry about. It's just a feeling."

"Isn't half of magic about feelings?"

Swift looked uncomfortable. "Well, yeah. Sort of. The dopey half."

Happy's silvered orbs locked on Steven. "Check again, Steven."

Steven emptied the remainder of his glass and swore. "I should've got some pretzels." At Happy's expressionless glare, he slumped down onto the table again. Somehow, Swift made the eerie business of separating his spirit from his body seem as spooky as farting. Happy scanned the room while he waited.

Steven jumped to his feet, his strangled cry bringing Happy's gun to his hand and snapping half the people at

Lobo's into defensive postures. "Shit a bleeding toxrat!" The mage was staring wildly round, then round again with the off-center gaze of a mage looking Elsewhere. Abruptly he stopped and shrugged, picked up the chair he'd knocked over, and sat back down. He leaned forward. "You won't believe this: it was an angel."

Happy put his gun away, noting Bander's crew pointing at the mage and making jokes. But the man's sudden pallor convinced him Swift wasn't joking. No mage was completely rational, but this kind of performance was far from Swift's normal idea of laughs.

"A glowing white, flaming-sword-in-the-hand angel. It flew straight up to me, right here in this room."

"And then?"

Swift shrugged. "Raised its sword, like in a salute, then vanished."

"You mean, flew off." Happy knew only enough magic theory to deal with it tactically, but one of the things he did know was that nothing 'just vanished' in the Imaginal realm.

Steven said nothing for a full three seconds. "Okay. It must've flown off."

Happy stared at him, trying to summon the massive energy required to drag more information from Swift. He gave up.

The mage frowned, looking around. "I can still feel it, you know. Not just after-echoes, either." Just then the team's second mage, Haggard, and the others entered the bar. "I think whatever it was is getting physically closer. It was strong, too."

-

The whistling stopped, and with it the footsteps. Leaning forward the two men saw the youth standing like a statue, apparently unaware of them. They eased back, waiting silently in the dark.

When his steps started again they were rapid, purposeful, heading directly into the alley. "Spawn of Lucifer! Take this message to your Master!"

Though the youth had kept back as he stepped out into view of those in the alley, the two men were already a blur of motion diving towards him. Yet somehow he was faster. Unimaginably fast. The night air *pulsed*, and two red clouds exploded backwards, the ghastly sound of meat ripped cell from cell echoing briefly through the darkness. Tiny gobbets of flesh dripped from white cloth like water off Teflon.

"You are very capable, Alpha." From one side of the alley a camo suit deactivated and an unapologetically robotic form stepped forward, its movements lazily graceful and its voice precisely controlled. Two other Shielded androids moved silently and invisibly to flank the boy. "Let us discuss your situation-"

"Satan himself!" hissed the boy. Face twisting into outraged anger, he flung out both hands in a strangely artificial gesture, sinews stretched tight.

The entire alleyway *rippled* as the androids jerked like puppets then crumpled to the ground. The boy *yanked*, then slapped both hands together, the metal and plastic constructs crumpling in on themselves, bursting into flames as their power cores breached. For a few seconds he stood, sides heaving with the massive exertion. His face no longer held any trace of playful humor.

Striding off angrily, his feet left a trail of red footprints for two blocks. Blood trickled off his coat, until it was once more snow white.

As the barbarian's sword swept down, gutting the cyberphage, an alert-window suddenly flashed into existence. Nelson swore, saved his game, and checked Ghost.

"Frying chips! Half the citynet's down. It's happened *here!*" A grin split his face and he enhanced reality to give him a net view, then portaled in through the first layer of defenses and looked around.

He was quite alone. Alone in his room, alone on this quantum peak, alone in the byways of the Tik Tek security system – to those who knew, the site with the most dangerous and perfect security on the whole friggin' net. Even the people who employed him, who thought he was god's gift, would have freaked if they knew he was trying this. Hell, *he* couldn't believe he was risking this! Especially now, knowing what he did.

Behind him, what he called his Ghost moaned and sighed. It'd seemed cute to program it like that, the groans letting him know how much counter-measure activity he was triggering in the systems he penetrated. It meant he got multiple sensory inputs, using the natural multitasking capabilities of the human brain. Usually the idea worked well, too. Ghost would detect the activity, he'd phase out and watch, then re-insert when the activity died away. Tonight, though, it was creeping him out.

Ghost made another almost-silent noise, and David Nelson had to resist the impulse to check behind him. He was alone in his rooms, deep inside the most secret inner sanctum of the most secret agency in North America. No one could get in here without him knowing. Unless Leeth-

His eyes widened and he spun around. If that crazy girl-thing had decided-

The room was empty. Of course she couldn't be here. That was why he was trying to hack into Tik Tek's Antarctic systems, after all. This was crazy! Why was he so twitchy? Maybe it was the creepy feeling his Ghost was trying to warn him about something. He forced out his breath and turned back to his comp, the adrenaline rush making his hands shake a little. People said Tik Tek was impossible to crack, but not for him. No password or barrier could stand against him and Ghost. It'd be like a two-dimensional being trying to build barriers against a three-dimensional intruder. In cyberspace, he was a god. Unfortunately, in Tik Tek he faced the digital equivalent of another god.

Behind him, Ghost went utterly, profoundly silent.

-

"Dangerous?" asked Happy.

Haggard collapsed like a shabby pile into a chair beside the large man. Bruce the neo-barbarian shifted the plastic battleax from his shoulder and plucked a chair out to straddle. Nick, in black as usual, ghosted into place against the wall, a pace or two from the table.

"Dunno," Steven said. "I've never met an angel before."

Haggard lazily eyed the ex-cop. The middle-aged slum mage straightened in his chair as he registered Swift's unusual emotional state. "Wuzzup 'im?" he asked Happy. "Wuzzy mean, 'angel'?"

Swift told him. "Feels like it's practically on top of us now," he added. Nick, with a sniper's eye, had moved to the other side of the room to cover them, Happy noted, and keyed his commlink so Nick could still listen in. He brought his own gun out, and opened a retina-link to their Hacker, who watched the meeting point's Net neighborhood. "Anything odd going on, Jake?"

"Bet your arse. I've had to link to a weather-sat – the entire net in your part of the city just went down. I've never seen anything like it. You're roughly in the middle of it."

"Situation," murmured Happy, and was pleased to see the team come instantly alert. "We're the targets?" he asked Jake.

"Can't say." Jake shrugged. "Maybe not. Someone who could do this'd have much juicier targets than us."

"The mages say something's-"

A glowing white figure stepped into the bar.

Happy blinked, and suddenly his tension fell away as the

pale kid in the fluoro-white trenchcoat took a step forward, looking around in wonder. Happy read the word 'Wow' on his lips. Steven swung around in his chair to see what all the others were staring at. "How did *he* find us?"

The youth saw them, and suddenly his gawkish nervousness evaporated. Looking almost dignified, he made his way to their table. He looked different to when they'd interviewed him for a possible spot on the team yesterday.

"Shit!" breathed Steven. "He's the goddamn angel!"

No one spoke as the kid, Mike, approached and sat down. "Sorry I'm late Mr Holliday. I had difficulty in remembering where you'd said to meet this evening."

The others all looked at Happy in surprise.

"That's because I didn't tell you. I didn't invite you, Mike. We only discussed the *possibility* of your joining us." Happy looked around. "Did any of you guys contact him?" They all shook their heads. "Our *client* contacted you?"

Mike smiled, paternally. It looked really strange on the sixteen-year-old's face. "Hardly. I sensed... a storm gathering. You need my help."

Haggard snorted, Steven looked confused, and Bruce looked worried. Across the room Nick just watched. "Cute answer, kid," Happy growled, "but I need to know how-"

Jake interrupted via commlink. "Client's here."

Happy swore.